The Great Lie DUP

The Great Lie

A Nick Talbot Adventure

M Stanford Smith

HONNO MODERN FICTION

First published by Honno
'Ailsa Craig', Heol y Cawl, Dinas Powys,
Wales, CF64 4AH

1 2 3 4 5 6 7 8 9 10

ISBN 978 1 906784 16 4

Published with the financial assistance of the Welsh Books Council

Cover image: Andrew Davidson
Cover design: Graham Preston
Text design: Graham Preston

Printed in Wales by Gomer

This book is dedicated to Rohan, Santa and Thomas the Tank Engine
– the 'Stanford Greys', and to Axel,
a great-hearted dog.

Heartfelt thanks to Gillian and Professor Rodney Coates for their support and encouragement, to my family likewise, and for rescue in the maze of technology; Simon Holloway for self-belief, to my actors and friends in the Rep who play Shakespeare so eagerly and well, and, of course, to my editor, Caroline, and all at Honno much thanks.

On 30th May 1593, a fight broke out in a private room on London's dockside. The brawl developed and knives were drawn. In the subsequent fighting a young gallant was stabbed through the eye and killed.

The broadsheets the next day bore headlines to rival our own tabloids

CHRISTOPHER MARLOWE MURDERED

FATAL STABBING IN DEPTFORD

And more soberly -

Our greatest poet foully done to death

There was a hurried inquest that day but no official ceremony.

Encrypted report from Master Edward Faulds to the office of Lord Robert Cecil, Clerk of the Privy Council.
30th June

All went according to plan, my lord.

As expected, Marlowe's friends hastened to see for themselves and pay their respects but unfortunately the body had already been taken to St Nicholas' church, seen by the coroner, shrouded, coffined and nailed down. The officials and jurors, as instructed, were carefully screened and briefed beforehand.

The other three men involved in the brawl, Frizer, Skeres and Poley were taken for examination. At the end of the week, Frizer, who had wielded the dagger, was pardoned by her Majesty and all three now have been quietly released, as arranged with your office.

After the burial in a corner of St Nicholas' churchyard (over-hasty to my mind), Master Ben Jonson gathered together the remains of the group calling themselves the University Wits, Messrs Nashe, Peele and Chapman, in the Mermaid tavern, Bread Street, to join the cream of literary society for a wake and an impromptu secular service that Christopher Marlowe would no doubt have enjoyed. Master Greene was no doubt there in spirit. Thomas Watson was there and Will Shakespeare and that unpleasant youth Webster. Kyd, of course, we have in custody. Master Shakespeare was seen to be in tears. He was pale and appeared unwell. Young Master Talbot, the victim's protégé, was not present. I understand he has gone abroad for his health.

Your obt servant, Phoenix.

By this time, Christopher Marlowe, bearded and dressed as a Jew, was halfway to entering the Bay of Biscay with a following wind, on his way to Italy.

Prologue

Two Gentlemen in Verona. Autumn 1597

Decision made. Decision uttered. Nicholas Talbot sat watching the pale, heart-shaped face brooding across the scarred table. Christopher Marlowe, playwright, gentleman-scholar and spy. Their corner of the tavern was dim, the nearest candle a table away, their own guttering in a pool of stinking tallow. They were a pocket of quiet in the din as Nick waited for a response. Around them bubbled the hell's kitchen that was Verona's answer to the Mermaid, popular and packed. The press and stink of unwashed bodies was miasmic: undertones of urine, spilt wine and worse vied with overtones from the questionable stew being manoeuvred between the tables by the sweating servingwomen. Nick leaned further back in his corner, peeling his leather jack away from the jerkin of the soldier behind him who was using him as a leaning-post, becoming aware of the ache in his thighs from the long ride.

Nick looked round. Courtiers on the way down rubbed shoulders with courtesans on the way up; thieves and dips jockeyed for position, a quartet of habitual gamblers threw dice obsessively at one table and the group of mercenaries next to Nick were celebrating having money in their pockets.

1

Across the room, Nick noticed a hairy man with a wall eye staring at him fixedly. He leaned down and loosened the dagger in his boot. He observed the man carefully for some time, until he realised that the good eye was concentrated on the be-furred burgher sitting to his left, picking his teeth. The noise was dense enough to lean on, and to Nick, who had ridden from Venice with only the wind for company, it was almost unbearable. Someone was actually strumming a battered guitar and trying to sing against a background of catcalls from the group round the fire. Nick was stifling and he pulled open his jack, bringing a whiff of horse and fresh air into the fetid atmosphere. He looked again at his companion. How could this sophisticated scholar sit there and produce these wonderful plays in these conditions? Not that he looked like a sophisticated scholar these days, no longer the perfumed man of fashion whom Nick had first met brawling in a London tavern. His linen was grubby and the velvet of his once-fine doublet was rubbed and stained. The man did not look well, he had aged. The black hair and unkempt beard was grizzled with grey, the round cheeks a little sunken.

Kit Marlowe was stabbing at the raised grain of the table with a ruined quill, his papers pushed to one side. He was hunched as if in pain, the greasy lovelock almost dangling in his wine. Nick shifted, easing the ache in his muscles, and the tip of his sword scraped on the flagstones. Marlowe looked up, his sloe-black eyes catching the light.

'Don't leave me, Nick.'

This happens every time, thought Nick, I'm too useful to him.

'Show me your hand, my dear,' came the soft voice. 'Let me

see where it is written.'

Heigh-ho, here we go again with the fortune-telling. Nick extended his upturned left hand onto the table, indulgent. Marlowe stabbed the quill hard into the middle of the palm.

'There, my mark! You are mine.'

Nicholas reached across and removed the quill and the clutching fingers with a firm grip. He hissed as he poured the crude brandy he was drinking into the wound. He was taking no chances, he knew what the ink was made of – oak-gall and hog's piss – this was his dagger hand.

'That's hardly the way to keep me,' he said.

'No, that was foolish dramatics. But what do you expect? You have chosen a bad time.'

'Why? Has Julio left you too?'

'You think that would trouble me? He grows fat and idle and is losing his looks. No, you are my lifeline, Nick, how else will my work see the light of day? I must have my audience, make them laugh and cry, or I am dead, Nick, truly really dead.'

'I have letters from home. Responsibilities.' And my woman, he thought. 'It's time I went back.'

'And do what? Dwindle into a landowner, a bucolic farmer tending your flocks, a hayseed, a Corin! Or is there some other pressing call – a siren, a Helen to lure you back – you with your absurd preference for women? You are so stubborn, my dear, I could—'

'Keep your voice down.' Nick squeezed the cut to make the bright blood run and closed his fist to seal it. He would have another scar to go with the missing joint of the middle finger. 'I'm telling you, our masters grow dangerously extravagant in their requirements. Careless. Little Robin Cecil isn't the man your old paymaster was. I was nearly done for last time. Think. If I were caught on my way there with your plays in my saddlebag, what then? It would be all up with you, you'd be exposed for the trickster you are.'

'How? Where is my name written? They would take it for a cypher.'

'And you think I wouldn't break under the question? I find I am not so brave.'

'Come, come, where is the young cock who crowed so loud in Southwark? What has changed? Have you fallen in love with something other than my words? Or some other impossible she?'

'Can you never imagine other reasons? This is my chance to live my life, not yours, to claim what's mine. And you haven't written for weeks—'

'No, listen, listen, Nick. That is my point. You have been an inspiration to me – you remember that little book you found to remind me – although I have it by heart – *The Prince*? By Machiavelli? My bible. So clever to find it for me again when those philistines have banned it. They called him Make-Evil, did you know? Of course you know, we all do, but do you agree with that? Of course not, he was one of us, a liberal, a freethinker, a little pragmatic perhaps, the end justifying the means, but—' Nick groaned, foreseeing one of those lengthy philosophic discussions he usually enjoyed with Marlowe, but he had other things on his mind. '…but think, a *dispossessed* prince, now. Dispossessed as you were, Nick, but a young man of mild disposition, a poetic even a melancholic cast of thought; what advice do you think our Niccolò Machiavelli would have for him? This starveling thing of poor Kyd's you brought me, what a chance the man had missed! In my hands it will be my greatest work – my philosopher-prince, the evil king! My Hamlet is a young man, faced with terrible decisions, but he is a scholar, a poet perhaps, who must justify his—'

One of the soldiers, drunk, lurched into their table, flailing for balance. The remains of Marlowe's wine slopped over his papers and he cried out, frantically mopping with his sleeve. Nick stood up, shouldering the man out of his way. 'We can't talk here.'

Marlowe got to his feet, stowing the manuscript inside his doublet.

'No, we'll go to my lodging, I want you to read this—' His last words were lost as the enraged drunk swung wildly at Nick's head. Nicholas swayed calmly to one side, brought up his knee fast and slammed the heel of his hand up under the man's nose with a crunch. He did not believe in half-measures when it came to a fight. The man screamed and the table went over as his companions got up. Nick flung his cloak over one shoulder, seized Marlowe's shirt collar, now liberally spattered with blood, and hustled him through the crowd to the door before the fight could start in earnest. No one followed. The cutpurse waiting in the shadows did not stand a chance.

As the night air hit them, Nick saw that Marlowe was a great deal more drunk than he had realised. Whether with words or wine was unclear but he was grinning and giggling to himself and could hardly stand. Nick set his shoulder under Kit's and put an arm round his waist just in time to stop him slipping into the slime of the kennel and half-carried, half-dragged him up the shallow flight of cobbled steps that led to the path along the river. Marlowe now had rooms above a paper-maker nearby, and the musty odour created by the process followed them upstairs.

Kit was still giggling helplessly as Nick hauled him through his door.

'What a man of action! No model for my philosopher-prince after all. Except…yes. Yes, there must be a hint to please the groundlings, a promise early on that we have a complete man in the making—' His black eyes were sparkling and intent. Nick recognised the signs with a sigh. Kit would have forgotten all about their discussion, if you could call it that. This new work had taken over.

He threw off his cloak and set about lighting candles and the floating wicks of the small oil lamps. The room was cold after the heat of the tavern and he stirred up the embers of the fire, throwing on more fuel. The store of wood was getting low, he must see about it. Marlowe was already at his desk by the window, finding and mending a new quill, flexing his fingers, oblivious. The remains of his meal were still on the table, together with a straw-covered flask. Nick found a goblet and polished it with the clean square of linen he liked to keep on him, and poured the wine. The droppings on the floor and table did not encourage an appetite for food. He looked round at the squalor in which the man lived these days. A straw palliasse had been dragged through from the other room; a chair lay on its side with a discarded shirt draped over it. That, the table and desk, and a winged chair covered in grimy brocade were the only furnishings. Nick glanced through into the next room. A four-poster bed took up most of the space, the sheets were tangled and stained, the pot beside it had not been emptied. The doors of the armoire stood open, clothes spilling out; a chest under the window was piled high with scribbled paper. Nick sighed again. The man needed a wife. Or something.

What did he do with all the money? His share of the plays so successfully rendered through Master Shakespeare was steadily increasing together with the demand for more. The funding from Francis Walsingham's successors was more than adequate: the Queen's legendary meanness compensated for by little Robert Cecil's canny management. Nicholas himself earned more than his keep nowadays.

Nick gazed out of the window at the round sugarloaf hill across the river, musing. Master Shakespeare now had property in London and was looking to build a fine new house in Stratford, and here was Marlowe in dreary lodgings seemingly contented so long as his plays were seen and applauded.

The early dawn light picked out the cypresses that spiralled with the road to the castellated buildings at the top of the hill, black brushstrokes showing the way. The copper roofs of the towers crowning the mound flamed suddenly as the rising sun caught them. It was a scene familiar from so many Annunciations and nursing Virgins, glimpsed through a painted window or in a distant landscape. It was beautiful, and Nick was momentarily overcome with homesickness. He was not the only one. He had recently had a letter from a colleague of Edward Faulds', an Intelligencer stationed in Venice. Poule had written;

'...the shadow of an English oak would give a more perfect refreshing to my whole body than all the stately pines of Ravenna.' Poule, lucky dog, looked like being recalled soon.

Marlowe looked up suddenly, feeling for a word, and caught Nick's eye. A smile of pure joy broke across his face like the sunrise, and he flung up his arms, making fists.

'I have it!' he crowed, and Nick remembered exactly why he could not leave him. He poured more wine and took it to the desk, leaving it in easy reach well away from the inkpot. He stood watching the quill spluttering its headlong way across the page, remembering the first time he had heard this man's miraculous words spoken in the theatre, and how they had fired him.

He saw now there was still more to come. The plays were growing in stature and maturity, the language refined to pure gold: all Marlowe's background and experience was now focussed and brought to life, his breadth of understanding deepening, his way of life mere defiance. It was as if he had died indeed and been reborn a wiser man.

'He is not the only one who's changed,' thought Nick. What had happened to the devil-may-care lad who had run away to join the circus that was the London playhouse? Too much. How different his life would have been had he not been ensnared by the gossamer weaving of this man's words. Not that he had any regrets. Save one. Marlowe waved him irritably out of his light, and Nick found his pack and sat down by the fire, his back against the chair, stretching long legs to the flames. His boots were still muddy from his last errand, and there was a new tear in his hose, goddammit. As he relaxed, growing warmer, with the scritch scritch of the quill in the quiet room for company, he allowed himself to reflect upon the changes of fortune that Kit Marlowe had done so much to bring about. A voice roused him, chiming with his thoughts.

'What is your motto, Nick? So newly elevated, your father must have had a motto to grace the new coat of arms. Or haven't they got round to that yet?'

Stung, Nick answered abruptly, 'The readiness is all.'

Transfixed, Marlowe fell back in his chair.

'But that is it! Perfect! My prince exactly! This is what he will come to find, the readiness. I can see it – a magnificent last scene, a duel.' He seized his pen and began to scribble, alight with invention. 'Such a waste, a tragedy to die before he can prove himself a great king, likely had he been put on—' The quill scratched on, Marlowe muttering feverishly to himself.

Nick bent to make up the fire, preparing to see out this new play. Marlowe would need feeding, would have to be reminded to eat, wash, change his clothes, be fed poppy juice to make him sleep. Nick went into the other room and emptied the chamber pot out of the window with a yell of ''Ware piss!' He shut the door on the mess, finished his wine and, spurning the grubby mattress, wrapped himself in his cloak and disposed himself on the floor, his head on his priceless pack. The pack was stuffed with letters and packets worth a small fortune in the right (or wrong) hands. And the cyphered stuff from his last mission, of course. It would have to wait… he slept.

Minutes, or hours, later he was startled from his exhausted sleep by a cry of fury. Marlowe was tearing and crumpling the sheets of manuscript, swearing and sobbing.

'Hell's teeth, I've lost it!' He turned on Nick with a snarl. 'You've broken the thread, damn your tripes! It was all in my head…'

'Leave it, Kit. Rest. It will come back.'

Marlowe flung himself back into his chair.

'Ah, no matter. I have others crowding into my brain – this lad, Orlando, you tell me of and your pretty, witty Kate.' He looked into Nick's tired eyes and stopped. 'I am a selfish bitch. Something has happened since I saw you last, my dear.'

Face and voice showed the new depth of understanding that made this mercurial man the great playwright he was. It was too much for Nick and he buried his head in his hands. Marlowe rose to pour wine for them both and came to sit by him. He listened quietly as the tale poured out…

Chapter One

Rokesby Hall. Late Summer 1590

The players had come! The cavalcade made its jingling way up the long drive. The faces of excited villagers pressed against the gilded iron of the tall gates as the keepers closed them out. Banners waved: scarlet, blue and gold; a famous clown jigged and capered in front. Nicholas opened the casement to lean out and noise flooded in, sounds of flute and tabor, rumbling wheels and bells and creaking harness, snatches of song and shouts of laughter. Signs hung from the sides of the wagons, gaudy posters for performances in the next town or village. Women did not perform on the stage, but women there were, waving and calling to the people left at the gate.

The noise died a little as they approached the forbidding doors of the keep, and Nick crossed the room to kneel in the other window and watch their reception in the courtyard.

The clown had stopped his jig and was sweeping his feathered cap in the dust, making a deep and respectful bow to the steward who stood in the doorway. Nick could see his guardian in the shadows behind, the white triangle of his face floating ghostly between tonsure and black habit. He sat back on his heels, easing the shirt away from his back. The old devil had drawn blood again that morning, and there he was, welcoming the actors as if he owned the place. Enough. He had waited and endured long enough. This was his chance. He rested his hot forehead against the wavy glass, watching and planning.

Nicholas Talbot, only son of the first lord of Rokesby was, at 15, a wiry lad of medium height, whose long bones presaged the big man he would become, given the chance. He had a mobile, bony face that should have been merry, long green eyes and a mop of tow-coloured hair. His mother, Marie, had died giving him to the air, and his father never spoke of her. When Nick asked, his face had closed with such pain that Nick understood it was forbidden ground. He had been reared by a succession of nurses who had done their best to spoil the rosy, chuckling baby. His home had been a series of army camps in England and France and the Low Countries, where he ran wild, following his father's rise from captain to commander. Jack Talbot, a young offshoot of a distinguished family, had his way to make.

Now, remembering, a vivid scene came into Nick's mind, a scene that had changed everything.

Brought before his father once again to be disciplined, he recalled standing very straight and sturdy and trying not to laugh. Jack Talbot had looked at his ten-year-old offspring with horror. Where had all the time gone?

'Does he know his letters?' he had asked the drill sergeant.

'That he does, sir, and he figures well. His sword-work is good and he shoots tolerable straight. But he can't seem to learn any rules, sir.'

'Or manners either, it would seem.' Jack had eyed the grimacing child and made what would be the worst decision of his life. He sent the boy away to be educated as a gentleman. Nick never saw him again.

When Jack Talbot was killed three years later, fighting in the Netherlands – knighted by Leicester on the field to become Sir James, lord of Rokesby Hall – his half-brother Paul took over unbidden as Nick's guardian and promptly removed him from his school in Stratford. He had installed himself as lord of the new Rokesby manor and at first meeting he decided Nick was aptly named as a limb of Satan and proceeded to try to beat the devil out of him. To Nick's great surprise, the world changed from the cheerful rough and tumble of army life and boarding school to a straitened existence of prayers, beatings and regimented lessons. He ran away twice and was brought back and punished.

He was not supposed to visit the stables and kitchens and storerooms but he became adept at evading his uncle and was a favourite with the servants. He practised his fighting skills with Jem, the old soldier who looked after the stables, and his arts of persuasion on the maids. He did not starve on the many fast days imposed by his uncle, sitting in the chimney corner by the spit, learning to flirt with Kate. Kate, a bonny girl, was in charge of the still room, and it was she who, when she was nineteen, took Nick into the haybarn to make a man of him. It was his fifteenth birthday and he thought it the best present he would ever have. You might say he made the best of things.

Now he rose, a little stiffly, and made his way down the winding stair and quietly through the darkening cloister which, with the ancient keep, was all that remained of the original building. The main dwelling was a brand-new manor house still being built on the ruins of a Priory near Stratford-upon-Avon, destroyed by Henry's Reformers. The house and demesne were a gift to his father for services to the Queen, but Jack Talbot had not lived to enjoy them. Now they had been stolen from his son. Nick slipped through the side door and, once inside the new main building, stood for a while, listening. There was a distant hum of hospitality, a bell was struck and joined by a ruffle of drums. The entertainment would start with an exhibition of juggling and tumbling and after the banquet would come the play. He moved silently to the stair that led to his room and had almost reached it when a sound from the shadows caused him to whip round in a feral crouch. What was left of the evening light glinted on the rim of a metal bowl and the white of a woman's cap. Kate came towards him in a whiffle of skirts and a tang of herbs.

'Where have you been? I waited for you when I should have been in the kitchens. How much has he hurt you – let me see.'

'Not much. He needed me held this time. It will be the last.'

'Jem told me. He wished me to tell you—'

'Never mind. Not his fault.'

She brushed past him into the room: the warm domestic smell of her body aroused him. She found kindling and lit candles, beckoning him to the stool by the banked-down fire. He found he was shivering, partly with pain and shock, mostly with excitement at the thought of escape.

'Sit down. Take off your shirt so I can look at you.' He did as he was told, unlacing his points and easing off his shirt with care as she began laying out cloths and salves, hissing angrily under her breath. She bathed his back gently, smearing

14

marigold ointment on the stripes.

'What do you mean – the last time?'

'I'm leaving. This is my chance… Kate, sweet Kate, I need your help. I'm going with the players as far as Stratford, to join the army. Jem says there's a troop there and he won't be able to drag me back from that. What sort of girl do you think I'll make, Kate? I mean to hide in the wagon with the women when they go.' He laughed suddenly, standing up. 'Thanks.' He stood there grinning at her, reaching for a clean shirt. The soft light gleamed on his narrow sweating body, highlighting the fencer's muscles, the strong neck and the apple in his throat.

With a sob, she threw her arms round him, pressing her face to his chest. He flinched and stood for a moment, then bent his head to nuzzle her neck, fingers busy with her laces.

'I need women's clothes. Help me, Kate, there isn't much time.'

'I can't. I dare not, I must go—' He was drawing her towards his bed, one roving hand inside her bodice, the other teasing up her petticoats. She did not resist for long, she had taught him too well for her own good, but this time their coupling was short and urgent, unspeaking.

Spent, he lay across her belly, eyelashes spiked with unshed tears. She lifted his head and stroked a finger across the soft down of his upper lip. They spoke together.

'I shall miss you.'

He laughed. 'I shall come back. When I am grown this place will belong to me. I shall make my fortune, Kate, and I shall take back what's mine.'

She looked into the young confident face and could have cried. Instead she climbed from under him and began to rearrange her clothes.

'We'd better make haste then. Come down to the still room when you're ready. I'll find someone to help. Don't worry.'

When she had gone, Nick dragged on shirt, hose and breeches and set about collecting his small store of possessions. Through Jem he had money gained from the sale of the few valuables left to him. He had a miniature of his mother – an auburn-haired beauty with laughing green eyes – painted on ivory and framed in gold, a hat brooch with a cabochon ruby, a jewelled comb and two rings. He took the key from around his neck and unlocked the precious box containing his father's papers. Taking out the records of his birth and his father's marriage to Marie Melville, he wrapped it all in a spare pair of drawers and crammed them into a pouch under his shirt. He pulled his father's sword from under his bed and buckled it on, folded his one good suit of clothes into a blanket, stamped his feet into his boots, buttoned on his doublet and was ready.

The still room door was unlocked, quite natural tonight because of the banquet. The cooks could hardly keep running for the keys whenever they ran out of raspberry syrop. The heat and noise was at its height, and no one had time to pay any attention to Nick's familiar figure as he sidled through. The heady mix of succulent smells, roasting meats, layer pasties, sweetmeats and freshly sliced pineapple, made his mouth water and his stomach rumble. His eyes glistened as he surveyed the loaded shelves. He unrolled his bundle again and carefully wrapped jars of honey and greengage jam in his best breeches, with bread and a piece of salted pork, cramming cake into his mouth. He found a cloth to hold a whole spiced and peppered tongue and a bottle of brandied plums to sweeten his welcome by the players, and some sacking to wrap the sword. He would not be parted from that.

He was still eating when Kate came quietly in, bringing with her a stranger in gaudy finery. The woman was immensely fat and tripped lightly on tiny feet, her face round and pink in the frilled cap and laced with cheerful lines. She was looking rather worried until she set eyes on Nick, guiltily caught with his mouth full of pastry. She turned to Kate with a roar of laughter, her little bright eyes pouched and creased.

'So this is your girl? He's pretty enough, I grant you, but the rest of him will be a nice problem.' She looked him up and down, taking his measure, while Nick grew slowly scarlet. 'And what about the size of his feet? He'll have to keep his boots on.'

'You'll help me? I'll cause you no trouble. Once we're away from here, I'll make myself scarce.'

'Kate tells me you're going for a soldier. That seems a waste of a fine-looking lad. However—' She walked round him. 'Very well. Sit you down and I'll see what I can do.' She nodded to Kate and floated off on dainty feet, light as a dancer, the layers of flesh bouncing slightly as she went.

'That's Mistress Molly, wardrobe mistress to the company. I told her all about it. She had a son about your age, I think.'

'I don't need a mother.'

'No. No, of course not, of course you don't. But, Nick, I shall sleep easier if I know someone is looking out for you. You will write to me? Otherwise you will have taught me my letters for nothing.'

Mistress Molly came back on soundless feet to find Nick with his arms round Kate, trying to soothe her tears.

17

'No time for that. Strip. You can keep your boots and hose and your modesty if you must, but I can tell you, in my job nothing surprises me, young man.' Nick started to laugh, as she intended, and submitted to being squeezed into shift and bodice and bum-roll, and trying several voluminous skirts to find one long enough. An auburn wig and a mobcap were clapped on his head and he was handed a shawl with a long fringe.

'Keep that over those brawny arms or you're done for. You'll do. Off with you, get into the second cart and keep your mouth shut. The play finishes soon, and there's little enough to keep us.'

Nick turned to Kate for a last kiss and was put out to find her giggling. He kissed her anyway, picked up his sword and his bundles, hitched up his skirts and followed Molly out of the kitchen. He parted from her in the Great Hall and stole across the stone floor to ease the massive bolts.

Heart pounding, he heaved open one leaf of the great studded door to find the courtyard brilliant with white light. A full moon shone bright through a rent in a raft of cloud, coating its edges and quilting its underbelly with strokes of silver. Nick stood entranced, watching and waiting until the slow drift should eclipse the shining disc and its single star. It seemed an age before he could risk crossing the cobbles to the wagons.

Possessed of a natural grace of movement, he made himself walk slowly, swinging his skirts, balancing his bundles on one hip as he had seen the women do. He even dared a flirty toss of the head at the man coming to close the door as he climbed aboard. He took his time settling himself and waited, quaking, for the players to come.

By the time the company straggled out, a thick bank of cloud covered the moon and the courtyard was dark. Nick's uncle had not extended hospitality beyond a barrel of ale and the leftovers of the banquet, and there was a fair amount of grumbling as they began to load up the wagons. Nick, in his mobcap and shawl, went unnoticed except for a sharp glance as he lent a surprisingly strong pair of arms to lift in the kettledrum. His sword tripped someone up, and to his horror it was tossed with a curse onto a pile of props. Mistress Molly stopped him just in time from leaping after it, and nudged him to sit down and keep out of the way.

The cavalcade, muted now and tired, moved off at last and lurched down the rutted road that led to Stratford, 10 miles off. Nick was huddled at the back of the second cart, wedged between the plump arms and generous thighs of two of the women who, from their giggles and pinches, were well aware of the game.

The cuckoo in Will Kempe's nest was not brought to his notice until the following morning. They were to play that day at the Wheatsheaf at the bottom of Stratford's High Street, and they jangled in about an hour or so after midnight. Knowing they were coming from Rokesby Hall, the landlord had assumed they would remain there for the night, and was not best pleased to find them on his doorstep in the small hours, demanding lodging. The inn was full, largely owing to their coming performance, and after a great deal of argument, the disgruntled players were given space in the hayloft over the stables.

Nick was exhausted, his back sore from the jolting cart and

he was beginning to be frightened by the enormity of what he was doing. Too tired to think about it, he simply went where Molly pushed him, lay down in the straw and fell asleep.

What seemed like moments later, he woke with a yelp to find someone's hand being very familiar under his skirts. He sat up with a jerk. His cap and wig had fallen off, his petticoats were rucked up and it was painfully obvious that here was a man where no man had a right to be. He was pulled down into a billowing mass of soft giggling flesh and was about to surrender when the dainty feet of Mistress Molly, now in a pair of workmanlike boots, waded in and he was hauled up by his hair. Molly laid about her with slaps and a vicious tongue until she had produced some sort of order.

'What are you about?' she hissed at Nick. 'Is this how you repay me? You'll come with me now and see what the master has to say to you. I was helping you for your sweetheart's sake, you – you profligate young hellhound!'

Red in the face and eyes watering from the pain in his scalp, Nick said nothing. He had learned very early in life not to make excuses. He took the bundle thrust at him, turned his back on the whispering girls and pulled on shirt and breeches, ignoring the rest of Molly's diatribe. Laced and buttoned into his clothes, he was ready to face whatever Will Kempe might do. Whatever happened he was not going back.

The flattened straw of the men's side of the loft was empty and the sound of hammering outside told where they were at work putting up the stage. Once down the ladder after Molly, he could not help grinning up at the row of faces peeping over the edge of the loft. Molly seized his arm with an angry shake and dragged him out into the yard. Annoyed, he pulled away from her and went to the cart to find his sword and buckle it on. The comforting weight of it made him feel better, and he retrieved the ham and the other offerings, raked the remaining straws out of his hair, straightened his shoulders and marched over to where Molly was speaking to Kempe.

Will jigged on the spot even as he listened, and his brown face was creased and seamed with laughter lines. Nick was taller by a head, but the actor's huge personality dwarfed him. He turned on Nick with a shout.

'So this is the worm in the apple! Came with the women, did you? I'd like to have seen that. A strapping lass you'll have made.' He made a skipping leap and squeezed Nick's biceps. 'You're right on cue, my lad, you'll work for your ride – unless you've been rewarded already? Eh? Eh? Noll over there has just broken his finger, damn him, take hold of that rope and sing for your supper.'

'I've brought supper, sir. I'll gladly work.'

Kempe seized the sack, glanced inside and thrust it at Molly.

'Give the lad a mug of ale and show him what to do, Noll. I'll talk to him later.'

Noll was a tall, lugubrious man with one wrist in a sling. His eyes were squinting with pain, but he had a droll way of walking – his shoulders slumped in terminal despair – and a wry twist to lip and eyebrow that made Nick want to smile. He found later that Noll was Kempe's counterpart, a foil to his clowning and a brilliant mime. Nick followed him into the apparent chaos at the end of the yard and for the rest of the morning was worked like a dog. The stage was a simple platform, easily erected at one end of the inn yard, taking advantage of the gallery running round all four sides. At the back of the platform went a wall with a central opening, constructed of lath and canvas and braced to the foot of the gallery, leaving room behind for the actors. A curtain of dusty red velvet was hung over the centre doorway. Hauling on ropes and fetching and carrying, it all seemed very plain and dull to Nick and it was not until later, when the performance began, that he understood the glorious flexibility of the acting area. The play to be performed was Christopher Marlowe's *Tamburlaine the Great*.

They worked until the framework was up, and then, just before they stopped to break fast, one of the young men fell off the balcony. Nick hoped he would not be regarded in the light of a Jonah or an albatross after this second accident, but actors had their own superstitions. On the contrary, a roll of paper was pushed into his hand and he was told to sit in a corner with the young man, whose knee was swelling up like a pumpkin, and study his part. The young man's name was Robin Ackland, in his third season with the company, and he was white with pain and furious with himself. Nick was horrified.

'I can't do this! How can I learn this?'

'This was my best chance,' Robin was moaning and rocking back and forth. 'If it went well, I was to play in town...' A wizened little man dressed all in black, with a dewdrop at the end of his nose and clutching a fat bunch of papers loosely sewn together, came hurrying up.

'Can you stand? Good. You cannot kneel, but you can stand and you can speak. You,' he pointed at Nick, 'you can kneel for him and draw the chariot and pull Badajoz in the cage. You are both of a height, it will pass. Go and see Mistress Molly for your costumes. Robin, show him the cues.' And he hurried off again, muttering and sniffing and sorting through his script. Nick and Robin stared at each other. Robin had cheered up slightly. Nick was totally bewildered.

'What did he mean?'

'You will stand in for me, in the parts I can't manage. Mother of Christ, this hurts.' He bent over, holding his leg in both hands. 'All very well, saying I can stand and speak. I can't think straight.'

'Let me see.' Ignoring the yelps of protest, Nick tore the rent in the stocking open further and examined the purple swelling. 'Wait here, I think I know what will serve.' He stopped a woman passing with a bucket, and asked where he might find Mistress Molly.

'She's busy, what do you want?'

'Arnica, if she has it, and some cloths.'

'I'll get it, love. Master Robin, you are a lucky fool, you might have broken your neck.' Robin gazed after her.

'I don't seem to be getting much sympathy.'

'When does the play start?'

'Three of the clock.' Nick glanced up at the big clock face on the wall. Two o'clock.

'There you are then. No time. Be thankful it's no worse.' He took the rags and the pot thrust at him as the woman scurried past on another errand, stowed them inside his doublet and stood up.

'Come on.' He seized Robin's wrist and pulled him up. Robin yelled as Nick turned and hoisted him up in a piggyback and set off out of the yard and down towards the river. There, he pulled off Robin's boots and propelled him thigh-deep into the water. Regardless of pleading, he kept him there until Robin's teeth were chattering, fetched him out and cut away the sodden remains of his stocking. The swelling was considerably down. Having nothing else to dry it with, he pulled off his doublet, put it round the shivering Robin and used his own shirt. Gently, he rubbed arnica into the bruising, soaked the cloths in the river and bound the knee in a figure of eight as he had seen the army surgeons do.

'There. Do you want me to carry you back, or can you manage?' He stood up, bending to pick up his damp shirt, and turned to see Robin gaping at him in horror.

'Who did that to you? Who are you?'

'None of your business. I'll be leaving after the play. We should hurry. Do you want a carry or not?'

'Certainly not. Not after seeing that. If you could just lend an arm—'

The two young men arrived back in time to be hustled into the crowded tiring room set up behind the stage, where Nick submitted to being daubed with brown dye and his face adorned with fierce eyebrows and long drooping moustaches. He was fitted with a slave's breechclout and tunic, and a turban and purple robe covered in fake jewels for his role as King of Fez, pulling the chariot. He attributed the sick hollow feeling to hunger, having missed breakfast and the midday meal, but he had no desire to eat. Trumpets sounded, and the noise of the spectators swelled and died. More trumpets and the sound of flute and drum, bells and castanets, and the actors formed in procession, swept aside the curtain and the play had begun.

Nothing had prepared Nick for the gut-wrenching excitement, or the organ-music of the spoken word – Christopher Marlowe's words – sonorous, lyrical: full of power. Phrases hung in his head: 'to entertain divine Zenocrate', repeated over and over. The rhythms beat in his blood, and the magnificent voice of Tamburlaine was a siren song in his ears. He knelt as a slave, crawled as a conquered king, hauled chariots and cages, not noticing the burn of the ropes on his sore shoulders until afterwards.

Terrified at first, he began to listen and watch Robin and his wooden face began to relax and give expression. He felt the bitter pride of a vanquished king, suffered as a slave, strutted proudly as a guard. The magic of the stage had him in its grip.

If he needed further reward, he was given it. Robin's tale had gone round. He was carefully embraced and plied with food and drink and welcomed with friendly words. Master Kempe sent for him.

'You have made yourself useful today, Master Whoever-you-are. Unless your heart is set on soldiering, there is a place here for you. You may not know it, but men came during the play seeking a runaway. I knew of none such and so I told them. They searched and watched and went away satisfied. You were pulling Tamburlaine in his chariot at the time, I believe, to the detriment of your stripes, and missed all the excitement.'

'I had excitement and to spare, sir. I have heard nothing like it. To read such words written cannot compare – my imaginings have fallen far short of the doing. They must be heard and seen and then read again with new eyes and ears.'

'You are easily seduced, young man. So, which is it to be, word-play or swordplay? Not that we don't run to both. The action and bloodshed was in most part offstage today, but tomorrow we play Henry Sixth. An extra stave would be of use.'

Nick did not hesitate.

'I would join you gladly, sir.'

'See Master Prompter, then get to your bed. There are rooms and to spare tonight, some with real beds in 'em. By the way, what are you calling yourself?'

'Nicholas Talbot, sir.'

'Very well. Enjoy your rest.'

Nick found Robin eagerly waiting for him, bursting with questions.

'Did he offer? Are you to join us? Did you accept? You must accept; this is the life, Nick... travel, girls... we are in London next week. What did he offer you?'

'How's the knee?'

'Well enough. What did he say?'

'I am to break a stave or two tomorrow. After that, who knows?'

Dear, sweet Kate,

I am to tell you I am safe and well and have not joined the army. This will make you glad, as I know you did not wish it. Mistress Molly, she who helped us, is kind to me, and Master Kempe – imagine the honour – has allowed me to join the company. I share a room with four of the players, lesser ones, and a mattress and a nail in the wall suffices me. It is quite like being back with my father's troop, except I have a roof and not a tent. One of the company has family in Stratford and I entrust this to him with my wages. This is towards a dowry, Kate. I do not think you should stay in that place and you may wish to marry. I will send more when I can.

Your loving Nicholas, one of Lord Strange's Men.

His messenger returned from his visit with a brief note and an address in the village of Lower Rookham, outside the Rokesby demesnes.

Nicholas, I have left the Hall and am staying with the minister here to help care for his babes. Do not trouble yourself about me. I am safe and well and pleased to hear you are too. Godspeed, Kate Archer.

Disturbed, Nick questioned his friend, who could only say that he had been refused entrance to the Hall by armed guards and had found Kate through an old groom in the local tavern.

'That would be Jem. How did she seem? Was she well? Why did she leave—'

'I don't know. She looked fine. I can see why you're interested. She wouldn't say anything, just gave me that note.'

'No other message?'

'No. Sorry.' Nick thanked him as best he could for the trouble he had taken, and tried not to worry.

Chapter Two

Once arrived in town with the troupe, there was no time to fret over a situation he could do nothing about. To a nose accustomed to country air, London was an assault: Nick's acute sense of smell almost shut down. Over a powerful underlay of unwashed, crowded humanity were smells of roasting and boiling meat, smoke from chimneys and braziers, decaying vegetable matter, yeasty smells of baking bread; scents of cinnamon, nutmeg and cloves from pomanders fought a losing battle with sewage, with a topnote of honeysuckle overhanging a wall. The smell would intensify as summer drew on but even now it was so thick you could slice it. Add to that the constant noise and press of people, iron wheels on cobbles, pedlars crying their wares, women shrieking from upper storeys, their breasts comfortably blowsed on windowsills, the rattle of harness and booted feet, with here and there a strand of music and song, and Nick was stupefied. For the first few days he could hardly think.

The life of the playhouse engulfed him. He found that the company he thought he had joined was only a small part of a much larger one, splintered into small groups when the theatres were closed, the players fleeing into the countryside away from the plague. The theatre world was a seething cauldron of conflicting loyalties: players and playwrights were poached and coaxed from one company to another, the companies themselves formed and re-formed according to the whims and fortunes of their patrons: theatres were closed down by the civic authorities as dens of iniquity, and straight away opened again somewhere else.

Bewildered, Nick now found himself an unacknowledged member of a company calling itself the Lord Leicester's Men, under the aegis of James and Richard Burbage. James had built and owned the Theatre outside the City walls, and now left the running of it to his son Richard, arguably the finest actor of his day. Nick was both exhilarated by the highly-charged atmosphere and concerned that he might lose his place. Kempe, who had hired him, was a star in his own right but he was not the top man.

'What should I do?' he asked Robin. 'Who does the hiring and firing?' They were squashed together on the end of a bench in the Mermaid, the actors' tavern of choice and, according to Robin, the only place to be. 'See and be seen,' he said. Although how anyone could see anything in that crowded haze of heat and noise was a mystery. A soft breast pressed against Nick's shoulder as Nell, Molly's helper, squeezed between them and squirmed onto Nick's lap.

'What are you two plotting?' she whispered in his ear. Robin spoke across her.

'You've made yourself very useful, for which much thanks, and you might be an actor one day, but you need something... what can you offer?'

Nick ignored Nell's suggestive little wriggle and thought.

'Languages. I have French and Flemish and some German – there were some Germans in my father's company. I don't suppose five years of classical education will be much use. A good memory—'

'Either keep your head down and hope no one clocks there's another mouth to feed, or do something spectacular, draw attention to yourself and become another star in London's firmament. Or join the army.'

'He doesn't want to join the army anymore,' pouted Nell. 'He likes us, don't you, Nick?'

'Kempe would speak up for you. Why don't you ask him?' This would not be necessary. At that moment there was a crescendo in the noise, a bench went over and someone screamed. There was the familiar rasp and rattle of a drawn sword, lethal in that crowded space, and a flashy red doublet was backing towards them, menaced by a pale-faced man with black ringlets and snapping black eyes, armed only with a dagger. Flashy doublet scooped up Nell and backed out into the street with her held yelling in front of him.

Nick never went anywhere without his precious sword, he was afraid of losing it. It was in his hand without a moment's thought, and he leapt on the table and hurdled to the door, pots and platters crashing in his wake. He arrived just before the black-eyed man, and his point was at the throat of Nell's assailant. Nell was pushed aside, and with room now to move, the man engaged. The setting was not ideal. Recent rain had overflowed the kennel and the cobbles were slick with mud and ordure, and of course the entire clientele of the Mermaid had come out into the narrow street to watch. Nick had no wish to do anything but disarm the man, and he manoeuvred lightly, his dagger out now, watching to see his opponent's style. The man fought in the French manner, as if he were using a rapier. He went for his own dagger and Nick's blade prevented him. There was a clash and ring of steel on steel, two rapid engagements, forward and back, the man in the red satin doublet slipping on the mud. A third fast attack and the man's sword was trapped between Nick's two blades.

It flew into the air and landed to stick point down at the feet of a handsome burly man in the front row of the watching mob. It hung there, elaborate hilt swaying like a metronome.

Of the black-eyed man there was no sign.

Nick stuck his dagger in his belt and walked across to pluck up the sword with his left hand. His own weapon pointing down, he laid the blade across his forearm and offered it to his opponent. The man, sweating and pallid in his gaudy doublet, took it cautiously and hastily stowed it away.

'I had no quarrel with you, sir, it was—' he looked round helplessly.

'You made it mine,' said Nick. Nell was still sitting where she had fallen, open-mouthed and muddy, her legs stuck out like a doll's. Nick went to help her up.

Her attacker bowed awkwardly.

'Your pardon sir, and – er – madam.' Nick nodded and the red satin melted away into the crowd. Robin pushed through, with Nick's scabbard still in its sacking, pulled his forelock to the burly individual and took Nell's other arm.

'Better get her home,' he muttered.

Half-carrying Nell, they walked off, the backslapping crowd parting to let them through. Two constables rounded the corner at a canter, scenting an affray, and Nick put Nell's arm round his neck and his own round her waist and they all three held their breath until they were safely away.

'Did you see who that was?' burst out Robin.

'Never saw him before.'

'Not him – come on, Nick, he owns our theatre – Burbage! God, I thought that point had gone through his foot.'

Nick stopped abruptly. 'Hell,' he said.

'You're a made man! I said do something spectacular.'

'Fool,' said Nick. 'More likely I've blown my chances. Who was the fellow started it – with the black hair?'

'Don't you know anything? Christopher Marlowe, you dolt.'

'Christ!' said Nick.

In spite of his worries, Nick strolled down Eastcheap next morning feeling pleased with life in general. The sun was shining, an infatuated Nell had been generous with her favours, his belly was full and he was in London, the centre of the universe.

A filthy urchin ran up to him and tugged his sleeve.

'If you're Nick Talbot, Master Burbage wants you,' he sniggered, and made off. A little of the gloss went out of the day, and Nick sighed. Shrugging he turned left instead of right, up Gracechurch Street, and went to meet his fate. It was a longish walk out to Shoreditch and the Theatre, and he strode out manfully, whistling to keep his spirits up, up past the busy grain market at Leadenhall, past the well at the top of Threadneedle Street towards the city wall. He had grown accustomed to the sight of Bishopsgate Arch, with its rotting heads stuck like lollipops on poles and the quartered limbs hung on hooks like a grisly butcher's shop and he passed under with the glorious immortality of youth, tipping his hat as he went. On past Bedlam and the artillery fields, where he lingered for a moment to watch, then down Hog Lane on his left.

He found Richard Burbage in his office behind a desk piled with scripts and scrolls and columns of figures on long strips of paper. This first actor-manager was a handsome man with an imposing presence and a beautiful voice, and in this small room he was overpowering. Nick could imagine his impact on the stage. He waited, and Burbage looked up.

'Talbot. Pretty footwork back there. Good timing. D'you want a job?'

'I'd like to keep the one I've got, sir.'

'One of Kempe's lads. I know. If you can teach the cow-handed individual I've got playing Mortimer to move his feet and handle a sword, there's a raise in it for you. Consider yourself hired. See Fox, the fight master.' Then, as Nick bowed and turned to go, 'But no more brawling in the street, mind. Gets us players a bad name.'

Master Burbage's Theatre was outside the city limits, but Nick found his way about the seething, stinking mass that was the City of London with glee. He celebrated his sixteenth birthday with his new friends, Christmas came and went and he settled into life in the theatre. He grew several inches that next summer, and began to broaden out. He heeded what Mistress Molly had to tell him, and avoided the worst pitfalls, staying away from the stews and the painted whores that haunted the theatres and called to him and pinched his leg as he passed. He had missed Kate at first, but his days and nights were too crammed with work and new acquaintance to repine for long.

Time flew by. He had entered the strange world of the theatre where men were whisked up into Heaven on fiery chariots, or tumbled into Hell through the floor: where actors dressed as bears chased boys dressed as girls across the stage and the smallest actor crouched in the nose of a fire-breathing dragon frantically puffing smoke. There were all manner of cunning contrivances so that a man could be run through, spouting blood or drop from a gibbet with a sickening crack and spring up smiling to take his bow.

Nick had visited the Commedia in Paris several times with his father, and had marvelled at the painted scenery that vanished to a distant perspective. Taken backstage he had been amazed to find the same scene was only twelve or fifteen-feet deep. Here in London the players set the scene with words, painting forests and deserts and throne rooms with a phrase. If they said so, it was night in the blaze of noon.

The other difference was that Columbina, in the candlelit Commedia, was a woman, with golden skin and eyes green as grapes. (Looking back, and remembering his miniature, Nick thought he understood his father's apparent passion for visiting the play.) On the London stage, slender beautiful boys dressed themselves as women and worried about puberty.

Nick happily suspended disbelief and set himself to learn the craft, how to pitch his voice and woo an audience. His status had improved slightly with his new job, and his cheerful willingness and natural exuberance earned him notice. Willingness did not mean he could be bullied, however, and his ability to amuse others and defend himself soon brought ungrudging respect. Apart from the arts of war and a fund of dirty jokes, he had one or two other small skills learned in the army, beating a ruffle on a drum and getting a respectable note out of a trumpet. All very useful.

But his greatest asset, unvalued 'til now, was a prodigious memory which would stand him in good stead all his life. To see was to know. A great help to a budding actor.

Nick found life with the company very like those formative years spent following his father from camp to camp: it was another extended family and he was grateful. The painful time under the guardianship of his uncle had taught him a great deal however, and the trusting extrovert child had gone. Nowadays, he remembered his early training but took nothing for granted.

Chapter Three

That autumn the threat of plague closed the theatres again and since hostilities in Europe had died down for the time, Kempe decided to take a troupe touring the Low Countries and northern France. Like Richard Tarleton, Kempe had found his style of farce and knockabout comedy went down well in those parts, language was no barrier, and he often took a reduced company across the Channel. Nick was chosen for his languages to help with the commissariat. No amount of fooling would find them food and lodging.

So it was that on a gusty, damp day in October, eight of them took ship from Rotherhithe on the afternoon tide and squashed themselves and their gear into two tiny cabins aft of the mainmast. The forecast was not good, and by the time they reached the open sea it was grey and choppy with a nasty groundswell. The wind was getting up and they were making good speed, but the master soon shortened sail and the ship began to pitch and heave, bucking into the rising waves. Nick had sailed before, on troopships, and was fortunate in possessing a strong stomach. Not so the rest of the company, and soon he and Kempe were the only men standing. It was a fearsome voyage, the North Sea was in a bad mood, and it was a miserable, whey-faced troupe that straggled ashore in Amsterdam. It took two days for them to recover enough to start their journey, let alone perform. Kempe was impatient and harried his unfortunate players along, and Nick found himself burdened with a great deal of extra work. He proved himself useful as interpreter. As a child, riding behind his father, he had soaked up local dialect and language – not always the most elegant usage, to be sure, but helpful. Once they had started, things improved, and they were well-received as they travelled the flat countryside, seamed with canals and dotted with windmills.

Politically, apart from trade disputes and the troubles in France, things had ostensibly settled down in the decades following the Spanish collapse and the appalling massacre of the Huguenots in Paris, and arriving with the company in Amsterdam on their way home, Nick took leave for a day or two to seek out the battlefield where his father had fallen. Jack Talbot had been serving under Lord Leicester during Parma's siege of the city, and had taken a ball meant for his lord commander. Robin offered to come with him, but Nick preferred to go alone. Always self-reliant, he felt he would enjoy his own company for a while.

Arrived outside Zutphen, there was little for him to find after all, although he wandered far outside the pock-marked city walls, and he discovered that a lone Englishman in those parts was both unpopular and vulnerable.

He stood vigil for a long time on the humped and mounded battlefield where the coarse grass blew, grey-green in the dying light. Presently he drew his sword in a last salute and turned sadly away, calling up his hired horse from where she grazed quietly by a ditch. Mounting, he rode along one of the many waterways that drained the land until he reached one of the countless little bridges. A tiny village straddled the narrow canal, and he found lodging for himself and his mare at the inn. He was sitting disconsolate in a corner away from the other drinkers with a meagre supper of thin soup, black bread and cold meat, wishing he had Robin to talk to after all, when he was approached by a rather effete individual who hailed him in English.

'A fellow-countryman or I'm a Dutchman! Which I'm not. May I join you? My ears ache for the sound of my native tongue.' He drew up a stool uninvited and called for a mug of wine. 'What they call ale here is undrinkable, horse piss.' He had a beguiling laugh, and Nick smiled in spite of himself. The man did not look English, except perhaps for something in the shape of the head and the set of the blue eyes. His fair hair was cut short and had a dead look about it. His clothes were of the extravagant Dutch cut and the hat he put on the table had a wide brim and a long curling feather. From his accent he was a man of Kent and his expression was roguish and equivocal. Nick reserved judgment.

'I'm waiting for a friend,' went on the stranger. 'You look as if you need a drinking companion, a young lad like you should not be drinking alone.'

'Not at all, sir. I am about to leave to rejoin my company.'

He was careful not to say what kind or where.

'A military man. I admire a military man.' This came with a sidelong look and a wink. 'Whom do you serve? I was in the army myself. Faulds, at your service.' He cocked his head enquiringly, and Nick, not liking any of this, got to his feet, glad of the sword belted round his hips.

'You must excuse me, sir. I have a long way to go. I trust your friend comes soon to keep you company.' He bowed politely, and left, threading through the tables and going out toward the stables. He intended to avoid the man and get up the back stairs to his allotted space in the communal sleeping room. The moon had not yet risen and it was a cold, starry night threatening frost later. He shivered. The privy advertised its presence as he passed, and he made use of it to save sharing the common pisspot in the dormitory. He came out lacing himself up, to find Faulds waiting for him. His hand went to his weapon, and the man's hands went out at his sides, empty.

'A ready young man, I see. And wary. That's good. I mean you no harm, I swear it.'

There was the sudden loud clattering of a body of horsemen on the bridge in front of the inn, and Faulds dodged quickly round the back of the privy. Nick looked across at the troop. They were mercenaries, mostly German by the look of them and could be in the pay of any of the three factions, Spanish, Italian or Protestant, that troubled the Netherlands at this time. Four of them dismounted and burst into the inn, weapons drawn.

Nick joined Faulds in the noisome slurry behind the privy. 'Are they looking for you?'

'Don't waste time, I need help. I'll make it worth your while.' He was fumbling in the leather satchel he carried. 'These *must reach London*. Can you read? Good. Get them to this man and you'll be rewarded again.' He pressed coins into Nick's hand. 'I have to trust you're a loyal patriot, I'm desperate. Don't tell me your name. If I'm taken, I would betray you as I have been betrayed. Everyone talks in the end. Go now, go quietly. Lead your horse through the fields until you reach those woods and then ride like hell. Get to the port and find the *Florizel*. Give the packet of papers to the master, or better yet, sail yourself—' Breathless, he seemed to collapse on himself. 'Oh God, you're only a boy... can you do it?' Annoyed, Nick nodded.

'What about you?'

'Never mind. Go!' The inn erupted in a tumult of shouting and barking, shots were fired and someone screamed. The door banged open again and Faulds pushed Nick to the ground, crashing away through the hedge and making a great deal of unnecessary noise. Nick had the sense to stay where he was, listening to shouted orders and the swearing clash and flurry of an armoured troop of horse trying to turn in a small space. If the men at the rear had less discipline and more initiative, thought Nick, they might have a chance of catching their man. As it was, he was probably safely away. He gave a thought to his own safety. He was spiked with adrenaline and shaking, his mouth dry. He made himself stop and think. Faulds' plan seemed a good one. If the soldiers came back and found an unclaimed pack, there was nothing in it that would lead to him; better to leave it than risk going upstairs to fetch it in the pandemonium.

It did not enter his head that he could simply dispose of the packet and walk away.

He crept swiftly round the edge of the yard, keeping in the

shelter of the low walls and bushes, through the opening to the stables. There was no one there: the horses were shifting and blowing uneasily, their ears flickering. Hell's teeth; his saddle was stowed in the inn with his pack. He would have to do without; there was no time to break into the harness room. He reached to unfasten the head collar and found his fingers were still clenched round the coins in his hand. They were gold. He stared at them, finally convinced the matter was serious. As he stowed them away, there was more shouting from the direction of the canal and, galvanised, he snatched a couple of blankets off the wall, threw one over the roan mare's head and the other over her back and led her silently out of the yard and through the fields, now rimed white with frost. He was leaving a trail on the sparkling grass, but it couldn't be helped. He kept to the edges as much as possible, walking in the ditch where he could, thorns and twigs tweaking his clothes. He didn't think they had hounds, the barking had been the house dogs. Once in the copse, he stopped to listen, trying to hear over the slam of his heart. All seemed quiet and he pulled the blanket from the mare's head and made much of her, pulling up handfuls of grass and whispering in her ear. She gave a soft snicker and rubbed a snotty nose down his sleeve. He made a saddle cloth of one of the blankets, vaulted on her back and wrapped the other round himself. She shook herself with a snort and they set off cantering into the dark, the little mare surefooted among the trees, Nick lying low along her neck. Back on the rutted track, he slowed to a walk and turned her nose towards Amsterdam.

By morning, Nick was falling asleep as he rode, the adrenaline buzz was gone and he was cold and hungry. He had seen no one. His mount was tiring, and he slid off to lead her the rest of the way. They had reached the outskirts of the city and before long were plodding across the cobbles of yet another bridge to find the hiring yard. Brought up among horses, Nick had a feel for a good one, and he had developed a real affection for this mare. She was a rose-grey roan of the cobby sort, with a good head and a kindly eye, well up to his weight. She looked as if she could stay all day. His father had always said that a good mare would outstay and outperform any other of her kind.

'I've got money,' he thought. 'I could buy her.' He had no time to think about it now, the packet was burning a hole under his doublet, and he had enough instinct for self-preservation to realise that he must exchange the gold pieces discreetly. He had no idea how to go about it, and reluctantly delivered the mare back to her owner. But he could not resist getting into a horse-trading argument, and arrived at a fair price, aided by the fact that the man had an anniversary in the offing and needed a pretty gewgaw for his wife. Nick never went anywhere without his little pouched store of wealth, and happily parted with the jewelled comb for the mare, the saddle he had lost and tack for himself. A good enough bargain. He arranged to leave Rowena, as he had named her, where she was for the moment and set off to find the harbour.

Nick stood in the shadows of a warehouse in a thin drizzle, chewing on a small loaf filled with sausage, and watching the ships and barges being loaded. A big galley was in; he could smell it from here, flying the Golden Lion pennant of Venice, alongside a roundship festooned with little flags and great silken banners, cannon sprouting from her sides. Both were surrounded by cranes and an army of workers, unloading crates and barrels and sacking-covered bales; small boats rowed to and fro. Nick caught a whiff of nutmeg and spices, with a grace note of urine from the group of men nearby with the blue hands and aprons of dyers. A seaman approached with the unsteady gait of one newly ashore, and Nick caught his arm. The man pointed out the *Florizel,* berthed at the end of a short pier, riding high in the water and flying an English ensign. Her cargo seemed to be loading now, and a few passengers were boarding. To Nick's dismay, a cluster of officials were at the foot of her gangplank examining the credentials of everyone going aboard. Another group was diligently checking the cargo and manifest. Faulds had not mentioned the possibility of customs officers. Nick wandered along the dock. Not every ship was being checked so carefully. Had there been a leak of information? Perhaps Faulds had been caught after all. He found a corner out of the rain and for the first time drew out the packets entrusted to him. They were wrapped in oiled silk and tightly stitched, with a grubby scrap of paper thrust between them. He took one look at the pencilled name and address scrawled there and sank down on his heels, aghast.

Lord Robert Cecil. Privy Counsellor to the Crown and the Queen's spymaster after Walsingham.

News of the Armada victory, when Nick was still at school, had been slow to reach middle England, and the populace had been in the grip of spy fever, every Catholic a Spanish agent in the pay of the enemy. The unmasking of the Babington plot to assassinate the Queen, and its dreadful aftermath, had rocked the country and Nick's old schoolmaster had made a terrifying homily of it – Robert Cecil, spearheading the discovery, was a name to conjure with.

Nick was out of his depth. And on his own. He tried to think what to do. What would his resourceful father have done? Open the packet. No. Lose it? The coward's way out. He set himself to recall everything he could about the man Faulds. If Faulds had ever been in the army, Nick was a flock of goats, but the change in him when the troop arrived was significant. He was a different man, crisp, authoritative. Genuine. He had certainly been an officer of sorts.

'That's why I took it on,' thought Nick. 'Wait a minute. What if it's a trick. What if he is an officer for the Jesuits?' This could be false information. 'No, doesn't feel right. Doesn't smell right.'

He remembered waking one night at Rokesby to a clattering and shouting in the courtyard. He had looked out to see a group of horsemen wheeling and turning in the starlight. One of them rising in his stirrups had turned, hissing, 'Apostate! Traitor! Gresham shall hear of this.' His uncle, grey-faced with fear, had driven them from the gates. Nick had been beaten with no less religious fervour, but Mass was no longer held and all his guardian's books and symbols of Catholic faith disappeared. There was nothing to find when the government men arrived to search, and the servants were too frightened to speak. There was a distinctive smell to it all.

'No,' thought Nick, 'it's politics. Might be really important.'

Faulds' instructions were impossible to carry out; all his own papers were back with the troupe, in Robin's pack for safe keeping. He had not needed them on his innocent little trip to pay his respects.

The troupe! Of course. There was one more performance in

the town square tomorrow and they were embarking for home that night. Surely he could find a safe place among all their paraphernalia for a small packet. No, no, he couldn't involve his companions in what had turned into a very dangerous adventure, he would keep them on him somehow. As part of the rag, tag and bobtail of a group of players, he could perhaps hope to escape notice.

'You're a fool,' he said to himself. 'No one knows your name, and even if he's taken, a description won't find me in so many. Brace up.' He tore the paper into tiny pieces – he would not forget that name in a hurry – and scattered them in a puddle. He rose to his feet and stowed away the packet, wishing he had not lost his cloak, adjusted his sword-belt and set off, much cheered by having a feasible plan, to find his companions.

He said nothing of what had happened, and the others, attributing his mood to the sad duty he had been engaged upon, left him alone. He found out the name of their ship, and slipped away to arrange for Rowena to be put aboard. He intended to stay quiet about her as well, he had no business to be keeping a horse in his lowly station, but some instinct was guiding him and he obeyed it.

After the performance next day he was kept too busy packing up to be nervous, but as the time came to board ship his mouth was dry and tasted of tin and he could hardly keep still. There was a large group of excisemen scrutinising the outgoing craft again, and Nick was very conscious of the sticky packet anchored under his shirt. Fortunately, Will Kempe was in full extrovert form. Pleased with the success of the trip, he had begun a jig outside the town hall and was intent on keeping it up until they reached Dover and possibly London. The weather did not bode well for him, but nevertheless he danced along the quay and up the gangplank, yelling to Nick for a beat on his drum. Plastering a broad and silly grin to his face, Nick followed him aboard and onto the deck, rattling on his drum for all he was worth past the excisemen, tailed by the others. In all the orderly confusion of readying the ship for sail, they could not have been more in the way amid coils of rope and heaps of chain, bales and boxes and all their own gear. There was a parrot in a cage, and a monkey, and a stately cluster of men in courtly dress surrounding a woman carrying a small dog. Seeing Kempe, the group opened, laughing, ready to be entertained. Kempe was a familiar figure in court circles, and to the shipmaster's fury he was welcomed into the group and encouraged in his antics.

Order was established after a while and the elements separated: the fashionable gentlemen and their lady to comfortable quarters near the bridge and the players to a dismal hole aft. Nick heaved a sigh of relief and relaxed, listening to the rattle and chant as they weighed anchor, the shouts and drumming feet of the crew making sail, feeling the surging lift of the keel. They were underway and he was safe.

Their ship this time was a Dutch vessel, the *Franz-Maria*, much lighter than their outward-going barque, smart as to her paint and brightwork, her canvas white as a gull's wing as they made sail through the broad canals to the sea. She flew a silk pennant of azure blue beneath the Dutch flag, and was carrying mostly luxury goods: furs from Muscovy, porcelain and embroidered silks, fine dyestuffs, with some superior livestock, including the blood-horses of the passengers and the lady's fine-boned Arab palfrey.

All was well until they left the shelter of the harbour and the sea wall and the full force of a north-easterly gale struck them. The lapdog lady and her escort had come back on deck, exclaiming at the windmills stark against the flat, water-logged fields. Nick did not like the look of the weatherglass and went below into the hold to settle Rowena. Judging by the screams as the ship heeled over, the party had been taken by surprise. Nick smiled grimly to himself. Perhaps Will Kempe should pick his touring seasons more carefully. The North Sea in winter was no playground. He wished he was on a good, deep-bottomed, well-ballasted troopship. He hoped the captain knew his job. He heard sails coming down with a rush, bare feet pounding the deck and the bosun roaring orders.

Below decks it was chaos, all lights dowsed and the hatch-covers slammed down as a slender figure swung himself through.

'Give us some light here,' someone yelled above the screaming of the horses and Nick stood where he was, holding tight onto a plunging Rowena's head rope, until a glowworm of light bloomed in the darkness, showing a man down and a horse cast in a tangle of flailing hooves and screaming panicking horses. Nick set about turning his mare to face forward, shoving his weight against her flank to get her balanced with splayed legs against the bulkhead, tying her rope tight to the ring. The man on the deck did not look like getting up, which left two grooms out of three, Nick, and whoever it was had dropped through the hatch, to deal with twelve frantic horses. The four of them fought to get the other animals steady and secured tight in their stalls, heads to the forward bulkhead, pulling the unconscious man out of the way. Working together, thrown about in the gloom, bitten, kicked and stamped on, it took them all their combined strength and skill to get the terrified cast horse on its feet. Once up, the ungrateful creature reared and struck out with both hooves and Nick leaped just in time to knock the man in front of them out of the way, taking a glancing blow himself. In the concerted effort to get the maddened animal under control and roped up with the others, there was no time to think what might be happening above deck.

Slowly things began to calm down, and Nick realised that, far from turning and running back to shelter, the little *Franz-Maria* was making headway. They had hit the tail end of the storm and sailed through it, and although there was still a heavy swell the pounding of the waves on the wooden hull was lessening and the big combers were no longer breaking over the bows and streaming down the decks. The bolted-down hatch-covers were opened at last and the shipmaster himself came down in furious disarray. Nick realised why when he saw that the filthy scarecrow next to him was the handsome auburn-haired gallant last seen playing with my lady's monkey.

'My lord, my lord, what were you about?'

'Having a care for my horse, sir. What were you about, putting to sea in such weather—'

'The weather is nothing, sir, my ship and my crew are my affair! Your grooms are at fault, sir—' Seeing a fine quarrel brewing up, Nick quietly got on with filling mangers, amazed as always at how quickly horses adjusted themselves. Balanced and reassured, Rowena nuzzled him as he adjusted her bridle, and he stood for a moment with his face pressed to her sweaty neck, beginning to feel his various aches and pains from the struggle. Not for long. There was still a great deal to be done;

the injured man to be attended to, the deck to clear and each animal checked over for injury and treated. Even the delicate Arab had come to little harm. The skipper and the gentleman had gone to settle their differences elsewhere and it was some time before the three could take time to tend their own hurts. An extra issue of grog came round and Nick, as an honorary crew member, was uncommonly glad of his. He spared a thought for the rest of his troupe, but he was too tired to do more than make himself a bed in a heap of straw and go to sleep just as he was.

When he woke, crusted and reeking, he got himself hosed down by a deckhand, and made his way, dripping, to report to Master Kempe. Most of the company was in a sorry state and Kempe waved him grumpily away. Nick was happy to return to seeing to the horses and eating with the crew. He spent the rest of the voyage as third man below decks, and when they finally dropped anchor in the Port of London, he was on excellent terms with his fellow grooms. Rob and Jamie willingly agreed to take Rowena with the other horses to stable at the Elephant until called for.

Coming up into the fresh air to watch the ship daintily manoeuvring alongside the wharf, he became aware of his ruined clothes. He stank.

'You stink,' said Kempe at his elbow. 'I hope you're getting paid for this.'

Nick shrugged. He had not given it a thought. Nor, he suddenly realised, had he thought about the packet since coming aboard.

'Indeed he is,' said the man standing behind Kempe. 'Such sterling work must not go unrewarded.' It was the gentleman who had helped with the horses, modish and immaculate in an azure blue doublet with crested buttons, jewelled and embroidered, his auburn hair lifting in the wind.

'I trust you took no harm,' he went on. 'I am aware you took a chance for me.'

Kempe was bowing low and tugging at Nick's jacket.

'It's Devereux,' he hissed. 'My Lord of Essex. Bow, you fool—'

Essex was bouncing a clinking purse in one hand, stroking his squared-off beard with the other.

'Not a groom, I understand. A player. Your name?'

'Nicholas Talbot, sir. My lord.'

'I knew a Jack Talbot. He served with my Lord Leicester, as I did. With some distinction.'

'My father, sir.' About to toss him the leather bag, Essex hesitated, lifting an elegant eyebrow. Nick shook his head slightly. Sensing intrigue, Essex smiled.

'It pleases me to make you this small gift,' he said. 'Enquire for me at Whitehall if you seek preferment.' He twisted a button off his doublet and dropped it into the pouch. 'This will find me. Little enough for my life and my horse. Come soon.' He tossed Nick the bag and turned away with a wave.

Nick bowed, speechless, Kempe open-mouthed at his side.

'You're a made man, lad! What will you do?' Nick shook his head. He was regretting admitting his parentage so carelessly. 'I don't know. Stay with you, I expect. If you'll still have me.'

Kempe wagged his head, despairing.

'You're a fool. Robert Devereux is the Queen's darling. If he takes you up, you could find favour yourself – make your fortune! Mind you, you need to watch him.' Nick was looking

49

in the bag.

'First thing I'll do is get cleaned up, Master Kempe – buy myself some clothes. All mine are now past praying for. Is Robin on his feet? He can show me the right place to go.'

'Aye, and help you spend your money, lad. You'd be better giving it to me for safe keeping.' Nick laughed.

'Don't concern yourself, sir. I'm not so green as I'm cabbage-looking.'

'I'm thinking there's more to you than meets the eye, my lad. Very well, if you want to lay low, it's naught to do with me. But I should warn you, there will be some changes in the company – you may want to look about you.' And he laid his finger along his nose with a droll grimace and a skip in the air. 'Word to the wise.'

The court party was preparing to leave the ship, and, never one to miss an opportunity, Will turned himself into their conductor, leaping and capering before them onto the dock, waving cheerfully to Nick as he went.

Nick felt a little cast down. Life was getting very complicated. Ah, well, one thing at a time. He went to find Robin.

Chapter Four

London. Winter 1592

Nicholas Talbot, second lord of Rokesby, son of Sir James Talbot of Rokesby Hall, just seventeen years old, star sign Scorpio, pulled down his good doublet of dark-green wool, and adjusted his new frieze cloak. He strode towards the imposing gates set in the tower wall protecting Whitehall, now sporting stiffly frozen standards and banners in immobile folds. He rather fancied himself in his fashionable Venetians. Softly falling snow outlined the elaborate iron scrollwork and clung to the armour of the men-at-arms, covered the icy slush underfoot. Far to his right the terrifying bulk of the Tower was silhouetted on the skyline: further towards the river was the Great Stone Gate, Traitors' Gate, hung with the severed heads and butchered limbs of those deemed guilty of treason to her Majesty, their horrors made grotesque with a festive cap of white. The dread reality of it suddenly struck home, and Nick's courage failed him for a moment. His fervent imagination conjured up screams and shrieks of agony as limbs popped from their sockets and fingers and feet were slowly crushed in a tightening iron press. He knew a little of that kind of pain. His own hand had been trapped under the iron rim of a recoiling cannon wheel when he was a child. Waiting to be freed had seemed an eternity of pain, but nothing to the agony as the feeling came back; his hand and arm and then his whole body on fire, fiery strokes pulsing with the beat of his heart. He looked at his left hand, missing the top joint of the crooked middle finger and shuddered. This was nothing to do with him. The packet had swollen in Nick's imagination to grotesque proportions, the size of a door, impossible to hide. A door to adventure or the way to suicide. He could turn away, destroy it, no one would know.

'I would know,' he thought. His father's face came between him and the guardians of the gates, with that faint smile and lifted eyebrow. Nick took a deep breath and turned again to his task, to be forestalled by a man brushing boldly past him.

'Master William Shakespeare, to see Master Tilney,' he announced. Nick was astounded. Was it possible then, to simply walk up and demand entry? But no, the guard wanted to know what business the playwright had with Master Tilney.

'I have two plays to submit to the Master of the Rolls,' said Shakespeare. 'A matter of urgency. Her Majesty requires entertainments for Twelfth Night. Master Tilney expects me.' Nick cringed, expecting him to be felled to the ground for his presumption, but the guard simply summoned a messenger and dispatched him with a word or two. Master Shakespeare turned aside and paced slowly to and fro, protecting the scrips under his cloak as the snow fell thicker. Presently the messenger returned with a tall man of clerkly appearance. The gates were opened and Shakespeare passed through. The men-at-arms closed the gates behind them and went back to their posts: they looked frozen. Nick took off his glove, fingered out the button from his pouch, summoned up his courage and approached the older man on the right.

'I am here at the pleasure of my Lord of Essex,' he announced boldly, the turquoise button displayed on the palm of his hand. The man looked him slowly up and down.

'I shouldn't wonder,' he said with an unpleasant smile. He nodded to his junior, who swung the gate open once more, pushing now against the gathering snow.

'I daresay you know where to find him, my lad. If not, just open your ears.'

Face burning, Nick entered the courtyard and hastened through the archway towards the great oaken doors of the building. More guards. Not one to make the same mistake twice, he stood panting and gasping for breath.

'I have a message for my Lord of Essex,' he gasped urgently, just as he played the messenger in *Tamburlaine*, keeping the button in reserve. The doors crashed open and he was in. Keeping up the illusion he sped along a passage lined with men-at-arms until he could turn a corner and relax. He leaned against the wall, shaking. The wretched button had got him in, now what? How could he find such an august person as Sir Robert Cecil? Try the messenger trick again? The long corridor stretched empty to either side, silent except for a burst of laughter and song from far away.

'Essex, I suppose, like the man said.' Nick only wanted to approach his putative patron as a last resort; he was not ready to put himself in a position where his uncle might find him yet. He tossed a mental coin and turned left, away from the laughter, trying to walk as if he had every right to be there. He had nearly reached the end of the wide passage with its columns and long diamond-paned windows, when a door opened and a man emerged in some haste, almost toppling Nick over. Turning with an apology, the man went as grey as the sky outside the window. It was Faulds.

'Body of Christ, it's you! Alive!'

'Did you fear I might not be, sir?'

'Have you not heard? The *Florizel* went down with all hands, blown onto the Goodwins in the storm – never mind that now, have you got it?' As Nick nodded, he went on, 'Of course you have, why else would you be here? What took you so long?' And he hustled an indignant Nick into a room with a blazing fire at one end, crying, 'He is here, my lord. Our man in Amsterdam! All safe and sound.' He rounded on Nick, 'Come on then, give it to us!'

At the end of the room, close to the fire, sat a small figure in black. The armchair was low but his feet still dangled clear of the floor, and as he turned painfully towards them Nick saw the twisted spine and the hunched shoulder. So this was Robert Cecil, the 'little beagle', the Queen's new spymaster and her 'elf'. After the cold of the corridors, Nick felt his face blazing in the heat of the fire as Faulds pushed him forward. He had almost to undress to find the packet strapped to his skin in the small of his back, and Cecil sat watching him, swinging his legs and twiddling his thumbs. As Faulds snatched the thing and brought it to him, he simply indicated the table at his side and nodded dismissal.

'Wait outside,' he said. 'I wish to speak to this young man. It would seem that a word of thanks is in order. Sit,' he said to Nicholas, who was stuffing in his shirt and attending to his points. Nick looked around. There was only a stool, so he sat on that, effectively bringing himself down to Cecil's eye level.

'Take off your cloak. You will lose the benefit when you leave.' Ignoring the package, he picked up a tablet and dipped a pen in the inkwell. 'Your name?'

Nick told him.

'Talbot, Talbot. Hmm.' He made a note. 'Why are you not at school or university?' Nick told him that too.

'What were you doing in Amsterdam?'

'Earning a living with the players, sir, to fill the time.'

'Tell me exactly what transpired after Master Faulds left you. Leave nothing out, however trivial.' Nick did his best and halfway through, when Essex came into the narrative, Cecil poured a goblet of wine and gave it to him. When he had finished, there was a long silence.

'Have you seen my lord Essex since, or spoken to him?'

'No.'

'Have you spoken to him, or to anyone of this task?'

'To no one, sir.'

'Hmmm— ' He sat for some time tapping his teeth with his quill. 'You have performed a useful service. Just for the fun of it, it would seem. You can be rewarded in one of two ways, Talbot. Money, or I can arrange for you to take up your rightful position at once, without let or hindrance. However, if you choose the latter, I should prefer you to install an overseer and remain incognito with the players until I tell you otherwise. You are too young to manage a large estate but in spite of that you have shown resource of a certain kind. You could be of further service to me and to your country. This is advice only, it is not a condition of your reward. Of course, if you prefer to take my lord Essex up on his offer of preferment, you are at liberty to do so. In which case, take the money. You will need it.'

Nick could hardly sit still for excitement. He had forgotten the fear and constant anxiety, and was about to speak when Cecil held up a hand.

'Take time, young man. You have shown yourself to be

capable of sensible decision-making. You are no hothead to rush into a choice that may affect your whole life: indeed may even shorten it. You are at the Elephant, you say. I will arrange for Master Faulds to meet with you there in an hour. Talk it over with him and he will inform me of your decision. I do not wish to see you again. If you are to be of use to me, go on as you have been, and do not be disappointed if there is delay. Although a beardless youth who can handle himself has obvious usefulness, I shall have some regard for your lack of years and experience. Your father, God rest his soul, would not thank me for getting you untimely killed.'

Nick scrambled to his feet and made an awkward bow.

'I thank you, sir.' Cecil waved him away.

'Be off with you. And remember, a golden opinion, once won, must be maintained.' And with these ominous words ringing in his ears Nick bowed himself out to keep his appointment at the Elephant tavern.

Chapter Five

Nick got himself out of the room somehow, his legs decidedly shaky and found Faulds waiting for him, leaning his shoulders against the wall and picking his teeth with the point of his dagger.

'He wants you, now.'

Faulds lowered the dagger, inspected its point, wiped it on

his sleeve and stuck it back in his belt.

'Wait,' he said, and pushed through the door.

Nick realised he was holding his breath. He let it out with a gasp, and moved along the corridor to look out of the window. Master Shakespeare was crossing the courtyard, a dejected slump to his shoulders. As Nick watched, he stopped and leafed through the papers he carried. Finding what he wanted, he shrugged, tore the scrips across and across again and tossed the pieces into the air. The remaining one he stuffed into his doublet, squared his shoulders and strode to the gates. He exchanged a few words with the man on guard, who laughed and let him through into the thickening snow.

'No doubt he'll be at the Mermaid later,' thought Nick. 'I'll catch up with it.'

Cecil's door opened again.

'I am to speak with you,' said Faulds. 'But not at the Elephant, thank you very much, too many eyes and ears. Do you know the Cardinal's Hat on Bankside, further along?'

'No, sir.'

'Don't "sir" me; you saved my bacon two weeks ago. I suppose you are too young and innocent to have found the stews, or perhaps you just haven't had time. Take a boat to Mason Stairs – best avoid Paris Gardens – and walk towards London Bridge down Willow Street. 'Cap Alley is a cough and a spit along. If you reach Goat Stairs you've gone too far. Ask for Meg, she's a good clean girl. Wait for me upstairs. One hour. Don't mention my name.'

'Yes, sir. Master Faulds.'

'You don't know my name. We do not wish you to be seen with me, be associated with me, or know of me. You are the

57

fresh face, let's keep it that way. Call me captain.'

Damned if I do, thought Nick.

'One hour. Don't be late.'

Faulds nodded and turned back into the room. His stomach churning with excitement, Nick was setting off the way he had come, when Faulds shot out of the room again and seized his arm.

'Not that way, Essex is just leaving. Don't want him to see you here. This way, come—'

He hustled Nick along the corridor, down some steps and through a long passage towards a smell of roasting meat that made his mouth water, down more steps and round a corner into a dimly-lit hall. A clamour of voices and clashing pots was coming with the cooking smells from further along, where a low door was outlined in orange light.

Faulds paused and listened a moment, then crossed the flagstones to a heavy iron-banded door with a massive lock. He turned the key and thrust Nick out into a small courtyard.

'There will be a guard at the gate. Password Phoenix,' and he vanished back into the gloom.

The snow was falling faster now and Nick pulled up the hood of his cloak, careful of his cap-feather. It all seemed unreal. Passwords and secrets, for God's sake. He trod across the unmarked snow and was instantly challenged.

'Phoenix,' he muttered self-consciously, not really expecting to be let go free. A frozen-looking guard in half-armour saluted, and unlocking the gate quietly dragged it open, the snow piling up around his boots. Nick passed through, grinning to himself. What a tale this was going to make! He could imagine his friends… he stopped in his tracks. He was not going to be able to share this with anyone. He was on his own in what promised to be a maze of intrigue, having to account for his absences with lies, answerable to men like Cecil and Faulds. He turned to the only role model he knew.

'What have I done? Father? Should I refuse—'

He was back in his father's tent, having taken his punishment and now, far worse, faced the disappointed gaze of the man who made him. As he looked, a gleam of amusement lit the steady grey eyes.

'We all make mistakes, son. You won't lie to save your own skin again. Listen to me, Nicholas. Your soul and your honour are your own to safeguard. We can lie for our country without dishonour but not for our own profit. God knows I have lied and killed for my Queen before now, and if I must suffer for it in the next world, so be it. It's a fine line. But if you ever become a leader of men, Nick, and you will, if you are a man of honour they will follow you into the cannon's mouth. You must earn that trust. You have mine.' The echo faded on a whisper, 'Remember me—'

Bewildered, Nick recalled Cecil's words. 'You can serve your country.'

Jack Talbot had commanded his own troop and died in battle, honourably, knighted on the field. Creeping about backstairs at the heels of men like Faulds hardly compared. Nick shook his head. He would see what Faulds had to say and then decide.

He looked about him. There were several passages leading off the small courtyard and he chose the one that had a whiff of river mud. It sloped downward with a low roof and slimy cobbles smelling of mushrooms, and he almost slithered into the two boatmen huddling for shelter at the bottom.

Begging their pardon, he asked, 'What stairs are these?'

'The Privy Stairs, o'course, wotcher think? And if y'wants ter cross, it'll cost y'double.' No saluting here. Past haggling, Nick paid, followed the man into one of the boats and they pushed off into the full force of the weather. He sat hunched in his cloak in the stern, snow beginning to stick to his eyelashes.

'I could have been warm and snug in the Mermaid by now,' he grumbled to himself, feeling sympathy for the ferryman whose purple hands were freezing to the oars. His enthusiasm for the enterprise was decidedly waning. Rafts of floating debris were drifting and freezing together making an extra hazard on the fast-ebbing tide, and when they reached the Mason Stair, there was an expanse of mud at the foot of the steps. The boatman sniggered as Nick almost slid back into the water, but he clawed his way up and started to pick his way past a row of houses already shuttered and dark.

Every sense was heightened; he smelt the sharp tang of vinegar from the tenting fields and a whiff from the bear pits before his considerable nose gave up from the cold. Small sounds of shifting animals, a pig grunted and there was a sharp cry, abruptly cut off, from behind in the Paris Fields. He eased his sword in its scabbard and threw back his cloak to free his arm. He went on cautiously, hugging the wall, relieved when he reached 'Cap Alley unmolested.

A few paces along, an open door threw a yellow rectangle onto the dirty, piled-up snow. A bulky man in a canvas apron was busy ejecting two quarrelsome drunks, with a deal of shouting and swearing. A lantern hung beside the door, lighting a sign painted on the wall, another sign swung in the wind with a wincing shriek. The Cardinal's Hat. Gusts of talk and bawdy laughter eddied from the open door with a snatch of song. Nick knew the song from campfire and march and the words were unrepeatable in polite society. Someone yelled 'Put the wood in it, Billy!' and the man in the apron turned, dusting his hands and saw Nick, hesitating under the sign.

'Looking for someone?'

'I was told to ask for Meg.'

'She's busy. If you want someone to teach you your business, lad, try Sue. If you can afford it.'

Flushing, Nick gathered his wits.

'I assure you, sir, I rise like the phoenix when required. I shall wait, if you please.'

The man went very still. Then, 'Of course, sir, of course. Come in, she will come to you presently,' and he ushered Nick through the crowded, noisy room into a small hallway with another door leading back outside, a stairway and two chairs, one occupied. The landlord jerked his head and the other man rose and scuttled off behind them.

'A moment, sir,' and the landlord disappeared upstairs. Nick waited, listening to the effortful grunts and creaks from above. After a while they ceased, coins clinked and presently a portly, sweating individual stumbled down the stairs still tucking in his shirt and lacing up his cod-piece. He looked Nick up and down and gave him a wave and a lascivious grin before pushing his way into the taproom. Nick wished very much he was safely back in Cheapside with Nell.

His host peered over the banister and beckoned him to come up. One of the two doors on the landing stood open, revealing a rumpled bed and a girl hastily pulling on her clothes. The landlord placed himself in front of Nick.

'Hurry yourself, girl, we have visitors.' He pulled the door shut and tapped on the other.

The room into which Nick was shown was not at all what he had expected. It was neat and clean, furnished with a tapestry-covered table and comfortable chairs, the bed tidy in a curtained alcove. Good wax candles and a bright fire discovered the velvet skirts of a woman sitting sewing in the window seat. Demure pleated lawn filled the neck of her bodice and her hair was tucked into a cap. The face under the starched frill was not young, but comely under discreet paint and her nails were clean oval filberts.

She put aside her needlework and smiled at him.

'Take off your cloak, sir, and warm yourself.' Going to the fire, she lifted a steaming jug; the aromatic smell of spiced wine reached him as she poured a goblet full and offered it to him. The rustle of her skirts and the ticking of the fire were the only sounds, the closing of the door had cut off the roar of the taproom; the explicit noises he had heard from the hall belonged to another world.

'Come to the fire, sir, you must be shrammed with cold.' Her voice was low and pleasant, and Nick was relieved of cloak and cap and settled in a chair by the fire before he had found his tongue.

'My cousin will be here soon.' Of course, he thought, the accent is Kentish, like Faulds. He found his voice.

'Thank you, mistress. My name is Nicholas—' She interrupted him.

'My name is Meg.' The latch clicked. 'And here he is.'

Faulds walked in, jaunty and self-important, knocking snow

off cloak and cap as he kissed his cousin and sent her out of the room with a friendly slap.

'Made yourself at home, I see. Not what you were looking for, I daresay. You got past Billy,' he said, pouring wine and sitting down. 'I'm impressed.'

'Phoenix seems to open a lot of doors.'

'To be used sparingly in future. Now, we have been speaking of you.'

'He thinks a lot of himself,' thought Nick, 'aligning himself with lord Cecil like that.'

Faulds went on, 'If you have decided to take the money and run, the matter ends here. No one would blame you. If you are willing to serve with us, here is the sweetener.' He placed a heavy chinking bag and a sealed packet on the table.

'Did he mean what he said? About my uncle?'

'I know nothing of that. What he says he usually means.' Nick picked up the packet and opened it. Inside was a warrant, signed and sealed, for his guardian's arrest. A note was enclosed. 'Use this or not, as you please. My bill will be presented in due course. The money you have already earned. Keep it with no obligation and our thanks.' He looked up.

'Take your time,' said Faulds, booted feet to the flames.

'I want my inheritance – to put things right. My father died fighting for this.'

'Do I take it that is your answer? If I were you—'

'I want to look after my people. I want it to be as my father intended – I can't be an actor all my life… I want the home he fought for—'

'You won't get much chance to live in it, my dear. And if you renege on the deal or prove a loose mouth, you won't live long at all, I warn you. I am being frank with you, son.' The condescending tone grated and Nick found he was grinding his teeth. Faulds went on.

'The Essex connection could be useful, or dangerous. Depends how you play it. That man is heading for trouble. If you want my advice, you'll settle for a quiet life in the country.' He caught Nick's eye and grunted. 'If not, settle your affairs and we'll be in touch. It may be sooner than my lord Cecil hinted. A valuable mutual acquaintance is sailing very close to the wind and you may be called on. Take back your blasted castle or whatever it is and be ready. If you need help, find this man. He's a pinching, nip-farthing man of law, but he knows his job.' He got up and stretched. 'Now, you won't get back over the river tonight. I suggest you stay here—'

'Thank you, I have friends in Southwark, sir.'

'Do as you please, stripling,' replied Faulds, sharply. 'My cousin would have been pleased to entertain you.'

'I feel I have had entertainment enough, Mr – er. There is much to think of and I believe I am playing tomorrow – today.'

'Young people have no stamina these days. As you will—' He picked up his cup and drained it as his cousin entered the room. 'This young cub spurns your hospitality, my dear. Detain him, if you please, until I am well away.' He turned in the doorway. 'Should we meet in public, you do not know me. Remember what I have said. Guard your tongue and be careful. Be very, very careful indeed.' The door closed quietly behind him.

The woman crossed to spread her wide skirts in the chair he had occupied. She smiled up at him, and Nick felt suddenly over-large and clumsy.

'I had no wish to offend you, mistress,' he stammered.

'No offence in the world.' She tipped away his untasted wine and poured him another from the jug by the fire. He took it gratefully. 'I would not thrust myself upon you, Master Nicholas, but if ever you are in need of a friend, you will find me here. Billy will know you again.' She paused. 'I am not so free with advice as my cousin, but I tell you this. He is very good at what he does – however irritating. I call him my mosquito. Heed him. War has many faces, Nicholas, and we live in interesting times, as they say. Think hard.'

She sat gazing into the fire, musing. Nick sat and watched her, warming his hands round his goblet. She puzzled him. After a while, she spoke.

'You must have certain qualities that make you apt to their purposes. My cousin is a good judge. He has to be.' She looked into his face. 'Remember, they are coming to you, suing for your service. Stay independent and keep your advantage.'

This chimed so sweetly with his father's favourite precept that he grinned at her in sudden amity. *Take the high ground, be it moral or geographic, and hold it...*

'I understand you, Mistress Meg. But first things first. They don't want me yet. They think I am too green a stick to lean on. I have time.'

'I shall watch with interest. Now, the bed is yours if you want it. If not, Edward is long gone and you may leave.'

She stood and Nick hastily collected cloak and cap, stowed away the parchment and bent to kiss her hand. She reached up and stroked his cheek. 'Take care, little one.'

Nick smiled down at her.

'I am glad to be of your acquaintance, mistress.'

Once back out in the driving snow he began to regret the ambiguously offered bed. Head down, he made his way east past the bear-baiting arena towards the darkened bulk of the theatre called the Rose, where he was pretty sure the night-watchman would be fast asleep. Sure enough he was able to climb over the gate and steal across the auditorium to the tiring room at the back, where he made himself a snug nest in a pile of cloaks. He was hungry, and with all he had to think of he expected to lie awake, but once warm and comfortable he fell off the edge of this frightening new world into a deep sleep.

He woke with a start and couldn't think where he was. Getting up, he peered out of the door to find the wind had dropped, the sky was a dazzling blue and everything was covered in a sheet of untrodden white. He would have to climb out at the back.

Edward Alleyn, Burbage's only rival for the actor's crown, leased this newly-built theatre and Nick liked it. He liked the bullring shape, open to the sky, the flexible acting area and the intimacy of the audience standing close on all three sides of the stage. He liked the smell of the new wood. He liked the repertoire. Alleyn had the monopoly of Christopher Marlowe's plays, Kempe had been putting on a pirated version. Marlowe was rapidly becoming a cult hero in Nick's imagination – as he was for many others.

'Perhaps I shall play here one day,' he said to himself. The events of yesterday came crowding back. His acting career looked like being fragmented, to say the least. The warrant crackled against his breast – his guardian's death warrant if he chose to use it. He thought of those rotting heads on Traitor's

Gate. No, not that way. For use as a threat only. Why not wait? He was enjoying life with the players – his time would come if he did nothing. He would be under no obligation to Cecil.

'Make up your mind.'

He was thinking more clearly this morning. As he climbed out of a back window and started walking towards London Bridge, the crisp cold air was invigorating. The bag of money was heavy at his waist as he strode along. He had said to Faulds 'I can't be an actor all my life.' He had said it without thinking, but it was true. It had begun as an interim measure and he had been drawn into it – it was like some drug. He loved it.

'But I want more.' Lord of Rokesby, his father's son, a travelling player? What sort of future was that?

'Don't want to end up like Faulds, either.' What about Essex and his offer of preferment? What sort of preferment – the handsome earl's own position looked decidedly shaky.

If Nick did as his instinct told him, he would do the first thing to hand – take back Rokesby. If that committed him to Cecil, so be it.

'Faulds has reached his ceiling – it needn't be mine.'

He suddenly saw with the clarity of hunger and brisk exercise, what he should have seen before. He had been behind the scenes already, seen and heard what he should not, knew one of Cecil's agents. His freedom and probably his life, hung on this decision.

'Very well. *Que sera*. I'll see the world and take my chances. Seize the day.' And with this, he hitched up his sword and went to find Rowena at the Elephant and eat the best breakfast money could buy.

Chapter Six

Once Nick had eaten his fill and was sitting back with a second mug of ale, another idea occurred to him. He fished out the paper Faulds had scribbled on.

'Nathaniel Fitzgibbon. Attorney at law. 13, Gray's Inn Road.'

He could go to law. Somehow this course failed to appeal. His uncle's name, his family name would be dragged through the courts and the thing could wear on for months, perhaps years. The notion was foreign to his temperament and he dismissed it on the spot.

He recalled Kate's message and the mention of the armed guard. After the episode with the fugitive Papists, a number of men had been employed and armed, set to patrol the grounds and repel boarders. His guardian was in possession and would not give up Rokesby without a struggle, even when Nick came of age.

A plan was forming in his mind. He put away Master Fitzgibbon and his litigations and reviewed his new programme.

One: fetch his horse and pay his shot.

Two: get himself to Chelsea barracks and find out where Sergeant Ponsonby was billeted these days.

Three: Seek out his old tutor, now retired at Jack Talbot's expense to a cottage in Richmond.

Reunited with Rowena, he left a message for Robin, rode across the bridge between the crowded shops and turned downriver towards Chelsea. One of the men on guard duty he knew. The man did not recognise him, of course, but when

Nick dismounted and gave his name, he so far forgot himself as to shout with laughter and beat him on the shoulder.

'Nick Talbot, by all that's holy! You young imp of Satan, you've grown a little! Corp, come and see who's here – the guvnor's boy, all grown up.' The angry face of the man emerging from the barracks relaxed as he recognised the profile.

'Master Talbot – or melord Rokesby I suppose I should say. Come to join us, is it? Your da wouldn't like that.' Nick grinned and shook his head.

'No, Taffy, I'm looking for Alf Ponsonby. Is he still with us?'

''fraid not, sir. Lost an eye at Arras. Retired now, he is, lives with his old 'oman – you mind his wife? Tongue like sandpaper, she has. Got three sons now.'

'Do you know where?'

'Got a smallholding out at Holborn. Whyfor d'you want him?'

'I've a mind to reclaim my father's property. I need some trained men. There's bound to be a spot of bother.'

'Wilson! Come and give a mind to this man's horse. Come you in, come in, there's men here would like to see you. We lost Murdo and Simmonds, if you remember them—' The reunion went on some time, and Nick left full of ale and goodwill and with some useful names and addresses. He rode westward, Rowena picking her way delicately through the drifted snow, musing rather drunkenly on the fortunes of war, his father's legacy of loyalty and trust and the blessed straightforwardness of fighting men.

Following directions, he had no trouble finding Ponsonby, where he was taking refuge in his pigsty from his wife's notorious tongue. Greetings and exclamations over, oiled by some potent spirit from the sergeant's secret cache, Nick got down to business. Ponsonby was easily recruited, black eyepatch and all, angered by what Nick had to tell him and spoiling for some fun and a holiday from his family.

Yes, he could find the men if Nick could supply the armour. Always prepare for the worst, lad. Yes, he knew a man to provide it. Yes, he would meet Nick in Stratford in a week's time with a troop. Have another drink. Who would have thought it? Nick tore himself away from his reminiscences at last, congratulated Janet on her trio of noisy children and rode off with one of her pasties in his fist and two more in his saddlebag (for the growing lad), setting Rowena's nose towards Richmond. The food and the cold air between them cleared his head and he began to enjoy the ride.

Ten years older and the drink taken, combined with the glare off the snowfields, would have given him a blinding headache. As it was, he rode contentedly along between the hedges whistling and singing to Rowena, and chewing his second pasty with enormous enjoyment. So much the worse then, when he arrived at the village where his tutor lived, to find strangers occupying the cottage.

The charming, erudite scholar who had taught Nick from infancy was not there. Jack Talbot had given him the cottage where he himself had been born, and a life-long pension for what he considered a job well done. When Nick introduced himself to the new occupants, the name Talbot triggered off a torrent of complaint. The rents went up each year and nothing was done about the roof or the cracks in the walls and the damp and what was he going to do about it?

When he discovered what had happened, Nick's resentment of his uncle hardened into rage. Unable to repossess the cottage, Paul had simply discontinued the pension and made it impossible for Doctor Knowles to live there. He had then taken it over and now let it to the present couple. Once convinced that Nick was not their rack-rent landlord, and would do his best to see that things were put right, they gave him civil answers.

Yes, they thought they had heard of an old gentleman called Knowles but he couldn't possibly be the man this young lord was looking for. He lived in a hovel at the edge of the woods behind the church. Oh, thank you my lord, thank you, you understand we had no responsibility—

Furiously angry, Nick galloped recklessly through the village, slithering on the snow, and found a dilapidated shack built, or rather assembled, between two large elms. A thin thread of smoke spiralled from a roof of turfed-over branches. Appalled, Nick flung himself from the saddle and hammered on the door so hard it sprang open. The squalor outside belied the Spartan neatness within. A small turf fire with a cooking pot, a bed of spruce branches and a blanket on the dirt floor, and a bodged table and stool was all there were. A pile of books, with pen and paper, was the only sign of the civilisation so dear to the occupant's heart. It was bitterly cold. And empty. Nick's heart was pounding, he was almost in tears. Rowena whinnied and a figure darkened the door.

'Who is there?'

'Nolly! Oh, God, Nolly, how could I have let this happen? I never thought—'

'That is never young Nicholas! So tall! Of course, you must be… let me see… sixteen! No, you have had a birthday. So like

71

your father, God rest his soul.'

The two men, old and young, met and embraced, tears flowing freely now.

'Forgive me, Noll. I have no excuse—'

'Nor do you need one. What could you know – a mere child. My dear Nicholas, I have been so worried. I thought you gone.' Presently, Nick drew him outside, where the lowering sun still gave a little warmth, dusted the snow off a tree stump, sat him down and gave him the last pasty.

'It ends here,' he said. 'I came with a request – a favour to ask, if you like. Now,' he choked on the words. 'I hardly dare to speak it.'

'This was none of your doing. Ask.'

'I wanted you to visit Rokesby and teach a young woman there. She is clever, she would be an apt pupil, Noll.' He stopped. 'I love her. She was good to me – I would repay her. Money is not enough. Now, well, you will have a cottage again, all will be as before, of course. Or perhaps you would live at Rokesby, and be cared for as is fitting.'

'How could this be? Your uncle…'

'Will be gone. Rokesby is mine and I shall take it.'

'You don't change, Nicholas. Except in inches. When is this translation to take place?'

'Next week. There are things to arrange. Until then you will come with me, we shall see you comfortably lodged and when matters are settled, I will come for you. Will you then stay at Rokesby until you decide?' The wise eyes twinkled.

'My pupil outstrips me. Which is as it should be. I shall be guided by you, my lord Rokesby.' Nick flushed and shook his head. The old man, brown, weathered and thin as a rail, laughed at him.

'The circle of life, my dear Nicholas. Accept it. You are in authority now.'

Chapter Seven

Nick made one more call the following week. He obtained leave of absence from the company 'on personal affairs' ('Don't guarantee your job back, mind.') and, through Ponsonby, located his father's second-in-command. Hugh Shawcross had been a high-flier, promoted fast and young, his career cut short when he lost an arm outside Beauvais. Now widowed with one small boy, he lived with his married sister in Sussex, near Horsham, eking out a tiny pension. A frequent arbiter between Nick and his father, he greeted him with the sardonic smile Nick remembered.

'So, my chickens are coming home to roost, are they? Which particular sins am I to pay for now? You will sup with us – do not think of riding out again tonight.' Nick accepted gratefully. Rowena was tired, his cloak was stiff with sleet and his eyes sore and streaming from the bitter wind. The mare settled and fed, Mistress Blyth insisted on finding him dry clothes and the two men sat either side of a blazing fire with a hot toddy. Shawcross' brother-in-law was a farmer in a fair way of business, the house was comfortable and well-found, and Nick began to doubt that his companion would favour the enterprise. He forgot for the moment that the eager young Captain Shawcross had been a strategist of great ability, his groundwork and forward planning always excellent. He was wasted here, his intellect rusting away.

Nick told his tale, leaving out lord Cecil, saying only that he wished to see something of the world before settling down.

'I have come to ask you to take on the management of Rokesby estate. There will be a lot of work. There would be Doctor Knowles – you remember him – to tutor your boy and you would have a completely free hand. I shall be away, and when I do come, I shall not interfere. I have in mind to install my – a young woman as housekeeper. If she will.'

'Have you asked her?'

'Not yet.' There was a long silence while Shawcross looked at him, measuring.

'How old are you now Nick? Sixteen? Too young to be settling in the country minding sheep. I accept with thanks. When do we start?'

Flushed with pleasure, Nick raised his glass.

'We go to unseat my uncle next week. There's a lot still to do. I hope to God the bloody weather improves.'

They were in luck. The following Tuesday dawned bright and clear and Nick and Shawcross made rendezvous with Ponsonby and his men in the shelter of a wood on the edge of the Rokesby estates.

Nick had decided to hire mounts for the fifteen men Ponsonby had found, to save time on the road. He had considered bringing in the sherrif and his men from Stratford, but decided he would keep the warrant for a last resort. He would fight his own battle and avoid bloodshed if he could.

He surveyed the troop of men waiting for him.

'Into the cannon's mouth,' he thought. 'Get it right.' Many of the men with Ponsonby knew Shawcross, and remembered Nick as an inquisitive harum-scarum child under their feet. They were prepared to tolerate him for his father's sake and exchanged sly grins as he rode up to face them. The grins faded as the tall, determined young man greeted them in a clear, carrying voice, sitting easily in the saddle. Nick outlined his simple plan, emphasising the element of surprise and his hope for a bloodless outcome. None of them were young, all experienced campaigners, musketeers and archers among them, and he was able to make a small deferential joke. Shawcross, amused, watched them warm to him, and exchanged a wink with the sergeant.

They set off as the low winter sun began to cast long lilac shadows, the white fields tinted with apricot. They rode in silence between deep hedges of hawthorn and may, bowed down under their burden of snow.

The old priory had been built in the lee of a forested hill, facing southwest, and they were able to skirt behind the hill and approach under the walls unseen. Nick's preparations had been comprehensive, he had hardly been out of the saddle all week. He had made contact with old Jem, and knew his guardian still kept a force of some twenty men.

The old groom was in the gatehouse with the keeper, looking out for Nick's approach. The gates were opened for them at once and they rode without pause into the courtyard and drew up smartly before the great doors to the main building. Nick looked up and round, checking the upper windows. There would have been no time for men to be set there, and he nodded to the trumpeter.

The trumpet sounded, its bold note echoing back from the four stone walls surrounding them. Out of the cloisters came the servants, the grooms and farm workers and formed two creditable lines. They doffed their caps and bowed. Jem had been busy.

'Sound the dismount, if you please, Sergeant.'

The doors opened and a steward appeared. Frost sparkled on the steps like marzipan and he trod carefully down, staff in hand. He walked to where Nick was standing and offered it gravely. Nick took it and handed it back.

'Where is my uncle? Ask him to come out to me here.' He was aware he was taking a risk. Time was passing, and his chief advantage was dwindling away. He feared his uncle's glib tongue and knew he could be made to look a fool, bringing such a force to break down a door that seemed already open. He would keep to his plan. He would rather look a fool than be fooled.

In the next second he was proved right. A ball whistled past his cheek and whined off the granite of the gatehouse behind him, burying itself in the ground. Before they heard the bang, he was giving his orders. Outside himself, he heard his actor's voice issuing a string of crisp commands.

'Gunners take cover and set up your muskets. You four archers, to the gatehouse roof. Jem, show the way. Shawcross, Sergeant, take your men and search the house. Start at the back. Grooms go with them. You three come with me.' The men dispersed like beads of quicksilver, and, covered by the marksmen setting up in the cloister, Nick made for the open door at the double. Up the steps and through the hall, up the stairs and into the long gallery where the premature shot had come from. With no time to reload the single musket, four swordsmen faced them beneath the oriel window.

Nick had practised for hours in this gallery, and he drew his sword with glee. The men with him fanned out, each choosing his man. Nick picked the one to the right, who looked most dangerous. His uncle's mercenaries had grown lazy in idleness, and had no real stomach for this fight, but they were not lacking in courage and came on with a rush.

Unfortunately, they all chose to attack the man they took to be most vulnerable and converged on Nick, getting in each others' way. It was short and sharp, over too soon for Nick, who had stuck to his target and enjoyed a fast bout with him. His men, after a quick look, left him to it and soon disarmed the others. Nick pinked his man in the sword arm and the weapon clattered to the floor.

'This is too easy,' he thought. But it was not over yet. They had herded their prisoners back into the courtyard to join those driven from the house, all nursing cuts and bruises, when a group of yelling swordsmen erupted from the doorway.

Four arrows planted themselves in the snow at their feet, followed by the hiss and twang of the bows. Those in front stopped so fast that the men behind cannoned into them and they slid down the icy steps in an inglorious heap. Nick felt that his first command was turning into farce. He flung up an arm to the archers grinning on the gatehouse and asked Jem, 'Is that the lot?'

Counting, Jem nodded.

'Sergeant, take command, if you please,' said Nick with a

straight face, and turned to the steward, who was cowering against the wall.

'I ask you again, where is my uncle?'

'In the library, my lord.'

Shawcross stepped forward and Nick shook his head. The fewer people who knew about the warrant, should he have to threaten, the better.

Despite himself, Nick was shaking as he walked the familiar way to the seat of punishment. The library, which should have been a room of peace and enjoyment, was to him a place of purgatory. There he had been whipped and scourged with tongue and lash, dispossessed and humiliated. He had decided to conduct this interview with his uncle in private however, knowing how skilled Paul was in manipulation.

He squared his shoulders and pushed open the door. Paul Talbot, as unlike his half-brother as he could be, was sitting behind the heavy desk, strangely shrunken. His eyes widened as Nick strode into the room and he strained back in his chair. Nevertheless, he spoke first, the nasal whine in his voice accentuated.

'My dear Nicholas! Such a fuss! Could you not have made me a civilised visit? Your coming-of-age is a few years yet – this resort to violence is unwise. I confess I fail to see what you hope to achieve. I have only to send for—'

'Send for nobody. I am here to ask you to leave. Quietly, for your own sake. At once. And take your men with you.'

'Nonsense. This reckless action, typical, I might say, is unlawful. The sherrif—'

'Your guardianship was unlawful. You misused my people,

my property and myself. You know it. Keep your dignity and go quietly. Or do you wish to be thrown out?'

'And what if I refuse? I am an old man, it ill becomes you to use force.'

'That cock won't fight. You are my father's younger brother, half the age of Doctor Knowles, the man you turned out of his home to starve. I am not here to bandy words with you. Leave of your own will, or I shall be obliged to execute the warrant I have for your arrest.'

Paul was white, his hands writhing together on the desk in front of him. Aware, he hid them in his lap.

'Arrest? What charge? I have done nothing except care for you, take upon my poor shoulders the charge of your estate and education, spend my days in the nurturing of my brother's neglected child.' He could not have taken a worse line. Sickened, Nick drew out the warrant he had hoped not to use.

'You are cited a usurper and a Catholic spy, harbouring Jesuit followers of Gresham. No, don't say it, I did not betray you. You are my father's brother: do not make me use this. Go now, of your own accord, and I will burn it.'

Naked hatred burned in his uncle's eyes. Always jealous of his half-brother, now robbed of his comfortable acquisition, impotent, he was beside himself. About to call his nephew's bluff, he hesitated. The implacable young man facing him was not a rebellious child any longer. Between a rock and a hard place, he had no choice.

'You will give me time? I must prepare—'

'Your belongings will be sent after you. You will leave here as penniless as you made my old friend. I will send men, now, to escort you out of my house.'

'The warrant—'

'On second thoughts I shall keep it. An insurance policy. I don't trust you, my dear uncle. I bid you good bye.'

Closing the door behind him, Nick leaned against it puffing out his breath. He felt he had not rubbed through that too badly. Now for Kate. If his uncle had harmed her in any way, he knew what to do.

He returned to the courtyard to find the wounded attended to and the twenty men being escorted, weaponless, out of the gates by an armed guard. The rest of his men were taking their ease with food and drink hastily brought from the kitchens. Shawcross, holding the staff of office, was talking to the trembling steward.

'This man elects to go with your uncle,' he told Nick.

'See he has his wages – no need for him to suffer for his loyalty.' Nick turned aside to find Jem and seek out Kate.

'Where is she, Jem?'

'Sent for, sir. She's right behind you.'

She was standing in the gatehouse door, smiling at him. His heart squeezed in his breast. She looked thinner and tired but nothing else had changed. To him she was still beautiful.

'I said I would come,' he managed, his voice husky.

'I saw it all. Well done, my lord.'

'I have plans – come—' He brought her to meet Shawcross and Ponsonby and was impressed to see how gracefully she conducted herself and saw to their comfort. His uncle emerged from the house, refusing to meet Nick's eyes, and the sergeant elected to go himself and set him and the steward on their way.

*

The threatened anti-climax was avoided as the men and women of the estate, crowding in, built a huge bonfire in the snow and set up spits to roast haunches of meat and tubers from the fields. Nick ordered up casks of ale and cider and the merrymaking looked set to last into the small hours. Jem was proving himself no mean fiddler.

Nick and Shawcross sat over the table in the hall with a flagon of wine and a roaring fire for company. Nick was disconsolate. He had failed to persuade Kate to join them – 'It would not be seemly' – and when he outlined his plan for her she had asked for time to consider. When his uncle banished her from the manor, she had sought sanctuary with the parson of Lower Rookham, a village on the estate bordering Rokesby, and had been helping with the care of his increasing brood. This village suffered extreme poverty under its absentee landlord and Kate's loyalties were torn.

'Don't be downcast, lad. She will come round. Today has been – surprising,' said Hugh. 'You were lovers? What do you want of her?'

'I fear for her health in that village. I shan't be here. I want what's best for her.'

'She may be confused as to what you intend. She is a well-looking woman,' mused Hugh, gazing into his cup. 'What is her breeding?'

Taken aback, Nick stared at him. 'I don't know. My father took her in. The daughter of one of his officers, I think.'

'Since my time.' There was a long silence. Then Nick said, 'What do you think, now you've seen the place? Is the project to your liking?'

'Indeed it is. There is much to do and room for expansion,

if you've a mind to it. I would take you up on the idea of employing Doctor Knowles, should he be agreeable. My boy would be happy here.' He paused. 'Let us drink to it. You did well today, Nicholas. Jack would have been pleased. And if your Kate decides to stay, you may be assured she will be kept safe.'

A worm of disquiet entered Nick's heart as he drank the toast and he took himself to task. What else did he want for Kate but a safe future? Why else was he providing her with a position and a dowry? He remembered her in his arms, her pliant body and warm, sweet breath, the way they had talked together and woven dreams, the pucker in the smooth forehead as she pored over books with him, hiding and making love in her still room or in the barn or out in the fields, and her secret ambition to learn music. Both orphans, they had comforted each other.

Disturbed, he drained his cup and stood, picking up his sword-belt.

'It's been a long day. Welcome to Rokesby, Hugh. I will bid you goodnight.'

Once in the silence of his empty bedchamber, he let his father's sword, now made his own, fall on the bed, his new dignity with it, and at last allowed himself the bitter luxury of tears.

It took Nick three days to persuade Kate to accept his offer of chatelaine of his house, and longer still to coax her back into his bed. Those days had also been spent at Hugh's side, riding over the estate, planning and reorganising. He learned a great deal. Oliver Knowles arrived ('my old owl') and Shawcross' son

Henry. Some of Ponsonby's men opted to stay and work, and Ponsonby rode with the rest back to town, well paid and well pleased. 'Any more little skirmishes like that, lad, and I'm your man.' Jem refused the purse offered to him.

'I've reward enough. There'll be good horses in my stables and good food in my belly. Can't ask for more nor that.' Kate watched and listened, and when Nick came again for her answer, he found it in her arms.

With no one to fear or hide from, safe and warm in his bed, curtained against the chill, it was a joyful reunion. The sun was reflecting a pink glow off the snowy fields before they slept that first night. A day or two later, Nick woke to find her stroking him, over and over, her fingers defining the muscles, the changes in him.

'You have found a sweetheart in London, Nick, I feel sure.' In a state of bliss, he did not answer at once and she took his silence for admission.

'Of course you have, look at you. I would expect it.'

He sat up. 'No, not a sweetheart, a friend, a girl in the company. A nice girl – Kate, I never – I could not make you a promise.'

'And I would never ask it. You are a young man, you have your way to make. There will be others. You cannot be thinking of me.' He picked up a tress of her auburn hair and arranged it to fall across her breast.

'But I do think of you. I miss your wise counsel and your quick wits and…you comfort me. These last days, free to spend with you, falling asleep at your side and waking with you, have been—'

'I don't ask what you mean to do. I have a sense that it will be dangerous. But you are not meant to spend your youth here minding your acres. Master Shawcross and I will work together and when you return with your bride, all will be in readiness.'

'My bride! I do not think of marrying—'

'Not yet. But the time will come—'

'Kate, let's not waste time with such talk. My life is uncertain – I can make no promises. But you will always be my first love and that must suffice.' She reached up to draw him close.

'I am well satisfied.'

A week later, goaded by Shawcross, he saddled up Rowena and prepared to leave. Passing under the arch of the gatehouse, he stood up in his stirrups and turned to wave. Kate and Hugh Shawcross were standing in the doorway at the head of the steps, Kate with her keys at her belt, her wide sleeve hiding Hugh's empty one, Hugh's small son at their side. They made a handsome group.

Nick almost turned back, but the beckoning of the wider world was too strong and, taking a last look, he turned a determined face towards London and adventure.

Chapter Eight

Early one day, soon after Nick's return to London, Edward Alleyn, actor-manager of the Rose on Bankside came to visit his rival Burbage in something of a temper. He passed in under the gallery and stopped on seeing a young man practising in the space in front of the apron where the groundlings would stand. The great actor drew back out of sight and watched the boy shadow-fencing, backwards and forwards, whirling a great sword first with one hand and then the other, stamping forward with a grunt and a two-handed sweep. He moved like a dancer, his face lit with enjoyment and effort. Presently, breathing fast now, he laid aside the heavy blade and took up a lighter Italian foil and stuck it through his belt. Alleyn sat down, fascinated.

Nick threw on his cloak, walked a few steps and whirled round to face an imaginary foe, sword out, a dagger in the other hand, his cloak wound round his arm as a shield all in a moment. This time he made good use of the space, sword and dagger flickering, body and footwork creating an opponent out of thin air.

The actor-manager did not know who this young man might be, he did not concern himself with the underlings who oiled the wheels of his rival's theatre, but this exhibition of skill and grace was entrancing. He withdrew silently and made it his business to find out Nick's name and send for him. He had not noticed the other cloaked and shadowy figure watching from under the gallery.

Nick received the summons with surprise. He was well aware of the poaching that went on, but had not considered himself worth stealing. He confided in Robin and Mistress Molly and Nell, and they encouraged him to the extent of turning him out in starched shirt with a new ruff and his brushed doublet adorned with fresh points and ribbons. He had his good cloak and a hat with a new feather and he took himself off to the ferry full of a lively curiosity. It was still bitterly cold and his boatman's fingers were blue. Well-wrapped in cloak and gloves and boots, Nick watched, with a sense of déjà vu, the dewdrop form like an icicle on the man's purple nose, and gave the poor devil a large tip when they arrived at the Goat Stair. He clattered off along the frozen ruts beside the river to keep his appointment, planning to visit Rowena in her livery stable that evening. The afternoon was clear and crisp and he revelled in a feeling of well-being as he strode along past the bear-baiting arena, pulling his cloak across his nose at the stench of the animals roaring in their cages. Further along was the space slowly being made ready for the erection of a new theatre, the Swan, and beyond that open country faded towards woodland purple in the falling dusk. There were still patches of snow lying in the fields and Nick began to long for spring, when he planned to revisit his home.

So far had his thoughts gone from the world of the stage that he was taken by surprise by the Rose in daylight. In shape it was vastly different from Burbage's theatre in Blackfriars; it seemed to echo the shape of the bear-baiting arena rather than the inn yard. The small space round the raised stage was open to the sky, and towards the back was a raked area, the ground slowly rising towards the rear, an innovation that seemed to Nick a very good idea. The actual platform had the familiar flexible arrangement of the inner and outer stage with a balcony supported by two columns. Above this was the musicians' gallery and the thatched roof which ran round to shelter the spectators' galleries. Nick revolved in the middle of the floor, seeing where parts of the building were still unfinished and admiring the general structure. A melodious voice spoke behind him. If Burbage's voice was golden, this was silver. Edward Alleyn was Dick Burbage's greatest rival; some said he was the greater, more sensitive actor. Nick had never seen him onstage, and was more interested in the fact that he had the monopoly on the work of his current hero, Kit Marlowe.

He turned to see that very man standing beside Alleyn, pulling a pair of doeskin gloves between long fingers and smiling at him.

'Yes, he will do very well, Ned,' he said. 'Take him.'

'I have prepared a piece, sir. Do you not want to hear it?'

'Blank verse extempore! He has a little wit as well as a well-developed sword-arm. We need a fight arranger, sweeting. But now I see you properly, my dear Master Talbot, you will add an undoubtedly decorative element to a scene. If you can act as well, we are trebly fortunate. Ned, I must go. Make sure you secure this Adonis for us.' He made an elaborate leg and departed, laughing, leaving Nick in a state of scarlet confusion.

'Pay no heed, young man. It is just his way. If you have a mind to join us, come along with me and we will make terms.'

Nicholas returned to his lodgings with a raise in pay and status as fight manager (play as cast), for the Lord Admiral's Men in Southwark, on the South Bank of the Thames.

Chapter Nine

London. Spring 1593

Nick rested his arms on the windowsill of the room he shared under the eaves with his friend and fellow-player, Robin Ackland. It was noon, and a ray of sunshine sneaked between the rooftops and warmed his face. Eagerly he scanned the bobbing heads, bonneted, capped and feathered in the crowded street below, looking for Robin.

He had ridden down once to see Kate, and had found her blooming; the house and estates running with military precision. He saw no sign of any developing liaison with Shawcross and she had come to him with confident ardour. She was benefiting greatly from the association with Oliver Knowles she told him, and he could see for himself how her new dignities became her. If his own future in London had not looked so promising, he would have found it well-nigh impossible to leave. There had been no word from Cecil, and he was caught up with his career in the theatre.

Entrusted with polishing the many fight scenes for Master Alleyn, and taking part himself, he had grown into his early promise and was now tall and broad-shouldered with a strong and pleasing baritone and a physical presence that had brought him a few lines and minor roles, courtiers and Second Murderer, a bloody captain or a rebel knight. Now, today, he was mad with excitement to see what Robin was bringing – his first real big speaking role. One of the players was sick and he was to take his part, he had only a few hours to brush up the extra lines written in for that night to accommodate him. Kit Marlowe himself had approved it.

The noonday sun was higher now and reflected into the window opposite. He could have reached across and touched the leaning casement, and he looked in for a moment, mildly amazed at what was going on in the previously darkened room. He looked away with a snort of amusement – such ingenuity – and glimpsed the broken feather of Robin's cap waving through the crowd.

He had snatched up his doublet and crammed it on, when his eye was caught by an eddy and a swirl in the melee at the top of the street. Moneypenny Lane joined the main thoroughfare at this point, leading towards the riverside and a crossing point for the theatres on Bankside.

There was an impressive cavalcade passing, men on horseback clearing the way and trumpets proclaiming people of quality. Nick craned out of the window to see. The horses were glossy and high-stepping, their harness powder blue and silver, saddle-cloths emblazoned with a crest he could not make out. The men-at-arms were followed by four guards on showy chestnuts and between them, on a grey gelding, its coat silver-white against the blue trappings, its mane a-shiver with tiny bells, rode the most beautiful creature Nick had ever seen.

His breath caught and something banged in his chest. If he ran the other way, Moneypenny Lane curved round to cross her path. Not stopping to think, he tore out of the house and began to thrust his way through the crowd, deaf to Robin calling from behind. Using his weight, he arrived at the riverside in time to see the little procession slowed by the press of humanity heading for the ferries. There was a garlanded barge waiting at the steps, presumably to take the lady aboard. Her escort was armed, as was the fat man at her side, but even the guard of a lady of quality could not do more than shoulder the people aside.

As they drew near, Nick gazed his fill. The rayed and jewelled gauze of her ruff fanned out behind her head to frame an oval face in which blazed coal-black eyes, staring straight ahead. Her skin was white, unblemished and unpainted save for scarlet lips and lids the azure blue of her skirts. Black ringlets escaped the twisted silver of her headdress, and as she came nearer Nick could see the delicate tracery of veins mapping breast and wrist. He could hardly breathe.

Her padded and pearl-embroidered oversleeves swung free of her silken arms and might brush him as she passed. Waiting and hoping, he stood his ground, ignoring the pushing and jostling of the playgoers trying to get out of the way. He was so intent that he almost missed the swift, furtive movement and the flash of steel at her side.

Instinct and training hurled him forward and he was between the horse's flank and the cutpurse who had slashed off the pearls. He went for the knife first and was wrestling the man to the ground, twisting back the hand with the jewels, when he was felled to the ground himself with a vicious blow that just missed the back of his head and fell between neck and shoulder with a crack. Someone was screaming, shrill above the roar of the mob, and he rolled desperately, trying to avoid the dancing hooves and the steaming dung of panicking horses. The thief had disappeared, the screaming went on over the shouts and commands and the neighing and trampling all round him. The knife was there on the ground and Nick picked it up automatically, grabbing for a stirrup and hauling himself up out of danger with an agile twist. Someone tried to seize him and he whipped round, bringing up the knife as he had been taught, realising what he was doing just in time to change direction. The blade passed harmlessly through the man's sleeve instead of up under the steel cuirass and the man snarled. He raised a mailed fist and Nick ducked under the belly of the nearest horse and smacked it hard on the backside. It reared and bolted off down the street, followed by another riderless mount. Part of his mind was intent on his lady and her safety; she was well back from all this activity, the best he could do was end it. He threw down the knife and headed for the river.

Of course, he didn't stand a chance, there were too many of them, and the mob joined in. They produced him presently, battered and filthy, to stand precariously in front of milady and her companion. Her maid had stopped screaming and was sniffling, the red mark of a slap on her cheek. The lady was obviously not so easily frightened. She sat straight-backed and calm, a curve to her lips and an interested gleam in her eye. The man beside her was not at all calm. He was, on close sight, not so much fat as bulky. His brick-red velvet doublet and tunic was puffed and quilted and slashed with saffron and made a monstrous slab of him, stewing gently in the midday sun. His padded trunks were fashioned to display to advantage handsome muscular legs in expensive knitted-silk hose. With clocks. They were muddy and torn. One of the guards was trying to hand him a vast pancake of a hat, brooched with gold and covered with muck. He snatched it and belaboured the importunate man with it, flung it to the ground and stamped on it.

Nick wanted to laugh and then changed his mind. The man's face was rapidly turning the same colour as his clothes, the nostrils pinched and white with temper. He was breathing hard and wringing his gloves between hands like hams. The lady's presence was obviously cramping his style. Nick could sympathise. The princely escort was in disarray, only now sheepishly reassembling round their prisoner, some trying to placate members of the public who claimed to be damaged, some trying to discourage those who thought this was a free entertainment. The place reeked of sweat and horses and their dung and someone's blood.

For Nick, things looked bad. He had picked up the knife, the thief had gone and two pearls were making dents in the palm of his bloodied fist. He was sure the big man had hit him, the blow had come from above and behind. He waited.

'Will this take long, my lord? We shall miss the play.' Her voice was silvery with bells in. Nick made her a graceful leg. Her companion swelled like a bullfrog and spoke at last in a strangled tenor, 'Not long at all. He will pay for this. You there, bind him. Take him to my house. I will deal with him later.'

'But is this the man? I saw another—'

'A crude trick. It failed. Take him.'

It was time to speak up. Nick opened his mouth and was forestalled by an exquisitely modulated voice at his side.

'An inept thief, indeed, my lord Mowbray, if this were he. My lady is right. There was another, foiled in the attempt. This in fact, is an actor in one of my plays. I know him well. I also saw exactly what happened. In *every* detail, my lord.'

Nick turned his head awkwardly. His bruises were beginning to stiffen.

Beside him, elegant in pleated black silk, stood Christopher Marlowe, his hero and most admired poet, the idol seen only seldom, hardly known to him at all. Marlowe went on smoothly, 'I feel sure he was, as we are, bound for the playhouse, when he was embroiled in this distressing affair.' He bowed with ineffable grace and a charming smile. 'My lady Rosalyne, your servant. I fear you are right, the play at the Rose has begun. Allow me to offer alternative entertainment. The Queen has ordered a performance to be held at the palace. We leave for Whitehall in an hour. Time for refreshment, if my lady pleases.'

Mowbray, in his spoiled finery, looked ready to burst. The lady leaned down and placed her hand on his puffed sleeve.

'A play in the Queen's presence. How delightful that will be, my dear. An interval to recover ourselves and all will be well. Don't you agree? Our promised outing together will not be spoiled.' She held out her hand to Marlowe. 'I thank you, sir, for your timely intervention. May I know your young friend's name? I feel sure he should be attended to.'

'And rewarded, my lady, for a gallant attempt. I believe he has something of yours.'

Nicholas assembled his wits and made his best bow.

'Rokesby…um…Nicholas Talbot, my lady. At your service.'

He unfurled his knuckles with some difficulty and proffered the pearls embedded in his palm. The crowd, still feeling part of the action, swayed and murmured. This stuff was as good as a play. The lady Rosalyne did not disappoint. She leaned forward and closed his fingers over the jewels.

'Keep them, Master Talbot. Or Rokesby. With my thanks.'

She turned to placate her angry squire and Marlowe seized

Nick's arm.

'Meet me after the performance at the Elephant. I will wait for you. There's someone I want you to meet.'

Next moment he was all smiles, helping my lady to dismount, and sending for a waterman to initiate his improvised programme. Nick skipped hastily aside as the disgruntled troop clattered past him the other way. The entertainment over, the crowd began to disperse; one or two who had handled him roughly clapped him on the shoulder to show no hard feelings. Robin, who had been hopping about on the fringe, ran over, still clutching his roll of scrip.

'You lucky madman! What were you thinking of?'

'Who is she?'

'The lady Rosalyne Hart, wife to Sir William that was. They say she probably "pressed" him to death. All right, all right, just jealous idle talk… What's that in your hand?'

'Why did he hit me?'

'Perhaps he was aiming at the other fellow. He doesn't know you, does he? No, well, he does now. I'd keep out of his way if I were you. lord Mowbray's well known for bearing a grudge, and you made him look a fool – in front of the lady, too. Hey, Nick, are you hurt? Shall we go and find Molly? You're bleeding.'

Nick found he was giddy and unsteady on his feet, and he was glad of Robin's arm to help him back to their lodging. He paid no heed to his friend's chatter, his mind was in turmoil, the woman's beauty and Marlowe's intervention vying for his attention.

Marlowe, Christopher Marlowe, the man who wrote those lines that rang in his head and fired his imagination, the legendary Kit Marlowe wanted to see him, had intervened and lied for him. Why? He knew all the tales and scurrilous gossip surrounding the man, with the hint of something darker. That did not worry him; he could take care of himself. No, he was wondering how he would speak to him, a man of such towering intellect. It was a level to which Nick did not aspire.

And the woman. What of her? She had looked at him in that certain way women had. He had first glimpsed her as a goddess, but her touch had taught him differently.

All the way back to his lodging, he went over and over the encounter. He had been lucky. He could be in the Marshalsea now, facing mutilation or hanging. He had certainly made an enemy in Mowbray. How did he come to have such an ally in Marlowe? It was true he had played a small part in *Tamburlaine*, but he had only met the playwright that once, at the Rose. You could hardly count the brief fracas at the Mermaid. He grew slowly hot, remembering how Marlowe had looked at him. An Adonis, he had said. Oh, well. He had watched the elite group of the Wits in the taverns and listened avidly to the wordplay and exchange of ideas, but as a lowly player of small parts, not expecting notice. Not yet, anyway. He never went less than wholeheartedly into whatever he was doing, often to his cost, and he was turning into a good actor. His flexible voice and skill with weaponry had gained him acceptance into the Company, and now, like his childhood with the army, it was his family. He was happy as he was. He was not sure about this appointment with Marlowe.

His one good suit was ruined, his hose in tatters and his linen stained with blood. He had protected his face and belly and his arms and shins had suffered as a result. There was no time to do more than bathe his hurts, stow away the pearls in his pouch and borrow some clothes from Robin before setting off back to the river. The players were bidden to Whitehall that evening to present *Doctor Faustus* to the Court, a circumstance that would normally have him in a fever of nervous excitement, but there was no time, and he ran down the hill to find a boat, conning his lines as he went. They were no problem, he knew the whole play by heart. Dickon, the ailing actor he was replacing, played Gluttony, the Deadly Sin least suited to Nick's lean frame. He would need a deal of extra padding if the costume were not to hang on him like a leaky balloon. He worried that the cheek pads would obstruct his speaking. Dickon had also doubled as Cornelius, Benvolio, (which would be Nick's largest speaking part to date), Alexander (with swordplay), and a demon. He was going to be busy.

The tiny room set aside as a tiring room was crammed with sweating actors muttering their lines and fighting over the mirror. Mistress Molly, much in demand, had followed Nick into his new company across the river. She spotted him and surged through the throng with her arms full of costumes.

'Hurry up,' she scolded. 'You're late! Oh my goodness, what is this! Whatever happened to you–'

'Never mind now, Moll, is this stuff going to fit?'

'I've taken them in round the waist. Come here, you are not going to bleed all over them.' And she insisted on binding up his cuts before helping him into Benvolio's suit. It was dark green taffeta, his favourite colour, faced and slashed with saffron and embroidered with lilies, and suited him very well. He buttoned Cornelius' robe over it, almost suffocating with the heat, crammed on the wig, and was ready just in time for his cue. It was exhilarating and he rose to the occasion, rejoicing in his chosen profession. This was the life. He was oblivious to the audience of courtiers grouped around the Queen, only faintly aware of her raucous laugh leading the applause. A relatively short piece, it played non-stop, and this audience was no different from any other, joining in the slapstick and sitting mute and terrified as Faustus shrieked in fear, pleading for his soul as he dropped through the trapdoor in the makeshift stage to groans of horror.

Nick took his bows with the rest, still in his demon costume, and came off to find Mistress Molly holding up Robin's third-best suit in dismay.

'You are sent for – by the Queen! You can't appear before her in these! Wait, you can borrow Benvolio's suit, come along, hurry—' she dragged him after her through the euphoric group of players, his fellow-actors clapping him on the back and offering to drink his health. Nell, who still helped Moll in the wardrobe, ran an appreciative hand over his sleek crimson flank as he passed.

'Later,' she whispered. The day already seemed the longest he could remember, but he nodded, and stole a kiss before Molly tweaked his arm and handed him a clean shirt with blackwork at collar and cuffs. A jaunty velvet cap needed only a brooch and Nick found the one in his pouch that had come from his father. He buckled on his sword and flinging a cloak over his shoulder, turned to survey himself in the glass. Nell crept up behind him and slid her arms round his waist, 'You look very fine, Nick. Fit for a Queen. You won't forget us?'

'Don't be foolish, sweetheart, I'm not going anywhere. lord Essex is behind this, I expect. I did him a small service once. I hoped he'd forgotten. Molly, I truly thank you. We shall come to a reckoning tomorrow.' He planted a kiss on both her scarlet cheeks, hugged Nell and went off to meet his queen, the meeting with Marlowe at the Elephant forgotten.

Chapter Ten

London. 28th May 1593

Elizabeth sat enthroned at the end of the long room, her courtiers standing about her or sprawled at her feet, a flower garden of colour. She dominated the scene, the light from what seemed like a hundred candles flashing from her jewels. Nick looked at his queen for the first time, the Queen for whom his father had died, who commanded his allegiance, and was amazed. She was an old, old woman in a red wig, face painted thick with white lead, hectic spots of rouge beneath hooded eyes. She had chosen to wear crimson velvet, quilted with pearls and brilliants, her stomacher and underskirts white satin criss-crossed with rubies. An enormous ruff and tiara of jewelled gauze framed the head poised proudly on a chicken-skin neck. On her breast lay a pigeon's blood ruby, long chains of gold and precious stones descended into her lap. She raised her lids and stared at him.

She seemed to him an eagle, and himself the smallest, most helpless creature, exposed in an empty field. She raised a hand sparkling with rings and beckoned him forward.

'We are pleased with you, Master Talbot. A young man of Parts.' She waited for the laugh. 'And I believe you were of service to my lord Essex here.' Her hand strayed to the auburn head of the man on the dais by her feet. 'It would have been a pity if, having obeyed me at last, he should have been prevented from coming home to us.'

Nick was slowly becoming aware of the others in the room, among them faces he knew. Essex, of course, and there was little Cecil by the pillar, Kit Marlowe in the shadows, the bull-necked form of the man Mowbray and – the lady Rosalyne! She was smiling at him and raising a discreet hand. He realised he had not heard the last part of what was being said to him. They were waiting for him. What was he supposed to do?

He bowed low.

'Your servant, your Majesty.'

'Indeed. What else can you do?'

'Fight, your Majesty.'

She gave a coarse crack of laughter.

'A lot more besides, I'll warrant. Approach.' He stepped forward and she pulled a pearl from her bodice.

'I hear you collect these. Go on as you have begun, Master Talbot.' She tossed him the pearl and bent to speak to her companion. Essex smiled at him and nodded, his black eyes strangely cold, Rosalyne put two fingers to her pursed scarlet lips, and blew. He was dismissed.

He backed out somehow and leaned against a wall to catch his breath. A servant was tugging at his sleeve to hand him a note.

'The Elephant. Half an hour.' Nick sagged down on his heels. He wanted nothing better than to find his bed and sleep till noon. This was no less than another royal summons. He would have to go. He opened his hand and stared at the pearl. How had she known about that? She must have a God-like knowledge of the fall of each sparrow in her kingdom. Or a good spy network. He remembered Cecil by the pillar, and suddenly cold, got up and tugged down his doublet. He claimed back his sword from the man-at-arms who had relieved him of it, who bowed to him this time. He stowed away the pearl and buckled on his sword. Another servant hurried up and pressed a packet into his hand.

'From my lord Essex, a gift. He requires no reply at present. This way, sir.'

Thirty-five minutes later Nick tipped yet another boatman and stepped ashore. His aches and pains were making themselves felt as he trod up the greened-over steps to the tavern.

At the top, he was stopped in his tracks. Outside the inn a glossy black stallion – a Friesian, if he was not mistaken, rare in these parts – stood restlessly in the charge of one of the ostlers. He was a magnificent creature, long in the back with a thick crinkled tail brushing the feathered hocks. The extravagant curve of his neck bore no fewer than twenty-five plaits, knotted and bound with silver, his forelock hung low over lustrous, well-set eyes. The quilted velvet saddle-cloth was as black and glossy as he, edged and stitched with silver. All the elaborate tack gleamed with polish, and silver bosses with tassels. Nick was familiar with the breed, much favoured as a warhorse or for any task requiring strength and stamina, but this was a splendid specimen, not often seen in Town.

As Nick stood lost in admiration, Marlowe emerged from

the inn, booted and spurred and drawing on elegant, silver-embroidered gloves, his face alight with mischief.

'A small spoke in our wheel – we are going to be late,' he said. The ostler relinquished the reins and picked up his lantern from the ground. The light fell on Nick's face and Marlowe exclaimed.

'My dear Nicholas! You are worn out. I don't wonder at it now I bethink myself. In all humanity I cannot ask you to ride through the night. We will rack up at Greenwich and go on in the morning.'

'Where are we going? The play – I must be back.'

'Your presence is not required. They are performing some trumpery comedy by Will Shakespeare, you have no part in it.'

'How far is this place?'

'Some thirty miles or so. We have been too long delayed—' Nick, to whom a forced march of thirty miles was commonplace, interrupted him.

'It's no hardship to me, sir, two or three hours at most. Ah, pardon me. You yourself are tired.' There was a long silence, then Marlowe suddenly laughed.

'Dare me, would you? Well, I daresay they will still be talking. We all talk too much, my dear. And too unguarded. Here is your horse, I believe.'

The ostler led Rowena round the corner, saddled and bridled and ready to go, snorting softly when she saw Nick. Next to the spectacular Friesian she looked what she was, a useful sort; any cavalryman would be pleased to own her. Nick took good care of her, her coat had come in early and shone with health and grooming, the diamond patterns on her hindquarters lovingly brushed in. Her tack was plain, clean and supple: the only flamboyant touch was his crest, a falcon, embroidered in bullion work on the saddle-cloth. Nick stopped to speak to the man, and Marlowe's voice rang out, impatient.

'Have done, time's a-wasting,' and he wrenched his horse round and was off at a gallop with a clatter of hooves. Nick swung into the saddle and squeezed the sturdy mare into a gentle trot.

'Don't worry, lass, he won't keep that up. We've got the legs of him.' And sure enough, about three miles further on, Marlowe was pulled up, waiting for him, his horse snorting and pawing the ground.

'How long have you had this horse standing?' Nick wanted to know.

'Not above five minutes.' Nick shook his head. 'Is this our road?' he asked, and at Marlowe's nod he set off at a steady trot. He did not trust Marlowe's estimate of distance. Marlowe objected at first, wanting to gallop on, but finding Nick unresponsive, lapsed into sullen silence, rousing only to give directions.

Nick rode on, relaxed and easy. Visibility was good. A gibbous moon rode high above a rising sea of cloud, a fitful breeze eddied among the new leaves, turning them inside-out. There would be rain later. Marlowe came up presently to ride beside him. He was fiddling constantly with the reins, shifting in the saddle. Nick glanced across at him and made no comment. His hero was nervous, disturbed about something, perhaps this mysterious meeting. He himself felt stupid with weariness, was falling asleep in the saddle.

Their road undulated gently between copse and dense

woodland, with stretches of arable land laid down to wheat and flax. As they went on, through occasional villages, more and more orchards and hop fields began to replace the woods and the country opened out. There was no sound but the breeze in the leaves and the beat of their horses' hooves. Nick nodded off.

He woke with a start, to find Marlowe's hand on his bridle, urging him onto the verge. A troop of men was galloping towards them in a cloud of dust, helmets and half-armour gleaming in the waning moon, pennanted lances at the carry. They were past in a thunder of iron hooves, leather creaking and the snort and jostle of the horses creating a blast of hot air and speed and noise. Then they were gone, and Marlowe relaxed.

'They were Cobham's men,' he said. 'We must be nearly there.'

'Cobham's men?'

'Henry Brooke, Baron of Cobham Hall – where we are bound.'

'Who's he?'

'What a strange mixture you are, my young friend. Wise to so much of the world, with pockets of woeful ignorance.'

'I am only a player, sir.' Marlowe laughed.

'A tiger in a player's hide. Very well. Hide your stripes if you must. Brooke is Warden of the Cinque Ports, a very useful man. Make yourself known to him. We may need him. Ah, there you are, Cobham Hall – as far as it goes.'

Nick saw two large buildings against the darkling sky, joined by a puzzling fretwork pattern like the rigging of a ship. As they turned between tall gateposts, Marlowe said, 'Are you a true Protestant, Nick?'

'I suppose so, I haven't had time to—'

'Not a Papist, then?'

An image rose in his mind of his uncle intoning prayers while wielding the whippy cane.

'No.'

'Of course, you would say that. An atheist, then. Have you thought about that?'

'They say no man is an atheist on his deathbed.'

'A good sophistical answer.'

'I have heard men cry like babes for their mothers,' said Nick. 'And on God. Like Faustus at the end.'

'And you? Who would you appeal to?'

'I never knew my mother. God? I don't know—'

'Let us hope you do not soon find out. I trust you will not speak so freely to anyone else, you young fool. You will find yourself making the acquaintance of the Duke of Westminster's daughter.'

'Who?'

'The rack. The press. Or the thumbscrew – another finger lost. Watch your tongue. Especially tonight. There is someone – I'm not sure. Be on your guard.'

They had reached the buildings now and Nick saw that the outline that had puzzled him was scaffolding. The centre part of the house was not finished. They rode round to the side where a lantern was burning and a large, squat coach was standing, its shafts resting on the ground. Marlowe gave a cry of delight and flung himself off his horse, throwing the reins to Nick, to hasten into the house. Nick slid wearily from the saddle and stood for a moment leaning his head against Rowena's sweaty neck, his hand caressing her nose.

The man waiting in the shadow of the stable watched him with interest, assessing. He saw a tall lanky youth, not yet grown into his breadth of shoulder. In the feeble light, Poley could not make out the colouring but as Nick's head turned, he saw the face. Not a handsome face, strong slanted brows, the nose high-bridged and bony, the features too emphatic. An actor's face, altogether too noticeable, thought Poley. He faded, nondescript, back into the shadows: it was not his decision, he simply liked to know what he might be dealing with. There was something about the way the lad carried himself. 'Petit' Poley thought he might be a bit of a handful. He slid quietly away to insert himself into the house by way of the kitchens.

A man ran up to take the horses. Nick made much of Rowena, feeding her a titbit from his saddlebag.

'Mind you rub her down well. And don't wash her legs.'

'No, my lord.'

Marlowe hurried out again, flung an arm round Nick's shoulders and led him into a shadowy, flagstoned hall. A banked-down fire slumbered in a fireplace big enough to put a tent up in, and watchman's chairs flanked either side. A man was sitting in one of them, his face in shadow. Marlowe bounded across the room and kissed his forehead, holding his hands.

'Here he is, my sweet Thomas. The instrument of your choice and my sorrow. Send him in when you have done with him. Ralegh wants a word.' He passed through a door in the panelling, saying airily, 'Master Nicholas Talbot – Thomas Walsingham,' as he went. The man rose from his chair. In his early thirties, he was a well-built handsome man with strong

105

features framed by a dark-brown beard. If Nick had known it, his resemblance to his uncle Francis was marked, though unmarred by illness. Sir Francis, spymaster extraordinaire, had died two years previously, leaving the Court and the world of intrigue for Cecil to bustle in. Nick had heard the name of the man facing him mentioned in the Mermaid, as a patron of literature and a man of letters, Chapman in particular singing his praises. The worlds of poetry and intrigue seemed close-meshed.

'My scapegrace friend might have introduced us more elegantly. Thomas Walsingham of Scadbury, at your service.'

'Talbot of Rokesby, sir. You wish something of me?'

'Come and sit down, Master Talbot. Take a glass of wine with me.' They established themselves in the two hooded chairs by the fire, and he went on, 'I will come straight to the point. I am told you may be trusted. Our mutual friend, Kit Marlowe is my concern. He is very dear to me. He stands in grave danger – his own reckless doing. You will know, Master Talbot, he is passionate in his ideas and impatient to inoculate others against what he sees as irrational dogma. He has now brought official notice upon himself. He has made enemies and I would protect him – save him from himself I cannot. But he can be saved from the executioner. I am being very open with you, Master Talbot, because it has come to my ears that you greatly admire my Kit and his work. I hope I am not mistaken?'

'It is true that I love and admire his work, sir. And I have heard him speak many times. But I have met him only once before tonight.'

'Once is usually enough. Your final choice in this matter will be your own. I ask only for your word as a man of honour, that you will not repeat what you see and hear tonight. That is, as far as you are able – Topcliffe and his torments can be very persuasive.'

'You have my word.'

Walsingham sat back in his chair, nursing his goblet of wine and staring thoughtfully into the fire.

'You are much younger than I thought. What lies in the other room will be strange to you. When you go through that door you will see men who are known to you in your own world, and faces you know only from cartoon and broadsheet. Others will be complete strangers, men known only among their kind for the great thinkers they are. These are the movers and shakers of our world, Master Talbot, or so they would like to be. Their ideas make them dangerous and feared, so they must meet secretly in each others' houses, calling themselves the School of Night.' He looked across at Nick. 'There is nothing of necromancy – or treason, either. It is a foolish, romantic name only. Ralegh began it, I believe. You are not drinking.'

Nick, desperately tired and fearing the wine would cloud his judgment, shook his head and covered his cup. Walsingham went on, 'The School of Night... I suppose you could call it a gentleman's club, where men of like mind can meet and talk and exchange ideas: air their views and discoveries without fear of prison or torture or repression. Look at poor Galileo...You might ask why only gentlemen? That is another of their frightening notions – that the common man should read and write and think for himself. Lunatics – this is anarchy and perilous stuff. But one cannot halt these ideas.' He stopped, as if he remembered something.

'Were you not taught by Oliver Knowles? Someone mentioned—'

'He was my tutor, sir. He is living now at Rokesby.'

'He taught my brother. A fine mind. Well then, these notions may not be so strange to you, after all. You will have heard of the Gutenberg press – a straw in the wind, young man. And there are great things for us. Drake and Ralegh and the New World; Master Dee, Dickon Chancellor and his maps and trade routes, freethinkers, all of them.' He sat forward, gripping the arms of his chair.

'I am content to make my differences closer to home, but my Kit will not be circumscribed. He will be taken and killed most horribly if he stays.' He struck the arm of his chair with force. 'That must not be, it must not. If he is to go on with his writing he must be free. His soul is too big for his body, Master Talbot, his mind is like quicksilver, it runs away with him, like his tongue – he needs time to grow – I need someone to take care of him, keep him safe.' There were tears in his eyes now, he was holding onto Nick's arm like a drowning man.

'I have been watching you since Kit first spoke of you and I have had reports. You speak his words, however few, with love. Young as you are, I pray you, accept this task. I will be forever in your debt.'

'What task, sir?'

'Go in now, listen to these great men, unworldly as some of them are. Ralegh will tell you.'

He was to meet Ralegh. In a daze, Nick allowed Walsingham to lead him through the door Marlowe had used and usher him into a much smaller, square room, new-panelled from floor to ceiling, smelling like a sandalwood box and lit by a blazing fire and branching candles. Nick recognised with a shock faces seen only in procession and on pamphlets: Ralegh, Harry Percy,

Lord Stanley and Thomas Harriot. The familiar faces of Nashe and Chapman grinned at him. Out of his depth, he tried to shrug off Walsingham's hand and efface himself, but he was drawn forward. Marlowe came to take his arm.

'Well, gentlemen, here at last. This young man was delayed by Gloriana herself – excuse enough, I think. Unfortunately, his own virtues have drawn attention upon him – she will know him again – but perhaps his beard will come in soon to remedy that.'

'Bitch,' said someone.

'Are you hungry, boy?' asked Ralegh. Nick, red to the roots of his hair, could only nod.

'Never saw a lad your age who wasn't.' He stood, a tall, well-built man with a full, pointed beard, handsome dark eyes and hair, and a strong West Country burr to his voice. He beckoned Nick to a table against the wall. Talking easily, he filled a trencher with bread and meats, poured wine and told Nick to eat his fill. Turning back to Walsingham, 'Master Dee cannot be with us, he is in poor health, but he lends himself to the enterprise. When we meet at Durham House, he may join us.'

Nick found he was indeed ravenous, and easing his seat further back into the shadows, applied himself eagerly to the food, listening hard and trying to understand.

A leisurely discussion was going forward. Chapman read part of a new work, Harriot's new discovery was applauded. Someone produced a challenging idea and placed it *en prise* like a chess move, tempting argument. The heat of the room, the food and the gathering smoke were too much for Nick. His head went down on the table and he slept, the whirling words of the School of Night flowing to and fro in his ears.

He woke with a start to a babble of raised voices.

'Master Dee could have had nothing to bring to our talk tonight. Matters are coming to a head.'

'They have broken Kyd. He will say anything now.'

'You are castigated too, Kit. Tom Baines testifies—'

Marlowe's voice rose, 'There is no sin but ignorance! Their holy book is nothing but a collection of myths, badly told and probably misheard. I could make a thing of Moses and his story better than any of those ramblings.'

'Yes, but Baines' testimony is dangerous. You were mad to get mixed up in that money-coining business last year and now this—'

'Politics!'

'Religion is politics—'

Marlowe's voice rang out again. 'I am heartily sick of this daily reporting to the Council! Every day a journey to Whitehall, every day more questions – my every movement watched – cribbed, cabin'd and confined! I tell you I cannot endure it!'

'It has only been a fortnight, Kit. It was that or imprisonment. If they let Topcliffe loose on you…you know too much.'

Ralegh's deep voice cut in. 'Was it wise to present your Edward Two at quite that time and in quite that way?'

Nashe broke in, 'Your reckless arrogance will be the death of you, Kit, never mind the rest. Baines has said—'

'Bugger Baines!'

'I don't think you would like him.'

Marlowe turned on him, cutting through the laughter. 'If I did not have words crowding my head clamouring to be heard, I would let them take me and be damned. What is a world where it is a crime to speak freely, think freely, live according to one's nature? When will mankind have the wisdom to shake off dogma...?'

'We are all converts here, Kit, save your rhetoric.'

A measured voice spoke. 'You say you live to write and write to live. Save yourself. You have been a useful servant – for whatever reason – and we would not lose you to make a wasteful political gesture. The Continent has been your cockpit before. It will be a new life.'

'I will be banished!'

'Over-dramatic, Kit. Save it for your plays.'

'My plays? What plays? I shall be alive in the world and dead to the world—'

Ralegh's calm voice cut through the hubbub.

'Gentlemen, gentlemen. This is a planning meeting. The die was cast long ago, and Kit, my dear fellow, you will be first to admit you have brought it on yourself. No amount of rhodomontade will change things. You will go and live, or stay and die.' He paused. 'Your Tom prefers you to live.'

Marlowe's eyes suddenly glittered with tears.

'I know.'

Ralegh went on, 'It is through him this is possible. The plan is made, Frizer and Poley are ready, Mistress Bull is prepared. We have the necessary body and Frizer's pardon is in hand. Is that right, Poley?' Poley nodded. 'It will be given out that there was a drunken quarrel over the reckoning and my friend here was stabbed through the eye. An accident.' Marlowe shuddered but Ralegh continued. 'Our body died so. I myself am under the cat's foot of her Majesty's displeasure: once the news of my wedding reaches her ear, I'm for the Tower with my poor

Bess, and can be no further use to you after tonight. Now, this young man you have brought us – I have good report of him and I like the cut of his jib.'

'I tell you I don't need a nursemaid!'

'He is too young,' put in Nashe. 'You will be nannying him – but perhaps you won't mind wiping his bottom...'

Ralegh frowned. 'You need someone who is not known to mind your back, Kit, and do the legwork,' he said. ' A new face. His background is interesting, he has good understanding and he has shown resourcefulness. He will do.' He looked steadily at Marlowe. 'Dramatics apart, there is no going back from this, Kit. Christopher Marlowe and all his works will be dead and buried.' There was a long pause.

'You are mistaken, sir. You may bury me, but my words are immortal. However, as I am an arrant coward, I do not wish to end my days like poor Kyd, broken and babbling at the hands of Topcliffe.'

'That reminds me,' said Nashe. 'The poor devil asked Greene to go to his lodging and weed out anything incriminating and sell what he could. He was desperate for money, poor fellow. Then of course, Greene burst himself with drink. Finally. Anyway, Kit, I found this among Greene's leavings. It's not in my line. Shakespeare's had a go at it – you might make something of it. Don't worry, I gave Greene's woman a shilling for it.'

'What use is this to dead Kit Marlowe?'

'Something to read on the boat?'

Kit aimed a cuff at him, but took the roll of scrip and stuffed it in his doublet.

'What part has the lad to play tomorrow?'

'He will be at the foot of Cockhill steps with a boat,' said Ralegh. 'He will take you downriver to Woolwich where you will both board the *Black Swan*. She is a well-found vessel and I know the captain. You will have no trouble.'

'All very bright and breezy, sir,' said Marlowe, who had gone very white. 'I am still to play the Jew? An ironic touch, I feel. And what of our young friend?'

Nick had become heartily sick of hearing his future arranged for him over his head, and stood up, dizzy for a moment.

'Have I nothing to say in all this?' he demanded, forgetting whom he was talking to. 'I am a mere actor, sirs. I have had no word from—' he stopped in time. lord Cecil was not a name to drop lightly, even here. Ralegh rose and poured wine into two goblets.

'I have had the office from Robin Cecil to protect his predecessor's investment in Master Kit here. Your uncle Francis, not you, Thomas. He mentioned you,' he said to Nick, handing him a goblet. 'Your time has come, lad. Through here. We'll talk.'

He took Nick by the arm and led him back into the hall. Nick set the wine down and turned to face him. He had begun to tremble.

'My lord, I am honoured by the trust you wish to place in me, but – but am I the one for the task? Master Nashe is right, I am young, people will not do my bidding – I don't know my way in the world. I would not want to fail you.'

'You will not fail, my lord Rokesby. Yes, we know all about you. It is as if you were made for the role. I am for the Tower, I fear, but the work must go on…see to it.' The iron fist was clearly visible, the wise eyes stern.

113

'My lord.'

Ralegh smiled at him. 'Sit.' Nick was glad to do so.

'The story is this. You have acquired a wealthy and influential patron. You will return to your lodging, pack up your gear, rejoice with your friends over your good fortune – you will not get drunk – and be at the steps from eleven o'clock tomorrow – no, tonight. You will row with the tide to the arsenal at Woolwich and take ship. Your new livery will be on board. Marlowe will become a merchant Jew – a nice touch, don't you think? Considering his views. You will not know each other. Your further orders are in your cabin.'

'But – who is to be my patron? My lord Essex?'

'Hardly. No, it will be the gentleman you upset this afternoon – yesterday now, yes? My lord Mowbray.'

'He hates me!'

'All the better, my lad. You know exactly where you are with him. He owes favours.'

Nick was appalled at the lengths to which these intriguers were prepared to go, but nevertheless a rising tide of excitement began to bubble up in him.

'A snug billet awaits you in Venice.' *Venice*, thought Nick. 'You will settle our volatile friend, do Cecil's errands and return. Then we shall see.'

Yes we shall, thought Nick. I'm not wearing anyone's livery if I can help it. Ralegh's shrewd eyes were fixed on him.

'You mislike the plan? The patronage, perhaps?'

Nick was never likely to underestimate this great man, but the insight surprised him.

'I should like to be independent, my lord. I would be free to move as I see fit. A livery would mark me. Could I not hint at some mysterious Personage, an illustrious name I cannot divulge – or, or, yes, I could be fleeing for my life from the displeasure of my lord Mowbray.' That would go down better with Nell, he thought.

'I see your friends will believe anything if sufficiently dramatic. I will leave it to you. Mowbray will be relieved, I imagine. Throw the livery overboard.'

No, thought Nick. It might come in useful. The thought brought him up short. He was enjoying himself. He was committed. He caught Ralegh's eye and grinned. Raleigh gave a shout of laughter.

'You'll do. Indeed you will. Your father would be proud of you. Now listen to me.' He sat down opposite Nick and took up his pipe. 'You are still wondering why we chose you. I had not the privilege of meeting your father, but Leicester told me of him once. He was a brave and loyal man. He would have gone far. You were badly left, young man, but you show promise and an adventurous spirit. I like that. Now, you must understand that few of our agents are gentlemen. They do not need to be. But it is sometimes necessary to infiltrate a level of society they are not bred to. Men like Marlowe can go anywhere. You are another such. And you catch the eye of the ladies – a distinct advantage. You think you want to be an actor, Nick – may I call you that? You will find scope for your abilities serving your Queen and country as your father did.' Yes, but he wasn't a spy, thought Nick. But if Ralegh had wanted to bind Nick to him and his cause he had succeeded. Nick had succumbed completely to the force of personality and the integrity of the man.

'Now, promise me you will govern yourself and be careful.'

'I will, sir.'

'Good. Now be off with you. Your horse is rested, but you will need another. Take Marlowe's nag. He won't need it, he's going back to Chislehurst with Thomas Walsingham, to take leave of him. Keep the animal. They will both be shipped aboard for you. Speaking of which, here, put money in your purse—'

Marlowe came in, pat upon his cue.

'Put money in your purse? Has he agreed then? I think you borrow the arts of Master Dee, my lord, witchcraft and charms. Not that he has much choice, mark you. He knows too much already. I'm glad we decided to keep him intact, Walter. I really cannot have ugly men about me. It would look so strange.'

'There is that, of course. Leave him be, Kit, he will be at the steps as planned. Be punctual.'

'I'm sure Death's fell sergeant – in the shape of Poley or Frizer, or is it Frizer or Poley – will be strict in his arrest... just a moment, that's rather good—' He got out a little notebook and jotted it down '...is strict, is strict.'

Ralegh shrugged and urged Nick to the door.

'You will be guarded (you mean watched, thought Nick) until you are safely aboard. Off with you, and may whatever god there is go with you.'

Chapter Eleven

London. 30th May 1593

Nick could never remember afterwards how he got back to Southwark. Nero, Marlowe's handsome black stallion, bore him back safely, nodding in the saddle, and he fell asleep for a while in Rowena's empty stable. He woke later in the day to settle his bill and go and find his friends down the road at the Rose. They hauled him back to the tavern to celebrate his good fortune. 'The playhouse will miss you, Nick—' Robin especially mourned his leaving. 'You were doing so well. You'll be back, you'll never make a civilian.'

Nell coaxed him out to the stables with tearful looks to say goodbye and then burst into tears when he tried to give her money.

'Put it away, you clown. I don't lie with you for money. Bring me back a present – if you haven't given me one already.' Nick grinned, Nell was too shrewd for that, and he put the gold angel back in his purse. There were crowns and angels and silver coins there, more money than he had seen in his life. He would need a money belt under his clothes.

He parted from Nell with some reluctance and took himself off to find Molly. He had decided to travel as a gentleman, he would have more clout if there were difficulties, and he needed clothes. Benvolio's suit was looking decidedly lived-in by now.

Mistress Molly, impressed with his mysterious hints and the gold coin he offered her, found him a suit of cramoisie velvet slashed with cream satin and another in green and gold brocade and velvet with a fur trim. Molly did not stint on her costumes and these were good cloth and well made. He kept on the Benvolio costume, still good enough for the journey, rolled embroidered shirts and fine linen in his frieze cloak and bought a money belt from Casper, the stingiest member of the company – never known to buy a drink. That done he sat down to write a rambling and confused letter to Kate.

It had grown dark, and by half past ten he was stealing along the riverside where Drake's *Golden Hind* still rode at anchor. The docks were dark and empty, the shipbuilding and hammering that went on all day had fallen silent, and he made his way unhindered to the steps by the inn at Deptford. A lad no older than himself was there, holding a small rowing boat to a ring in the wall: Nick paid him off and he slithered away into the darkness. Bursts of laughter and shouting came over the dark water from the north bank, and a cascade of fireworks went up with a sudden bang from Westminster, upriver. More fireworks were glittering galaxies in the water, more bangs, and Marlowe crept quietly down the steps and made him jump.

Nick was ready, casting off quickly and settling to the stroke. The ebb tide was running fast and Nick was glad he had not to shoot the Bridge. Before very long the loop of the Isle of Dogs was behind them and the bulk of a roundship loomed up amongst all the other rigging, black against the starlit sky.

Marlowe hailed her and a rope ladder splashed down. Nick was surprised at the agile way the playwright swarmed up, a rope ladder at night in a fast-running tide is no easy thing, but he remembered that the man had been an intelligencer longer than he had been a playwright, and prepared to hoist himself and their baggage on board.

'There are undoubted advantages in living on an island,' breathed a voice in his ear. 'This is not one of them. Do not speak to me hereafter, you are a gentile. I shall be – God rot Ralegh's soul – a Jew. Ha!' He picked up his carpet bag and vanished. Nick was shown a minute cabin according to his status as gentleman and he went at once to see to his horses. They were stowed safe and comfortable, nosebags full and stalls clean. Rowena appeared to approve of Nero. He tipped the man in charge of the livestock and, feeling the lift and surge as the ship got under way, found his bunk and fell thankfully into it.

The journey was not a comfortable one, the Bay of Biscay was at its worst, and he spent much of his time concerned with his poor animals. A horse cannot vomit and he had seen more than one trooper heaved overboard. He had either been lucky, or chosen wisely, both seemed to be standing the journey well.

He did not remember the packet from Essex given him at the palace until well into the voyage when he was looking among his belongings for paper to write to Kate. Essex and the Court seemed far away. Curious, he broke the seal. A heavy gold ring fell out, inset with a cabuchon emerald. A tight-folded paper came with it.

'A further token of my regard, Master Talbot. Wear this ring if you will and so acknowledge our future friendship. RD.' Nick cursed. Why in God's name had he not found this before he left. Now, with so much time gone by, Essex would either have taken mortal offence or assumed Nick was complaisant.

To send it back now, taking weeks in the delivery, would add insult to injury. He didn't know what to do.

If there was one thing a classical education and army life had taught him, it was an understanding and tolerance of the relationships between men thrown together by their trade and inclination. In Thomas Walsingham he sensed it in its purest form. Never ambivalent about his own inclination, Nick had been hopeful of being able to deal tactfully with Kit Marlowe.

The powerful Robert Devereux was a different kettle of fish. From what he had learned of Essex since the episode on board ship, he would make a bad enemy and a doubtful friend, never mind anything else. How would he look on Nick's sudden disappearance? Nick could only hope that Essex would infer his enemy Cecil's hand in it and leave well alone. It was too late to mend matters now.

Once through the Straits, the weather improved dramatically and Nick was able to spend time on his own interests and study his orders. The arrangements so far had been impeccable, not surprising when you considered they were made by a man who had been to the New World and back. Nero and Rowena were to be stabled outside Venice within easy reach and it was left to him to find a safe haven for Marlowe in the Veneto. There would be work to do in Venice first, however, and he sat in his cabin, writing up his journal and perusing his orders for the hundredth time. These were quite clear. He was to keep Marlowe in sight and out of mischief, meet with the Antolini brothers, the local spymasters, and take charge of whatever budget of news that was to be brought home. Their own messages were to be delivered and he had letters of introduction to a bank on the Grand Canal. Ralegh seemed to have read his mind. He was to establish himself in Venice before moving Marlowe: he did not know what Marlowe's orders were. They had not spoken and he had seen that the elderly Jew was shunned by officers and crew alike. He feared poor Kit had a very wretched time of it. He need not have worried. All was grist to Marlowe's pen, and he spent the entire voyage scribbling in the dismal kennel allotted to him.

Dear Kate,

I saw a marvellous sight today. Great pillars and bastions of stone rising out of the sea and on them swarming, pygmy-like, yellow-brown monkeys that have no tails, chattering and playing like children. I have seen dolphins too, many dolphins, and pilot fish leading the ship. The flowers of these parts are abundant and tumble down the houses and streets in colours and scents to gladden the eye and tickle the nose. The rocks and fields are full of the herbs you like and some we have never seen. I have gathered some camphor and balsam for the rheum. I send some seeds and a drawing of the monkeys. I hope you like the belt of Spanish leather to hold your keys, my dearest chatelaine. Please do not address me as my lord Rokesby. I am, as ever, your loving Nick.

Chapter Twelve

Nick was bewitched by his first sight of Venice. She floated in a shifting mist between mother-o'-pearl sea and mother-o'-pearl sky, evanescent, veiled with seduction. As the sun rose, the mist dissolved in wispy spirals and tendrils, floating like smoke above the reflections appearing in the waters: roofs and domes copper-tipped with rose. The city slowly became real, Palladian facades resting on their upside-down foundations. Marlowe had been here before, but Venice never repeated her effects.

Poet and player leaned together on the ship's rail, rapt. Kit was the first to collect himself and put distance between his Jewish gaberdine and Nick's furred velvet.

As the morning wore on, a variety of boats, skiffs and gondolas came out to meet the ship and Nick was able to board an elegant black and gold gondola bound for the Grand Canal. The gondolier stuck his pole in alongside the pillared frontage of the Banco Medici for Nick to step ashore. Nick had not been this far south before and he was too hot in his cramoisie velvet. The canals and narrow walkways were crammed with a noisy throng, mostly dressed in the extreme of fashion: some of the women were bare-breasted, nipples tipped with rose, some wore fantastical masks, and Nick noticed several faces hideously disfigured, noses eaten away by the French disease. The universal beggars and pimps eased through the crowds and the stink of the canal mixing with the many perfumes and pomades was overpowering.

Nick was quaking inside. His usual confidence seemed to be deserting him. He caught Marlowe's eye on him from further down the quay and pulled himself together. He paid off his gondolier and, stiffening his spine, trod with a lordly air up the green-stained steps to the tall, carved doors. Flunkeys bowed him in and he stood on the marble drawing off his gloves and looking round, playing the part. The bank seemed a cross between a private mansion and a cathedral, veined marble pillars soaring up to an impressive dome painted with floating clouds and frowning deities. It was very quiet inside: soberly clad men paced to and fro with sheaves of paper, heads bent, looking not left nor right. Nick slapped his gloves negligently against his leg and one of the clerks looked up and came over.

'Attend to me, please. I have letters of marque and packets for Signor Fratelli,' said Nick boldly. 'Messire Rokesby, from Lord Burghley of London.' The man bowed.

'If the Messire would come this way.' It seemed to be working. The notorious close-fistedness of Elizabeth's government was not evident here, and Nick transacted his business, arranged for money to be available to him and accepted a glass of wine served in a handsome goblet of Murano glass. All was conducted with dignified courtesy. He left the bank considerably encouraged and set about finding his billet. This turned out to be rooms in a palazzo painted a faded pink with blue shutters, and facing the Rialto. Their dunnage had been delivered surprisingly intact and a servant appeared with a platter of cheeses and bread, fruit and wine. Nick wandered about chewing, a goblet of wine in his hand. The apartment was spacious, the high ceilings coffered with gold, the walls hung with damask: tall, narrow windows looked out on the busy canal. Nick noted with interest the small door hidden by a tapestry that opened onto a noisome little tributary to the main waterway. 'Handy,' he thought.

Pleased with his progress, he chose one of the two bedchambers and started making himself at home, stretching out on the bed dropping grapes into his mouth and watching the rippled reflections on the ceiling.

Presently he heard the little door open and close and Marlowe appeared in the doorway, cat-footed in his felt slippers. He pulled off his yarmulke and gaberdine and kicked them into a corner.

''sblood, I'm glad to be rid of those! Did you see that fat merchant spit on me? What it must be like – do you know, I begin to have a sympathy for the wretched race.' He stood there in shirt and hose, scratching. 'They are flesh and blood after all. They must have feelings, like us. How do they endure it?'

'They take their petty revenges, no doubt,' said Nick.

'Never again. At least I can take a piss now without looking to see who's watching. Uncircumcised dog that I am. I shall keep in touch with my new friend Malachi. Where are my clothes? And pour me some of that wine, you selfish creature.'

He had grown a full beard on the voyage, worn in a spade cut that changed the shape of his face and hid his full red lips. His hair was in long greasy ringlets and he had darkened his skin. As Nick got up to do his bidding, Marlowe fell into a slouch, rounding his shoulders and poking his head forward, sliding his hands one over the other.

'Signor Martelli, at your service,' he lisped. 'Will this serve, do you think, until we leave here?'

Nick was doubled up with laughter.

'If you can keep it up.'

'Christopher Marlowe was well known in Venice. I can keep it up. Have you contacted the Antolini?'

'Tonight.'

'Tonight is Carnival. One of the many. I shall come with you to make sure you don't fall in the water.'

'I shall be glad of your company, sir.'

'You did not sir me just now.'

'Your pardon, sir. I forgot myself.'

'We are colleagues and fellow-conspirators, *Master Talbot*. But I will wait until my name falls naturally, trippingly on the tongue. Meanwhile, Nicholas, I shall go and procure for us some masquing gear. I fancy you would make an enchanting girl, if a little tall, and wide in the shoulder. Or a dashing pirate, with that scowl. What a pity you left your demon garb behind.'

'You may find I brought him with me... Sir.'

In the event, it was Marlowe who wore the skirts, a bold Circassian, black eyes sparkling behind a mask of sequins and feathers, a veil covering his beard. Nick was Arlecchino, a thing of patches and spangles and mirror-glass, unnoticed among a hundred others. He was glad of Marlowe's company, albeit he was behaving atrociously.

The crowds had swollen to suffocation point. Jostled and caressed by men and women either merely merry, drunk, or falling-down drunk, fleering, sneering masks thrust into his face, bewildered by the noise and laughter and stench, he was glad to be pushed stumbling between two dark houses out of the crush and din and the glare and smoke of the torches.

Marlowe propelled him through a door into a cell-like room lit only by the flickering stub of a candle. The air was fetid with sweat and fear and the reek of loosened bowels. As Nick stood for a moment, his eyes adjusting to the dark, he was aware of a noise that made the hair rise on his head – a noise of panting and heels drumming. There were three men in the small space, one of them a fat man of about forty, eyes bolting from his head, pinned up on the wall by a hand at his throat and a knife to his belly. A second man was searching him, slashing and stripping to the lining of his clothes and the flesh beneath. When he got to the soiled breeches, the man on the wall whimpered and the searcher slashed the points and pulled them down. What he wanted was strapped to the man's groin. The fat man yelped as the packet was ripped away, and the man holding him changed his grip to slam his victim's head hard against the wall, twice. He let go and allowed the body to slump to the ground.

Marlowe coughed gently.

Two identical faces swivelled round, mouths agape, bodies crouched, a knife in each man's hand.

'Marlowe, risen from the dead, at your service, gentlemen. And this is the ferryman from Hell. You must pay him, you know.'

The two men straightened, as like as two peas in a pod, tall, thin and cadaverous, in matching clothes. They sheathed their knives, and Nick noted automatically that they were mirror-image twins, one right, one left-handed. The left-handed one had a small mole under his right ear. No one looked at the body gently twitching on the floor. Marlowe was squeezing Nick's arm, holding him back.

There was a board across two barrels pushed against the wall, serving as a table and littered with papers. The stub of candle guttered and the man on the floor appeared to writhe. One of the brothers found another candle and lit it while his twin poured wine and offered it. Marlowe gave

Nick's arm a 'don't interfere' shake and sashayed across to take the proffered mug. He had pushed the gilded mask up on top of his head and pulled down his veil. The effect was paralysing. Nick kept his mask in place and slanted a glance at the man on the floor. He was obviously dead, or as good as. Marlowe waved a scented handkerchief.

'Foh! Could we not lug the guts elsewhere. I swear I feel quite faint.'

One of the brothers picked up the body by the heels and dragged him out. The other rolled up the spoiled clothes and followed. There was a splash and ripples of water gurgled against the side of the canal.

Nick's face felt stiff under his mask and he surreptitiously eased his dagger in its sheath. Marlowe was sitting at the table by now, sipping his wine and looking through the papers. So far neither of the brothers had uttered a sound. Now the one who had disposed of the corpse cleared his throat.

'Is this what you're looking for?' He threw the packet torn from his unfortunate victim onto the table.

'Possibly, Tonio – or is it Francisco? Possibly, but there was no hurry you know.'

'Hurry enough. The man was on his way to lay information.'

'Ah.' Marlowe ripped open the oiled-silk package with fastidious fingers and cast his eye rapidly over the contents. 'Yes.' He rummaged under his skirts and a clinking bag changed hands. 'Now for your business with my friend, here. Arlecchino, the papers, if you please.'

Nick fumbled Cecil's sealed packet from inside his tunic and handed it over in exchange for a small ribboned bundle of letters. Marlowe tipped the rest of his wine down his throat and rose.

'Our thanks, Messire, as efficient as ever.' He pulled up his veil, adjusted his mask and with a flirty wave of the hand pushed Nick out of the door. There was no sign of the murdered man but a knot of sodden clothes slowly sinking.

The heat and noise and stink hit Nick like a blow, almost overpowering him, the gondolas crowded with gaping, crowing, fantastical faces wavered through the fog rising inside him. Something unspeakable rose and rolled in the water and sank. Nick wrenched off his mask and vomited into the canal.

'Come, faint heart, no turning back now,' murmured his hero's voice in his ear. 'More than you bargained for was it? A little aqua vitae will set you to rights.' He piloted Nick to a crowded tavern with tables and stools spilling onto the cobbles and disappeared inside. He came back with two small crystal glasses full of some golden liquid.

'Get that inside you. Those two are hard to stomach, I agree.' He waited until some colour had come back to Nick's face and went on, 'You kept your head in there. It is as I thought. The information is not complete. You will have to wait for another messenger. There is trouble brewing in the Levant and the people here will be the first to know. If you wish to have no further dealings with our twin evils, approach another, whose name I will give you. He is homesick, poor fool, but until you can speak the language, you will be able to converse with him, at least.'

Nick, who had applied himself on the long voyage to mastering Italian, merely nodded.

Marlowe grinned at him, the mischievous eyes the only

feature visible in the masked face.

'I am never wrong,' he said. 'A playwright watches, Nick, learns to read men – not from their faces, there is no art for that, but the signs and actions that give them away, unwitting.'

Nick turned away. 'There is a lot to do,' he said. 'What will you do with yourself while I am away? I am to ask you not to show yourself here, disguise or no disguise.'

'We won't talk of it here. If you are more yourself, we will go back and be private.' Nick swallowed the rest of his brandy and nodded.

Once back in the comparative quiet of their rooms, Marlowe stripped off his costume and walked up and down with a cup of wine, half-naked, clicking his fingers.

'What will I do. Good question. I should have plenty to occupy me. I need a fair copy of my writings on the ship and even now I have an idea stirring. No wonder Italy is the birthplace of so much enlightened thinking, Nicholas. The warmth, the light, *the life!* It suits me.'

'I have a place in mind for you, sir. There was a traveller on board ship – he makes maps – and there is a small town in the Veneto—'

Marlowe flew into a sudden passion of rage.

'A small town! Some provincial village! Are you trying to kill me? Is it not enough that I am exiled with a 17-year-old dolt who won't even let me love him! What possessed me to do this – I have sold my soul and gained nothing—'

The 17-year-old dolt could only stand and watch as Marlowe's despair escalated into a fury of words and tears. He worked himself into a frenzy, beating the walls and banging his head until Nick, frightened and desperate, put his arms round him and used his young strength to subdue him and sit him down. Marlowe was shivering and sobbing now, his white skin gooseflesh, and Nick pulled up the coverlet and wrapped it round him, his heart wrung with pity. He sat beside his maestro, petting and gentling him as if he were his horse, and the man gradually grew calmer, nestling his head into Nick's shoulder.

'Niccolo, Niccolo…you could make life bearable… I miss Tom—' Nick smoothed back the tangled hair and kissed the high forehead where it showed white against the dark stain.

'Your life is in here, sir, in your head. You don't need anything else. I am here merely to make all possible amends, smooth the way.'

'Help me bear it, Niccolo…' Nick eased away and piled the pillows behind Marlowe's head.

'Rest easy, sir. All will be well. Let me go and spy out the land. A secure base we must have. You must have a new identity – a name, a position. Wander Europe at your leisure, sir, but I must have somewhere to find you, where you can find friends—'

'Where am I likely to find like-minded men in some benighted village!'

'There will be educated men in Verona, sir. If not, I will look elsewhere.'

Marlowe sat up.

'Verona! Why didn't you say so! I know Verona, I have friends there. They know me as M'sieur Parolles.'

Why didn't you say so, thought Nick. Good name, though. Marlowe was excited now.

'The very place. Arrange it.' He jumped up, dragging the quilt toga-like about him, and began to pace the room like a caged animal, talking, talking.

Nick could see that Marlowe was facing the brutal fact of his exile for the first time. The words of Mephistopheles rang in his ears. 'Why, this is Hell, nor am I out of it.' No, he thought. Kit Marlowe must not be allowed to dwindle into the drudgery of a paid hireling, spying for Cecil. It would not do for either of them. That brilliant intellect must be given nourishment, a purpose.

An idea was forming in Nick's mind. What were those papers Marlowe had brought in with him yesterday – Christ, was it only yesterday? Perhaps he was working on another epic poem. No, he could not look now, there were more urgent things to be done. He heard his father's voice, 'Establish your base before aught else.'

He set himself to persuade a fretful Marlowe to take some food and more wine, finally getting him to bed as sequins of sunlight began to dance on the ceiling, disengaging the clinging hands and gently tucking him in.

No one had warned him he would be playing nursemaid. He looked at the dark ravaged face on the pillow, and almost wished he could do more. Shaking his head, he found the maps he had copied and sat poring over them, working out distances and times. Finally decided, he rolled himself in his blankets and, muffling his ears against the noise still rioting outside, fell asleep.

When he woke it was late afternoon. Marlowe, who had drunk far more than he, was still asleep and woke in a sullen, sombre mood. Nick only waited to exact a promise that he would be patient and stay within doors, before taking to the water to go and find his horses.

Chapter Thirteen

Nick set off across the plain of the Veneto strangely light of heart. The spirit of adventure, a little daunted by the encounter with the Antolini brothers, sat up and stretched, rubbing its eyes and pricking its ears. He had a good horse between his legs, a task he felt he could accomplish and a new country to explore. He sang as Nero bore him easily along, Rowena trotting behind, both horses glad to stretch their legs. Nick rode them turn and turn about, his sword handy in front of the saddle, passing wagons and carts and more wagons taking produce and livestock into the city. Many drovers smiled and raised a hand to the young gallant in his sleeveless leather jerkin, trotting so purposefully on the fine horse, his russet hair lifting in the breeze.

The sun rose and grew hot, and Nick turned into the shade of a small chapel beside a stream, hobbled the horses and let them graze. He ate a little and drank, then sat for a while, elbows on knees, chewing on a succulent stem of grass. He could see for miles, through a shimmering haze of heat: field after field of vines, orchards and pastureland, punctuated by the exclamation marks of poplar and cypress. Groups of red-tiled houses and barns kept their distance from the classical splendour of white colonnaded buildings: a landscape totally new to him.

He would have liked a closer look at some of the fine buildings and promised himself that once his errands were done and Marlowe settled he would spend time here. For now, he was bound for Florence, to the palace of the Medici on the first of Cecil's errands, and he mounted up and headed west once more. He reasoned that the dispatches had been delayed so long already, he need not lather his horses for the sake of speed and there was no dearth of decent inns along the way. Trotting contentedly across the Lombardy plain and through the hills of Tuscany, stopping where he fancied and marvelling at the vistas spread out before him, he nevertheless kept a wary eye out for trouble and was no doubt fortunate in arriving at the outskirts of Florence unhindered. He was surprised by the wide, paved streets that separated even the meanest of dwellings and as he approached the city centre in the early light, there was already a constant background noise of sawing and hammering. New buildings, in the classical style he had already noticed, were still in the process of completion and a haze of brick dust hung in the air with the smell of new paint and drying stucco. Impressed with the light and space after the huddled streets of London, he clattered over a splendid bridge up an incline and drew rein to consult his notes. He leaned over to question a passer-by.

'Piazza della Signoria?' The man jerked a thumb over his shoulder and Nick rode on to come into a wide square surrounded with buildings the size and style of which took his breath away. In front of one of them was the largest chunk of marble Nick had ever seen, sculpted in the shape of a naked man with a sling for hurling stones thrown casually over one shoulder. Nick's mouth fell open. The huge sculpture – it must be all of seventeen feet high – was so full of raw energy held in leash that it felt like a punch in the gut. It was sparkling crystalline white and Nick saw a small man with a crooked shoulder and a ladder beside him washing pigeon droppings from the strongly planted foot. He drew closer, fumbling for his notebook. The old man looked up with a toothless grin.

'Stranger here?' Nick saw that he had the scarred and muscled hands of a mason and opened his mouth, but the man went on, 'My father saw him put here before I was born, I'd like to have seen that. Trundled him round in his wooden cage for four days they did, before they decided. Puts old Neptune there in the shade, don't he?' He waved a dismissive hand at the fountain further down the colonnade. Three men were working on a group of nymphs and satyrs round the edge of the basin dominated by a marble figure. 'You know what they say about him that made that? Eh? Pity he ruined so much marble! That's what.' The old man went into a paroxysm of wheezy laughter that turned into a coughing fit. Nick jumped down but was waved away as the old craftsman sank down on the plinth wiping his eyes.

'What is this statue called?'

'Don't you know that? Where are you from? David, he is, that killed the giant. Tell me something. Has he just slain Goliath? Or is he planning how to do it? Some say the head's too big, but I don't know—'

'Doesn't it have to be big to look right so high up?' ventured Nick, thinking of the playhouse. The old creature seemed to feel possessive of this marvellous piece of work. He had gone back to his cleaning, nodding thoughtfully. Nick put away his notebook. Perhaps there would be time later. He looked round at the array of impressive buildings. They all looked equally important.

'If you please, which is the Palazzo Vecchio?'

'Right in front of you.' It looked more like a fortress than a palace, with a single graceful tower. There seemed to be building work going on even here. Dusty and travel-stained as he was, Nick felt he had better use the tradesman's entrance, and giving the old man a coin he led the horses through a narrow passage and round to find the usual domestic activity, stabling, hens scratching, people shouting above the clash of pots and pans. He asked for the steward and by degrees was passed from hand to hand through magnificent apartments with painted and coffered ceilings to be left to kick his heels in a small chamber hung with tapestries and with one tiny window. Suddenly nervous, he investigated behind the tapestries and found nothing but a recess behind one holding a bed and a chamber pot. He still felt someone was watching him, and pulled a chair under the window, easing his sword. He stood as the door opened and a tall man with an aquiline nose and cold grey eyes entered. A guard stood behind him.

'Signore Talbot?' He gave the name a flat A. 'You have words from England?' His accent was atrocious and Nick tried his Italian.

'For the eyes of the man who can show me a sign. Signore.' He held out the hand with the missing fingertip.

'You are new. And wise to be cautious. Were you told to know this ring? You need a name. Dottore Vassili Fioreste – secretary to the lord Ferdinando.' Nick unbuckled the sealed leather wallet from his belt and handed it over.

'This will take time. There will be a response – perhaps tomorrow. Do not attempt to leave this chamber, signore. Your baggage will be brought, make yourself comfortable. Your horses will be taken care of.' He turned and went. The guard locked the door behind him.

Nick did not like this at all. He had no idea what might have happened in the state of Florence since he left London. He had a hazy recollection from listening to Noll of the turmoil going on here as the people fought for a Republic, but no certainty of the outcome. Yet if a Medici was back in power, surely things must have stabilised. He felt distinctly under-prepared. His brief had been clear. See Marlowe safe and settled, deliver a few messages and report back. Nothing about this kind of reception.

'Let's hope there's nothing inflammatory in that wallet,' he thought.

His bags were brought, and later an excellent meal. Always one to make the best of things, he stopped worrying and used the time to write up his journal and a separate report. It grew dark and sufficient candles were brought in. Before he rolled into the bed in the alcove he tried to put down on paper some of the wonders he had seen. His last thought before he slept was of the expression of the great statue in the square.

The next day, after a good breakfast that came with hot water and cloths, he sat down clean and shaved to write to Kate, struggling to keep his dislike of enclosed spaces at bay. The morning wore on and he had begun to wonder what Marlowe would do if he didn't come back, when the lock rattled and the same official returned. Unsmiling, he held out a bulky wallet dangling with seals, and a leather bag. Nick bowed and took them: the bag was heavy. The secretary said, 'The money is yours. Show me your writings if you please.'

'So there is a spyhole,' thought Nick. 'Good thing I was careful.' There was nothing in journal, letter or report that could be taken exception to, he had kept neutrally to facts. A faint glimmer of a smile crept into the man's face as he read and looked at the little drawings.

'You used your time admirably, Signore Talbot. We shall know you next time – I think you should do well. Go as discreetly as you came and God speed.'

Nick had much to think about as he rode quietly out of the beautiful city, a city that set such store by its art and civilised buildings and hid such menace. He could admit now to having been very frightened. He hefted the bag of money.

'I'm worth robbing this time, Nero,' he said. 'We had better beware.' He returned by different ways and rode into Verona a few days later to find lodgings for Kit.

He was anxious that the volatile spirit he had sworn to keep safe should have room to spread his wings, away from the mood of self-destruction. He liked the feel of the mediaeval town of Verona, as yet untouched by the hand of Palladio, though by the gap-toothed look of some of the squares, it would not be long coming. It took some time to find what he wanted. He settled at last on a small balconied house in a tiny square courtyard, tucked away behind one of the main streets of the town. Marlowe would not have far to go to find company, and the place was well-found and clean. Nick took the house, engaged a cheerful young woman to keep it and set off back to Venice. It was an exhausted young man who arrived on the Rialto to find Marlowe spitting but writing.

In his absence, Marlowe had been busy. His young companion travelled light, and had left his baggage behind. Marlowe had been through it and found Nick's journal. His orders Nick had prudently taken with him. He had a small aptitude for accurate drawing, and the book was full of tiny sketches; the interior of the Rose, a voluptuous beauty in Oporto, the rocky heights of Gibraltar and Marlowe himself as a Jew. There were more practical diagrams, maps and notes, not so much a journal as a campaign notebook. Marlowe read on avidly, piqued to find little reference to himself other than his health and the state of his bowels. He found the little drawings charming however, especially those of Malta. He was admiring one of heavy-laden donkeys climbing the parched hillside to the fort, when he noticed something else. He peered closer, and made out some fine detail as to the disposition of guns.

Marlowe was beginning to have a healthy respect for Nicholas Rokesby.

Venice was well documented already. Hosts of miniature piazzas, bridges and grand porticos filled the margins. Some little maps were adorned with tiny crosses, each with its minute cypher.

'You have been busy, my lad,' said Kit aloud. Turning a page, he found a whole sheet devoted to more elaborate attempts at a portrait. He recognised her at once – the lady Rosalyne. There had been several stabs at this and a despairing 'crapaud' scrawled across. 'My foolish boy,' said Marlowe, putting the book away as he had found it. 'I see you are a lost cause.'

To Nick's relief there were no more hysterical outbursts. The expected dispatches had arrived, together with news from England. As Ralegh had feared, the jealous Elizabeth had confined him and his new wife to the Tower. Marlowe shook his head.

'He knew he was risking the Queen's anger. For a man so wise in her ways he has handled this affair badly. I hope he considers the world well lost for love or whatever it was,' and he turned his attention to his letter from Thomas. For Nick, there was a letter from Kate and another from Hugh, both full of domestic detail, painting a picture of a green and peaceful landscape so far from present surroundings it gave Nick a stomach-ache.

He stowed them away and turned to the problem of smuggling his dispatches back to London. He had it in mind to see Marlowe safely established in Verona, deliver his messages, pick up whatever he was supposed to take home and travel back over the Alps. He had found out there was a well-established trade route and he planned to join whatever party was using it. If he was going to be making this journey often, he needed to see for himself the various ways of tackling it.

On arriving back in Venice, he had found the Rialto in a fever of excitement and anxiety. A number of argosies had been lost and fortunes with them. Only two had been due to bad weather or the other misfortunes encountered at sea, the rest had fallen to pirates. Studying his maps, he sighed. Surely in this new age of science and engineering, it was not beyond man's ingenuity to find a way of tunnelling under the Alps or crossing the Narrow Sea? However, he applied himself and found several possible overland routes for future reference. This first trip would be a learning experience, he could do without pirates.

Dear Kate,

Your letters make me almost as homesick as my poor acquaintance here. I take heed of your concern for the villagers of Lower Rookham, tell Hugh to do what he can. As for your other concerns I am in good health and want for nothing save your company and good counsel. I have no worry unless

you spend yourself too freely in your good works. You have a
great heart, Kate and a generosity of spirit that cannot but
command my continuing affections. Look to yourself, Kate.
I pray you may find one worthy of you though to my mind
that would be most hard - hardest of all perhaps on your
loving Nicholas.

I enclose some drawings of the fashions now obtaining. Do
not worry, I shall not be ballooning my britches with vast
amounts of stuffing, I prefer to have the use of my limbs as
nature intended. The tires for the head would become you, I
think. N.

Venice was as riotously noisy as ever, and he found he could
not look at the canals without expecting to see the bloated
body of the man in the cellar bobbing on the sluggish tide.
Nick was still too young to see these things other than in black
and white. In a year or two, he would fall in love with Venice
again, able to appreciate the subtle ironies, the elegant forms,
the excitement and glamour of a great trading port. He would
stand on the quays watching a great galley row in fast from
the East, drums beating, oars feathering at the last moment to
glide with accurate grace to its mooring, bringing exotic spices,
silks and fabulous embroideries worked the same on both sides.
The full-bellied sails of galleons and roundships would grow
from small white puffs at the edge of the world to mountains
of canvas towering over the docks, unloading dyestuffs, alum,
bolts of woven fabrics, coal, pig-iron and slaves. Men of all
colour, race and religion would disembark to trade and treat,
and Nick would rejoice in the infinite variety.

At this moment, embroiled in a milieu foreign to his nature

– he was a born adventurer, not a spy – Nick was not happy. He needed to get out of the city for a while. He left Marlowe well supplied with ink and paper, and a handsome acolyte to wait on him, and took a boat to the island of Murano. He felt that watching the glassblowers might exorcise the demons that were plaguing him in the city. And so it proved.

He stood sweating in the heat of the blast furnaces, watching the teardrop of molten glass swell and blossom at the end of the long rod, forming, as if by magic, beautiful hollow shapes. Flasks and glasses, decorated and plain, thin and transparent, thick and serviceable, all from the lungs and brawny, scarred arms of the blowers. They had some showman's tricks, twisting and tweaking the coloured glass into fantastical creatures: dragons, horses with wings, horses prancing, small animals, rabbits and cats, dolphins – many dolphins, all created in a moment and cut off from the rod with brutal shears. The speed of it all was entrancing and Nick stayed as long as he could, watching and asking questions.

Trawling the shelves for something to take back, it occurred to him that a well-packed load of the glass animals and figurines, together with the eyeglasses he discovered, might be a commercial possibility to conceal his real purpose in returning home. Sitting in the boat on the way back, refining the idea and balancing the risks, his attention was caught by a sumptuously decorated barge making its stately way towards a neighbouring islet. The islet itself was worth noting; half hidden by stands of pine and cypress, a rose-pink building raised fairy tale turrets and cupolas, silken pennants flying from each one. As the barge floated slowly by, he saw, under its jewelled canopy, a woman in gauzy draperies beaded and festooned with pearls, lying back on cherry-coloured cushions, listening to a young Moor playing a lute. The sheer ostentation amused him. She was a beautiful creature, needing only the simplest surroundings to complement her beauty.

'Who is that?' he asked idly.

'Dream on, young sir,' grinned the boatman, with the easy familiarity of one who thinks he is indispensable. 'That's my Lady Julia, worth all the ducats in the Doge's war chest. Besieged with suitors, she sets 'em tests and riddles but I reckon she's holding out for one she fancies, never mind her father's will. She'd give him a clue, alright. Try your luck – if she likes the look of you she might tip you the wink. If you ask me this business of the riddles is all a hum.' He cast his eye over the plain leather jack and workmanlike breeches and boots Nick had chosen to wear, and shook his head. 'You'd need to dress it up a bit, mind, the peacocks I see having a go.'

Nick frowned him down and the man, mindful of his tip, applied himself to his oars. The sight of the languid beauty trailing her hand in the water reminded Nick that he had not lain with a woman since they had changed ship and rested awhile in Sicily. The wild countryside and the ferocious men had impressed him deeply. There had been a young girl, his own age for a change, seemingly intent on bestowing her virginity upon him. Her stated reason had been that she wished to please herself before obeying her fearsome brothers in their choice of a match. The Sicilian women were spectacular and Nick had done his best to please: the fear of discovery lent a delicious frisson to the affair. If he had known then of the ruthless and powerful network of the Sicilian clans, even then spreading in influence to mainland Italy, he might have thought twice. That had been weeks ago. Stirred by the vision in the barge, Nick lay back in the stern of the boat, musing. Still disenchanted and bedevilled by what he had seen of the spying game, it struck him that a rich wife with her own island could be a two-fold blessing. It would scratch his itch and release him from the need to earn his living spying. An answer to both his problems.

He shifted uneasily, shocked at himself. It was a contemptible idea, to sell himself and his name for a life of security. It was not the way forward. He thought a little guiltily of Kate. True to his word, he had given Kate enough money for a dowry, and made her the housekeeper of his home. She would be able to marry well – perhaps Hugh Shawcross was already a suitor. For some reason this gave him a pang, he loved his Kate. And he had loved others too.

'Calf-love,' he told himself. 'Grow up. She'll have moved on. As I must. As I have. But this is not what I want to be, a man to stand by and see murder done.' Death in battle was one thing: the casual slaughter of an unarmed man still shocked him. The idea of winning this rich prize, snatching her from under the noses of all her other suitors began to take hold. Why not after all? Contracts of convenience were made every day. He started thinking. The money he had been entrusted with was not his, except the handsome tip from the Medici. These rewards, however carefully husbanded, were dwindling fast. This was a city of usury. He began to plot ways and means, naively prepared to gamble on this one throw.

He arrived back at their lodging set on this new plan, to find Marlowe writing, driving his quill across the paper to the detriment of both.

'I need to borrow a lot of money,' he announced without

ceremony.

'Mournful music and a muffled drum,' muttered Marlowe. He drew a line with a screech of the quill and a shower of blots, and sat back, stretching.

'What did you say?' he asked with a huge yawn. 'It's finished.'

Exasperated, Nick said it again.

'I need money – a lot of money.'

'What for?'

Nick explained what he had seen.

'It would take care of both of us. I thought I would borrow the money to outfit a barge and some – some retainers, buy myself the right clothes, and then—'

'From whom would you borrow this money?'

'Well, I thought – Malachi? You could borrow it for me, you have connections… I would be able to pay it back.'

'And if you failed, the bond would be forfeit. What do you suppose would happen then? Make no mistake, Nick, I would pay any forfeit for you gladly, if I thought your scheme had legs. No. You have an important job to do. Rich Venetian ladies do not come into it.' He stood up and called for wine. 'Stop pacing about and sit down and listen to me.' He had shed his usual dilettante manner. This was a Kit Marlowe Nick had not seen.

'You have carried yourself so well thus far, I had forgot how young and untried you are still. This is a hare-brained scheme, Nick. If you had fallen in love, it might be understandable, but you are thrashing around for a way out. I know the Antolini episode troubles you. It was nasty, and I daresay you will see worse, but remember this. The work I and others like me undertake is necessary for the peace and safety of the realm. I started off for the hell of it, and the money, and to put two fingers up to the Establishment, but now I see the usefulness. My own usefulness is almost over, but I am still to keep my web spread to catch what I can. And first and foremost, I am still a poet.' He pushed a cup of wine into Nick's hand.

'Drink. You are not an intelligencer, Nick, that weasel word for spy. You have not the temperament, and so I shall tell Cecil. But you have nerve and intelligence and are undoubtedly a brave young man of considerable resource. You will make a superb courier, an item always in short supply. For some reason.' He lifted a quizzical eyebrow and Nick had to smile. 'You came into this for the adventure and, I like to think, for my sake. I pray you, for my sake, let us continue.' The man's magnetism exerted its usual pull, and Nick found himself nodding agreement. He had been shown a picture of himself he did not like – a foolish, callow boy seeking a coward's way out. Marlowe had dealt the wound and then applied the balm. Nick saw that he could continue with his honour intact, serve his country as his father had done, albeit on a different battlefield. He looked up to find Marlowe lost in a brown study.

'And there is something else,' he went on slowly. 'You seem to bring me luck, Nicholas, inspiration – what you will. The words, the forms, have never flowed so sweetly, so free. Tell me again of this rich lady and her riddles.'

Dear Kate,

I saw today on the lagoon a most marvellous and assured beauty in a barge like to that of Cleopatra. You would have been amazed at her puffed-up consequence, Kate. I had thought to make her my wife and my fortune, but my master thinks we would not suit. I shall have to think of something else. I am pleased to hear you are making good use of my library, Kate. I am sending a parcel of books and some tall tales for your enjoyment. You will particularly like the tale of Don Quixote, I think – peruse it carefully, for we are meant to read between the lines, I believe, for the true message. I send also a piece of silk come from the East and a bolt of velvet for your Yuletide gift in case I am not home. I remember well the chill of Rokesby's halls.

I am glad to think that you have Hugh to share in the responsibilities of my inheritance. Remember, sweet Kate, you had first call on my heart, but should another come your way among your many suitors I shall be first to wish you joy. If he deserves you. Choose wisely, Kate, if he proves unworthy of you, he will answer to me. I am sending this by fast galley, it should reach you soon, and by then I shall be preparing for my journey home. I cannot arrive before November, but I hope to be home by Christmas.

Nick.

Chapter Fourteen

'Excellent staff-work, my dear,' said Kit Marlowe, swivelling on his heel to survey his new kingdom. The little house was sturdily built of stones plundered from the ruins of the Roman amphitheatre close by, with a sunny walled garden at the back. The furniture was sparse but polished and the beds comfortable. 'And now you will abandon me to be off on your travels. You can't wait, can you?'

It was true, Nick had certainly been looking forward to it, but now he was not so sure. Autumn seemed a good time for the journey, before the first snows, and he was joining what had looked like a well-organised group of twenty travellers. His own arrangements were made: he had maps, a mule, a spare horse and the dispatches cyphered in invisible ink wrapping a consignment of glass. He had also invested in a brace of pistols, two throwing knives and a crossbow. Marlowe had laughed at him.

'My dear Nick, you are positively bristling with weaponry! You have arsenal enough for a small army. Who is going to attack such a large party?'

Nick did not know, but he was beginning to have a bad feeling about this trip. He had glimpsed the wagons and merchants beginning to assemble, and the sight had not filled him with confidence. He was worried about one of his horses. Nero had a slight colic, and still seemed listless. Nick had not found a better animal, and at least Nero had started eating up. He was dosing him and hoping for the best.

'We should order a special supper to send you on your way.'

Nick shook his head, uneasy. He was finishing unpacking Marlowe's belongings and came across a bundle of scribbled paper. He picked it up.

'May I read this?'

'Outpourings of a dead poet. Romantic trash. Do what you

will with it. Hang it in the privy for all I care.'

Nick, feeling he deserved a break, took a hunk of bread and cheese and settled down to read in the garden. It was a reworked version of the play Nashe had brought to Cobham. He had hardly read the prologue when Marlowe burst out of the house.

'I've changed my mind!'

Nick held the manuscript up out of his reach, and began to read.

'Starts with a fight – that's good. Grabs the attention—' he read on, immediately drawn into the story. 'Who's the hero?'

Marlowe snatched back the pages.

'Too slow, too slow! Plays are meant to be acted, not read by the light of a candle, at snail's pace – my words must be spoken, shouted aloud – stay there, I am Juliet, that is my balcony, you are my Romeo—' he bolted into the house to emerge on the balcony and lay his cheek artistically against his hand.

Exhorted by Marlowe, Nick found himself posturing in the garden, fighting in the street, up and down the stairs and in and out of the rooms, caught up in the drama, and swept away by the music of the words. At the end, they flung themselves down, breathless and laughing.

'Well?'

'It's like nothing you have ever done! And yet the words, the sounds – "take him and cut him out in little stars"' Nick struggled to express himself. 'Where is your mighty line? What have you done to it? It's – it's like, like – elastic!'

'It is a small story. No kings and queens, no demons and emperors. No pampered jades of Asia here. A domestic.'

'I had not thought you could enter into—'

'Do you think I know nothing of this kind of love, Niccolo? Of the feeling of one human being for another, passion, tenderness? How little you know me. What are you afraid of?' He stretched ink-stained fingers to caress Nick's hand. 'You sit there with your round brown arms and your green eyes and say I cannot feel?'

Nick pulled away his hand and stood up hastily.

'These are young lovers, untried babes, innocent—'

'I was young and innocent once,' said Kit quietly. There were tears standing in his eyes. Nick gazed at him, helpless.

'There is not a word written in derision or cynical hypocrisy, Nicholas. Christopher Marlowe is dead. I have found a new beginning here, with you.' He turned away and poured wine. 'Don't be afraid. I have not changed my spots, but I shall not harm you, youngling. Well,' he lifted his goblet. 'To the unknown, unseen Tragedy of Romeo and his Juliet. What a Romeo you make.'

'Not Romeo. I'd play Mercutio, me. Oh, yes, that's the thing. The best character dies in the first twenty minutes! What were you thinking? The play dies with him a little – can you not contrive some way to strengthen Romeo? He seems to me a feeble thing, weeping and wailing, making love and running away. Or change Mercutio.'

Marlowe was laughing.

'A critic now, are we? Mercutio is modelled a little on you, Nick. I shall not change him. Do you not realise that Juliet is my hero? Perhaps one day, if women are allowed to play, she will dwindle and the balance will change. Women are frighteningly strong, Nicholas. I prefer my life without them. But what does it matter, the play will not be seen.'

He picked up the scattered pages and went towards the fire.

'No, no! Wait—' Nick leapt forward and snatched the pages. 'There must be a way – let me think—'

'A lost play by Christopher Marlowe, discovered after his death?' mocked Kit. Nick was at the desk.

'No, that won't serve, you are already embarked on another – what is this? A comedy? You don't do comedy.'

'I told you. The juices flow in this place, something about the light, the warmth…the company. You make me laugh.'

Something overheard in the Mermaid surfaced in Nick's mind. What had they been talking about? A production of Henry Six, that was it. Robert Greene, fat, sweating and half-drunk as usual, had been complaining he had not been paid for his part of it. That's right, and his companion had been laughing at him. 'Everyone knows Kit Marlowe wrote the best bits,' he had said.

'Will Shakespeare!' he muttered.

'What?'

'Nothing. Let me think.'

Nick had remembered Will Shakespeare at the printers' where he had been picking up some pamphlets. Shakespeare had been trying to sell some play or other, seeking to break into the magic circle. A man from no particular background, no university education and little to recommend him but a dulcet tongue and an ability to please, he was finding it hard. He had had some small success, but so far had not taken.

The great idea was forming in Nick's mind.

Marlowe was speaking to him. Unheeding, he stuffed the manuscript in his shirt and went to find Rowena. He saddled her up in a daze and set off, thinking. He thought better when he was doing something else. By the time he got back he had worked it out. All that remained was to persuade Marlowe. He had no doubts of his ability to persuade Shakespeare: the impression he had formed of him was of a man ambitious, envious and slightly venal. He was always short of money, with a wife and family to support and wanted to rise in the world. Nick had heard rumours that he was setting his cap at a lady far above his touch.

He found Marlowe sitting in the garden, an almost empty bottle at his elbow. Nick found another and poured himself a drink, trembling, sitting down on the grass at Marlowe's feet.

'I wish I had not come,' said the poet. 'I should never have agreed to save my miserable skin at the expense of my art. What is it worth to have a life that is a lingering death? I was afraid, Nick. Afraid of torture, afraid to die, to lie in cold obstruction and to rot. And now I am to rot here, unrecognised.'

'It need not be so.'

'What are you saying.'

'I'm saying, let me take the plays to London, get them put on. Not in your name, another's name, but they will be heard and seen and applauded and loved. You will know of it, I will bring you news of it – your *work* is you, Kit, your words are your life, your children—' Nick was looking up into his beloved poet's face, his eyes shining, on fire with his desire for the work of creation to go on.

'You called me Kit—'

'I have it all planned. Let me try. It will be a huge hoax, the greatest lie, the best joke ever played, and only we will know of it! And when the time is right, we shall reveal it! And in the meantime, your genius will be heard and sung and talked of – the whole world shall hear you, Kit, and yet you will be safe. Let me try—'

'You do love me.'

'I have been in love with your words since I first heard them. I cannot bear to hear you talk as you do as if everything is finished. You said yourself this is a new beginning, let us publish it abroad. What's in a name? The work is what matters – and in the end it will be known!'

'You say I am my words. You love my words, you must love me.'

'Yes.'

The silence stretched on. At last, 'This is a real, honest and true love, Niccolo. It is worth having and I am honoured. You have placed trust in me and I shall not abuse it to live in a waste of shame. I am learning.'

'Then I may try it?'

'Do what you will. Just don't get yourself killed. That would be too much to bear.'

Nick leapt to his feet.

'What about that feast you promised me? Now we have something to celebrate!'

Marlowe looked up at him with a strange smile.

'What a boy you are. Very well, let us put on our best finery and see if we can find you a girl.'

Chapter Fifteen

Nick had carefully pricked the letters of their address in Verona – and other private things – in the pages of *Don Quixote*, but nonetheless when the final packet of letters arrived before he left, he was greatly surprised to see Kate's handwriting. He picked it up at once, he always read Kate's letters first, and since she had obeyed his instruction to make use of his library and the books he sent, they had become a delight to read. They were full of domestic detail, told with the delicate irony and sense of fun that attracted him to her; he felt he knew every person on his estate through her eyes. She would write of the beauty of the changing seasons and the latest controversial or scientific discovery almost in the same breath and had been quick to pick up his hint at a secret message. She wrote now:

Dear Nicholas, my lord of Rokesby.

You are good enough to refer to my many suitors. I assure you I do not lack them, sir; thanks to your generosity I have an excellent dowry and position. I am reckoned a good catch in these parts. But I am Penelope, weaving her web, waiting for her Ulysses to return. Do not fear, this is metaphor only. I ask nothing more of you than you have already given me. I am content to mind your house and hearth and keep all in readiness for when you have done with your adventuring. As I said to you, there will be nothing wanting when you bring home your bride. No man has yet presented himself that pleases me. Your books and travel tales have spoiled me, I fear, and yet I find in them and in your letters world enough.

Save your concern for yourself and your health. Rokesby wants its master but will wait in good heart.

Yours in all obedience, Kate.

Standing in the doorway with his baggage heaped around his feet, Nick read this letter in bewilderment. Tone and words alike revealed a new Kate. He read it again. He seemed to have annoyed her in some way. He got out the letter he would leave with Marlowe, to be given to her only if something were to happen to him, and wondered. No, leave it. He would write again on the journey and perhaps give it to someone travelling faster than he, there was no time now.

He shook his head and stowed away her letter, bade farewell to Marlowe who stood in the hall disconsolate, disposed his baggage tidily and mounted Rowena, Nero's lead rope in his hand. Marlowe came to look up at him.

'You will be careful.'

'Of course. Haven't I your next great play to look after?'

Arrived at the starting-off point, Nick looked at his fellow travellers with disfavour. They were a mixed bunch: four wealthy merchants with their servants, two with wives and their maids, one obvious soldier of fortune, four or five craftsmen carrying the tools of their trade – bound for home after working on the new cathedral in Milan, now ten years in the building – the rest traders with heavy-laden wagons drawn by bullocks. Altogether twenty mismatched targets for brigandry. Nick felt he might be being unduly pessimistic, but he was not taking any chances. Pistols, never his weapon of choice, rested loaded and ready either side of his pommel, the twin throwing knives occupied a tiny scabbard at the back of his neck, another nestled in his boot. His sword and dagger hung at his belt and his favoured crossbow was slung behind the saddle. If all this seemed ostentatious, he did not care. He was new to this and it was a trial run. It was on the advice of the Antolini that he was joining a baggage train – safety in numbers and he would not get lost, they said, grinning. Nick was not sure. The company seemed to him like an army on the move – 'Might as well shout "Here we are, come and get us",' he grumbled to himself. He had his own horses and a sturdy mule miscalled Bella, for an uglier brute he had never seen. Bella carried the consignment of glass wrapped in the pages of invisible cypher and packed in shavings, sawdust and an outer layer of oilcloth. His copy of Marlowe's play he carried openly in his satchel with extra paper, pen and ink. He had on a woollen shirt and small-clothes, under a well-worn boiled-leather tunic, and leggings bought from an old soldier, and a heavy-duty cloak. A spare suit of clothes was rolled into one of Bella's panniers, with the spices, silk and alum for trading. He felt he had allowed for most eventualities.

There were six wagons, four sumpter mules as well as Bella, and seven spare horses, three of them thoroughbreds with breakable legs. One of the women had a linnet in a cage, and a servant was leading a pair of shivering greyhounds with jewelled collars. To Nick, brought up to army discipline on the move, it looked a thoroughly unhandy expedition.

The soldier lounged over to him, chewing on a slice of pomegranate. He was a tall, lanky individual, dressed much as Nick himself, with the addition of a quilted jack. The rangy walk could not quite disguise a limp. His brown face had long creases in the cheeks and his eyes were very blue with blond lashes. What hair Nick could see under his cap was streaky fair.

'What do you reckon?' He was English, his accent the drawl of the South Country.

'Unchancy lot,' said Nick. The man chewed and spat a pip politely to leeward. He inspected Nick's armoury.

'Expecting trouble?'

'Always.'

The man choked, his eyes disappearing for a moment into glimmering slits. Nick thumped him on the back. He spat more pips.

'Thanks. Pity about the llama,' he said.

'The what?'

'Present for the Queen – just turned up its toes. It would've been better going the whole way by sea, I reckon. Want to take a look?'

Nick studied him for a moment, suspecting a hoax, and realised the stranger could only be a few years older than he. He led Rowena after him round to the back of the inn yard, where a strange creature lay on its back with all four stumpy legs sticking stiffly into the air. It had a long neck and a face like a camel. Nick had seen engravings of camels and a thing called a giraffe, but nothing like this. He got out his notebook and began to draw. His companion stood looking over his shoulder.

'Reminds me of a company commander I had once,' he said. Nick turned to grin at him.

'Tobias Fletcher. Ex-cavalry.'

'I thought so. Nicholas Talbot.' The two young men stood

looking one another over.

'You've seen action,' said Nick.

'A spot of trouble outside Naples. You've never seen such a shambles, the buggers nearly had us. I decided to take my money and run – too young to die for some poncy prince who doesn't know his arse from his arquebus.'

Nick snorted with laughter, saving up this gem to share with Kit. He put away his drawing, and, much in charity with each other, they strolled back to find one of the horses had cast a shoe and the wheel was off one of the wagons. By the time they started off, only three hours late, the two were well on the way to being friends.

Nick chose to bring up the rear, but after an hour of eating dust, spurred up to ride by Tobias. Tobias was munching an apple now.

'Don't you ever stop eating?'

'Not if I can help it. What d'you reckon now?'

'Too slow. I think I might go on ahead. Why haven't these people got a guard?'

'Guards cost money.'

'Let's hope it doesn't prove false economy.'

Tobias slanted a blue eye at him. 'Don't worry,' he said, 'I'll look after you.'

Nick aimed a cuff at him and the two jostled happily for a few moments, drawing disapproving glares from the leading merchant. By nightfall, they were still only traversing the foothills of the mountains and the women were complaining. Fortunately they found a hospitable inn and racked up for the night. Nick was still chafing at the slow progress, but Tobias shrugged and proceeded to win sums of money from the traders and artisans drinking and gambling in the alehouse. Nick rolled himself in his blanket and wrote to Kate.

The next day was better; the weather was kind and the scenery magnificent. The inn at their next resting-place was more than adequate and Nick began to relax. He had discovered that Tobias Fletcher had in fact commanded a small troop, twenty men, and his forebears had been bowmen at Crécy. For his part, Tobias had known someone who had fought alongside Nick's father. Both familiar with army life, they got on with making the journey as easy as possible, and things went smoothly as a result, if not very fast.

So on into the mountains. The altitude began to tell on man and beast alike, and Nick continued to fidget at the leisurely pace.

They were climbing to the saddle between two high peaks when the weather suddenly shut down. A thick mist rolled down from the heights above and in an instant they were half blind. The path was narrow, with a downward slope on one side and as one man Nick and Tobias called a halt. Nick dismounted, gave his reins to Fletcher and walked forward, feeling his way. He had almost reached the head of the column when the mists parted in a gust of freezing wind and the thing Nick had been dreading was upon them.

The robbers were a tatterdemalion crew, but well organised. They had been watching as the travellers idled along admiring the view. The mist had given them their chance and now they swept down, yelling and screaming, heading straight for the most vulnerable, the merchants who had insisted on riding at the head of the cavalcade.

Nick cursed and ran for his horse. Fletcher tossed him the

reins and grabbed Nick's two pistols, cocking and discharging them to good effect, giving himself a chance to draw his sword which was slung across his back.

Startled, Bella shied and lost her footing, sliding down the slope with a mournful bray, to the musical accompaniment of breaking glass.

'There goes my profit,' thought Nick as his throwing knives came into play, downing one brigand attacking the women, and putting the other into the throat of the man behind Fletcher with an upraised axe. He fought his way to the hapless merchants and with sword and dagger began to drive the robbers to the side of the hill where Fletcher and the others were fighting. The masons were giving a good account of themselves, one mighty fellow swinging a huge mallet round his head like a hammer-thrower: another was engaged in close-work with a pair of chisels. The traders were mostly under the wagons. Up at the front, the youngest of the merchants was struggling with his furs to get at his sword when he was felled by a blow to the head. The fighting was fast and furious until, confronted with two such determined young men and confounded by the fury of the masons who had not toiled two long years to see their wages stolen, the attackers wavered. Nick's strategy in herding them together to join with Fletcher in driving them towards the edge, finally told, and those still on their feet turned and ran. The mist rolled back and Nick could hear some of their party giving chase.

'Stand still!' roared Fletcher in a voice made on the battlefield. 'Wait!'

There was oil and tallow in one of the wagons and a veteran trader tore off a strip of his shirt to make a torch. It did not make much difference to the visibility but it was a rallying point. The screaming of the women began to die down and men started to shuffle together. The fickle wind got up again and this time blew steadily straight from the north off the frozen heights above them.

Nick and Tobias and the mallet man looked around to take stock. The column was in complete disarray: the wagons all over the road, bullocks lowing, the horses and mules bolted in different directions, a knot of sobbing women clustered round the injured merchant and three of their men down. The linnet had died.

The attackers had left several of their number behind, some dead, some not.

Nick was white and sick. He had seen dying men brought from the battlefield, and watched one murdered, but he had never before killed a man himself. While it had been going on, there had been no time to think, he had simply followed training and instinct, it had seemed like one of his play-fights to amuse the groundlings.

Tobias gripped his arm.

'It will pass,' he said. 'You saved my life. I thank you.' Nick shook his head.

'What are we to do with—'

'Leave them for their fellows to dispose of. We have no time, we must get on.'

It went against the grain, but by the time they had rounded up the horses, found the mules, set the wagons to rights, calmed the ladies with the stolid help of their maids, attended to their wounded and finally coaxed a protesting Bella back up the slope, Nick was ready to drop. He slumped to the ground beside Tobias, who was sitting with his back to a rock with a hunk of bread and cheese.

'What d'you reckon now?' said Tobias, indistinctly. 'Want some? Keep your strength up?'

'No. Those men are too sick to go on and two of the women look pretty poorly. They want to go back with their blasted dogs. That last inn was a good one, they could go there, it's not far. We could unload one of the wagons and put them on that.'

Tobias raised an eyebrow.

'Yes, my organising friend, and who is to take them? Not you, I take it, no doubt you have reason for being in such a hurry.' He looked up.

The merchant who had insisted on leading, setting the leisurely pace and behaving as if he were on a picnic, stood before them. The gold chain he wore round his shoulders hung awry in the wet ruin of his furs and he had lost his cap. He had not troubled to introduce himself up till now.

'Arturo Agostini, sirs. Gentlemen, I am prepared to pay well for my wife to be taken safely back. My colleague also. And to compensate for your loss of time, and in some way thank you.'

'The others fought bravely,' said Nick.

'Indeed. They shall be rewarded. But, sirs, I beg you, it is of prime importance that the ladies should have safe escort. Name your price.'

Nick and Tobias exchanged glances. Tobias gave a faint wink and a nod, and whispered, 'I'll catch you up.'

Nick said, 'If we are to split our forces, sir, I will come on with you and my friend will see your ladies safely back.'

The two of them worked together to reorganise the party and made a plan to meet again in Basel: Nick wanted to keep in touch with his new ally. The crossbow had not been much use on this occasion: it took too long to bring it into play in the close fighting and Nick felt that if this was likely to be the pattern if they were attacked again, speed was all-important. He gave it to Tobias – 'for the look of the thing'.

So it was that Nick rode into the small village nestling the other side of the Alps at the head of a reduced column of travellers. It had been raining steadily for the past three hours, that nasty, cold, fine rain that works itself into every crease and corner. One of the horses was lame and the whole party was in desperate case. The one inn they had passed had been shuttered and dark.

Nick surveyed the one down-at-heel tavern with a jaundiced eye. It looked terrible. The roof had developed a saddle-back curve and the outbuildings were in a state of advanced disrepair. The lights in the windows were dulled by the filth on the yellow talc of the panes and the yard was a sea of mud. He stood up in his stirrups to look back at the column. Even those uninjured looked half dead. No help for it, they would have to stop.

He sat for a moment listening and watching. A thin mangy dog rattled its chain in the yard and barked a discouraged bark. No other sound.

Swinging out of the saddle, he led his horse forward and rapped on the door. The low hum of voices within ceased: there was no sound but the inn sign keening in the rising wind and the hiss of the rain. He tried the door, to find it bolted: the broken gutter over the portal dripped down his neck. Highly irritated, he drew his dagger and hammered with the hilt, driving the dog to further efforts. There was a shuffling footstep and a screeching of bolts. This was beginning to be like one of those stories told round a fire on a winter's night to frighten the children, he thought. The door opened a crack and a head peered through about on a level with his middle button.

'Open up,' said Nick sharply. 'I want food and shelter for fifteen men and horses.' The door began to close, and Nick kicked it open. Behind him, one of his party gave a low moan and slid into the mud.

'Tuh!' said Nick and dropping the rein, advanced into the room. Rowena tried to follow him and the little man at the door squeaked.

'Take my horse round to the stables with the others,' Nick told him. 'I'll see to her later. Now, where is the innkeeper?'

The little man drew himself up another couple of buttons.

'I am, sir, and I can tell you, sir, there is no room. We are full, sir, and the kitchens are closed.' The gutteral accent was hard to follow, but Nick got the drift.

'Nonsense. We are a party of travellers shortly to be benighted and you are obliged to take us in.' He looked round at the five or six customers sitting frozen on their benches and picked a likely one.

'You, take my horse and help those outside and there's money in it for you. You,' turning to the innkeeper, 'stir yourself and find hot food and drink for my companions. Unless you want me to do it.' He strode to the fireplace where a sullen fire did little to warm the room, and kicked it into life, throwing on a generous helping of wood. The innkeeper, about to protest, caught Nick's eye and subsided. Nick felt in his purse and produced a gold coin.

'This for your kind assistance.' He tossed the coin into the air and six pairs of eyes followed its glitter as he caught it and stowed it away with a clink. There was a sudden scramble of activity and in a surprisingly short time, the exhausted party was provided with hot soup and bread, tankards of mulled ale and a room upstairs with mattresses where they could spread their blankets. Nick went back out into the rain to see the animals attended to and decided to bed down in Rowena's straw rather than on the inn's dubious floor. Once he had chivvied his helpers to complete their tasks and paid them, he went back to find food for himself and see how the sick man was faring. He was asleep, dry and warm and Nick let him be. The men from the inn had taken their money and vanished into the mist and rain.

He went to look for the landlord and found him disappeared too. Nick shrugged, past caring, it could all wait 'til morning. The taproom looked decidedly more welcoming now with the fire blazing up the chimney, and he took his bowl of soup and went to sit by it, beginning to steam gently. He had almost finished when someone hammered on the door.

Wearily Nick heaved himself to his feet. What now.

A bedraggled figure in soaking-wet livery stood shivering on the step. He looked up at Nick with pitiful relief.

'Please, sir,' he said in a soft West Country voice, 'do you speak English?' Considerably startled, Nick stared. 'Yes.'

'Oh, thank God. Please sir, will you come to my lady?'

'Now? Where?'

'If you please, sir, not far.' The man was elderly and looked worn and worried to death, plainly at the end of his tether.

'We can go no further and my master is sick. I beg you—'
Nick shrugged and fetched his cloak that had been drying by
the fire. It had better not be far, he wasn't going to turn the
horses out again.

About a hundred yards further on, a miserable-looking
horse stood with drooping head and splayed legs, harnessed
to a makeshift litter. What looked like a young woman was
huddled over it, trying to shield its occupant from the rain.
The manservant hurried forward.

'My lady—'

Nick caught him up.

'Nicholas Talbot, at your service.'

'Oh, thank God,' and she burst into tears.

Nick waited, thinking longingly of his nice bed of straw.
This was not even a tale that would amuse Kit. The story that
emerged however was shocking and Nick forgot his bed in a
growing anger.

It was a sorry tale. The grey-haired man on the litter was
her father, a scholar who had been visiting a monastery in
the mountains to study one of their manuscripts. He had
succumbed to a fever on the way back to their inn – the one
that had been silent and barred when Nick passed the day
before – and had come out in a rash. The innkeeper, terrified
of the plague, had refused to let them come near and turned
them away with threats of violence. All their belongings were
at the inn and one of their horses had run off. And of course
Nick's innkeeper had not even answered the door.

'A rash?' asked Nicholas.

'It is the chickenpox only – but my father is not strong—'

'Are you sure?'

'Of course, look, it is scabbing over – my little brother had it—' Nick had had it himself: unpleasant, but not usually fatal to a healthy body. In an old man, though—

'Leave the litter,' he said. 'I'll carry him back. We must get him warm and dry. Can you walk? Or wait for your man to ready the horse. I'll go on ahead.'

He picked up the old man and set off back up the track.

Much later, the sick man attended to, Nick sat with the young woman by the fire. She could be pretty, an oval face framed by fair hair that was frizzling into ringlets as it dried. He had been told their name was Challoner, Sir Bertram and Caroline.

'Why were you travelling these mountains alone? It isn't safe.'

'Our new escort was to meet us – the other men wouldn't wait. I can't think what has happened to Sergeant O'Dowd, he is so reliable always. Do you think he met with some accident?' Remembering his own recent encounter, Nick thought it highly likely, but did not say so.

'Your bedchamber will be warm by now. Go and rest. If your father is well enough, you can come on with us tomorrow.'

Chapter Sixteen

It was still mizzling with rain. Nick wondered when he would ever be dry again. He was riding at walking pace along a narrow path beside a precipice, looking where he was going. The lady rode on one of the wagons beside her father, the servant Anselm plodding beside them. The rest of the party straggled along behind. Nick stood up in his stirrups for a moment to ease his aching backside and in that moment came a fearsome yell and a clashing of swords, followed by pounding hooves.

Round the spur of the mountain came a wild figure – a giant of a man in a helmet and breastplate, with a mane of red hair, galloping recklessly on a splay-footed Cleveland and whirling a sword like a claymore round his head. With no room to manoeuvre Nick could only duck and snatch up his pistol. Before he could level it, a tight cluster of horsemen swept round the bend in pursuit of the first, screaming like banshees. The big man's horse reared up and lost its footing, crashing down in front of Rowena who skittered and almost went over the edge. Nick flung his weight the other way and leapt down to stand astride the fallen man, both pistols cocked. The great horse had scrambled up and was rearing, striking out with both enormous hooves, throwing the first pair of attacking horsemen back into the others. This was no place for a skirmish. One of the horses was down across the path and two of the riders, unseated, went over the cliff with a despairing shriek. Their mounts, scrambling to save themselves, completed the shambles.

The robbers at the back of the melee abandoned their frightened horses and came on. The big man, cursing and shaking his head, climbed up Nick to get to his feet.

'Gimme one of those,' and he seized one of Nick's pistols. It was damp from the everlasting rain and misfired. He reversed it with a grunt and waded in using it as a club. Nick dropped the other pistol which perversely went off with a bang, took a moment to pick up the man's great sword and hand it to him, then set his back to the cliff and got on with it. There was no room for swordplay as Nick practised it, but the man at his side was using his huge weapon two-handed, like a scythe. One of the attackers broke away and headed for the wagons. Nick dropped his sword and threw a knife, aiming low. The man dropped with a cry, and Nick closed with another who had ducked under the flailing blade. There was hard hand-to-hand fighting for a few moments, getting perilously near the edge, until Nick, with a desperate twist, hooked the man's legs from under him, grabbed him before he went over and thumped his head on the ground hard. He looked up to see the big man thoughtfully cleaning his sword on a wisp of grass and whistling through his teeth. The rest of the assailants were gone. It was all over so fast that no one with the wagons had moved.

Time began again and Nick became aware that he was bleeding quite heavily from a deep gash in his thigh. He held it together and looked at the swordsman warily, hoping he had chosen to fight on the right side. The man's weather-beaten face was seamed and creased, a white scar pulling down the lid of the right eye. His forehead was white above a red line where his helmet had been and, under bristling ginger brows, sharp grey eyes were assessing what they saw. Seemingly satisfied, he nodded to Nick and made his way to the wagons, greeting the lady Caroline with a bow.

Anselm closed his mouth and pulled himself together.

'Sergeant, where have you been! Where are your men? Not killed by those—'

The sergeant shook his head.

'Chickenpox,' he said glumly. Nick would have laughed but for the feeling coming back into his leg. He sat down rather suddenly. Caroline had jumped down and come to kneel by him.

'How bad is it?'

''Tis not so deep as a well—' murmured Nick with a wry smile. Marlowe had a word for everything. O'Dowd – presumably this was he – came to squat down.

'I'll see to this, my lady,' he said. The various horses had clustered together and were standing nose to nose in the drizzle. O'Dowd went to his saddlebag and brought back an oilskin wallet, of the kind odiously familiar to Nick from his early days. After a painful interlude, the sergeant professed himself satisfied and stood up.

'Lucius O'Dowd thanks you,' he said.

'Nicholas Talbot. I'm obliged.'

'Can you ride? It's a couple of miles.'

'I can try.' O'Dowd helped him up, and he hobbled to where Rowena was patiently waiting. She stood like a rock while Nick fumbled his way into the saddle and over the next part of the journey seemed to do her best to pick her way carefully.

By the time they arrived at the inn, Nick's leg was on fire, and he was only too glad to let O'Dowd take over. It was decided to rest there a while to allow the injured and sick to recover a little. Basel was twenty miles further on, where the merchants and traders would leave them to go north to Dijon. Lady Caroline came to where Nick was lying on a makeshift pallet in a room on the ground floor.

'Are you in much pain? Will you let me look at it?'

'It is not for you, my lady. O'Dowd has sent for a surgeon—'

She gently pulled aside the blanket to find the straw palliasse under his thigh soaked with blood. She caught her breath, rose and swiftly left the room, to return with her hussif and a servant with bowls and cloths and a steaming kettle. Nick got up on his elbow to object and succumbed to a wave of nausea. She pushed him back with alarming ease, and set about her preparations, dropping tweezers and needles and silk thread into the hot water and cutting away O'Dowd's rough-and-ready field-dressing. It was stuck and she bathed it away from the gaping edges of the wound. The cut had gone through the leather of his breeches into the muscle and was still bleeding.

'I fear there may be dirt, Master Talbot. It should be cleansed.' She went to the door to call O'Dowd, who came with a flask of brandy. He forced a fair amount down Nick's throat, gave the rest to Lady Caroline and grasped the leg firmly between his enormous hands. Nick gasped at the bite of the spirit in the wound, closed his eyes and set himself to endure as she tweezered and stitched. What with the brandy and loss of blood, he passed out towards the end and missed most of the argument with the surgeon who bustled in wanting to bleed him – 'to get rid of the humours and avoid the ague.' Lady Caroline, a practical and determined young woman, stood her ground, and Nick came to himself as she bandaged him up, tight-lipped and angry. The surgeon was standing with a grubby hand outstretched and O'Dowd paid the man to get rid of him.

'A lovely job, my lady, all right and tight,' he said. 'Couldn't have done better. Not much of a hand with a needle myself.' Cold and clammy at the mere idea, Nick wordlessly submitted to being undressed and wrapped in blankets, gulped down more brandy and slept.

They rested a day and then, because the rest of the party was anxious to get on, saddled up for an early start. Nick felt it would be easier to ride rather than suffer the jolting of the wagon he would share with Sir Bertram, trusting Rowena to bear him smoothly.

Nevertheless, as they approached Basel, Nick began to feel very poorly. He was in a lot of pain and the wound was looking angry. The constant movement kept it from closing, and by the time they rode into the city he was running a fever. Caroline did not like the look of him and insisted that he see the physician who came to attend her father. The man also advised cupping and Nicholas refused, he had lost enough blood already. But the fever mounted until he was verging on delirium, and Kate's sweet face kept coming to him in dreams. She seemed to be trying to tell him something – they were in her still room and she was teaching him the properties of her herbs and simples. 'Spiders' webs to stop bleeding, Nick, and mouldy bread to draw out bad humours—' He came to himself for a moment and grabbed O'Dowd's arm.

'Mouldy bread,' he muttered. 'Make a plaister.'

Caroline heard and remembered something her old nurse had taught her. She sent Anselm to find stale bread that had grown mould and went herself to gather feverfew. She made a hot poultice with the bread, and came to kneel by his pallet. Nick was in agony, the leg was swollen and inflamed, weeping pus around the neat stitches, and the girl looked up at O'Dowd.

'This is going to hurt very much,' she said. 'Can you help him keep still?' He knelt beside her and took a firm hold of Nick while she cleaned the wound again with brandy and strapped on the steaming poultice. Nick, in and out of consciousness after the first sharp intake of breath, bore it all in silence, drank the decoction she gave him and lapsed again into feverish dreams. The sergeant was deeply concerned, this youngster had taken the blow in his, O'Dowd's, fight and had fought well. He and Anselm and Caroline took it in turns to sit up with him, change the poultice and bathe him in cold water, a shocking procedure to O'Dowd. Gradually the fever abated, the inflammation lessened, and the wound started to heal. He was enormously grateful to Caroline and said so.

'You saved my leg and I think probably my life,' he said. 'I've seen far less than this kill a man. You were very brave to do what you did.'

'My nurse was a wise-woman – a white witch, they called her. She was a great believer in using common sense rather than astrology. How did you know about the bread?'

'My mi— A friend is a wise and sensible woman also.'

'Was her name Kate, by any chance, Nicholas? Or Kit? I'm afraid you talked a great deal in your fever, my dear.'

In the midst of all this, Tobias Fletcher walked in. It turned out he knew O'Dowd – the world of mercenary soldiers is a small one – and he was pleased to make the acquaintance of the lady Caroline.

'We shall make a fine pair of jigging fools,' he told Nicholas who was recovering rapidly with all the dedicated nursing. 'Yours is the opposite leg to mine – we can run a three-legged race, no problem! D'you reckon?' Nick was delighted to see him and hear all his news. He made a fine tale of his return with all the women, kept for a time when Lady Caroline was absent, and very soon the three men were on excellent terms. Once Nick's stitches were out and he could stand and walk after a fashion, they visited Bertram Challoner's bedside and kept him entertained with their tales and lively company. The old man was convalescent now, and content to fall in with Caroline's plan to travel back to London with them.

Basel was the furthest up the Rhine seagoing traffic could come, and barges and other vessels made the quays a bustling centre of commerce. Fletcher went down to see if passage could be arranged for themselves, their horses and their baggage and came back with everything organised. They had only to get themselves aboard.

The barges might be slow but the river was not, the currents flowing onward to the sea, and Nick was able to relax and hobble round the ship on an improvised crutch, enjoying the mediaeval towns that floated by: the villages each with their little bell-tower, and the glimpses of grey castles perched high in pine forest. He was entranced by the way a steeple or a tower would appear first on one side then the other: the landscape rearranging itself as the river twisted and turned. Thickets of holly and hazel overhung the banks, fat with bright berries and nuts, alive with birds and quicksilver squirrels. Signs of a harsh winter to come.

As his strength returned, he took his share of caring for the animals, and the three men would wrestle and exercise on the flat expanses of deck, watched with amusement by the Challoners and dour cynicism from the crew. After one such bout, lying in the weak late-autumn sunshine, listening to O'Dowd's tales of his exploits, Nick noticed Fletcher paying particular attention to the lady Caroline. He was aiming high. He would need money.

Nick began to mull over a scheme that had presented itself to him on his sickbed. The sheer inefficiency and muddle of the journey had offended him, and that evening, forgathered with the other three men in their cabin, he floated his idea.

'Is a trading trip always like that one?'

'Probably. Like you, it's my first. An army on the march doesn't get much interference,' said Tobias.

'Or the chickenpox,' growled O'Dowd.

'Plenty of the other kind of pox.'

Nick stuck to his point. 'It seems to me there's an opportunity here.'

'For what?'

'A business venture.'

Sir Bertram took his pipe from his mouth and pricked up his ears. Nick went on, 'Why not set up a reliable courier service—'

'There are plenty of those.'

'Not one that guarantees safe passage, comfortable, efficient – fast. There would be an armed escort, arranged stages, everything planned ahead – instead of the haphazard undisciplined rabble we had.'

'Deals with the innkeepers,' said Fletcher, his agile mind leaping ahead to ways and means and stratagems.

'A deterrent force, armour, trained men,' said O'Dowd, seeing himself in magnificent armour, riding at the head of a dazzling troop, their blazon flying from a standard stuck next his boot. There was a long silence, each busy with his own thoughts.

174

'It's an idea,' said Sir Bertram. 'Piracy is on the increase – there may be a niche. More overland trade for those in a small way of business needing security—'

'Jewellery, bullion—'

'Glass,' said Tobias, grinning at Nick.

'You would need capital.'

'I've still got my eyeglasses,' said Nick. 'I would put in some money – I have some armour – perhaps men.'

'It would take time to set up,' said Fletcher. 'Routes to plan, inns to arrange, post-horses – we'd need contacts—'

'What men?' said O'Dowd. 'There could be livery, our own device—'

Nick could see the plan had caught their fancy, they were identifying with it. He caught the amused eye of Bertram Challoner.

'What do you think, sir?' Sir Bertram blew a smoke ring.

'I think you should visit my cousin on Goldsmith's Row. I will give you a note. Present him with a plan and costings and he may back you. You three are a force in yourselves.'

'I'm a bit at a loose end,' said Fletcher. 'I'm on.'

'Let's drink to it,' said O'Dowd.

Later on, Tobias joined Nick on deck.

'Can't help thinking there's more to this,' he said. 'Are you out to make your fortune, friend? There's something else, I reckon.'

'Neither,' said Nick. 'It just seemed a good idea. I'm an actor... I wouldn't be taking an active part. Once it's set up it would be you and O'Dowd.'

'An actor? You never said – I thought you were freelancing like me.'

'In a way. To speak truth, I have not made up my mind. Making it up as I go along.'

'Mind if I go along with you a way? Mind you, I'm in it for the money. I'm done with honour and glory.'

'Thinking of settling down?' said Nick slyly. 'Mistress Caroline is a lovely creature.' Fletcher grinned.

'Not yet. I've my way to make, like you. I like the sound of this scheme. Use it as you will, Nick. No questions asked.' He put out a hand and Nick took it. There was great comfort to be found in this friendship.

Much of the rest of the journey was spent scrutinising possible routes and working out costs and profit margins. Like Hugh Shawcross, Fletcher had a gift for organisation and a head for figures, O'Dowd kept their feet on the ground. As the river widened and the traffic increased, they changed to a faster, lighter vessel and made better time.

Nick's eighteenth birthday had come and gone, he was now officially entitled to bear arms. He wondered how Kit was getting on. Winter was closing in and the sunny courtyard seemed very far away in time and distance. No wonder that crazy artist in Florence had wanted man to fly.

Chapter Seventeen

During those first few weeks back in London, Nick was busy. Before he did anything else, he sent a message to Faulds and, with Tobias, saw the lady Caroline and her father safely to their door. Leaving Tobias to look for temporary lodging, he took O'Dowd out to Holborn to introduce him to Sergeant Ponsonby. It seemed they had already met at Douai. He left them happily carousing and catching up on history and rode back to the Elephant to see if there were any messages, hoping O'Dowd would stay sober long enough to recruit Ponsonby and his crew to the enterprise. There was a note from Faulds bidding him go to the Cardinal's Hat. Marlowe's manuscript was to Nick a matter of urgency, but he took a room in the tavern and, having carefully separated the eyeglasses from their ciphered wrappings, set off on foot to the rendezvous.

Faulds was alone and his eyes widened at the sight of Nick. Then, 'You have foiled me, Master Nicholas! I was wrong. You are not the faceless, inconspicuous go-between we were looking for! What growing powders are you taking? Foreign parts must agree with you.'

'I have done what you asked of me, Master…er—'

'I did not ask you to turn into a head-turning giant, Talbot!'

'I cannot help my breeding, sir.'

'You are required, stripling. Where in God's name have you been? Your mission was simple enough: a dispatch to Florence, make your contacts and home. What took you so long?'

177

Nick had not been told whether Faulds was privy to the whole of the plan to save Marlowe, and confined himself to a mention of his injury. He kept his other plans to himself. Faulds grunted and held out his hand. Nick put the bundle of papers into it and fragments of glass tinkled to the floor.

'I won't ask,' said Faulds. He shook out the papers and stowed them away in his doublet. 'You may be needed again very soon. Hold yourself in readiness.' He tossed Nick a heavy bag. 'And don't get into a fight next time, speed may be the essential.'

Free at last to pursue his main object, Nick went to look for Master Shakespeare.

Nick's first arrival on the scene three years before had been one small eddy in the swirl and bustle that was the London playhouse. His disappearance with talk of a mysterious patron had been met with a shrugged shoulder and shake of the head.

'Probably annoyed someone.'

'Nah, stands to reason, likely lad as he was, he got a better offer—'

'He'll be back,' said Robin, missing him. Nell had wept, and when her time of the month came round as usual, for some unaccountable reason, had wept the more.

'Foolish girl,' said Molly, who knew about the correspondence with Kate, 'you won't catch a man like that. What's more, he's above your touch and you know it. Sent for by the Queen! Did he make you any promises? No? Well, then. He has his way to make in the world. Forget him.'

And when Nick walked into the Mermaid, tall and weather-beaten, looking for his friends and Master Shakespeare, the first thing he saw was Nell on the lap of the latest addition to the company, busy forgetting him. He was relieved. Battered and hugged by Robin and the others, he called for a round of drinks and settled down to catch up on the news. It was as if he had never been away. Master Jonson had written a new play, that spotty youth Webster had got a girl into trouble, the new fight manager was hopeless. My lord Essex was out of favour again and Ralegh was in the Tower – apparently writing great things. They finally got round to looking at him properly.

'Where have you been? Are you back for good?' He fended off the eager questions as best he could, and enquired for Shakespeare.

'I thought to find him here.'

'He's dangling after his ladylove. Poor fool, wasting his time writing sonnets – she'll never look at him, just keeping him on a string.'

Nick laughed, calling for more drinks all round.

'What lady is this?'

'The lady Rosalyne, would you believe,' said Robin. 'I say, Nick, you're pretty free with your money. Have you made your fortune? What have you been up to?'

'You wouldn't believe me if I told you,' said Nick, getting up. He winked at Nell, who was now sitting on a bench with a red face. 'See you in the morning.'

He went the rounds of the taverns, enduring more backslapping and buying more drinks, until all the theatrical world knew he was back and looking for Will Shakespeare. He found him at last, drowning his sorrows in the Leg o' Mutton and Cauliflower, a run-down alehouse near the horse-ferry. He was sitting on his own in a corner, nursing a tankard and scrawling listlessly on a piece of paper. There were crumpled-up scraps all round him and Nick saw that he had taken to writing on the backs of old playbills. His receding hairline emphasised the high rounded brow, and the long upper lip and pursed rosebud mouth gave him a mournful, llama look.

Nick took two horn tumblers of brandy over to him and sat down. He pushed one of them across.

'Master Shakespeare, I have something for you.'

'What could you have that I would want?'

'A play?'

'Oh, one of those. People think they have only to pick up a quill to write a play.'

'You already know of this one. Read it again – just these scenes.' He pushed the scrip across the table. Reluctantly, Shakespeare picked them up, and with a shrug, began to read. As he read, his breath quickened and his hands started to shake. He went back and read it again. He looked up, the hooded eyes luminous.

'You did not write this!'

'No. A friend. Are you interested?'

'It is – wonderful. Who wrote it – tell me.'

'Not now. Are you interested? Would you see it put on? It's yours.'

'Mine?'

'Put it on in your name and you have ten per cent.'

'What! But why—'

'Let's say we have a fancy to see it performed. Don't worry, it isn't stolen. We have the author's permission.' Nick bent close, conspiratorial. 'He has his position to consider – you follow me?'

'In my name and ten per cent?'

'Yes.' Shakespeare picked up the brandy and drained it. Nick signalled for another.

'It is great writing,' said the playwright. 'It could be a major success. Your patron – Lord Bacon or Oxford or whoever he is – might change his mind.'

'He will not. He cannot.'

'How do I know that you are speaking the truth? It may be stolen, it happens all the time. I myself have had my work stolen, plagiarized—'

Nick drew himself up, looking offended.

'You have my word on it, sir. Never mind, I will take it to Master Alleyn myself. It matters not whose name is on it, so long as it is performed. You will agree it must be performed?' He reached for the scrip and Shakespeare snatched it up.

'No, no! No one will come to a play by an unknown! I am an established playwright, my name means something – you need me—'

'Are we agreed? There will be others.'

'Other plays! Like this?' His face was red and contorted, he was sweating.

'Like nothing ever written before. But this one first.'

'Where is the rest?'

'If you want it, sign this receipt. It is a binding agreement between us that you will produce the plays, alter nothing and take ten per cent of the gross. Is that fair?' In fact it was a confession. 'Oh, and one other thing. I want the part of Mercutio. Agreed?'

Nick waited, holding his breath, but Shakespeare had taken the bait. His face was rapt, he could see his name at the top of the playbill; he could hear the applause, the adulation: 'Another new play by Master Shakespeare – the new Marlowe—' he stopped abruptly and looked sharply at the text. He did not know the hand.

Nick had copied it left-handed. Carried away by his dreams of glory, Shakespeare did not reason that this might be so. They would eat their words, he thought, those dullards who called him an upstart crow! He would have recognition, wealth. He had no doubt that this play would make him. His dark-haired beauty would love him.

Nick saw that he had won. He had been relying on the man's vaulting ambition.

'We are agreed? On all points?'

Shakespeare nodded, speechless.

'Sign.'

The day after this interview with Shakespeare, he made another important call. He rode Nero out to Chislehurst to visit Thomas Walsingham and deliver Marlowe's letter. The man took it into the window embrasure to read it, leaving Nick standing. Walsingham stood for a long while gazing out, the letter hanging loosely in his hand, then, turning, he said, 'Is this true? Kit tells me you have it in mind to see his work performed. He makes a jest of it. Is it simply a device to keep him from despair? That would be cruel.'

'It is done, sir. I have found the man who will ride on his coat-tails. The play will speak for itself and be heard. Your friend is writing like a madman, there will be others.'

'Others! And you are willing to bring them?'

'Yes, sir. And play in them, I hope.'

Walsingham dropped into a chair, gazing at him.

'Is it in his own hand?'

'I copied it, sir.'

'And the original?'

'Here.' Walsingham snatched the sheaf of scrip and took it back to the light. He read a few pages, his lips moving, leafed on and read more. He looked up, unseeing eyes shining, holding the papers close to his breast. Nick stood quietly, watching him.

The man came to himself with a start.

'Sit down, sit down, what am I thinking of!' He went to the table and poured wine, spilling a little.

'And who is this man who will lay claim to them?'

'Master Shakespeare, sir.' There was a long silence. When Walsingham spoke again it was in a different tone.

'Kit refers to you as his Niccolo. I trust I may use your name? You shall not bear this burden entirely alone, Nicholas. You shall bring the works to me and I shall employ a scrivener to transcribe them and a go-between to deliver them. You are taking risks enough.'

'With respect, sir, a go-between is an unnecessary risk, a link that could be traced. Master Shakespeare is a party to the present arrangement, he will not pry further for his own sake, as long as it is between us.' Nick grinned at him, flexing his fingers. 'The scrivener I would be glad of, if he is to be trusted.'

'You realise that if Cecil hears of this, he will take steps. The deception and his part in it would ruin him if it came out.'

'The scrivener is the only doubtful one.'

'Leave that to me. He shall have only a few garbled pages at a

183

time among my own work. He is no poet.' He looked at Nick, a broad smile lighting his face, tears standing in his eyes. 'Oh God, to think he will live on, immortal…come, Nicholas, we will celebrate! A toast to Marlowe's ghost!'

'To Shakespeare's ghost!' And the two conspirators clinked their glasses to the scam of the century.

Chapter Eighteen

Fletcher had found them a room near Cheapside, and now it was time to call in a few favours, looking for backing. Nick had considered lord Essex's ring, still in his pouch, and decided against using it. His instinct told him not to involve himself with Essex. In this, he was wiser than he knew. Instead, he made an appointment to see Sir Bertram's cousin off Lombard Street. O'Dowd was fully occupied arranging for armour and men and training with Ponsonby, so Nick, in new indigo wool doublet trimmed with rose, walked down the Street of the Goldsmiths with Fletcher, trying to look as if he did this sort of thing every day. They passed windows crammed with gold and silver plate, jewelled goblets and fancy chains, each with its armed man standing guard, and found Edward Challoner's establishment under a discreet sign. They were admitted to a small, dark room with a counter at the back holding scales and balances. More gold plate gleamed behind wire mesh. The two young men took up most of the available space and Tobias shifted uneasily, showing the whites of his eyes, his padded sleeve brushing the mesh.

'I'll wait here and admire the scenery,' he murmured. 'You handle this – it's your idea.' As Nick's eyes grew accustomed to the gloom, he made out behind the counter a small circular man with a quiff upstanding on an otherwise bald head that made him look exactly like a gnome.

'I am here to see Master Challoner.' He held out his letter of introduction and the gnome took it and disappeared. After what seemed a long wait, he popped up again and nodded Nick through into a back room. By contrast, this was a lofty apartment, well-lit by latticed bay windows and comfortably furnished. A tall thin man rose from behind a desk and with a courteous gesture indicated a seat.

'So, young man, my cousin tells me you wish to establish a courier service. Are you aware that such services already exist?' He obviously had no time to waste and Nick plunged in.

'Yes, sir. Ours would offer a better, faster and cheaper service. We would offer the greatest possible comfort and convenience to our travellers, and an escort of armed men. We would canvass suitable inns to be assured of decent hospitality and the routes would vary for greater security. At each staging post there would be a change of horses, and a man who speaks the language to take the party on.' Nicholas paused to take breath. 'Our men are selected for their skill, courage and intelligence, sir. Incidentally, they know how to behave.'

'These paragons are handsome as well, I suppose. Well, you seem to have thought of everything. How, in all this excellence, are you going to make it pay?'

'Organisation, sir. The main cost of a secure service like

ours is the manpower. Our armed escort is made up of men of skill and experience – we need fewer. The advance preparation means fewer costly delays. My partner and I are both putting in our own money.'

'And have you put all this to the test?'

'In a negative way, sir. The journey from Venice was fraught with avoidable mishaps and delays. It was enough to make the angels weep.'

'You are an intolerant youngster, Master Talbot.'

'I warrant you don't tolerate bumbling inefficiency in your business, sir.'

Challoner sat back in his chair and laughed till the tears came. Nick grinned at him cheerfully.

'Of course, there's always the weather or an Act of God. But there could be insurance for that, if you are a betting man. I have the projected plan here, sir, with the costings.'

Challoner was still chuckling.

'Leave them with me. I am inclined to back you. One thing occurs to me. The cost. In my experience a thing is more highly prized by a certain slice of society if it is known to be expensive, provided, of course, it is also value for money. Perhaps you should consider both possibilities, a luxury service and a commercial one.'

Nick gazed at him. 'I should very much like to work with you, sir. I mean, do business with you.'

'Have you considered a career in the army, Master Talbot? Or politics? I feel you would go far.'

'Thank you, sir. I did think of the army briefly. From what I have seen of politics that is not for me.'

'Very well. You shall have my formal offer in a few days. In the meantime go ahead with your plans. I advise you to take your time and aim to launch your venture in the spring.'

Nick was dumbstruck. He jumped to his feet, scattering papers in all directions.

Challoner took pity on him.

'Rest easy, Master Talbot. I am a business man, and this seems a sound proposition, if properly carried out. This first venture will be a probationary one. If it fails do not look to me for further finance. Incidentally, I am not influenced in this by any service you did my cousin.'

Nick gathered up his papers and placed them on the desk.

'I thank you, sir.' He shook the proffered hand and bowed himself out.

Toby was outside, leaning on the wall opposite.

'Well?'

'He'll finance the first trip. At least I think that's what he said.' Toby banged him on the back.

'Let's go and get drunk.'

Chapter Nineteen

Shakespeare wasted no time in presenting the play to Master Alleyn, who grabbed it with both hands, in spite of the fact that there was no leading role for him to tear a cat in. It would be put on at once, in time for Twelfth Night. Nick began to plan a visit to Rokesby.

Unfortunately for both these excellent plans, a minor plague scare flared up and the theatres were closed. The players accepted it philosophically and took their wagons out into the country with a revival of *Ralph Roister Doister*. Shakespeare was distraught. His wife had written demanding him home and he had no excuse. He would have to wait a little longer for fame and fortune.

Nick was sent for to the Cardinal's Hat.

Faulds was in a foul mood.

'We have a very nervous man in the Netherlands with sensitive information. He will not carry it through the ports himself and I can't say I blame him, he is known. We need a new face and yours is it. You are recovered? Good. Here are your orders – read and destroy. Get yourself to Antwerp as soon as maybe and don't dally on the way back. What form the information is in, I don't know, you will have to disguise it as best you can. Papers. Your name is Noel Trimmer. Money. This should suffice. Your man is usually to be found at the Tulip, don't look for him, he'll find you.'

'How—'

Faulds reached behind him for the heavy cloak that hung over a chair. 'Here. He will know the fastening. Anything else?' He was dancing with impatience. Nick shook his head. 'Off with you then. Make haste. Contact me as usual through Meg.' There was no arguing with him and Nick allowed himself to be bundled off the premises fuming to himself. His own plans in disarray, he sent a message to Toby and went to find Molly. She had a letter from Kate waiting for him.

Dear Nicholas,

So you have travelled as far as Venice! Hugh is impressed. I thank you for the too-generous gifts. I shall make of the velvet a cloak for the winter but when and where I shall wear it I cannot think. There is enough also to make a fine coverlet for the best bedchamber - fit for a queen! The silk is exquisite, the stitching so fine, and on two sides - I cannot yet think how it is done, or how to display it. Perhaps a screen for the great hall. All is in readiness for your return, it will be a Yuletide such as Rokesby has never seen. The Yule log is in and we have fine geese fattening for the prodigal's return.

The harvest was good and the hops. Hugh tells me the brewing is one of the best. Jessamy has foaled, a fine colt. You will be pleased to see all in fine fettle and the land in good heart. The sad news is that old Jem died last Wednesday. He was a good age and he spoke of you at the end.

In all our preparations, I am sad to see the plight of the village where I stayed. You will remember Lower Rookham lies on the estate that abuts your own demesnes. Their lord, Hugh says, is close to ruin and the land and the people are in a bad way. We hear his chief creditor is a lord Mowbray - from the pan into the fire, Hugh says. We do what we can from our plenty, and give employment, I feel sure you will not mind.

Thus, there are some new faces you will find and all look forward to seeing their lord at last.

In loving obedience, Kate.

When Molly came back, she found Nick sitting with his head in his hands.

'Bad news, my love?'

'An old friend gone, but it's not just that. Oh, Molly, I am so torn. Between my duty and my desires and – and what was waiting for me at home. I don't know what to do.'

'Your duty, my dear, whatever you have undertaken. The rest will wait. You can't have it all ways.'

'No, but this next task – never mind. A cup of sack and I'll be on my way. Is our Stratford friend going home for Yuletide? I'll have a parcel for him to take to Rokesby. Get him to come to you for it. And this is for you, Merry Christmas.'

Molly opened the packet of fine Brussels lace and burst into tears.

'Oh,' she wept. 'If only Kate – if she would – no,' she said, mopping her eyes. 'You must go. Come back safe, Nick. Godspeed.' She gave him a tearful hug and went to find John, the actor from Stratford.

Nick downed his mug of sack rather quickly and poured another. He found ink and paper and sat down to compose a reply to Kate's letter. When he had traded his spices and alum from Venice for Russian furs in Bruges, he had had them in mind for Rosalyne, the woman who still haunted his dreams, but now he changed his mind. Kate's sweet face, the way she laughed, her tough, enquiring mind and her eager body rose up before him. He wiped his nose on his sleeve and wrote:

Sweet Kate,

I am bidden abroad again. Please ensure a Yuletide feast for all at Rokesby. I am instructing Hugh the same. Extra help for any in want, I know you will have it in hand. None are to go hungry or cold. The furs are for you, a gift from a fellow trader from Muscovy. Do not put them on the beds, they are for you, to keep you from the cold. I am sad not to see you, Kate, but I shall imagine you warm and snug - wrap them around you and think that they are my arms in love and gratitude for all you do and have ever done for me. I kiss your eyelids,

In haste, Nick.

This done, he sealed it up, gave it to Molly with a kiss and went to find Nero for the ride to Dover, where he would take ship for Antwerp.

On the journey he had time to compose his thoughts.

'I shall not be a mere messenger boy for long,' he told himself. 'Sir Thomas is behind me now. Essex is in France, thank God – long may he stay there. Toby and Lucius can handle the other thing.' A thought occurred to him. If there was time, he could combine this trip with a money raising foray to Bruges and perhaps Paris. He caught himself up.

'What am I trying to do?' he asked himself. The courier business was an exercise in logistics. He and Fletcher were alike in that they hated to see a job bungled for lack of foresight, but he could not see himself as a business man. Yet money was the engine that drove the State and fired the ambition of men like Cecil and Essex. Money was Power. Is that what he wanted? There seemed so many paths open to him.

'I don't know what I want,' he thought. 'Not yet. I'd better make my mind up soon.' The long philosophical discussions with Marlowe and the wisdom of Oliver Knowles were working in him like yeast, fermenting dangerous ideas. He knew what he did not want. He would not be a cat's paw for men jockeying for position at Court. He thought of Marlowe as he had seen him that last evening, sitting outside the tavern, talking and laughing and jotting things down as they occurred to him.

'That's it. The play's the thing. Get this job done and the play on and I'm going back.'

The grey sea held at bay by the walls of the Antwerp docks bobbed with ice from the frozen rivers and canals. Winters seemed to be getting colder.

All the waterways were frozen, the boats and water-taxis imprisoned in the ice. He remembered again Verona and the sunshine, the warm evenings spent over a dish of olives and a glass of wine in the garden, swimming naked in the river, and he shivered, glad of the heavy cloak. Not knowing what he might be required to bring back, he had decided to pass as a young trader, just setting up, in search of new business, and had no trouble with the many officials scrutinising the new arrivals. He noticed they were just as careful with those embarking for England: a scuffle broke out as he was waiting for the final stamp, and a harmless-looking individual was dragged off, protesting, silenced by blows. The customs officer looked round and sniffed.

'Papist,' he muttered, and hawked and spat, just missing Nick's boot. Stamp in hand, he looked over Nick's papers again. They were immaculate, just new and ambiguous enough for his purpose – Noel Trimmer, dealer, from Cripplegate. He looked Nick up and down. Nick gave him the slightly anxious smile he thought appropriate and the stamp came down with a bang.

'If I have a say in the matter, I'll do things differently another time,' Nick said to himself. 'No play-acting – I'll be myself.'

He hoisted his pack over his shoulder and set off, sliding on the icy cobbles, to find the Tulip. The dock basin was crowded with shipping, barges and caravels and huge merchantmen towering over the quayside, their masts and rigging taller than the three-storey buildings that lined the canals, a marine forest. Nick slowed and craned his neck, staring up at four decks of cannon, a wealth of gold paint and sails swathed and tucked like a courtiers' sleeves. The anchor chains were thicker than his body and heavy ropes coiled fat round bollards: and over all the smells of cinnamon and nutmeg, tar and humanity. Bells rang, men shouted, the cries of gulls drowned the sound of someone singing. This northern port had an excitement and personality all its own, different from the glamour of Venice and yet the same in essence.

Nick felt like an adventurer, a Cortez or Magellan. He remembered Dickon Chancellor and his maps and grinned. He was enjoying himself. As he left the dockland, he passed little shops lining the side of the canal, under the overhang of the tall red-brick buildings, selling everything from socks to souvenirs. Some stalls spilled out onto the cobbles, fish glittering scaly on white-enamelled trays, crabs and lobsters crawling out of buckets, fruit and vegetables displayed on broad leaves, bread, in baskets, all shapes and sizes. The smell of the bread was irresistible and Nick bought some to munch on as he went along. His attention was caught by a tiny shop window full of trinkets and tourist-catchers, a grockle shop they called it at home, and in spite of the urgency imparted by Faulds, he stooped for a closer look. What had caught his eye was a collection of green glass bottles, each containing a little ship in full sail, complete down to the tiny flags flying stiffly at the masthead. He had never seen such a thing. How did they get a three-masted galleon through the neck of a bottle? He lingered there, chewing his bread and puzzling, until he thought he could see how it might be done. He decided to stop on the way back and buy one for Kate. A light fall of snow started, bringing him back to his purpose, and he asked the next passer-by where he could find the Tulip.

It was quite close, a middle-sized tavern catering for travellers, and he went in, beating the snow off his cloak and laying it over a stool with the clasp showing. He asked the serving-maid for the ordinary, fish pie with oysters, and a mug of ale. Looking round, he saw that the place was not overfull, most of the clientele probably, like himself, fresh off a ship. There were one or two beggarly men moving amongst the tables trying to sell trumpery souvenirs. His meal arrived. It smelt wonderful, spiced with dill and nutmeg and came with fresh-baked bread. He seemed to have lived on meals snatched in passing for the last few weeks and he spread his elbows and prepared to enjoy this one. He was just scouring the last crust round his bowl when a dirty hand appeared over his shoulder with a fan of tinted cards.

'A picture to whet your appetite, young sir?' whined a voice in his ear. 'Look at them.' came a whisper. Nick looked at them. He had seen such pictures passed round campfires and wondered what they meant. Now he had a much better idea and surveyed these with distaste. He was about to shrug the man off when he felt a hand steal round the front of his doublet and made himself sit still. The hand withdrew, and Nick pushed away the cards with a curt refusal. He tossed the man a penny and got up. The beggar gathered up his cards and shuffled off without a backward glance. Nick paid his reckoning with a word of appreciation and went out to the privy. It was a three-holer with no doors and he went round the back with a sense of 'I've been here before', to unbutton his doublet and see what he'd got.

A grimy cotton handkerchief was wrapped round a cube of paper about two inches square. Nick riffled the tiny pages. They appeared to be blank. He cursed gently to himself: this was a ridiculous thing to have in his pack on the way back. The pages screamed 'espionage'. They were also eminently loseable. He would have to think of something. The problem made any idea of going straight back untenable, and he pushed the scraps inside his shirt and went to enquire for decent lodging.

The next day dawned fine and sunny, snow reflecting dazzling white on his ceiling. He had covered the little block of paper with some drawings torn from his journal and packed it with his pen-case, but still had no better idea what to do about it. He stuck his head out of the window to sniff the clear air. It was a public holiday and the frozen waterway was thronged with people in gay clothes, bright woolly hats and mittens, calling to each other and laughing, making elaborate figures on the ice with their skates. It was too much for Nick. He ran downstairs, grabbed some bread and meat and went to find himself some skates. It didn't look too hard. It looked like fun. His problem went to the back of his mind to simmer.

Always accomplished skaters, the Netherlanders excelled themselves: the depth and extent of the ice giving them fast and easy thoroughfares. Markets had moved out onto the ice, fairs and booths spread themselves, groups of purple-fingered traders and burghers thronged round braziers roasting chestnuts and capons and cheese. Nick spent a little time finding his balance on the twin bones of his skates, and presently attached himself to the end of a long weaving line of laughing skaters. Single file and hand-in-hand they skated faster and faster down the centre of the canal. Nick found himself whipped from side to side as the speed built up, not daring to let go. A rosy-faced girl, shapeless in her bundled clothes, grabbed him round the waist, shrieking with delight and almost unbalancing him.

Faster and faster. His eyes were streaming and his nose running in the freezing air and he yelled with the rest with the sheer exhilaration of it. His fingers were achingly numb as he held on for dear life to the man in front of him.

The line was swerving round stray obstacles in its path and the inevitable happened. Nick saw the black limbs of the frozen tree sticking up from the ice ahead as the line broke and centrifugal force hurtled the skaters in all directions. The man clutching Nick's hand was heading straight for the dead branches. Nick tore free, grabbed the girl who was still hanging onto him and veered off to hit the bank with a crash. Something sharp speared through his doublet and scraped along his side, there was the warm trickle of blood. The girl landed on top of him and he lay for a moment unable to breathe. She was still laughing as she levered herself up and stopped abruptly, her hand to her mouth, at the sight of the spike skewered through his clothes. Feeling was coming back and he grunted as he carefully sat up and disentangled himself.

'Are you hurt?' he asked her.

'No, you cushioned me – are you?' He put his hand inside his doublet to feel a deep gouge along his ribs, bleeding freely.

He found a smile for her and shook his head.

'Nothing much – could have been a lot worse—' he looked across the ice and she followed his gaze. The laughing skaters were in scattered shrieking heaps of tangled limbs, two of them impaled on the branches of the dead tree. Others were flocking to the scene, and Nick forgot his hurt and struggled up and, holding on to his white-faced companion for balance, staggered unsteadily across the ice to help. They worked in silence together until the worst was over. Mercifully no one had been killed but there were broken limbs aplenty and the two who had been skewered presented a pretty problem. There was soon experienced help and Nick's own injury began to make itself felt. He fumbled with his shirt to stop the bleeding, and his diminutive helper grasped his arm.

'I live just over there,' she said. 'Come, my mother will tend you. I could have far worse than bruises, she will wish to see you.' She glided off, beckoning, and he followed her. They had come some distance down the canal and she led him to the very house where he had been musing over the bottled ships. He had to stoop to enter; the doorway and rafters were low, the little shop dark and smelling of woodshavings and glue. The girl led him up some stairs into an airy room, high-ceilinged and lit by an enormous window with squared panes, such a contrast that he blinked. A comfortable-looking woman, her hair tied in a sky-blue kerchief that matched her eyes, came to meet them, and the girl began rattling explanations at her. Before she had finished, her mother had Nick on a couch and half-undressed.

'Katje, warm water and cloths and the salve we used for Hans. Quickly, now.' 'Faulds won't believe this,' thought Nick.

The gash was not serious and was soon dealt with by Katje's capable mother. She lent him one of her sons' shirts and would not hear of him leaving without a meal. He sat down presently with the family to a dish of herrings and a savoury mutton stew with dumplings, prepared to be sociable. One of Katje's brothers was apprenticed to a bulb-grower and the other worked with her father. The dialect they spoke was not too difficult to follow and the meal passed in pleasant talk. Nick had a lot of questions: he was interested in the trade in bulbs and especially interested in the little ships. He was hatching the germ of an idea, and when invited into the workshop, went eagerly.

Johann van Cuyp settled down to work at once and did not stop to talk to him, content to let him browse, no doubt sensing a customer. Nick sat fascinated watching his host's hands fashioning the rigging and fixing the sails of a miniature galleon. Nick had not been far wrong in his guess, the sides of the hull could be sprung wide once in the bottle and the masts raised by an ingenious method he had not been able to imagine. He sat a long time admiring the delicate work, and presently asked to try his hand. He was given the simple task of varnishing, and he brushed away, watching Johann manoeuvre a galleas into an eighteen-inch bottle and raise the masts, wondering how he could introduce his little scraps of paper made into sails.

'I'm a trader,' he thought. 'I could order a shipment of these, and take some samples in my pack. As long as I remember which is which.' The bottles came in different sizes, some on stands, and he noticed all the ships had names, some on the hull and some on the wooden support. Perhaps it would work. Bidden to supper, he wondered where the day had gone.

Without her bulky outdoor clothes, Katje was a buxom young woman with a pretty figure and Nick was surprised when, after they had eaten, he was permitted to take her for a walk without either one or both of her brothers. There was a full moon and they walked side by side along by the canal, at ease with each other. Katje pointed out the wreck of a boat, its broken masts thrusting up out of the ice.

'That could have been us, on that tree.' Miles away, fiddling with tiny sails, Nick did not respond. He would have to make his substitution himself, after the purchase, away from the house. Perhaps Johann would let him practise.

'There's probably a quicker way to take those wretched scraps, like stuffing them up my arse,' he thought. 'For two days? Perhaps not.' Katje was shaking his arm.

'Noel, what's that?'

'Ouch! What?' There was a confused noise of shouting up ahead and a cry of agony. Not looking for trouble, Nick turned.

'Back to the house, Katje.' She pulled away from him.

'No, someone's hurt—' She was running up the street. Cursing, Nick followed her, naked without his sword. There was a derelict boat pulled up on the strand and he paused to pull out a couple of staves – just in case, he did not mean to get into a fight.

The strand opened out into a square and to Nick's relief Katje was standing rigid, her hands to her face. A yelling group of men were ringed round a figure kneeling on the ground, pelting him with stones. Nick could not make out what they were shouting and, as he watched, a particularly large stone struck their victim above the ear. He dropped: the signal for a howl and a deluge of missiles.

Nick couldn't just stand there. Wishing for Tobias, he waded in, swinging his staves like a whirlwind, battering his way to stand astride the man on the ground. He glanced down to see if he was still alive and then went on the attack, not giving them a standing target. He had taken them by surprise, and though he was hit by one or two stones, by the time a few of them had taken the edge of a stave, they scattered and ran. Katje had gone for help. Nick had got the senseless young man up on his shoulder when her brothers arrived. Between them they got him back to the house and laid him on the floor in the kitchen where Katje's mother was already preparing. Nick's chest wound had opened again.

He pulled open the man's shirt to assess the damage and Hans started back abruptly at the sight of a large wooden crucifix. The emaciated body was laced with thin scars. Nick looked up.

'What's the matter?'

'He's a Catholic! That's why they—' Mevroux van Cuyp interrupted him.

'And we are Christians, Hans. Get your father. Katje, stop your crying and go to bed.' She set down her bowl and calmly proceeded to deal with the stranger's hurts, much as she had done for Nick.

Johann came, looking grave, and took Nick on one side.

'We cannot keep this man here. You, it was different. There is a tide of bad feeling here just now, you understand. I must think of my family.' His timetable in ruins, Nick could only nod.

'I do understand, Mynheere. I am sorry to have brought

this upon you.'

'No, no, you could not pass by. But he cannot stay.'

'I will take him to wherever he lives, Mynheere, as soon as he can tell us where that is.'

The first wandering words the injured man spoke were in English. Nick knelt beside him.

'No one will harm you here. Tell me your lodging and I will see you safely there.'

The dark eyes fastened on Nick's face.

'You are English. I thank my God. He has answered my prayers.' Nick did not quite see himself as the answer to anyone's prayer, but having found out the man's lodging, he carried him out and set him down gently in van Cuyp's cart. Hans refused to touch the poor man and Katje was still in tears.

'You will come back?' Nick smiled at her.

'Of course. I have business to transact with your father – and your brother's shirt.'

Arrived at a mean-looking lodging house near one of the docks, Hans watched impassively as Nick hauled the helpless man out of the cart, and then drove off at a smart trot. Cursing, Nick could not bring himself to abandon this unlooked-for responsibility, and heaved the man over his shoulder and up three flights of winding stairs to a wretched little room under the eaves. Settling him on the thin mattress, he disturbed the rolled-up robe serving as a pillow and several objects slid out onto the floor. They were horribly familiar: a scourge, a missal and a thing that looked like a large bracelet stuck with thorns. Paul Talbot had had similar things he used on himself and Nick remembered well what the scourge felt like. He kicked them aside with disgust and looked at the unconscious man on the bed. He was young, in his early twenties perhaps, but looked older, thin. Nick covered him up; made sure he could not choke, flung on his cloak and went to find the nearest tavern. Much later, he came back with his own belongings, a bottle in his hand, to find his patient sprawled on the floor, the missal clutched in his fist.

'Tuh!' said Nick, angry with himself. 'For God's sake!' He got him back to bed, dribbled a little wine between his lips and gave a thought to his own hurts. He pulled off the borrowed shirt – now as blood-stained as his own – and strapped up his ribs again. His side was black and blue from hip to armpit and he had a fresh cut on his chest and another across the cheekbone. Furious, he roved about the room relieving his feelings with swearing and kicking the walls until a bang from the room below brought him to his senses. He slumped down in a corner, considering the next move. He still had not found a safe, quick way of carrying the bugswords, apart from the embryo idea with the little ships: this development did not help. He spent a sleepless night thinking, drinking, tending the young man's hurts and calming his frantic dreams. In the morning, his mind made up, he put the first part of his original plan into operation. Ignoring an unpleasant hangover and sore ribs, he went back to van Cuyp's workshop and ordered a consignment of ships-in-bottles to be sent to the docks and took half-a-dozen samples away with him, two or three unfinished '…to try my hand.' He had brought gifts and took courteous leave of Katje and her mother. No one mentioned the Papist.

He found his fellow Englishman much improved. A wan face smiled up from the pillow.

'Whom must I thank?'

'Noel Trimmer, merchant. And you are…?'

'Gerard Hawkin. I will be round with you – Father Gerard Hawkin. There, you may disown me if you wish, you have done enough.'

'What are you doing here?'

'Seeking a way back to England.'

'What for?'

'You were best not to know.'

'I see… you seem very young to be a priest.'

'There are many like me go to Spain for their training. Now I go back to do God's work.'

Not just a Catholic then, a Jesuit priest. Horrified at what he had got himself into, Nick still did not feel he could leave him in that state. Gerard was not much older than himself. He got on with the task in hand, feeding them both and making Gerard comfortable, waiting for him to sleep before getting out his bottles.

Over the next two days the two young men spoke together a great deal, Gerard regaining his strength and Nick struggling with his rigging. Gerard had most to say, speaking of his vocation and his mission and his faith, lost in his dreams until a piece of blasphemy from Nick as the thread broke for the umpteenth time attracted his attention.

'Why are you bothering with that, if it distresses you?'

'Sheer bloody-minded curiosity. I want to see how it's done.' The cypher was made into sails now, all Nick had to do was persuade the masts to stand up.

'When you sail for England, will you take me with you?'

'No.'

'May I know why not? I know you are not of my faith, but you kept me from death – that means something.'

'It means that I'm not prepared to help you kill yourself. You owe me a life. Have you any idea what will be done to you, a Jesuit priest, if you are taken?'

'I intend no one harm. I am to spread the word of God, hold masses for the faithful. I am a soldier of Christ, but I carry no arms, you saw that. If God asks the ultimate sacrifice I am ready.'

'Ready to be a martyr.'

'My teacher was martyred. Christ was crucified.' Nick looked at the thin white face and shining eyes and sighed. He was beginning to know himself and he had grown fond of Gerard in spite of his proselytising.

'Do you really know what you are facing? I'll tell you. First you will be tortured to make you tell the names of others like you. Your body will be stretched until your joints pop, and your hands and feet crushed. They will hang you by your wrists and put weights around your neck. Your arms and ankles will be tied and strapped to your waist behind your body and they will leave you so for days. And at the end of it all, there is the stake. The people are not so keen on burnings these days, so it will likely be the scaffold, where you will see your own entrails held up and burned in front of your living face. It is barbaric. I hold no brief for them, but is that how you would use the life your God gave you?'

'I am ready.'

'You think you are.'

'You don't shake me, Noel. I pity you for your lack of belief. Pray with me.'

'No. I have seen the scourge you use on yourself and it sickens me. And don't say you'll pray for me or I'll puke.'

There was a long silence. Each of them had gone further than he meant.

Presently Gerard said, 'I'll tell you my worst fear, my friend. It is that I shall not have the strength after all. That I shall deny my faith and recant. That would be the very worst kind of damnation.'

'Don't do this, Gerard. There are other ways to help mankind surely. Could you not work elsewhere among those who share your beliefs?'

'This is the way. Let me come with you, Noel. I shall pray for the courage to endure—'

'Then your God help you, because I won't.'

The last tiny mast slid into its bed and stood up. Still angry, Nick got to his feet, found his cloak and went to book his passage for the next day. He spent the evening drinking alone, and came back to find Gerard sleeping. He rolled himself in his cloak, found his corner and passed out.

In the morning he woke with an aching head to find Gerard gone, with all Nick's baggage save the pack with the sample bottles in it. Nick swore long and comprehensively, flung on his clothes and made all speed to the dock. As he expected, Gerard was already aboard, gazing down from the rail.

'Your servant is come before you, sir.' The excise man gave a cursory look through his pack, stamped his pass and waved him aboard. Gerard was like a naughty child awaiting his punishment. Nick had nothing he could say to him and brushed past him to find his bunk.

The crossing was rough and Nick spent most of it on deck

wrapped in his cloak, rather than below with a horribly sick Gerard. The only obstacle on reaching Dover was the customs man who took a fancy to the little ships and gave Nick a bad few minutes choosing two of them. Nick's presence gave credence to Gerard, who of course was an English national. Away from the harbour, Nick confronted him.

'This is where we go our separate ways. If you have friends here, find them. God save you, Father Gerard. Be vigilant, and if you need to betray anyone, let it be Noel Trimmer.'

Gerard flung his arms round Nick and kissed him on both cheeks.

'God will reward you.'

'I doubt it,' thought Nick, and turned away to find his horse.

Chapter Twenty

When he arrived back in London, he rode straight to Southwark to stable Nero and send a message to Meg. There was a note for him summoning him to Scadbury to see Tom Walsingham. He made much of Rowena, who was pleased to see him, and went to find some food and wait for a summons from Faulds. This came very soon and Nick stayed just long enough to make himself presentable before walking along Bankside to the Cardinal's Hat.

It looked slightly more prepossessing in the weak sunshine,

the rooms swept and garnished and the clientele quiet. He knocked and was admitted at the side door. He mounted the stairs carrying his padded sack of bottles wondering what Faulds would make of them. He had dressed carefully for this next meeting with Mistress Meg, but there was no sign of her. Faulds was surly.

'Hm. Not bad time. Did you bring it?'

'Yes.'

'What were you doing last sennight with Thomas Walsingham?'

'Do you have me watched?'

'Not you, no. Though it seems you will bear watching. My master likes to keep his finger on the pulse.'

Nick noted the pronoun with relief. It was *my* master not 'ours'. Obviously he had quite literally outgrown his usefulness as a potential spy. Faulds was watching him.

'It was not to your taste, was it? You can still be useful though, my boy, out in the open. You will be more exposed, mark you.'

Nick heaved his bundle onto the table and began to unpack his bottles. Faulds began to roar with laughter.

'Do you expect me to take these toys to my lord Cecil? Where are the reports?'

'On the sails, the size I was given them. I didn't want to lose them. I sold two of these to the excise men. They were scrutinising everything.'

'Sold—'

'Two plain ones.' Faulds sat down and slapped his knees.

'I hand it to you, young man. Meg! Come and see this! Are there any more "plain ones"?'

'"The Revenge" is for Mistress Meg.'

Faulds' cousin came in, elegant in grey wool, and clapped her hands at sight of the little ships flying their flags so bravely in their bottles.

Faulds was like a terrier at a rat hole.

'You have not answered my question.'

Nick had his answer ready now, and shrugged.

'Sir Thomas? A wasted journey. I am setting up a sideline that might be useful and someone suggested him as a likely patron. He wasn't interested. He will use us, though, might invest later when it's up and running.'

'When what's up and running?'

'My courier business.'

'You should be careful, my lad. You will be getting too big for your britches,' said Faulds spitefully. Meg looked up from admiring her little ship.

'Come, Edward. Master Nicholas is spreading his wings. Think.'

'What's so special? There are courier networks and to spare.'

'Why not wait and see?' said Nick. 'It will give me cover if nothing else. If I am needed again.' Faulds was examining the bottles.

'This shows imagination. I think my master will feel you wasted in this kind of work. There's your money. I'll be in touch.'

Nick left them arguing how to rescue the reports without smashing the glass, and set off for Chislehurst much richer in pocket and a little easier in his mind.

Walsingham had a packet of letters for him.

'I took the liberty of writing to your steward, Nicholas. I feel I shall be a safer postbox than whoever you were using before. I have a plan – I trust you will approve it and not think I am interfering in your affairs.'

'My affairs seem to be entangled with yours, sir.'

'Indeed they are, and I would not see you suffer for it. There is a bedchamber made ready for you. Bestow your horse and read your letters – we will speak presently.'

Nick sat in the comfortable room prepared for him and broke the seal on Kate's letter.

Dear Nicholas,

You are moving among the great ones now. I wonder what I should call you these days. Hugh says you will need money and is looking for new ways to make your acres pay. He says he will not now further his plans to drain Parson's Patch. He tells me not to bother you with our small news but I cannot think you are grown so grand. Spring is come early this year, the orchards are in beauty. Do you remember the bank of white violets? There are a multitude. I made me a nosegay like the one you gave me, so few will not be missed.

Have you found a bride among the grand ladies at court? Send us news of your health, so many have come from London to flee the plague, I fear for you.

Hugh was unwell just after Christmas, the wet weather troubled him, but you will be pleased to hear he is now in robust health and busy about the estate. Young Hal grows apace and Noll is pleased with him. You will be glad to know

I have outstripped him in my studies, and enjoy many long talks with his tutor and mine. I have learned much about your escapades, Nicholas. You do not change.

The letter went on to flesh out the dry bones of Hugh's letter with a dry wit and observation new to him. 'Bless you, Noll,' he thought. It ended on a more serious note.

The village of Lower Rookham where I stayed is in a parlous state. Hugh says the lord who owns it is close to ruin and owes money to a lord Mowbray. He says he hears no good of him. I fear for the people there. We will do what we can.

You are not forgotten, Nicholas, you are in all our prayers. I pray you come home safe when you are ready.

Your obt. servant. Kate.

The letters from Shawcross were mostly accounting, crisp reports of his stewardship. One thing Nick found of interest was a further reference to the parlous state of the adjoining lands and the ominous appearance of a bailiff. Hugh's concern was the possible spread of disease from neglected cattle, but he seemed pessimistic about the possible new landlord, Mowbray.

Nick went back and read the first letter again. Presently he found his pack and the bundle of letters from Kate. Perusing them, he thought for a while, then fished out his pen-case.

Dear Kate,

If you ever call me other than your dear Nick, I shall want to know the reason. I am writing to Hugh. As he well knows undrained land grows rank and sour. We saw enough of it in the Low Countries – land neglected by war is useless for a generation. There is money enough for Parson's Patch. As for the great ones – I am among them and not of them, nor would I be at present. The Court seems a place of warring factions, men jealous of their positions and wary of any incomer. I fear, Kate, that while there are fortunes to be made and heads to be lost, power will stay in the hands of those who least know how to use it, to the detriment of the common people. Ralegh, as he feared, is confined to the Tower with his new wife. His crime is marrying Bess Throckmorton in secret. The Queen was very angry. Ay me, marrying for love is a fine thing indeed, but all this matrimony brings in sore trials. So hey nonny nonny and a riddle-me-ree, as Master Shakespeare – a much-married man – will persist in saying, a bachelor life for me.

Make of our domain a small Utopia, Kate, a model state, where no one lives in fear. I have told Hugh to spare no expense, and to acquire if he can those lands you speak of. I know something of lord Mowbray and would not want him as a neighbour. In my travels I have seen a new type of ploughshare and I hear Master Tradescant has brought back from China plants that would flourish in the good soil Hugh tells me of. You will make a husbandman of me yet, Kate – though not a husband, I have seen none yet who would match the vision I carry in my heart. Nor am I in one place long enough to grow roots let alone set seed. As far as I know.

Do not worry if you do not hear from me a while, I am cast in a new play and will have much to do. I am glad Hugh is better, how could he be otherwise with you to care for him. He knows where to find me, love, Nick.

As he finished and sanded his letter there was a tap at the door.

'Sir Thomas would speak with you, sir, if you please.' Nick nodded and waited only to stow away his letters before following the servant to Walsingham's library. Sir Thomas was at his desk, writing, and rose as Nick entered. He gestured to a chair by the fire and poured wine for them both.

'I trust you had good news from home?'

'All is well, I thank you. Although I can hardly think of it as home.'

'My house is yours, Nicholas. It is of a matter approaching this I wanted to speak.' He took the chair opposite and sat forward, his hands on his knees. 'I have seen the care you lavish on your horses. Where are they bestowed while you are away?'

'At the Elephant, sir, handy for the docks.'

'Expensive. And you, yourself?'

Nick had been giving some thought to this. When Robin had followed him to the Rose, they had found cheap lodging nearby in the New Rents, between the Clink and the church of St Olave's. 'Handy for both,' had said Robin. In his absence, his place had been filled and he felt some aggression from Robin's new friends. Robin himself had been cool until he had been offered the part of Romeo. In his present circumstances Nick felt it would be more politic to be independent, even if it cost him friends. The rooms Tobias had found were temporary only.

'I have been thinking, sir, that my comings and goings may cause some remark. I shall continue to rack up with my friend until I can look about me.'

'I also have been thinking, my young friend. I should like to offer you the use of a house with stabling, more suited to your circumstances. I have some property adjoining Browne's lands in Deptford and it would please me to offer you some small addition to your privacy and comfort.'

'You are kind, sir, but—'

'But me no buts. I insist. If you have some companion you wish to join you, there will be no questions asked. It is arranged. You can go there in the morning.'

'I hardly know how to thank you, sir—'

'I need no thanks but what you are doing for Kit. I know the dangers better than you, Nicholas. No matter how useful you may be to him, Cecil will play the Judas and betray you the moment anything threatens him and his schemes. The one loose-mouth in the enterprise, Skeres, is already being watched and Cecil will if necessary have him – dealt with. Be warned. Now, our dinner is ready. Come in and tell me again how Kit looked—'

Chapter Twenty-One

Nick covered the distance from Scadbury next day in record time, eager to see what the generous Walsingham had in mind for him. He came into Deptford from the south and turned west to pass the church of St Nicholas, patron saint of those in sudden danger. The supposed body of Kit Marlowe was buried somewhere near. He passed the two stone skulls grinning on the churchyard gates, and rode on past the distant shipyards and the skyline laced with rigging. Following directions he turned down a narrow lane, and facing him was a small, square, solidly-built house of grey stone. Behind it were fields adjoining the property of Sir Richard Browne, who owned half the docks and shipyard area of Deptford. At present it was all fields and open country with scattered rows of cottages and small houses like this one, the largest buildings the church and Sir Richard's manor house.

Hearing his approach a well-set-up man of about forty came out to meet him, followed by a younger woman who would have been handsome but for a few scars of smallpox.

'Michael Turner, sir,' he said, bowing. 'M'wife Alice. Welcome to Crosstrees. We keep the place tidy for Sir Thomas and are to serve you, sir, if that is your liking.'

Nick dismounted and shook his hand, bowing to his wife.

'Sir Thomas is most kind,' he said. 'I had not looked for this. I think – I hope we will suit each other very well. I have a friend may join me – er – we will both be away a good deal—'

'M'wife cannot speak since the pox, sir, and I'm not much one for talking. You will be private,' with which he took Nero and proudly led him off, leaving the woman to curtsey and conduct Nick into the house that would be his home at intervals for the foreseeable future.

There were two pleasant bedchambers and, on the ground floor, an all-purpose room, oak-floored and wainscoted with large diamond-paned windows and two fireplaces. Outside was stabling for four, an orchard and paddocks. In short, a gentleman's residence. Nick felt he was living two lives at once.

Sitting down to a well-cooked meal that evening he could hardly believe his good fortune. Alice had poured him hot water without being asked, and Michael had fetched Rowena from the Elephant and left a message for Tobias.

'I know quite well what you would be at, Thomas.' Nick fully understood what Walsingham was doing. 'You have given me a discreet base, and you can keep an equally discreet eye on me.' How all this would fit with the life of a poor player was a bit of a puzzle. As far as possible, Nick would keep it from Faulds as well.

In the morning, he treated himself to an enormous breakfast, chose warm and workmanlike clothes and went to see what was happening at the Rose. He found rehearsals had started again for the new play. There was a buzz among the actors; the piece had taken hold of their imaginations. It was so different, so new – a great romantic tragedy about small people in a small town. As Marlowe had said, no kings and queens and emperors here.

There was an intensity to the rehearsals: Alleyn had stopped grumbling and was busy training up Robin in his first big role as Romeo, and Shakespeare had kept his word in spite of the inevitable grumbling from the other players. Nick was to play Mercutio and deal also with the all-important fight scenes. He threw himself back into this milieu with zest and amusement – the petty intrigues of actors were a welcome contrast to the real thing. Real enough to them, no doubt, but if they only knew—

Robin was delighted with himself in his new role and disposed to be friendly again. 'Of course it is good you're playing Mercutio – it needs a real show-off swordsman and anyway he's killed off almost at once. Now, how do you think I ought to react to that—' Nick had to admit with some sadness that he seemed to have outgrown Robin. He listened to him with patience and it was from Robin that he heard the first hints of suspicion about Shakespeare's claim to the play. It seemed it appeared to the other playwrights as a sudden leap forward. They were waiting to see if he could keep it up.

Fletcher arrived with a stalwart horse and a satchel full of maps and names and addresses, and drily professed himself willing to bear the hardship of sharing the house and grounds with Nicholas. O'Dowd had elected to lodge north of the river, working with Ponsonby, drilling his men as if for a military campaign.

Nick worked hard on his part and tried not to fall in love with Juliet. The boy playing the part was a new addition to the company: the previous female lead was now sporting a wispy beard and an uncertain baritone. Orlando, the lad taking his place, was an actor in the making and once in costume he was irresistible. Out of his skirts, he was a spotty youth with his feet on the ground, who needed a pair of Nick's eyeglasses to con his script. He got into a great many fights and Alleyn had to threaten him with fines if he let his face be marked. Nick liked him enormously, he was obviously destined for great things. Nick remembered Marlowe's concept of Juliet, and suggested to the lad that Juliet might be seen as the real hero of the piece. Orlando ran with it, making Robin work very hard to keep up. Actors who would normally just turn up to go through their parts and leave – 'swan in and sod off' – as Robin put it, took to hanging around the theatre to watch, actually allowing themselves to be dragged into Nick's crowded fight scenes. Word got out, and Alleyn put a guard on the theatre to keep out spying eyes.

Nick felt he may have found the key to his Mercutio in the 'dancing feet with nimble soles'. In the exuberant gaiety of the Queen Mab speech, he would parody the formal steps of the dance and the fencing school, using the stage and teasing it out. The other speeches fell into line – he could tread the edge between wit and lewdness, funny without being vulgar, flamboyant. Nick saw him as a man so full of energy and love of life that he could not keep still or be quiet, interrupting and bursting into speech, delighted with his own cleverness. The fact that most of his part was in prose made this easier, the words could tumble over each other in his eagerness. Nick worked hard at this, he must still be intelligible, and he went to Alleyn for help with the technique. The great actor picked up on what Nick was doing, and began to direct his cast away from the poses of rhetoric towards a more natural style, made possible by the supple writing. Nick began to understand why he must die so soon: it was not only to further the plot, Mercutio was such a charismatic character that he was likely to turn the whole piece on its head. More importantly, he seemed to Nick a lightning conductor, the speeding catalyst that set the whole tragedy in motion and spurred Romeo into growth.

He was an actor again and loving it.

He abandoned the usual formalised stage fights and choreographed much larger skirmishes, concentrating the formality on the duel between Romeo and Tybalt, aiming at showing Tybalt's greater skill and experience and highlighting the younger man's fury and determination to avenge his friend.

He felt Romeo might not really have expected to win this fight, and worked it out accordingly.

During all this activity, a grimy package arrived at the theatre from Venice. Nick tore it open eagerly. Under a stitched layer of oiled silk was a length of the most expensive black double-velvet, carefully packed in layers of an old, stained manuscript. Nick looked in vain for a covering letter and was about to discard the bulky packing when a phrase caught his eye.

'Ill met by moonlight, proud Titania—' It had an unmissable echo of 'divine Zenocrate'. He scrambled the pages hastily together, reading snatches here and there. It was written in a vile hand, but it was unmistakeable. A new play from Marlowe – and some other hand had copied it: Kit was being careful.

It was Sunday, a fine sunny day with no rehearsal, and his partners in the courier business were both in Europe, reconnoitering their first trip. Nick took the pages with him to find Rowena, who was in foal to Nero, and take her for exercise. They made their way into the fields around Richmond and, knotting her reins to let her graze, he settled himself under the flame-tipped branches of an oak, sorted the pages with some difficulty and began to read.

A Midsummer Night's Dream. What? He read on with growing amazement. He began to laugh. The twists and turns, the delicate beauty and the broad comedy held him spellbound. The coarse comedy of Faustus was here refined; the characters were as well defined as ever, the maypole dance of the plot intricate and well-nigh faultless. The language was exquisite. But fairies? From the man who wrote *Tamburlaine*? Worried, Nick read it again. A midsummer night's dream. Was it a fever dream? Nick remembered his feverish dreams in Basel. They were not like this: not funny at all. He had been given opium to keep him still when the pain and swelling had been at its worst – his dreams then had been fantasy much like this— oh God, had Marlowe succumbed to his isolation and turned to opium? Nashe had gone the same way for a while. Nick leaned back against the comforting bark of the tree, pondering. He would have to go back, he had been away too long. He picked up the pages to look at them again. No, there was order here: the interweaving of the four elements – the fairy kingdom and the three separate strata of society, was too skilfully handled to be from anyone but a man in full possession of his wits. The dialogue was fast, slick and witty, no blurring round the edges.

Perhaps the man was simply happy.

Nick knew he would have to go and make sure. The other pages contained passages to be inserted into Shakespeare's current opus, another history – Richard the Second this time. This abundance of riches would keep the players busy for a year. Nick got up and whistled Rowena, who had strayed off, wondering which part Alleyn would choose for himself in such a well-balanced piece. Still no kings and emperors. Oberon? Possibly. Tarleton would not allow him to trespass into Bottom. Nick rode back grinning to himself as he visualised the wonderful set-piece of comedy at the end – what a gift! He began to be reassured, but made up his mind that as soon as might be, he would return to Verona.

Chapter Twenty-Two

The day of the first performance of Romeo and his Juliet dawned fine and clear. They were more ready than they had ever been. The enforced closure of the past two months guaranteed them a full audience hungry for entertainment and they were ahead of the game with a new play. Everyone was out early keeping an eye on the weather. It continued cold, but dry and very bright and the flag went up at eleven.

Backstage there was mild hysteria. Robin was convinced he would forget his lines and Orlando was worrying about a spot on his chin. Nick checked all the weapons again for safety buttons and crossed his fingers no one would get too carried away. They had two chipped teeth already. He was pleased with his costume, plain emerald green velvet with no pinking or slashing. His reading of the part had darkened and become more cynical, and he wanted nothing fancy. The rival houses of Capulet and Montague were tricked out in opposing colours, Montagues red, Capulets blue: it would be easy to distinguish them when the fights started. It was all kept simple, nothing would distract from the words.

The trumpets sounded for the second time, the entire cast breathed in and the Prologue made his entrance. They were off.

From the first clash of words and swords, the groundlings were unusually quiet.

'Is there anyone out there?' muttered Orlando, adorable in pale blue.

Nick's lines had quite gone out of his head and the blood

was drumming in his ears, his hands freezing. His cue seemed to come too quickly and he was on. Everything fell away, he was in Verona, acting it out with Kit, and he was the cock-sure young wit fighting it out on-stage, with part of him keeping a watchful eye on the others. It was going well: he was wounded and helped off-stage. 'Send for me tomorrow and you will find me a grave man—' whereupon he bolted round to the front of house to watch. He stood at the back of the crowded gallery, watching the faces of the audience as the Tragedy of Romeo and his Juliet moved to its conclusion. They were absolutely silent, rigid, wide eyes fixed on the stage. The man in front of him was openly crying. There was still hope, Romeo might not be dead after all, but as Juliet drove the knife into her breast there was a collective moan.

'Just the tidying up now,' thought Nick. 'Don't drag it out.'

But the spell held to the end and there was that ineffable moment of silence before they came back to themselves and began to clap and shout themselves hoarse.

Satisfied, Nick slipped out to take his place in the line-up. As he made his bow and turned to go, a rose dropped at his feet from the box above the stage usually occupied by courtiers. He had not noticed that a woman had been sitting there, veiled and apparently alone. He looked up to see her narrow back as she left.

As he went towards the tiring room to change, he was stopped by a man-at-arms in a livery of powder-blue and silver. lady Rosalyne's livery. The man was offering him a note. Nick took it and tipped him, his hands trembling.

A heady scent of lilies and frangipani rose from the paper.

'Six, St John's Walk. 10 of the clock.'

He was still standing there, flushed with excitement, when the players erupted around him, triumphant and shouting, slapping each other on the back, Will Shakespeare borne along on their shoulders.

'A success! We have it! We are the best! That fight – that scene in the garden – in the tomb – that bit where you die, Nick – they loved it! They loved us—' Carried along by the tide of jubilant players, Nick was suddenly appalled at what he had done. Kit should be here. This should all be for Kit. Watching Shakespeare exultant, waving his arms and conducting the adulation, accepting it all as his due, Nick wanted to stand up and shout *It's a fraud – can't you see, can't you hear? Are you deaf, you fickle fools!*

The strange smile on Kit Marlowe's face in the garden swam into his mind and he understood.

'Very well,' he thought. 'It has begun. You might think you did this for me, Kit, but I shall go on doing it for you. And there will be a reckoning.' He would not go to drink Will Shakespeare's health, and he turned away to shed his costume and go home to make ready for his assignation.

As he sent for hot water and towels, he warned himself not to read too much into the invitation. She might send for him for all manner of reasons, he was a courier after all, not a courtier, she might have some secret errand for him. Nevertheless, he bathed himself and shaved and trimmed his neat new beard carefully, putting on his best linen and the suit of russet cut-velvet acquired in Bruges. His hair had darkened to much the same colour, his beard had come in a little darker still. A black cap edged with fur, gloves and a heavy cloak and he was ready. He consulted the watch Toby had brought back from M. Corner himself in Paris and decided to walk rather than advertise his presence by arriving on horseback. He cursed to himself – he was due to leave in three days on another errand for Cecil. If this was a beginning, a courtship, he needed more time.

'Of course it isn't, you fool, don't get your hopes up,' he told himself, but it was with a thundering heart and trembling hand that he rapped on her gate.

The same man-at-arms opened to him. The house was as narrow and elegant as its mistress, set in its own walled precinct, silent. It would appear there were no other guests, light burned only in one room beside the blue-painted door. Nick trod across gravel paths through a parterre of box and lavender: there would be roses here in the summer. He handed cloak and gloves to the maidservant who opened the door and waited to be conducted to the richly-panelled parlour he had glimpsed from the garden. Instead, the girl beckoned him to follow her up the polished staircase.

His heart beating in his throat, he climbed to a landing, where the maid lit a branch of candles for him and left with a smile. There were two doors and a further staircase. One door must be the one to the room at the front of the house, which had shown no light. He discerned a crack of light from the door facing him and he knocked gently: it swung open onto firelight flickering softly on tapestried walls. He pulled off his cap and took a step forward.

His lady was lying at ease on a daybed before the fire, in a fine linen shift and a furred bed-gown, brushing her hair. It rippled past her waist like a river of night.

Nick was speechless, he could hardly breathe. He had not been lacking in female company on his travels, but this was something he had dreamed of in the long night watches on the ship, and in the crowded bedchambers on the way back, thoughts of his gentle Kate banished by lustful desire for a more sophisticated and seemingly untouchable beauty. He had whispered some of these dreams to Rowena in the warm straw of her stable and now he was off-balance, tongue-tied. He had come in his best clothes and on his best behaviour hoping for some small sign of favour. Even now he was reluctant to presume.

Putting down the brush, she rose and came to him, taking him by the hand.

'That was a fine dashing performance, my lord of Rokesby. That is your name, I'm told. The Queen will enjoy it, I know.' She turned to a carved table set before the curtained window and poured a goblet to the brim with a liquid glowing red-gold in the firelight.

'A wine from Oporto, my lord, much like a sherris-sack, but sweeter, I find.'

'Yes, my lady,' he stammered. 'They drink it with a sweet biscuit dipped in—'

'Ah, I had forgot. You are a much-travelled man these days. Come and sit. Tell me of your adventures.' She drew him down on the couch beside her. 'I am minded of the tale of Scheherazade, who told tales all night to keep from death.'

The huge black eyes sparkled, she was teasing him. Nick sought for a witty reply and said haltingly, 'Perhaps a short tale and a little death, my lady.'

She laughed and raised her cup.

'A riposte! Will you go for the hit, sir?'

'I am here at your bidding, my lady. To do with as you will.'

'Then be comfortable, sir. Drink. Unbutton that excellent doublet and unburden yourself. I would hear all your doings, your exploits and conquests – even second-hand adventures arouse me. Indeed, what else is there, immured here, a woman, you men have all the excitement. Court is so dull. Come, tell me – where have you been, whom did you meet, what dangers have you passed—'

Her sophisticated fingers were busy at his points, undoing his laces, undoing him quite. But not so much that her guileless questioning did not strike a warning note.

In the event, it was easy to mind his tongue, it was busy elsewhere. The heat of desire made only broken words possible, words of wanting, passion for once made him incoherent. He eased the fur of the bed-gown from her shoulders, the shift fell away. Her body was redolent of all the perfumes of the east, rising in musky waves from white skin warmed by the firelight to a faint rose. She drew his head down to hers and he saw that she was older than he had thought. Tiny crows' feet adorned the corners of her eyes and underlined the full lower lids. Small creases would soon bracket the voluptuous mouth.

Her cat-like tongue flickered between his lips. On fire, he traced with his fingers the delicate lilac tracery of veins marbling her temples and the fullness of her heavy breasts. Marvelling, he mapped them with tongue and fingertips, stroking her smooth belly and exploring the heat of her and she teased him, withholding herself until, wild with desire, he thrust into her, almost driven to lose control. He lifted his head to gaze into her face, wanting to see her, to share the moment, and in that moment glimpsed a mocking light in her eyes, fleeting and quickly disguised, but he had seen it. Desire died a little and he mastered himself. He was not any longer the romantic idealist who had sought to put this woman on a pedestal. His illusions were being stripped away, one by one. He set himself to arouse her, using every art of lovemaking he knew, until, no longer teasing, she joined him in the sweet madness.

It was a lustful, night-long frenzy and the sun rose between angry streamers of cloud to outline their bodies entwined on the bed, the crimson of the tumbled coverlet reflecting madder-pink on the coffered ceiling. Nicholas roused as a shaft of light between the curtains touched his face and he raised himself cautiously on one elbow to look at this woman who had so bewitched him. Her hair spread in ebony tangles over the pillow, and her face was rosy in the morning light. The mocking eyes closed, she was a young girl, dreaming. Nick could almost think he had mistaken those telltale moments of the night before and he fell back on the pillows trying to think. He smiled ruefully, remembering his notion of courtship. There had not been much of that. Or any words of love. The young man who had fallen so easily in love with a powder-blue beauty on a white palfrey seemed to have gone. He suddenly remembered Marlowe's words when he had spoken of his passion for Rosalyne.

'Many a hopeful barque has foundered between those silken thighs, Nick. Don't look at me like that – you sail those seas at your peril… Let Master Shakespeare have her, he will write a sonnet to her eyebrow.' Nick had been furiously angry at the time, making the same mistake as many infatuated young men his age. He was a little wiser now.

She had begun to stir and he slid off the bed and began to pull on his clothes. There were a couple of topaz buttons off his doublet.

'Going so soon? Have you nothing to say to me?' He went to kneel by her side. She was beautiful, her face softened and appealing, the coal-black eyes drowsy with pleasure. She held up languorous arms to him and Nick, still in his shirt, was lost in lust.

Chapter Twenty-Three

Later, just after noon, Nick was making his way through St Paul's Walk, a little light-headed and extremely hungry. He was lost in his thoughts, avoiding the knots of arguing students, and with a hand automatically on his purse, bypassed the scholars each lecturing at his accustomed pillar and the dips and cutpurses mingling with the crowd, to make his way towards Cheapside, where he expected to meet with Tobias at the Mermaid. He was late and he turned into the dark network of lanes unthinking. He was blinded by the sudden dark and before his eyes had adjusted, at the point where Fleet Street crossed Chandlers' Lane, he was set upon from both sides and knocked to the ground. He had not worn his sword to his assignation last night and these were not footpads, they were armed men. He was trying to protect himself and get to his feet but another blow to the head scattered his wits and he went down again. He rolled desperately to avoid a knife and someone kicked him viciously hard. More kicks and blows followed, he felt something go. It would have gone ill with him had not a measured tramp of booted feet and a cry of 'Two o' the clock and all's well,' signalled the approach of the Watch.

His assailants disappeared, and Nick was on his feet, weaving about and retching blood into the gutter when the constables came up with him.

'This man is drunk,' said the first.

'And about to be Disorderly and Disturb the Queen's Peace,' said the other. They were like some dreadful double act.

'The Law says he must be taken up and give a good opinion of himself,' said the first voice. 'I warrant he is a desperate villain.'

A quire of printers' devils, a stare of bystanders, the rag tag and bobtail who always seem to scent what looks like becoming an incident, was already gathering to watch.

Nick could hardly see for the blood streaming from a cut on his head, he was sick and in no shape to help himself as he was dragged off. He came to himself in a cell just big enough to house a pig and smelling as if it did, with three other ragged unfortunates staring at him. He was filthy and hurting and his purse was gone. Where was he? He could hardly think for his aching skull and he suspected a cracked rib or two. He felt distinctly odd and he closed his eyes for a moment.

Images of the night danced in his mind. Had Rosalyne known? Had she kept him late by design? With a wry backward look, he had to concede that it was not unlikely.

'A fool and his lust well repaid,' he thought. Chalk it up to experience. Mowbray's men? So they might have been but he had a feeling a more powerful man was behind it. Mowbray was Essex' cat's paw, that much was common knowledge...he had offended Essex.

He must have slept, for the next thing he knew he was being hauled to his feet by the jailer and hustled along an evil-smelling passage into a room with a high bench bearing the Queen's arms. He was pulled and pushed to stand squarely in front of it, while a face like a sheep in a long grey wig peered over the edge at him. The two men who had arrested him were there. One was running to fat, with a fringe of frizzed ginger hair escaping from his cap, and the other was thin and stooping with a scooped-out chest like melon-rind and a bad attack of rheum. He had a distressing habit of sniffing and hawking with a liquid gurgle of phlegm. Between them the two described Nick's disgraceful behaviour, constantly arguing and contradicting one another.

The Justice appeared to be as bone-headed as his officials. He wrote down carefully, with a wretchedly spluttering quill, everything the constables told him and refused to listen to anything Nick had to say, delivering instead a long lecture on the evils of drink and the dissipation of young men of fashion. At the end of the rigmarole, he pronounced judgment that the prisoner should be sent to the Fleet until he could produce some credentials. Chains were brought and at this point Nick lost his temper and put up a fight.

On cue, the doors were opened with a flourish, and a tall, grave man in lawyers' black mitred cap and velvet bands paced sedately into the room. Nick had never seen him before. He surveyed the frozen tableau and addressed himself to the magistrate.

'I am here to address a serious mistake, sir. This man is—'

He was interrupted by two new arrivals, one an imposing figure in scarlet, a huge-bellied tun of a man, and his companion, a tiny, very old man in lawyers' bands, a skiff to his galleon. Nick cheered up.

'What is this?' roared the giant. 'lord Rokesby, by God! lord Rokesby, or I'm the Grand Cham of Tartary! Hah! I don't even look like him. What do you do here, eh? A peer of the realm to be chained! Loose him at once, or I'll not be answerable! Master Shallow, the writ if you please.'

'Is he charged?' piped the little man, who was dangling a lengthy scroll of parchment with an enormous seal and a number of ribbons. Nick recognised it from a recent production and fought not to laugh. The watchmen goggled.

'One moment, gentlemen,' came the voice of authority. 'Let us establish the facts. I am here to represent this man and I have a warranty for his release signed by the Honourable Sir Thomas Walsingham.' He was interrupted by the two constables, falling over themselves to justify their actions. He raised a white hand.

'Your names?'

'Gull, sir, melud—'

'And Tickle, sir.' Nick snorted and the lawyer gave him a cool and quelling glance.

'As I was saying, there has been some confusion. As my colleagues so rightly assert,' here he bowed solemnly to Nick's fellow-actors, who bowed in return with commendable aplomb, 'this gentleman is indeed lord of Rokesby, and even were he guilty, he cannot be tried in this court. As I understand it, he had gone to the rescue of a fellow-citizen when he was mistakenly arrested. No doubt, Masters Gull and – er – Tickle are guilty only of an excess of zeal and may be pardoned.' He placed a single sheet of parchment before the trembling magistrate and turned to gesture Nick to the door.

Andrew Agutter, last seen as Juliet's friar, took his arm.

'Don't laugh now, you fool,' he muttered. 'Off with you, go with Peter, I'll tidy up here.'

The little man in lawyers' garb drew Nick through the crowd at the door; the onlookers parted respectfully and pulled their caps to the bedraggled figure they had been ready to pelt with rotten fruit a moment ago.

'What will Andrew do?' gasped Nick. He was feeling it now.

'Ply them with drink 'til they can't stand up, let alone remember anything.'

'How did you know what happened?'

'You were late. Your friend Toby came to look for you and saw them haul you off. He had the sense to send to your landlord. Will thought of us to hold the breach. By God, yon man were quick off the mark.'

'Thank Will for me – brilliant idea, he should put it in a play.'

'We will enact it for him, never fear. And he will use it, as he uses everything that comes his way.' Nick shot him a sharp glance but the little actor's face was bland and smiling. Tobias came loping up the street.

'Body of Christ, look at you! I've a carriage here, come on.' He put a shoulder under Nick's arm and helped him back the way he had come. 'Are you hurt much?'

'A cracked rib or two, I think. My head's the worst. Listen,

Toby, those weren't footpads that set on me. It feels like trouble.'

'I gather you had a little note after the play. Those were Mowbray's men. You have made yourself an enemy there, my friend. I hope it was worth it.'

On the whole, given the outcome, Nick thought it was. He became aware of a growing hubbub in the street.

'God, what day is it – what's going on—'

'Some poor devil of a priest is getting the full treatment today. For what good it will do.'

' A priest! Where – let me see—' Tobias stared in disbelief. 'You want to watch?'

'No, you bloody fool – I need to know who it is—' He was pushing through the growing press of bodies, his hurts forgotten. 'Please, please, let it not be Gerard—' The thin immature face rose up, 'My greatest fear is that I shall recant, that would be the worst thing—' Nick forced his way to the front of the crowd as the cart came under the archway from the Tower, and he could see the man being dragged feet first on the hurdle behind, his fair head bumping the cobbles. Gerard Hawkin, almost unrecognisable. A cleric bent over him, murmuring. Weaponless, Nick looked up at the scaffold and its ominous table.

'Pray to your God that I am not too late if you need me,' he thought as he pushed on through the gathering sea of bodies. Once through the last stragglers following the cart, the streets were empty and he bolted through the twisting byways to O'Dowd's lodging. He wouldn't be there but the thing Nick wanted was. He tore up the dusty stairs and burst open the door. The familiar crossbow was hanging on the wall and he snatched it down. Running out again he thrust past the protesting landlady and up the street. He was hindered by the crowds as he drew near the place of execution, but he forged his way through, the hunting crossbow under his doublet. They were manhandling Gerard up the wooden steps now, a misshapen leg trailing. Nick gulped down nausea and looked up and round. He saw a likely spot and forced his way back through the massed crowd into a narrow lane empty of people. He found a drainpipe, set his foot on its barrel and started to climb. He ran and jumped across the rooftops until he had a good view of the scaffold and the boards laid like a grisly dining table with hooks and knives and saws. Gerard was to be taken to the very edge.

Nick unslung the crossbow, set the bolt and wound it to its full extent, at home with the weapon like most young men of his kind. It was not in his mind to rob Gerard of the martyr's crown he had pleaded for so eloquently. If Jack Flood was merciful, and let the rope kill him, Gerard would suffer little more than he had already. As for the rest, if he could not endure it, Nick was ready. Gerard would die with his faith intact.

There was a rolling of drums and a roar from the crowd as the young priest was thrust up to the scaffold. Nick could see he could not stand and had to be supported as the noose went round his neck. His lips were moving but when the prelate at his side asked him a question, he feebly shook his head, making the sign of the cross. The steps were kicked away and Gerard was taken down after only a jerking moment. Nick groaned, lifted the bow and sighted along the shaft. Laid struggling and alive on the table, the young priest's body went stiff as the hooded executioner picked up the hook that would first emasculate and then disembowel him and he screamed. And screamed. The prelate moved forward. That first scream had unsettled Nick and he found he was shaking. If anyone looked up he was in full view. He blinked away the difficult tears, once, twice, and took fresh aim. Gerard screamed in terror.

'Take me, oh my God take me – Sweet Mother Mary take me now, or I will—' Nick loosed the merciful bolt. There was a groaning sigh from the crowd, cheated as the quarrel found its mark. A man on the far side gave a shout and pointed. The sea of faces turned to look up as Nick dropped the crossbow and ran. He ran and leapt, stooping low, scrambling and jumping over the rooftops and across the ravines of the streets, outdistancing the guards below. It was unfortunate that as he slid down to street level and turned the corner he ran straight into the arms of Tickle and Gull—

It would take more than actors and advocates to get him out of this.

The manhandling was worse this time. He was hauled through the angry crowd and thrust down to lie on the hurdle that had brought Gerard, spreadeagled and tied while they flung the priest's body into the cart, a fair target for whatever the frustrated people chose to throw at him. He kept his head from the cobbles as best he could as they bumped back towards the looming bulk of the Tower and caught sight of Toby's white horrified face in the crowd.

Once under the arch, the great portcullis ground down and he was seized once more, bundled through and along, down and down into the bowels of the prison where only the occasional flaming torch showed the way. They stripped him of doublet and breeches and boots, tripping him to sprawl forward in his shirt and hose onto the wet stone. The door clanged shut and it was dark as pitch. He lay for a while, trying to breathe, the pain in his side making it difficult. He appeared to be sticking to the floor and presently he understood he was bleeding. A deep shudder took him as the dank cold seeped in and he began to be very afraid. Time to regroup, he thought. He had no doubt what lay ahead, only, like Gerard, he doubted his ability to withstand it.

After a while, he got to his knees and blindly explored the tiny space, hands encountering only harsh stone and nameless filth – no water, no straw. He tried to stand and found no room to straighten up. He was desperately thirsty and hungrier than he had ever been. He curled up away from the stream of cold air under the door and shivering, withdrew deep into himself. He was lying in his bed at Rokesby and Kate was bathing his hurts with snow. He told her to stop and the bed was the lush green grass by the river, the sun burning his bare flesh as he reached for her. He looked into her face, seeing it as never before: the little freckled band across her nose, the fine-grained skin that flushed apricot as she gave herself to him, the tiny baby hairs corkscrewing pink at her temples, the rest a silken mass of auburn in his hands— Her eyes seemed to look deep into his soul and he left his juddering body to lie on the stone and went to meet her.

Time passed.

It was almost a relief when they came to fetch him. He had lain so long, no knowing how long, conserving his strength and what warmth there was left in his body that he could barely stand at first. Up steps and round corners and there it was. A round arched room with the fire and the rack and the other things. They pushed him across to stand against a wall beneath a hook. Iron cuffs linked by a chain were locked onto his wrists and one of his tormentors stood on a stool to pass the links over the hook. He was at full stretch, the balls of his feet just touching the floor. One of the men went away and the other stood warming his hands at the brazier. It was hard to breathe except in small gasps and he tried to regulate it and ignore the pain in his side.

A short, bald man with a heavy belly and red fleshy lips stood in the doorway and his assistant hastened to close the door behind him. Nick recognised him. Topcliffe, self-appointed inquisitor to the Queen. She was said to turn a blind eye to his methods.

Topcliffe stood in front of Nick with his hands on his hips.

'Names?' He did not wait for an answer, clicking his fingers. The assistant brought two thick lengths of chain and stood on the stool again to drape them across Nick's shoulders. The cuffs dragged cruelly on his wrists.

'Names?' Another chain. Another. The cuffs were lopsided and Nick had difficulty taking the uneven weight. Topcliffe nodded and both men left.

Nick had heard of this treatment being meted out to one of the leading Jesuits and his stomach cramped. He could be left hours or even days. His arms already felt heavy and throbbing and he feared for his hands. He tried wriggling them through the cuffs and only succeeded in tearing the skin. He tried to hook the stool towards him and it disobligingly toppled out of reach. The chains bit into his shoulders. There was no sound but his own jerky breathing and the settling of the coals in the brazier. This was like no pain he had ever experienced: the crushed finger, his uncle's vicious beatings. It was grinding, crushing, increasing. Increasing at a mathematical progression the longer it went on. He struggled to construct a formula – time the main factor plus weight plus whatever force anchored men's feet to the ground.

His mind was wandering. He wondered what Kate was doing now and remembered lying with her in the long grass of the orchard, holding a buttercup under her chin and teasing her with a tassel of the wild timothy. They had made daisy crowns for each other. Had Kit ever done that? He set himself to recall lines from the Dream and from that to recite all he could find in his capacious memory. He could not feel his hands any more, only the remembered rasp of his sword hilt and the crumble of a stick of charcoal…it was going to take too long.

Unimaginable time later, Topcliffe returned. He surveyed the taut figure stretched against the wall and smiled. As they had said, this man enjoyed his work. He turned away and carefully selected a length of chain and weighed it thoughtfully in his hands, whistling through his teeth. Nick was fighting for breath now. How many chains would it take to tear the sinews and loosen the joints…the Queen's questioner approached.

Boots sounded in the passage and Edward Faulds ducked under the lintel, Tobias Fletcher at his heels. He looked with loathing at the chain and held out a piece of paper.

'Out of luck on this one, friend,' he said. 'I hope you haven't damaged him too much – he has the Queen's eye on him. Get him down from there – sharp! Transport at the West Gate.' You're too late, thought Nick. Can't fight without… I don't know how long. His arms came down and the chains slid off.

He almost fainted, and the next thing he knew Faulds and Tobias were half-carrying him down the steps to where a boat was idling at the landing stage, its owner lying back in the stern spitting date stones at a flotilla of ducks. Tobias lifted Nick and carried him into the boat and the boatman spat the last of his dates and took to his oars. Faulds stayed grimly watching at the head of the steps.

Nick fell back against his friend's shoulder, trying to ride out the pain, feeling every movement. His hands were bloodless unfeeling weights, his neck and shoulders and back on fire. Tobias put a flask to his lips and he gulped greedily. He didn't remember the rest of the journey. He recovered his senses on a gently heaving bunk. He appeared to be on board ship.

A grey-faced Walsingham was standing, his head bent under the low rafters, watching him. Toby covered Nick with a blanket and went for another pillow.

'You knew the boy – the priest.'

'Yes.' A pause. A breath. 'He was a fool. But he had the right to die as he wanted.' Breathe. His hands felt like balloons filled with lead. Feeling was creeping back into them and he wanted to be alone when it did.

'You make a good friend, Nicholas.' A shake of the head.

'An even bigger fool.'

'Do you think so?'

Tobias came back with pillows and more blankets and a leather bottle. 'He needs time, my lord.'

'Yes. You have Cecil to thank for your escape, Nicholas. I quote. He dislikes waste and he has invested time and money in you. He sends you on this mission to the Scottish court to give time for the dust to settle. For recovery, not punishment.

Or banishment. I argued for Italy, but he would have none of it. I must leave you now, Niccolo. Tobias has your orders and will go with you as far as Harwich.'

'He is not hearing us, my lord. All this talk of missions and reasons should wait.'

Walsingham nodded; his eyes red with fatigue. The last few days had cost him dear. Nick's eyes were closed and his face withdrawn and rigid. Toby pushed the flask against his teeth and kept it there until the throat moved in a convulsive swallow. Nick rolled over to face the wall and dragged his knees up to his chest, cradling his hands.

'It will be bad, sir. We can only wait it out.'

It was bad. The first tingling was welcome, he had not been left too long after all. The tingling grew to a burning then to a bursting sense of pressure and a relentless agonising hammering as the pulse drove the blood back into his fingers. Someone was groaning. Some sort of crisis came and went. Tobias brought a short stocky man with a bristled scalp under a nightcap who probed and prodded with iron fingers, bound up wrists and ribs and departed, muttering, 'As much water as he can drink. Nourishment.'

For those first long hours, Nicholas neither knew nor cared where he was. His mind was like a rat in a trap, thrashing uselessly to find a way out. He was well and truly in Cecil's power now, everything dear to him hostage for his own behaviour. Tobias said little, keeping him warm, feeding him until he could hold a spoon. He was infested with lice and could not lift his arms. Toby helped him scrub his body and shave his head and beard.

'Pity,' offered Toby. 'The beard was coming along nicely.'

Nick said nothing. Rosalyne had admired it. Had she kept him late that morning for Mowbray's men to find? The aftermath was his own fault; as usual he had not stopped to think. He wondered if he would have acted differently given time. He could not tell. He lay in his bunk, staring at the hypnotic swaying of the lamp, squeezing, squeezing at the orange in each hand.

Gradually the resilient young muscles began to respond and he could make himself smile at Toby's effortful jokes and was rewarded by seeing the strain leave his friend's eyes.

'They won't let me come to Edinburgh with you,' said Toby. 'I can't see why you couldn't simply have come with us on the next trip – Innsbruck and back, nice and restful—'

'I am meant to feel the iron heel and be grateful, I think. It could be worse. They could have left me to it.'

Toby shuddered and shook his head. 'Your friend Walsingham would have moved mountains to get you out—' He looked into Nick's face, hoping for answers.

'I'll tell you one day, perhaps. I am a sufficient danger to my friends at present. You were best leave the ship and forget about me.'

Toby straightened up and banged his head on a beam.

'God damn it! I've done it again. Your wits are wandering, man. Here, see if you can hold your knife.'

Nick missed Toby's rough kindness when he left the ship. He had even thought to bring Nick's belongings from the house.

Slowly, as his abused body recovered and the strength came back to his fingers, he regained his tone of mind, and began to be aware of his surroundings. The cabin was surprisingly spacious and well-found, he saw, beautifully fitted with oak and brass: a skilled cabinetmaker had made use of every inch of space. This was not some leaky fishing vessel plying the North Sea. The cabin boy who now brought his meals was spruce and clean, fresh-faced and smiling. He began to take an interest. The next time the door opened, he found a nod and a smile of thanks. The boy grinned cheerfully back, setting down the tray on the gadrooned table where it immediately slid to one side and back.

'You're feelin' better, sir. Cap'n bids you dine with him, if you're up to it.'

'What ship is this?'

'The *Northern Star*, sir, bound for Archangel.' Nick felt the familiar lift of excitement.

'Thank you.' He found an appetite and could handle his knife well enough to cut his meat and hard cheese. He set himself to peel an apple.

He presented himself laced, buttoned and groomed at the captain's table, very different from the fugitive huddled aboard at Greenwich. The fine bones of the shaven skull were picked out by the swaying lantern, the features drawn and unsmiling. Captain Webb shook his hand. The skin was dry and cracked and the captain was surprised by the firmness of the grip. Webb had specific instructions regarding the future usefulness of this young man, and he watched as Nicholas moved to take his place. A roll of the ship took Nick by surprise and he flung out an arm to save himself. A gasp of pure agony escaped him and he stood for a moment, eyes closed. Webb moved forward.

'Congratulations on your recovery, Master Talbot. We

had not looked for the pleasure of your company so soon. Jonathon Webb, at your service.' Webb was a burly man, as tall as Nick, stooping under the beams. His beard split in a gap-toothed grin as he led Nick to the table and introduced his officers, in particular Gadsby, their chief navigator. There was excellent roast fowl, amber wine, fruits and cheese, good talk and laughter. Nick remembered where he had heard the name of the captain.

Jonathon Webb belonged to the Muscovy Company, one of those dedicated to finding the north-east passage to Cathay – round the top of all the Russias! Nick sat quiet and listened, speaking when spoken to. These men were like those of the School of Night, witty and knowledgeable, explorers, with that far-seeing look in their eyes.

Webb turned to him and raised his glass.

'You met Ralegh, I believe, Master Talbot. We miss him. His imprisonment is shameful, though I warrant his quarters in the Tower are more comfortable than were yours.' Conscious of the keen eyes on him, Nick found his voice.

'We must all act as we see fit, sir, and take the consequences. I was rash. His lordship wanted freedom to marry where he chose. I hear great things of his writings,' Burough sat back.

'Indeed. And he has his good wife with him.' He indicated his first officer. 'Gadsby here, and Carlisle, were with him on his first voyage.'

'I should like to hear of that, sir.'

'In good time.'

Nick returned to his cabin feeling a blast of fresh air running through him. These men were survivors, adventurers. They reminded him there was a world apart from torture and intrigue and religious persecution. He had survived, and he did have a choice, of a kind. If he had to work for Cecil he would do it his own way.

Given the freedom of the ship, he found his way about her. She was a galleon, a three-master of over a hundred tons, armed with cannon and culverin and she was flying north under full sail, a glorious sight. He learned that she bore a cargo of fine woollen goods, china and coal and tin, presents of beautifully crafted silver and gold, on a voyage to keep open the new trade route with Russia, and ratify the treaty with the Tsar initiated by the great Dickon Chancellor. A tremendous venture. Nick regretted very much that he was to be set down in Edinburgh.

For three days the sun shone and the south wind blew, a false spring. The towering white cloud of canvas carved the blue sky and Nick began to recover. As his strength returned, his grip improved and the last fears slunk back into their kennel. He listened eagerly to the nightly talk at dinner, and when Webb asked about his travels to Venice, Nick made tentative mention of the courier service. It caught their interest and there was much discussion of ways and means, sledges and barges, to be poled or drawn by horses, or by the huskies of the north. Intoxicated by all this, Nick began to draw on the tablecloth and Gadsby moved round to sit next to him to correct his notion of the Americas. Talk moved to finding new ways to the Spice Islands and the fabled north-west passage. To these men everything was possible. It was the best possible medicine.

At the end of those few halcyon days, the wind changed, the temperature dropped and the fog rolled in. They were already well past the furthest point north Nick had ever been. He was woken that night by the doleful clang of the bell on the headland and he went on deck into a cold blanket of white, tinged with pink from the watchfires. The shipmaster shortened sail and headed east away from the coast. They wallowed along in an eerie silence, the ship's bells sounding oddly muffled, all her lights burning. A ghost ship. It was a new phenomenon to Nick and he went below to find words to describe it to Kate. The letter was long in the writing and as he paused for a word he felt the ship heel and change direction: the keel lifted and the sea began to hiss past the bulkhead. He found his cloak and left the cabin to find a flurry of activity. A strong easterly gale had got up to blow the fog away and he could only admire the spectacular seamanship as they came about to beat into it. Flakes of snow danced in a wind coming straight from Russia, and he pitied the barefoot sailors swarming the rigging as they rode out the storm.

Once things began to calm down and the hatches were open, he went below to check on the animals. He was still there when a message came, summoning him to the captain's cabin. He entered the cabin smelling like a farmyard, and Webb looked up and smiled. Nick saw he had some familiar-looking papers spread out in front of him.

'They stood the journey well?'

'Yes, sir.'

'As have you.'

Nick waited.

'You are fortunate in your constitution, Master Talbot. Now, my orders leave much to my discretion.' Someone gives this man orders? thought Nick. 'I may put you ashore at Edinburgh where I understand you have a duty or, if I consider you in any way unfit, I may use you in what capacity I choose.' Nick had a sudden flash of being dropped discreetly overboard.

'I confess, Nicholas, I have a fancy to take you with us. You would enjoy the venture, and would be of much use. But you appear fit and well and have your own orders. I shall exercise my discretion and leave the choice to you. Sleep on it.'

I am not good at choices, thought Nick. And really, there isn't one.

'I have no choice, sir. I am grateful for the offer and sensible of the honour, but I must leave dreaming and go to the Scottish court.'

A slow smile lit Webb's face.

'Which shows I was right in you.' He held out a hand and Nick took it. Webb turned the hand over and looked at the bruised nails.

'If we should not meet again, remember me to Ralegh.'

'I shall remember.'

As they rounded St Abb's Head they began to shorten sail for the run up to the Firth of Forth. Nick went to his cabin and looked again at his orders. They were simple. Deliver the messages, contact the Earl of Mar and watch. He scrutinised the maps he had copied from those of Gadsby and began to form a plan.

The great ship sailed up the Firth and dropped anchor out in the river with a salute of guns. The fort responded and presently small boats began to make their way across. Nick stood with his baggage at the head of the ladder and made his farewells. 'There are no words to thank you, sir.'

'Keep out of trouble, young Nicholas. If you can. Somehow

I feel we have not heard the last of you. God speed.'

Nick climbed down into the boat and as it drew away, he sat enviously watching the activity as sails came down and the ship began making ready for her fabulous voyage to Russia and points east.

Chapter Twenty-Four

It had snowed in the night, and the hired horse trotted gamely up the steep hill to the castle. Challenged, Nick produced papers and guarantees and was passed from hand to hand, arriving at last in the chamber leading to the Chamberlain's office. Here he was left to wait until a gentleman of the Court came to relieve him of the dispatches for the Earl of Mar. Food and drink was brought him and he thought of the *Northern Star* winging her way to Archangel. He thought of Kit Marlowe in his banishment. He thought of Kate working with others to keep his home safe. No Toby, no Robin, no players. He felt small and alone in this bleak place. He went to the window and peered down at the sprawl of Edinburgh in the low sun. Banks of cloud heavy with snow gathered on the horizon and he shivered. Squaring his sore shoulders he told himself to brace up.

'You've made your decision,' he said aloud. 'Take them on at their own game – give them something to reckon with. Or go down fighting.'

He was still unsure whether or not he had been sent here to be quietly and discreetly disposed of, in a way that Thomas Walsingham would have to accept. A fatal accident, perhaps. Webb had had plenty of opportunity but had proved a friend.

'As soon as may be,' thought Nick, 'I'm for Italy out of harm's way. And where I am no danger to anyone else.'

His natural buoyancy was still a little subdued. He could not believe Faulds had spoken the truth: that the Queen had her eye on him. He had done little to merit such attention. He saw quite clearly however that finding her favour could be a way to the top, where he and his could be safe. Perhaps.

But first he owed a duty of gratitude and loyalty to Walsingham, and he had not forgotten Kit and the strange magical play.

'A magic carpet is what I need,' he thought. 'Or a ring to summon a genie.'

Beautifully timed, a tall, well-set-up man was bowed in, dressed for the hunt.

'Come, Master Talbot, we stand on scant ceremony here.' He bowed. 'Robert Campbell, thane of Cawdor. We leave today for Broxhill Castle and you are bid welcome. Tomorrow we hunt boar. Find yourself a better horse.'

Nick's belongings were in the tiny bedchamber he had been allotted to share with another – suitable to his lowly status. Hurrying there, he found a stranger frantically packing.

'You Talbot? Yes. Hand me that, will you? We're going to be late – I hate being at the arse-end—' He was not much older than Nick, his face prematurely lined and now pinched with worry. 'Your gear's gone on ahead. The King's taken one of his starts – this is the weather he likes for hunting. Give me a hand, can't you—'

'I've to find a horse. Where—'

'Oh God'a mercy, you'll have to catch up.' Halfway through the door the young man paused. He had a brush of wiry ginger hair and orange freckles standing out against a round face pink with haste. 'Look, go out the West Gate, turn left and ask for Fergie. He won't cheat you – tell him I sent you—'

'Who—'

'Charlie Seaton,' he yelled back as he clattered down the stairs and was gone. Annoyed at having to ride out in his good clothes, Nick followed instructions and once the horse-coper understood he wasn't to be bamboozled, hired a raw-boned grey with an intelligent eye, iron tendons and feet like soup plates. The tack was clean and that was all that could be said of it. Nick swung into the saddle thinking regretfully of Nero eating his head off in a warm stable in Deptford. He followed the trampled tracks of the royal party heading west.

So far north, it was snowing again. There was no wind, and fat lazy flakes drifted down to settle deceptively fast. Inappropriately named Mercury, the grey proved steady rather than fleet of foot and what with having frequently to dismount to pick packed snow out of those soup-plate feet, Nick trailed in long after the rest of the court, to find Charlie Seaton dancing with impatience. The task of nursemaiding the new arrival was evidently not to his taste and he grew surly and irritable as Nick insisted on seeing his horse bedded down with hay and water before following him into the granite-walled keep. The chamber they were to share was at the top of one of the two towers, spartan and chill.

'You've missed supper. I'll get something sent up. Is this all your gear? Where's your armour?'

'I have none—'

Seaton rolled his eyes. 'You were best stay well back tomorrow, out of the way. The King will leave before sun-up so be ready. You can have my bed, I've found a better.' And with a toss of the head he was gone.

Not at all displeased to have the room to himself, Nick ate the food when it came, looked out his gear for the morning and rolled into bed, thankful that at last it had stopped rolling to the rhythm of the waves.

The air in the pre-dawn was clear and bitter cold, the stars close and brilliant. When Nick walked into the courtyard, there was little sign of the promised early start, and he stood astonished, gazing at the gauzy curtains of light moving in the sky to the north until the bustle and clamour began and the light of the torches diminished the wonder of the sight. The deep crisp snow was soon trampled brown and the man Campbell came up to him.

'Found a nag? Good. The King is anxious to be off. Dougal here will carry your gear.' A small man with a face like a walnut and legs you could drive a boar through came up, carrying a bow and quiver and two long spears shaped like tridents, the cross-piece partway down the shaft.

Nick had only seen a boar-hunt but once, in Germany, peeping from the safety of his father's arms and he prayed he wouldn't make too big a fool of himself. He shrugged into his leather fighting jack, and Campbell looked him up and down.

'Imphm. Your first? Stay back with Seaton.' Charlie's face lengthened, and as the chief walked away, he snapped, 'Try to keep up, Talbot.' On his mettle, Nick swung up on Mercury and followed the lines of horsemen and servants out of the gates, his worn leathers drab and insignificant among all the polished breastplates.

The sun off the snowfields dazzled the eye as they trotted towards the dark belt of Ettrick forest. It was a fine sight. Hounds of all sizes and shapes streamed ahead across the snow, making their music, followed by bright-coated heralds and trumpeters with banners flying, gaily caparisoned horses, the King and his party in furred cloaks and burnished breastplates.

They entered the woods at a canter, jinking between the trees into a large clearing. Nick's eyes widened. A tented pavilion had been set up, open on one side, the inside hung with embroidered arras and brocades. A chair was placed on a dais, cushions scattered on the carpets. A table stood nearby, loaded with platters of cold meats, bread and fruit, servants were bringing round goblets of hot spiced wine.

No one dismounted.

On horseback the King showed to advantage, his spindly legs part of his horse, his disproportionate upper chest and shoulders impressive. He was talking to a tall, lean man with a grizzled beard and presently the man made his way over.

'A stirrup cup with you, Master Talbot. John Erskine, Earl of Mar.'

Nick bowed.

'His Majesty is pleased to invite you to dine tonight. Pray do not get yourself killed this afternoon.' He wheeled and trotted off, leaving Seaton staring with his mouth open.

'I think I spoke out of turn back there,' he muttered. Nick shrugged. 'I don't know one end of a boar spear from the other. What do we do?'

'We wait. The servants and hounds drive the hogs out into the open and we stick 'em. If we're lucky. Those tusks are deadly – rip out a horse's belly in a trice.' Nick leaned forward to pull Mercury's ears.

'I shall keep well out of the way in that case.' He could hear a great clattering and shouting, the deep-throated baying of the hounds. A frisson ran down his spine. He nodded at the collection of terriers and whippets, tugging at the leash, yapping and belling with excitement.

'Why are they here?'

'Hare-coursing, later.' A groom was offering Nicholas a spear and he shook his head. He was looking at three magnificent hounds leashed by a herald next the King, one tawny-red, one brindled, one blue. They stood at seven hands, their heads level with the King's boot.

'Deerhounds,' said Seaton. 'Royal – brave as lions. You really haven't done this before have you?'

A tremendous thrashing of undergrowth drowned his speech, squealing, shouting and a high-pitched cry. Two huge boars crashed out of the bushes making an extraordinary noise. The larger of the two, tusks dripping blood, careered straight across the clearing, scattering men and horses. The table went flying, the cloth caught on a tusk and the animal swerved, shaking its head, on course straight for the King's party. The herald, the only man not rooted to the spot, loosed the hounds.

They leaped forward, a blur of red and grey and blue, one to each flank and the third, the tawny one, straight for the throat. One maddened slash and he was tossed aside, to recover, sink in his teeth and hang on. Inexplicably, the one man left shielding the King moved aside, leaving James exposed to the attack. Everyone else seemed frozen. There was a single moment as the boar was hampered in its onslaught, before it roared and went on, straight for the King, and Nick grabbed a spear and spurred forward before it. The point drove deep into the animal's chest. The jar of it went right up Nick's arm to his bruised shoulders and he almost lost his grip as the boar turned on him. It squealed again and came on. The crossbar was across its chest now and still it came. Nick dropped the reins to use both hands, Mercury skittered under him and he jumped off, to be flattened by the charge, his foot twisting awkwardly. Two more spears skewered the animal and it dropped in its tracks, its huge head on Nick's boot, hot blood gushing over his leg.

Winded, the spear still quivering in his grip, the haft driven deep in the ground, he looked the length of his body into the hot little eyes, glazing now, at the bristling jaws and fearsome tusks of quarter of a ton of hate.

'By God, that was close,' he thought. It had all taken no more than a minute.

'That was close,' said the man next to him.

Distant shouts showed the course of the other boar. Nick dragged out his foot and struggled up. 'I think I'll stick to hare-coursing,' he said. The herald was bent over the deerhound, bleeding from a gash in its shoulder. The King had dismounted and came to make much of the animal. He straightened up, nodded to the herald and came to where Nick was standing, testing his ankle. Nick made to kneel and was prevented.

'Timely, if a little foolhardy, Master Talbot,' said James.

'Take your pick of the hounds that gave you your chance.' Nick hesitated, unsure of the protocol.

'I would choose the tawny one, your Majesty.'

'He is spoilt.'

'He will mend, sire.'

'Take him then. You are hurt?'

'None of this blood is mine, your Majesty.'

'We are glad to hear it. You are excused. Attend to your animals.' Trumpets sounded, other game had got up and James remounted and cantered off. The herald, his knife out to dispatch the 'spoilt' hound, held his hand and found a pad instead to bind the wound. Nick knelt beside him.

'His name?'

'Fearghas. It means 'excellent choice'. It's true, he's the bravest of them.'

The two boars were being strung on poles to take back and the table set to rights. The young man who had been at the King's side lounged across, leading his horse.

'You stole my thunder, Master Talbot,' he said. 'I was about to skewer the brute.'

'If I was over-eager, sir, I must pray pardon for a raw novice.'

He slapped Nick on the shoulder.

'No matter. No doubt I shall have another opportunity.' To do what? Nick's eye met Campbell's. The man shook his head slightly. So he had seen it too.

The young man strolled off, whistling, as Robert Campbell rode over, a broad smile on his face.

'My cousin will ride back with you.'

'I would not spoil sport, sir. I believe it was his spear that saved me.'

'The creature was dead already. It is the nature of the beast to fight on to the last breath. Let us drink to your first boar, young man.' And my last, thought Nick.

Young Jock Campbell came across and the two men shared a flask of wine while a litter was made to carry Fearghas. Water was brought for Nick to wash off as much blood as he could so as not to further alarm Mercury, who was snorting and rolling his eyes, not liking the smell.

Riding back with Young Jock, he learned a little of the composition of the court and made note of a few names. David, Master of Ruthven was the man who had moved aside. Re-enacting the scene in his mind, Nick still had the feeling the move had been deliberate. Ruthven's spear had been in his hand, the King had yet to grasp the one offered. It had all happened so fast. Had he moved to save his own skin or to expose James? Ruthven would bear watching.

His own action had been pure instinct, precipitate. No doubt the King would have been safe enough, his other nobles nearby. 'Cost me a good pair of boots,' he grumbled. He remembered the speed and weight of the charge and the wicked tusks and shivered. 'Safe? Perhaps not.'

In his room, he found his hussif and a piece of silk thread and apologised to Fearghas for binding up his jaws. It had been hard to prise them from the boar's throat. He stitched the gash in the shoulder as carefully as a field surgeon.

'We are a fine pair,' he told him. Fearghas looked at him with fathomless eyes and licked Nick's hand as he was released. 'Rash to the point of stupidity. I was not supposed to get myself

254

noticed. You are a trifle conspicuous, too, my friend.' The plumy tail thumped the floor. Nick sent for a servant to cut off his boot and was pleasantly surprised to find a valet had been allotted to him and his quarters had been changed to a pleasant small bedchamber on the ground floor. Apologising profusely for not coming sooner the man Angus took over operations and Nick let him deal with the swollen ankle and take away his clothes for cleaning. Suddenly tiring, he stretched out on his bed. After a moment, singing low in his throat, Fearghas climbed up and lay beside him.

'A royal bedfellow,' murmured Nick and dozed off.

It was late when Angus reappeared, bearing a new pair of boots and Nick's clothes, clean and pressed, ready for the evening. The boot would not go over the ankle and a pair of soft, square-toed slippers was produced. Fearghas would not be left behind and Nick entered the hall with the hound at his elbow, groomed to perfection and trying not to limp.

Trestle tables covered with carpets ran the length of the room, heaped with dishes and flagons of wine. The centrepiece was a glazed and bristling boar's head, its tusks gilded and an apple in its mouth. Nick felt sure he recognised it.

Trumpets sounded and the King and his nobles entered and took their places at the top of the table. Seaton beckoned from halfway down and, mouth watering, Nick made his way over. Fearghas joined the heap of hounds snoring before the roaring fire and a consort of musicians struck up in the corner. The Earl of Mar stood and proposed an elaborate toast to the King's health and his safe deliverance from harm. Murray rose with another and they drank to a successful hunt. Nick noticed the

King's eye was often upon him and when the meal finished and the entertainments began, Mar came to speak to him.

'His Majesty wishes me to present you. You will be sent for in the morning. I have a question or two myself. Be ready.'

Morning came and Nick was sent for, but not to be presented to the King. A dispatch rider had come with the dawn, his horse blown and dripping. Among the letters was a sealed package for Nick, and Mar handed it over with a frown. The writing and seal were familiar and his heart sank as he took Fearghas outside with him to break it open. Having read it, he sat with an arm round the deerhound's neck, lost in amazement. The summons chimed so sweetly with his own plans he felt there must be a snag.

His orders were explicit. As Special Envoy to the ambassador in Venice, he was to find out if there was any truth in the rumour that Ossuna, Spanish viceroy of Naples, had designs to close in and annex the city. Ossuna had built a fleet to be reckoned with, said Cecil, harassing Venetian ships in the Adriatic, and Venice was surrounded on all sides by Spanish-dominated country. The effort to tidy up the map was supposedly supported by the numbers of foreign men said to be infiltrating the city, aided by the marquis Gallio, Spain's ambassador in Venice. If it was more than a rumour, Cecil wanted to know. The loss of Venice as a powerful independent trading port would be disastrous.

Nick was expected to watch and inform, not take action. Kit, in his accepted persona as M'sieur de Parolles, was by now established as a party animal and a provider of masques and had his ear to the ground below stairs. Apart from all this, Nick had dispatches from the Treasury to the Medici in Florence.

He should go there first, money had been lodged for him and he should dress the part.

'Good,' said Nick to Fearghas. 'That's where we were going anyway. I have Kit on my mind; I have things I must ask him. "Inform, no action." Excellent. We shall stay out of trouble this time.'

Some of the time on the *Northern Star* had been usefully spent picking Gadsby's brains for alternative routes for the couriers, from the wilds of Scotland, where he was now, to the eastern Mediterranean. Time to test one out. Sail fascinated Nick, and he resolved to try the way that involved least riding on hired horses. Edinburgh to Carlisle was a matter of a few days riding post, and he would take ship from there.

He spent some time writing a report to go back with the messenger in which he emphasised the Ruthven incident: if not an actual attempt on the King's life, it had been a piece of blatant opportunism. Unsure whether Cecil or Walsingham's influence at court had been architect of his deliverance, he omitted any word of thanks. If the spymaster had engineered it, no doubt he would exact payment. Nick had no complaints. He would lick his wounds, spend much-wanted time with Kit, and then he would go home. He obtained leave to go from an irritated Earl of Mar, collected his hired horse and set off westward. The deerhound bore him faithful company, making little of the snow-covered miles. In fact, Nick made him the excuse for taking the rests his own body still needed.

Arrived in Carlisle he enquired for a ship heading for the Continent. A three-masted schooner called the Merryweather was lying in the Solway preparing to get underway and Nick secured a passage as far as Brest.

The ship was a misnomer, Nick's first encounter with the tempestuous, unpredictable Irish Sea was – interesting. One day the sea would roar and toss the ship like a shuttlecock, wind screaming in the rigging; the next the sun would shine and seals would climb out of the water to lie sleek on the rocks, white gulls crying overhead, shoals of fish flashing silver through the waves. They stayed away from the coast, where there were apparently rocks and treacherous currents, and bucketed uncomfortably south. They rounded the westernmost tip of England to the accompaniment of squalls and beat slowly across that part of the Narrow Sea where the Spaniards had made their first big mistake. The shipmaster of the *Merryweather*, a Belgian, was a surly brute of few words and Nick was careful to keep himself and his hound as inconspicuous as possible.

Nick disembarked at the busy port of Brest and found a serviceable inn. He was a little more circumspect this time and took trouble finding a berth for the rest of the journey. It was time well spent, and he was lucky enough to find a well-found trading ship, a galleon bound for Genoa and points south and east. The captain and his officers were English and educated men, the ship belonged to the new East India Company bearing goods to trade for silks and spices. Nick dropped the names of Webb and Gadsby into the negotiations for a passage and found himself allotted a decent, small cabin in the stern, windows opening onto the sea. He was invited to mess with the officers, who greeted Fearghas politely. The dinners were excellent and the wines French. Things were looking up.

Wind and weather stayed favourable, even the Bay of Biscay behaved itself and if there were pirates, they were busy elsewhere. They docked at Lisbon without mishap. Nick had got back into the habit of shaving now and he went on shaving his head as well. The weather grew warmer, and he left off his clothes to bask in the sun. Eyeing the marked body, no one asked questions.

Lying there drowsing, he realised this was the first interval in his headlong career when he had nothing to do. He had not even a horse to look after. Rowena would probably have foaled by the time he got back. Michael would take care of her. So he made drawings and kept his journal, dealt with the hound and his requirements, wrote letters and learned to shoot the sun. He studied maps and charts and listened to the captain and his officers and their yarns. He played a drum to the first mate's fiddle and envied the men shinning up the ratlines. When they were becalmed after passing the Straits, he dived and frolicked with those of the crew who could swim. And gradually he allowed himself to sink beneath the surface and think about what had happened to him. He understood finally that his had not been a rash and foolish action: it came from a deep-seated hatred of man's inhumanity and ignorance. The words of men like Ralegh and Marlowe and their fellow-thinkers had confirmed it. He had a sense that what was to come from Kit Marlowe was of great importance. His task was to see that the work went on and was heard and spoken about. He must not fail him.

He had been taught things about himself in the Tower and after, and now he could begin to come to terms with it. Life went on.

His pen ran smoothly writing to Kate, letters full of the trivial detail she enjoyed, margined with little drawings. The letter to Rosalyne caused him much trouble, his words a jackdaw stealing of other men's verse. He tried a sonnet of his own and tore it up. The infatuation was over. He was no longer the downy youth who accompanied Marlowe to Venice, nor the dazzled boy who rescued her pearls. It had been lust, plain and far from simple. In the end he treated it as an academic exercise and expressed himself honoured by her notice, captivated by her beauty and begged her to accept this humble gift in token of his heart. The humble gift was a pair of jewelled and embroidered gloves of the finest Spanish leather and workmanship bought and dispatched with the letter from Cadiz at some expense.

'I can be as cynical a lover as you, mistress,' he thought.

Hugging the coast of Spain, the ship sailed on to Barcelona. Here they stayed for some necessary repairs, and he begged Captain Turner's permission to go ashore and find himself a horse for his journey from Genoa. He obtained it, promising to take the responsibility and care of the animal on himself. He had heard great things of the Spanish horses. Hostility and the Holy Roman Emperor apart, there were large areas of the Iberian peninsula that simply got on with things. Poor men who hoed and planted vines, corn, olives, less poor who pressed the grapes and olives for oil and wine, men who bred the fighting bulls and the sacrificial horses, and the men who bred the famous Andalusians, equine aristocrats with their liquid, blue-shadowed eyes and haughty athleticism.

It was well into Lent, and with this and the uneasy peace there were none of the fiestas and bullfights he had heard about. He drew no attention as he hired a mule and went upcountry to an estate he was told of that bred horses for the Spanish cavalry. He was impressed by the size of the arid country, and by the peasants who scraped a living from the stony soil. He passed tiny villages where black-clad women washed their linen in cisterns outside their doors or carried jars of water balanced on their heads, upright and graceful caryatids.

He found the place at last, and spent a congenial few hours finding a way to converse and then barter for what he wanted. The animals were magnificent indeed: in particular a huge stallion that he coveted but was not for sale. He found instead one of the offspring, a splendid high-stepping grey, 17 hands and pure white with sinews of steel, a good, open eye and a richly curving neck. He snorted and pawed the ground as Nick approached him and the handlers stood around smirking. Nick stroked the soft blue muzzle and spoke to him, looking him in the eye. There was no hardness to the mouth, and the animal did not seem ill-disposed. Nick asked for a saddle to be put on him. The horse submitted quietly enough, and Nick gentled him and walked him round, lying over his back before vaulting into the saddle. Everything went very quiet. Then the world exploded. The horse reared and bucked and sunfished, all four feet off the ground, he whirled round in circles, bolted for the gate and stopped. Nick went over his head to hit the sun-baked ground at a roll.

'You would, would you,' he mumbled. He picked himself up – nothing broken – and went to where the creature stood peacefully, looking innocent.

'A joker, I see,' he said to the men standing round convulsed with laughter. He took the reins back over the horse's head and stroked and petted him. He ran his hands down his legs to bring up the feet to examine them, talking all the time. He asked for a brush and brushed him, especially in those places horses like. The laughter died away as he gathered up the reins and prepared to remount: he had taken to this animal and he didn't like to be beaten. He had no sooner settled himself in the saddle than the whole performance repeated itself except that this time Nick was ready for him. He wrapped his legs round and stayed on, and when the horse went for the fence, bore heavily on the left rein, dragging the head round with an iron grip. Puzzled at finding himself thwarted by this human who brushed him as he liked, and talked all the time, the animal tried his other tricks again, rather half-heartedly, but Nick stayed on his back. Patiently, Nick worked on him, putting him through his paces until presently his bidding was done willingly. Nick walked him round quietly to cool him off, and when he dismounted, unsaddled and rubbed him down himself.

'How much?' There was a burst of excited noise, and much throwing up of hands, but eventually, Nick insisting that he had done all the work for them, they arrived at half what he had expected to pay. He gathered they were glad to find someone mad enough to take him off their hands. Rubbing a sore shoulder, Nick had the gall to ask for the tack to be thrown in and got it.

Well pleased with his bargain, Nick drank on it with the breeder, paid over the money, and elected to ride his new mount and lead the mule. Shaking his head, the man saw him through the gate and waved him off down the hill.

'Well, Oberon,' said Nick. 'I think you and I will do very well, now we've sorted all that out. You are going on a ship, but I will look after you. You have cost me a few bruises, but no hard feelings.'

Oberon swivelled his ears and swished his tail, blowing softly.

They arrived back at the *Ariadne* to find lowing bullocks being swung aboard for fresh meat. Nick anticipated trouble but in the mysterious way of horses, Oberon had decided to trust his new owner and caused little upset. Nick saw him fed and bedded down with plenty of straw in a snug stall and slept the night next to him.

They called at Marseilles and then on to Genoa and Livorno, where Nick bade goodbye to all his new friends, left his baggage to be sent on and set off on Oberon, Fearghas tireless at his stirrup, to find his beloved poet.

Cecil and his accursed scheming could wait.

Chapter Twenty-Five

There was no curfew in Verona. It was a warm spring night and there were still plenty of people about as Nick rode in to where Marlowe kept his horse. Oberon had served him well. The visit to Florence had provided money and the required clothes and he had made few other stops on the way. Aching with tiredness, he unsaddled Oberon and wisped him down, saw he had clean straw and a full manger and went for a bucket of water. He set it down and leaned his head for a moment on the satiny neck, listening to the steady munching.

'Well, Oberon,' he murmured, 'I wonder what kind of changeling boy we shall find here.' He was tempted just to lie down in the straw and sleep, but the fretting that had cost him many sleepless nights on the voyage would not let him rest. He stroked Oberon's neck and the horse turned his head to nuzzle him.

'Better go and find out.'

He walked down the moonlit street, spurs jingling, and he stopped to take them off before turning into the little cobbled courtyard. There were lights and music and laughter: someone was playing a lute and a surprisingly strong soprano voice was singing. He pushed open the door to the garden. Candles hung in the big olive tree like fairy lights, others floated in the pool. A naked youth with vine leaves in his hair and holding a home-made trident hung over the balcony calling to a group of nymphs below. Nobody seemed to have many clothes on. Fearing the worst, Nick went into the house.

The first thing he saw was Marlowe, immaculate in clean shirt and hose, lying back in his chair with his eyes closed, motionless. The soprano voice soared effortlessly up and up, mellow, round and beautiful, and stopped.

Marlowe opened his eyes and saw Nicholas, tall and broad, a tawny pelt furring his head, filling the doorway, the hound at his side singing quietly in his throat.

His arms flung wide.

'What an entrance! Superb! And you, Signor Catalini, magnificent! This, pat upon his cue, is Nicholas Talbot, my dear friend. We were just singing of lost love, Nick, and here you are. Meet Signore Andreas Catalini from the opera house in Rome.'

The castrato, beautifully tailored in burgundy brocade, swept a terrific bow.

'Delighted, sir, to meet a friend of my friend.' His speaking voice was a pleasing tenor.

'I hope, sir, to hear you sing again. I have never heard such a voice.' Fearghas lolled his tongue and grinned.

The youth from upstairs had come down to join the others in the garden in a bacchanalian dance, and there was a shout of laughter from the other room. Suddenly irritated, Marlowe shouted for quiet.

'My friend is here from London! He will have news – Nick, you have news? Did you do it?'

Nick grinned at him and nodded. He was pushed into a chair and plied with wine and questions. There was a platter of cold beef nearby and he annexed it. Kit seemed different, but not in the way he had feared.

He swallowed a mouthful and told the tale. The performance of *Romeo and Juliet* seemed a very long time ago in another life. He told it as well as he could without giving anything away, embellishing it, acting out the parts until Marlowe, howling with laughter, looked round at his revellers with sparkling eyes.

'We will enact it! Go and put on some clothes and I will give you your parts. Nick, you and I know ours, Andreas, you shall be audience for the Italian premiere.' He was in tremendous form, and as Juliet's words fell softly into the garden, Nick was reminded of the sunny afternoon that had started all this.

Marlowe quickly tired of the ineptitude of his actors, and imperiously called a halt.

'Out, away, all of you. My friend is worn out and I want him to myself.' Signore Catalini had gone long ago and he shooed out the rest with scant ceremony.

Nick was asleep in his chair before the last complaining guest had gone. Kit stood watching him for a minute or two, stroked a hand over the velvety skull and then put a cushion under his head, covered him up and went quietly upstairs.

In the morning it all had to be gone through again: the play, the acting, the audience. Marlowe was not particularly interested in his travels or even how Shakespeare had been persuaded. When he did sober up it was to speak of Venetian affairs or the trouble brewing in the east. Nick said nothing yet of the Tower or Scotland. He handed over the letter Walsingham had left with him on the ship, and the poet bore it away to read and thereafter was very quiet.

Nick at last dredged up the subject of the fairy play and remembered his concern.

'Where did all this moonshine come from, Kit? Have you been smoking opium? Or herbals? Make no mistake, it is sheer delight, but from you—'

'Opium? No. But since you ask, that was a dream indeed. I was troubled with a raging tooth, and you know how I dislike pain, Nick. The thought of having it drawn – eugh! I took opium. A dream that comes in the night vanishes in the morning light, but this was a waking dream, it stayed with me, like music. The pain went and the pleasure remained. A trifle, a tangle, but it became something more. Four different worlds, each complete in itself, touching at a tangent, briefly. Magical.'

'You are happy here, Kit.'

'As you saw, I have friends. I have ideas, coming so thick and fast I fear they may vanish before I can grasp them and set them down. I have new plays here already, scribble, scribble…

But what of you, Nick – it has been so long. You have grown so. You have changed. Hector now, not Paris. Have you found a wife? Or are you still in thrall to that arch-witch, Rosalyne?'

Nick flushed.

'I have not found a wife.'

'I am answered. You are a fool. But here is our Hebe with our sops in wine. Let us take our food into the garden while you tell me of this latest venture that is to make your fortune.'

Nick made a good story of his journey and the companionship of Fletcher and O'Dowd. He still could not speak of what troubled him. When he had finished outlining their plans, Marlowe, who had sat unusually quiet and attentive, remarked, 'A friend brought me a new toy from Venice, Nick. It is a round ball of wood, in two halves, called a farmuk. It comes from the East, and it climbs up and down its string and to and fro, like magic. There is a skill to it, and sometimes the string tangles and it stops. Then, rewound, it is off again.'

'On a string? Like a puppet?'

'No, not a puppet. Just the smooth ceaseless to and fro, up and down at the pull of the player. Look at the miles you have travelled, Nick, and will travel, to and fro, up and down. At the pull of the string and the forces that move it. Why will you not stay here, and be at rest?'

'Who would see your plays, all these ideas you speak of, who would see them into the light?'

'Why, Thomas, of course, or your wonderful courier service.'

'I would not ask it of them. This is our secret, Kit, until you choose to reveal it.'

'But you need only make one journey a year, Nick, two at

most. I have no means of knowing when my fountain will stop playing. It began when we met. Stay with me.'

'As much as I can. I have business in Venice and with any luck I shall be in this snug billet for a while yet.' Marlowe was silent for a while. Then.

'I am a hypocrite. I have plays for you to take back. There are three, in fact. Although if you will be patient awhile I would make alteration to one of them: the history. I have conceived a new character, one who will make a sea change to the whole piece. He will be a magnificent drunken fool of a knight, we shall love him and scorn him and pity him – we shall see him again and again, I think – he is too good to part with. I should like to meet your giant in scarlet and your other sergeant, but you have painted them for me, that shall suffice.' He sighed. 'I wish I could have seen your Mercutio. When you are more in the mood, you shall show him to me, flesh on the bare bones of my words.'

'That is the last thing that can be said of your words, Kit. They come rounded and fresh, alive in the rhythms. I told you, this was not played as rhetoric – these were men and women – real as you or I.'

'I wish I could have seen it.'

Nick felt they were approaching dangerous ground and hastened to ask, 'What is the other piece you speak of? May I see it?'

Marlowe got up and went into the house. He came back with a sheaf of manuscript, saying, 'This will keep you amused until I have my new mainspring pinned to the page. It was almost finished and you might have taken it with you last time, had you not been in such a hurry.' He grinned a mischievous grin.

'I must insist to you that all these characters are of my making only, and bear absolutely no resemblance to anyone living or dead.' And with that he whisked into the house, laughing to himself.

Supplied with bread, a bunch of grapes and a dish of olives, a carafe of wine at his elbow, Nick settled himself to read. Well warned, he wondered only briefly who the merchant of Venice might be, and began to laugh, a little ruefully, as the tale of the self-seeking lover began to unfold. Compared with the love of the merchant Antonio, Bassanio's seemed shallow. He flinched, sensing what was to come as Antonio pledged his body and his friend gaily spent the money and went a-courting. He had to laugh aloud, however, at the misfortunes of the other suitors and the song with the rather heavy-handed clue.

'I think I was the blinking idiot,' he said to himself. 'You devil, Kit.' The twist that brought down the vengeful Shylock was clever. All ended happily, it was a comedy, after all, but reading it a second time, Nick began to wonder. He remembered Marlowe's words on arriving in Venice, after his long impersonation of a Jew, and saw the risk Marlowe had taken. Shylock's humanity stood out like a sore thumb – spat upon, betrayed – 'I would not have parted with it for a wilderness of monkeys' – how would their audience see him? Would they take it at face value, and rejoice at his humiliation? Throw things? Given his easy capitulation, Nick thought on balance he would stay the despised Jew, but to the broader imagination of a player, the ambiguity was there. 'If you cut us do we not bleed?' No actor in any theatre in London would dare to play it for sympathy, but it was possible. Nick had a dozen questions to ask, but Kit was in the grip of his new character and they would have to wait.

'We have another heroine/hero,' he thought. 'Orlando will love this. No part for me – I would not dare play the Jew, not now, I'd be hissed off, and I'll be damned if I play Bassanio!' The play had left him uneasy. The young man on the lagoon seemed a lifetime away, a stranger. He shook himself. Perhaps there would be something for him in the history. He reflected that, after all, he did not look like being able to play anything at all.

That evening, sitting under the stars in the garden, Marlowe broke the uneasy silence that had fallen between them.

'Thomas has told me what befell you, Niccolo. He writes that you tried to save the soul of a young priest.'

'Not so. I thought I would speak of it to you, Kit – ask you... but I can't. It is too soon. No matter.' He leaned forward on his elbows. 'I lost sight of my main task – to bring your words to their audience. I won't again. These other errands serve our purpose. I am well paid, don't worry.'

'That you should speak in that way worries me. Where is my romantic young idealist...?'

Nick shrugged and stood up. 'Older. I'm for bed. Venice tomorrow. A sinecure, I'm not expecting trouble.'

Chapter Twenty-Six

Venice. Two days later

Coming into the city on a clear day, the sky a cloudless ultramarine, the sun bouncing off little wavelets in the harbour, Nicholas experienced its true magic for the first time. It wasn't the beauty of the buildings or the fact that, instead of clattering cobblestones, water lapped softly at their feet. It was something in the glittering air, the light, a sleight of hand that deceived the eye and hid what lay beneath. His gondola slid smoothly under the recently completed bridge on the Rialto, crescents of light rippled the underside of the smooth stones so that they appeared to move. They were making good time until their way was blocked by what looked like a fleet of gondolas clattering and clashing together, filled with elaborately-dressed men jostling and shouting and waving their caps.

'What's going on?' asked Nick. His gondolier spat.

'The latest craze, signore. La Bellissima, the new courtesan who has them all by the ears – to put it politely. She shows a different portion of herself every day. You might be lucky, signore, you might see more than an ankle. Me, I've seen it all before.' This last came with such a world-weary sigh that Nick had to smile. He was going to be late. He didn't think the Council of Ten, let alone his superior, would accept La Bellissima as an excuse.

'Make haste, if you can get through.'

Piqued, the man shot through a closing gap and Nick caught a glimpse of a shapely high-nippled breast, thinly veiled. He looked back at the men gazing upwards. One face he was to remember.

'They say she'll be choosing her lovers soon. Three for use and one for play. You'd have to be as rich as Croesus. Or well connected. Or...' He looked at Nick consideringly, 'something—'

'A florin if you get me there on time.' The man put his back into it and Nick stepped out in front of the Doge's Palace just as his ambassador arrived. Lord Stanley nodded approval of his envoy's discreet blue velvet, slashed and embroidered with violet. Not a man of fashion, he was oblivious to the exquisite tailoring and the expensive tabby silk lining the cloak, the line of the soft boot hugging the leg. He hastened into the building crying, 'Make haste, Master Talbot, make haste!'

They were admitted to the last part of the meeting only. Nicholas presented himself and his dispatches, which were glanced at and set aside. Evidently Vanni had already carried the day. Within the Council of Ten only three held any real power, and of this Council of Three Alessandro Vanni was the prime mover. No notice, official or otherwise would be taken of the rumours of attack and infiltration, he told them. Venice would not show weakness, she could defend herself against her enemies. Enemies there had always been, envious neighbours, the motto of the city bore witness, Venice was ready. Stanley dared not point out that the heyday of the city was over, her power slowly waning. Nicholas, watching faces, was convinced there was more to it. The crippled Vanni was far too complacent.

They bowed themselves out, Stanley quietly fuming, and took water for the Embassy. Nicholas was dismissed and went to exercise Fearghas, thinking. This was where he missed Kit, he would know all the gossip, new arrivals, strange faces. At his lodging he changed his clothes, whistled up his hound and went to look for the Antolini brothers.

He ran them down in a noisome bar so like the cellar where they had first met that he shuddered. He brought over a jug of wine and sat down. Nervous of the bristling hound at his elbow, they shifted along the bench and kept their distance. Nicholas kept his questions general, but learned that there was indeed an influx of strangers.

'Mercenaries they look like to me,' said Tonio. Or Francisco. 'Ones and twos here and there, but building up.'

'It'll be a walkover if Ossuna gets serious. Our man in Naples was arrested last week, no help there,' said his brother.

'Who are they reporting to?' asked Nick.

'We think Gallio, but without proof—' he shrugged. 'The Councillors have their noses so far up their own arses it would take the city falling into the sea to shift them. Oh well, it's their city. We're off home.'

'Where's that?'

'Sicily, near Messina.' Of course, thought Nick. Where else.

'I'll try to get near Gallio,' he said. 'Don't go just yet.'

'Try that new courtesan. I hear he's got in there.'

'My water tells me things are moving,' said Tonio. 'We don't want to be here for the bloodbath, good pickings though there might be. They might take us for Venetians.' I don't think so, thought Nick. He wished them well and went to find better company.

Preparations for the coming carnival were well under

way, streets and buildings already decorated with flowers and garlands. He had no difficulty obtaining invitations to a number of events where he might meet Gallio. He enjoyed himself hugely but was no nearer to his quarry until Stanley, casting around for a presentable young man, requested his presence at a prestigious banquet.

Anticipating a long night, he chose the lightest of his new clothes, and in quilted cinnamon silk accompanied his ambassador up the receiving line, hoping for a glimpse of his man. The endless meal gave him no chance and he was kept fully occupied by the flirtatious ladies on either side. The usual entertainments followed and he stationed himself by a small balcony, half-hidden by the curtain, making the most of the tainted breeze coming off the canal. The heat in the room was stifling, lit by hundreds of candles and crowded with men and their wives and attendants from several embassies. Gallio had been pointed out to him at last and he leaned there watching the man he had last seen gazing up at a courtesan's window.

There was something about the way Gallio stood, balanced and easy, his hand light on his sword-hilt. He was brown-haired with well-opened dark eyes, a swarthy complexion and a piratical cast of feature. His clothes were dapper and subtly coloured, the pose elegant. A swordsman. Nick had dropped a few remarks into his conversations during the evening and learned that Gallio had the reputation of a womaniser and was indeed a fine swordsman. Apparently he visited a fencing master most days, Andreas Cavalli, a man of formidable talent. Gallio was rumoured to be a strong candidate for the favours of La Bellissima.

Next day, comfortable in his well-worn leathers, Nick rode

Nero out to Callisto where Cavalli lived, Fearghas loping by his stirrup. It was a low, square white house, built in the Moorish style, set in a well-kept garden, its orchards pink with plum and cherry blossom. He followed the clash and slither of blades through a colonnade shaded with vines and found two men fencing in a sanded arena. One of them was a slight, wiry man with close-cropped silvered hair and a seamed brown face, the other young and athletic. He watched for a while. It was immediately apparent which was the master and shortly, disarmed for the third time, the pupil, red and sweating, threw up his arms in despair.

'Must I tell you again? It is too easy to make you lose your temper, Julio. Come again when you can master it.' The silver-haired man turned and saw Nick standing with his hound by the pillar. Nicholas bowed.

'Your pardon. I have brought no introduction, signore. I have been told of your excellence and ventured to come unannounced.'

'Your weapon?'

Nick unsheathed the blade that had been his father's and offered it. Cavalli bowed to his crestfallen pupil and, accepting a bag of money, threw it onto the bench serving as armoury. He selected a weapon of similar weight.

'I accept no pupil except on ability. Show me.'

The next twenty minutes exercised all Nick's skill and agility. He made a mistake and the master's sword flicked off a button.

'Maestro,' said Nicholas, point down.

'Indeed. You took your eye off mine – a split-second. I can polish your technique – the style is a little rough. Let us try with the rapier, it may lend elegance.'

Unused to the lighter blade Nick found Cavalli's point at his throat almost at once.

'The rapier is not to be used as a cutlass, signore. It is the extension of your arm, your forefinger. Try a different stance, so…and so…back and to, so…your body sideways, *bend* your knees and forward and one and two and back—' It was like a glorious ballet; the blades flickered and danced in the sun.

His rapier spun out of his hand.

'You became entranced, signore. That is good. Now concentrate. Again.' Breathless and sweating hard, Nick shed his leather tunic and picked up the foil. After another fifteen hard-fought minutes and several rips in his shirt, Cavalli dropped his point and saluted. 'I will teach you. The same time tomorrow.'

There was a slow clap from the archway. Gallio was leaning against the pillar.

'Well done, signore. Andreas here is very selective.'

'*Buon giorno*, my lord. We have here a fencing partner worthy of your skill. Give me a week with him and we shall see.'

'A bout with him now, Cavalli?'

'This man has kept me busy nigh on an hour, would you take an advantage?'

'With the sword, then.'

'I would not advise it. Your name, signore.'

'Nicholas Talbot, maestro.'

'You have been well taught. At present, you are a fighter, not a swordsman, you lack refinement, but you have all that is needed. A diamond in the rough, Signor Talbot. Until tomorrow.'

'My thanks, Signor Cavalli.' A servant brought lemonade and Nick drank thirstily. 'May I stay and watch?'

Cavalli raised an eyebrow, Gallio shrugged and stripped off his doublet. Nick sat on a bench in the shade, his hand on Fearghas' head, and watched Gallio put through his paces, noting that he had a habit of dipping his shoulder before a lunge. The lesson ended with Gallio's sword on the ground and Cavalli's buttoned foil against his chest. He was laughing.

'One day, Andreas, one day.' Cavalli smiled and nodded. He threw his rapier to the waiting servant, bowed to them both and departed. Mopping his face, the Spaniard observed, 'A man of few words, our Cavalli. I have been admiring your dog. Worth a king's ransom, if I'm not mistaken. Would you sell him?'

'Not for a king's ransom. He was hard-won, my lord.'

'A beauty. And I suppose that is your enviable horse outside. I would like to see your woman.'

So should I, thought Nick.

'A simple signore? I don't think so – a princely company.'

'A mere underling to the English ambassador, my lord. I find there are times when a good horse and a companion like Fearghas are more valuable than a woman.' He grinned and Gallio burst out laughing.

'I like your choice of words. More valuable but not so rewarding, eh? Come, we'll ride back together. If I am to fight you, I would talk with you.'

Men of a kind, in spite of the difference in age, they rode back to the city chatting easily, and prepared to go their separate ways. Gallio put out a hand.

'Dine with me this evening. There is someone you will like to meet.'

'A pleasure, my lord.'

'My given name is Gaspare. I shall call you Niccolo. Ten

of the clock at La Camiglia. I usually bring a gift. Oh, and leave your fine hound behind, he might alarm the ladies.' He cantered off with a wave and a laugh. Nicholas gazed after him, confused. He had not expected to like the man so much.

Gallio was waiting for him at a table set on the paving outside La Camiglia, with a flask and two goblets of cut crystal in front of him. He had abandoned his discreet colours in favour of doublet and breeches in Tyrian purple, paned and embroidered with silver, the high collar and turned-down ruff of silver lace sparkling with amethysts. Nick, in his favourite dark green was quite in the shade. Gallio waved and raised his glass.

'Hey, Niccolo! Come and drink to the happiness of a successful lover!'

'I will, with pleasure. I wish you joy.' Nick raised his glass. 'To a long and happy marriage.'

'Marriage! Who said anything about marriage? Ah, your Italian is so much better than mine I had forgot you are an Englishman. They do things differently there.' He was laughing and Nick flushed.

'I am half a Scot,' he said lightly. 'A claim that I admit makes me peculiarly English. Am I to meet the fortunate lady?'

'I am the lucky one. Of all the suitors at her gate – half Venice! La Bellissima has chosen me to take her maidenhead.'

Nick was not so naïve as that. He knew how many times and with what stratagems a whore would sell her virginity. But in Venice, a woman of quality and great beauty, badly left with no dowry, had only two choices: the convent, or the life of a courtesan. A woman like La Bellissima need only take three or four regular lovers to live in great style.

He smiled and sat down.

'That explains the peacock finery. I congratulate you – and the lady on her choice.'

'Not on the strut yourself, young Niccolo? Fine upstanding lad that you are.'

Nick shrugged. 'If fortune comes my way, who knows?' Gallio upended the flask over his glass.

'I shall leave Cavalli to teach you how to use your sword, Niccolo. But I will show you where to couch your lance.'

Nicholas laughed. 'I believe I shall choose for myself.' Gallio stood up.

'Come then, you shall squire me to this battle. She may have a friend to take your fancy.'

La Bellissima had a magnificent suite of rooms in the house fronting the Grand Canal, where Nick had first glimpsed her. They walked up a wide marble staircase, the baluster ornamented with gilt cupids, the walls hung with silk and gold-framed depictions of the conquests of Zeus, the shower of gold the most erotic. Through high carved doors, the long room opened onto a balcony overlooking the water. Reflected ripples on the painted ceiling deceived the eye and Nick had to look twice to believe what he was seeing. Not that he looked until later – the woman standing before the fire took all his attention.

Her beauty was of the kind to bring a man to his knees. Steeled to resist, nevertheless, Nicholas felt himself stiffen.

He bowed over the delicate hand, lost for a moment. He looked up to see Gallio's triumphant eye on him. Pox on the man – this was just another dangerous game to him. The woman's fingers tightened in his, a definite squeeze.

'Gaspare tells me you are an ambassador from England.' Her voice did not disappoint, low and musical, the accent refined. He could not help himself, 'Not quite an ambassador, lady, unless perhaps for your favours.' She laughed, a delicious gurgle in her throat, and still holding his hand led him to a table loaded with sweetmeats and bottles of Murano glass winking in the light.

'Careful, signore, my gallant Gallio will call you out.'

'I had hoped you might do that, my lady,' he murmured. She pulled an embroidered handkerchief from her sleeve and put it to her lips, turning to where Gallio stood with narrowed eyes. The growing tension in the room was palpable.

'How shall your young friend amuse himself, Gaspare?'

'As best he may,' growled Gallio, his hackles up. The handkerchief dropped. Nick bent to pick it up, and as he handed it to her with a bow, a folded paper slid into his palm.

'My friend grows impatient,' he said. 'I shall leave you, *mia bella* Bellissima, and try to find consolation elsewhere.'

Gallio had recovered his composure, and waved an airy hand.

'Off with you, you young dog, or I shall wish I had not brought you.'

The woman extended both hands and Nick kissed them, his nose and all his senses assaulted by her perfume. He placed his gift on the table and she smiled.

Gallio had the door open and Nicholas passed him with a nod.

'Cavalli's at noon,' said Gallio.

'At your service. *Buona notte*, signore.'

'There goes a promising friendship,' Nick said to himself, brushing blindly past the woman waiting for him on the stairs. 'Why in God's name did he bring me?' The actor in Nick recognised the showmanship in the man, a Mercutio born, a ruffler who would die with a jest on his lips. He just had to boast of his conquest.

'Dammit, I could really get on with him.' Nick leaned on the wall outside under the flickering torch and unfolded the note. 'Please God, not an assignation.' It read, *Four of the clock, here in my garden.* He would just manage it back from Callisto, if Gallio hadn't killed him first. Nick grinned. The promised night of passion would not leave Gallio in much shape for a duel. 'I'll be gentle with him,' he promised.

Nicholas let himself quietly through the garden gate, punctual to the minute. A decidedly smug and languid Gallio had given him a half-hearted fifteen minutes and then sat watching Cavalli work him mercilessly for an hour, calling out helpful advice with a cynical gleam in his eye. They had ridden back together in perfect harmony and Nick had had to listen to a detailed inventory of La Bellissima's charms. It was the Queen Mab speech all over again. His eye on the time, Nick had refused to accompany him to his lodging, agreeing to meet next day.

He waited under a fig tree, its palmate leaves figuring their ancient pattern on the wall. The soft fawn of his leathers was perfect camouflage and he saw her before she saw him. She stood in the sunlight looking about her, gossamer silks lifting and lovingly folding a rainbow round her body. Nick had to fight down a growing desire for this woman. She was fair, not dark like Rosalyne, her skin delicately tinted, her nipples dark buds under the gauze.

He moved forward and she started, her hand going to her mouth. He drew closer and could see the lilac shadows under her eyes, the bruises circling her neck thinly covered with paint. Her mouth was swollen and tender and he felt a quick anger.

'What do you want of me, lady?'

'Your help. Not here. If you would help me, come—' She took him into the house, up the back stair to the room he had seen before.

He was able to look about him now, at the inlaid chests and richly-upholstered chairs, the decorative fan of swords over the mantel, their blades damascened, their hilts encrusted with jewels, the sculptures and pictures, the enormous bed in the corner with a tester and curtains of crimson silk. He crossed to her, weaving his way between innumerable embroidered stools and little lacquered tables, to where she stood pouring wine. It was a light golden wine, tasting of flowers, and she took hers to sit on the bed.

'I must trust someone, Niccolo – is that right? Gaspare called you Niccolo.' He nodded, standing by the table.

'I could write a letter, but who from the Council would heed a letter from a courtesan, even La Bellissima, the Cardinal's whore. Oh yes, did you think Gallio the only one?' She paused to compose herself. 'This is my city, my birthplace, I fear for her, Niccolo. There have been rumours, but what can one do?' She patted the bed and he went to sit beside her.

'These rumours – they seemed to centre on Gallio. I chose him for my lover because I thought – but it is too soon, it will take time. Oh, he hinted, he will soon be powerful and important, he made promises—'

'What do you wish me to do?'

'We must wait. I have two other lovers, but Gaspare – he wishes to live here, with me. He has already brought his belongings. He may – I might find an opportunity—'

'You run a terrible risk, bella. This is an intelligent man, with a great deal at stake.'

'You know of it then, it is true, they threaten my city.'

'It would seem so. I can tell you one thing. My ambassador – and others – have done their best, but the Council will not move without proof.'

'Proof? These were just words, Niccolo. Pillow talk.' Nick thought for a moment.

If he were in her place, what would he do?

'If, as you seem to say, you would serve Venice, you are in an enviable position, signora,' he said, fishing.

'What do you mean?'

'You cannot lose. Gallio is in lust with you, if Venice falls, he will protect you. If he is discovered by your hand, you would be rewarded.' She gave an exaggerated start.

'Betray him?'

'Overdramatic, *bella mia*.' Her face hardened.

'How much will your masters pay?'

The sudden dropping of the mask was disconcerting and Nick stared for a moment. Then, 'Not a groat,' he said cheerfully. 'You were best go to the Council.'

'Will you be my messenger, Niccolo – I dare not be seen in this.'

'You would trust me?' Her hand stroked his cheek and strayed to undo his laces.

'You seem kind,' she said. 'And I need a friend.' Slowly Nick stood up and moved away.

'Find me evidence, Bellissima, and we shall see. There may be letters, instructions—'

'He keeps them locked away.' Nick raised an eyebrow and she gave a harsh laugh.

'I am glad I am not your enemy, Niccolo. Have you a wife at home?'

'Not yet.'

'And you refused me. Formidable. Very well, I shall find your proof. Just remember, everything has its price.'

'I am never allowed to forget it.'

'An honest woman would be one to prize forever,' he thought as he ran down the stairs, back the way he had come.

Days passed. He visited Cavalli every day, sometimes meeting Gallio, sparring with him, most often he stayed talking with his teacher. He understood Gaspare spent most of his time with his celebrated new mistress, it was the talk of every gathering Nick attended. It was difficult to gain access to her. What talk he had with Gallio was wide-ranging but general and, on the whole, amusing. At no time would he be drawn into specifics. Nick could only wait.

After two weeks of this, dancing attendance on the ambassador, with no opportunity to visit Verona, at last a note was waiting at the embassy. 'Noon. He is away.'

Fearghas was content to be left behind to sleep, and Nick went immediately, as before, staying only to buckle on sword and dagger, through the garden and up the back stair. He was late. She was bending over an elaborately inlaid chest, feeling at the back of a drawer.

'There is a catch – ah!' A panel sprang open and she pulled out a bundle of letters. 'He writes here every night with a little book…here it is. Is this what you want?' She was breathless with fear, her words tumbling out. Nick looked at the book first. As he hoped it was the key to a cypher. Gallio had left letters and transcriptions jumbled together and Nick looked up.

'How long have we got?'

'He is at Callisto. An hour?' Nick sat down at the desk.

'These will be missed.' He got out pencil and journal and set to work copying the cypher and two of the most crucial letters. She was pacing up and down, hands clasped at her lips. Nick had almost finished when light feet ran up the stair and the door was flung open.

'Cavalli was sick—' Time stood still. Nick distinctly heard the slap and grind of a gondola under the balcony.

Then Gallio's sword was out and Nick was up and away from the desk, thrusting the woman behind him. There was no more time to think of her, Gallio was upon him, attacking fast. Nick dodged round the table, dragging out his weapons. He parried and whipped to the side away from the corner. A small table stood in Gallio's path and he leapt it, blade meeting blade. He thrust forward as he landed and Nick swayed aside, parried and struck in his turn. Gallio had a silver jug in his hand now and knocked aside the point, leaping in. Nick's dagger deflected the blade, he feinted and lunged. Gallio kicked a footstool in Nick's way and he stumbled, only parrying a blow with his crossed blades in time. Gallio swung the jug and caught Nick a whack on the elbow. The dagger dropped from his paralysed hand and he reeled back fighting for balance. The two were well-matched in many ways except the left-handed Gallio had lost his temper and seemed to be using whatever weapon came to hand. He came on like a fury, blade striking sparks, Nick dodging a storm of objects thrown and kicked in his path. This and Gallio's left-handed stance had him on the defensive and he found himself driven with his back to the fireplace. Gallio snatched up a heavy footstool and brought it down with all his weight on Nick's attacking blade. Veteran of many battles, it broke at the hilt.

'Hah!' And Gallio lunged. Nick twisted and the point drove deep in the carved wood behind him. Gallio dropped his stool to wrestle it out – his first mistake. Nick snatched up the stool and whipped it down, sending the sword splintering across the marble to disappear over the balcony and clatter into the gondola. He seized a weapon from the array on the wall.

A rapier, hell. His opponent was disarmed and Nick hesitated. His mistake. Gallio plucked the twin to Nick's rapier off the wall and slashed him across the chest. Nick went on guard, flicked his wrist and darted in to cut deep.

'Touché,' panted Gallio, blood pouring down his leg. 'But this is not your best weapon, no—'

'I've been practising,' said Nick, breathing hard.

The fight was on. To and fro, back and forth, *bend* your knees, thought Nick. The slender blades, unbated, shivered and flashed. The thin whine and clash of steel and the sound of the men panting echoed through the room, their soft boots slid and stamped on the marble. At last, hard-pressed and bleeding, Nick saw the opening he had been waiting for. After a dazzling barrage of feint and counterfeint that cost Nick a cut on the arm, Gallio dropped his shoulder to lunge and Nick, anticipating, thrust in. He engaged and twisted: Gallio's rapier flew across the room to land quivering in the head of the bed.

Nick's point at his throat, Gallio laughed and spread his hands.

'I enjoyed that,' he said. 'Cavalli should be proud of you. I was just going to have to fight dirty.' Not fool enough to lower his point, Nick grinned at him.

'With furniture – or feet? Go, Gaspare. There's the balcony. Go while there's time. Venice will soon be too hot to hold you.' Standing with his back to the window, Gallio shrugged, stepped back and eased his injured leg over the railing.

'Venice will survive without me.' He dropped from sight and Nick moved forward, conscious now of pain.

Gaspare looked up at the balcony and brought his sword up in the salute.

'We shall meet again, young Niccolo,' he called.

Nicholas stood and watched the gondola slip away down the canal.

'I hope so, indeed, indeed I hope so,' he said.

Turning back into the room he saw La Bellissima with the sheaf of papers in her hands. She held them up.

'These are sufficient?'

Still fetching his breath, 'I shall take the book if you please. I have my copies. Find another messenger.'

'I thought you would look after me, Niccolo…why did you not kill him?'

'I think you are able to look after yourself, signora.' He mopped at the shallow cut on his chest and went to pick up the two pieces of his father's sword. 'I will take a replacement, if you permit.' He stuck the rapier through his belt, found his dagger and reached down a sword from the wall. It was fine Toledo steel, the blade chased and inlaid, the hilt bound with gold wire and topped with an emerald. 'A fair exchange for an unwanted lover, I think.'

Chapter Twenty-Seven

Special envoys are allotted body servants. Nick, for once was glad of it as he peeled the ruined shirt away from his cuts and started them bleeding again. None of them were more than scratches; he swabbed them with brandy and let Paulo bind up the awkward one on his arm. The man dealt tactfully with boots and buttons, and turned Nick out clean and presentable in midnight-blue velvet, immaculate frills hiding the scarred wrists, to report the mission accomplished. He found Lord Stanley adrift in a sea of papers, a pile of new dispatches on the corner of his desk. He listened to what Nick had to say with astonishment and took the offered proofs in trembling hands.

'But this is superb! Vanni shall have this without delay. I congratulate you Master Talbot. Indeed, I shall be sorry to lose you.'

'Lose me, my lord?'

Stanley threw him a packet of letters and a folded sheet bearing a familiar cypher. Someone had carelessly decoded it between the lines and Nick frowned. He was ordered post-haste back to London. He looked up.

'Do you know anything of this, my lord?'

'Nothing at all, my boy. No rumour but a fluttering in the dovecotes over the Queen's health. God bless her,' he said absently. Nick was fuming. He had hoped for more time in the sun, more time with Kit. A puppet on a string, for certain. He took up his letters.

'I have leave to go, my lord?'

'What? Oh yes, yes of course. Orders are orders. I shall see your work here is noted, never fear. Wait – where is this man Gallio now – you have him safe?'

'I fear he escaped me, my lord.'

'Ah. A pity. Well, we have exposed him, his usefulness here is done. I shall make good report of you, Master Talbot.'

'I'll believe that when I see it,' thought Nick. He went slowly back to his quarters to read his letters and pack. Kit was not going to like this. He took Kate's letter out on to the balcony the better to read it in the dying light.

Kate had written,

Dear Nicholas,

You must have struck a rich vein! The purchase of the adjoining land is accomplished, not without trouble - Hugh will tell you - and I am pleased to say we have been able to amend the condition of many of the poor people in the village. Hugh has taken one of the men who can read to assist him and Noll and I have begun a school to teach the children. I fear you still have lord Mowbray as a neighbour, we have only pushed out the boundary. He owns all the surrounding lands; we must be a great thorn in his side.

Last time yon droll fellow Ned came with word of you – I would like to see that one upon the stage – he described a being I hardly recognise. I have no portrait of you, Nick, except the one in my heart. Could you not have one made? You must have changed greatly, outgrown us perhaps.

Your letters are a great joy to us and I thank you for the books. Is this poem really what is read in Town? And the play you speak of – how I wish I could see it; and you in your part. You are in your world, Nick, and I in mine. One day, perhaps soon, they will meet.

Yours in waiting, Kate.

Nick read it a second time, then stood for a long while with it crumpled in his fist, gazing out unseeing across the lagoon.

There was nothing now to keep him in Venice. The whole business had taken but a few weeks and the Council would now take action. Marlowe had plays for him to take back or a letter would have sufficed for him, whether he liked it or not. Nick faced another wearisome ride out to Verona and back and he was in a black mood when he clattered up the street in the chill of the evening to Oberon's stable. Fortunately Marlowe was entertaining two of his more sober cronies and they soon left. Kit came back into the room to survey Nick's uncompromising back as he stood gazing into the fire with his boot on the fender, nursing a cup of wine.

'I have not seen you like this. What troubles you, sweeting?'

'Don't call me that.' He drank off his wine and poured more.

'Very well. We are friends. Tell me.'

'I am recalled. I am sent hither and yon – I see no end to it. And I am in love.'

Unaccountably, Marlowe flew into a sudden violent rage, throwing the ink pot, stools, anything in reach, stamping and shouting.

'You want to leave me stewing here – and go to some whore! You treacherous hound, vile, vile – get out! Leave me, if that's what you want—' he suddenly dropped down and burst into hysterical tears. Fearghas was growling and showing his teeth. Nick stood for a moment staring, then turned on his heel and went out. So much for hoping to speak of his own inner turmoil to Kit Marlowe.

All his angry frustrations came flooding back. He strode down to the riverside and drew his new sword. There he practised like a man possessed, whirling and stamping, oblivious of pain, until streaming with sweat, he flung down the sword and plunged into the river, Fearghas at his heels. When he climbed out, calm now and dripping, Kit was waiting on the bank.

'I was wrong to speak as I did.'

'It is no matter.'

'You are different, Nicholas.' Fearghas climbed out of the water and shook himself vigorously all over them. Nick laughed.

'What do you expect? An hour or two with Topcliffe would change anyone. Is the piece finished? No? Then why are you wasting time out here – in with you. The fate of the realm may hang in the balance while I dally here!'

Relieved, Marlowe laughed with him and followed him back.

'I treat my dog better than this,' thought Nick.

He came down next day to find Marlowe riding his Muse like a maniac, until finally coming out of his trance, he came to find Nick and said, 'This fellow's girth has burst my play and split it in two! I would beg you to stay until the second part is complete, my Niccolo, but I have written a part for you that you and you alone must play. Tell Shaksper or however he spells himself, I said so. It won't matter about the second half; you're dead by then, died on a W!'

'On a—?'

'W! Worms! He can't get it out, poor fellow, he's dead!'

'Not right at the beginning again, I trust.'

'Trust me, at the very end. The man's a scene-stealer, I promise you.' He sat down abruptly. 'Oh, God, if I could only see you play it.'

'You will be busy, Kit, writing the next. And, please, now we have tapped this rich vein, another comedy. One I can stay alive in?'

Marlowe laughed.

'I think the actor may triumph over the adventurer in you in the end, Nick. You may find enough excitement playing to your audience. Whether Cecil will let you go is another matter.'

Nick shrugged. Neither man had mentioned the outburst of the night before: Nick doubted Marlowe even remembered it. These mood swings were beginning to worry Nick.

'*Que sera*. Another urgent packet came today. If you are finished, I should leave. Our escort leaves Venice on Friday, I would go with them, see our venture at first hand.'

'Do your partners know of me?'

'No. Nor will they. It is between the four of us, and so it must stay – you are not out of danger, Kit. Listen, I will tell you something for your ears only. When I get back, I am sent to the Scottish court. The Queen begins to think in private of the succession. The intrigues have begun, everything may change. Kit, be patient, follow your new star. It may not be long.'

'Nobody tells me anything these days. I don't like the sound of the Scottish court. James has favourites and behaves like a quean in heat. Don't get entangled, Nick.'

'I'm just a messenger.'

'The Greeks would kill a messenger bearing bad news. And you are playing larger parts than messengers these days. Be careful.'

'I will be back in the spring. Have a comedy for me. I will write to Master Poule – you will have news, I promise.'

The timing was good, Nick hoped to meet with the party to be escorted by O'Dowd and his men and return with them. It was a difficult parting.

'Don't leave me, Niccolo. What am I to do?' Still tired and sore, Nicholas was short with him.

'You'll think of something. I have to go. You remember the Antolini brothers – didn't you have some bright idea about twins? A comedy? Not that there's anything remotely funny about them, the Gemini from Hell.' Kit sat up.

'You're right, I did. Now, where have I put it—' Nicholas breathed a sigh of relief and embraced him, leaving him rummaging through piles of manuscript, muttering to himself and waving him away.

In spite of all the delays, Nick arrived at the rendezvous

outside Venice early. Nick saw Oberon stabled and went to sit in the wide piazza to wait. He was enjoying the bustle of travellers hurrying to and fro, a tankard of good ale in his hand, when a hiss and a tug at his sleeve surprised him. A stooped man in a Jewish gaberdine stood at his elbow with a note. There was an address in the Jewish quarter and a polite request. A rich Jew's widow required an escort as far as Basel. Nick was amazed. This was unheard of – a Jewess travelling alone with a company of Christians? The protocol and dietary requirements alone made it out of the question, let alone all the other difficulties. About to shake his head, Nick hesitated. Wasn't this prejudice what he had been thinking about? He knew O'Dowd, for one, would not contemplate it and his men would certainly object, but might there be a way to arrange matters? He would have to think about it.

'I will consider,' he said to the little Jew, who was standing with his eyes cast down. The man nodded and moved away quickly as someone sounded a trumpet, and with a great clatter and jingle and beating of drum, Nick's courier service came to town.

They were a splendid sight. It had been agreed that the Rokesby colours and crest should be used for the enterprise. 'It means you will have a legitimate reason for all your comings and goings,' Tobias had said, with a sidelong look. So there they were. The men were dressed in black with his crest of a hooded falcon in gold on the breast, or on sable. In shining half-armour helmets and lances plumed and pennanted with black and gold they rode proudly into the square, O'Dowd at the head, scarlet with suppressed triumph. The party they were bringing seemed in good heart, chatting and easy.

And they were on time.

It was certainly a sight to gladden the heart, and Nick stayed where he was, grinning till his face hurt, letting them reap the reward of all the hard work and meticulous planning that had gone into this. It was not until much later, after all the greetings and backslapping, that Nick had the tale of it. It had gone well, all Toby's forethought and reconnaissance had paid dividends, word had started to go round already and there were more commissions coming in. It was apparent that the impressive turn-out insisted on by O'Dowd was an effective deterrent. Nick decided to keep his embryo plan for the widow to himself.

A day or two later, the escort reassembled in the square for the return journey, civilian travellers and their baggage organised and ready. Fletcher would meet them in Basel and take them on. Nick had messages and dispatches for Cecil from the Medici, the Embassy and the Antolini brothers. Feeling advertisement was often the best concealment, Nick had solved the problem of smuggling documents in his own way.

They set off, and as they left the town behind they were joined at a discreet distance by a small party of two men on white mules drawing a palanquin with closed curtains, followed by two others, armed and on horseback, in yellow livery. Nick would ride as connecting file, with an extra man of his own. As he passed to speak to the men-at-arms, the curtain was drawn back and the lady looked up at him, pulling aside her veil.

'You are the picture of a parfit gentil knight, Master Talbot,' she said. 'On your magnificent white charger with your hound at your side.'

'I hope my services will not be needed, signora,' he said. 'Trust our escort.' She smiled and withdrew and Nick turned to see

O'Dowd glowering.

'As far as you are concerned,' he told him, 'they are simply going our way. We give them the same assistance as we would any other poor devil if there's trouble. The money goes into the funds.'

O'Dowd grumbled. 'All this liberal thinking will get you killed one day. I don't know where you get it from.' Nick grinned at him.

'No, Kit, never mind,' he thought. 'One day, one day…your day of public enlightenment is not quite yet. Write on.'

It was a feather-bedded trip this time. The stages ticked away like the accurate seconds on M. Corner's expensive watch. The small difficulties of accommodation for the Jewish widow were pressed away with the smoothing-iron of money. Even the weather behaved. The widow bade him farewell in Basel and tried to reward him.

'Only the usual fee, signora. Paid to Master Fletcher if you please. If you are satisfied, tell your friends.'

She unfastened her girdle, finely embroidered and tasselled with gems, and pressed it on him.

'Take it…take it, Master Talbot. If ever you are in need, sir, as I was, my husband's name still opens doors. Mention Reuben da Gama.'

Nick bowed and kissed her hand. 'My thanks, Signora da Gama.'

'And what are you going to do with that lewd creature we travelled with?'

'Entertain, my lady.'

Chapter Twenty-Eight

London. 1596

The sweetish reek from the Barbary ape was particularly cloying tonight. It had cleared a space round Will Shakespeare's table in the White Harte, where it persisted in playing with his pens and paper. Will wished Nick would choose a different meeting place, one without exotic pets to draw attention. He was tired of the threadbare jokes suggesting the ape wrote his plays for him. Nick seemed to find them amusing. He was late and the playwright was beginning to feel conspicuous and slightly worried. He always worried at this point. The handover, to him, was fraught with danger and his dramatist's mind saw a succession of 'what ifs' cross the stage of his imagination. It was far too late to withdraw from the arrangement but he made up his mind that the next meeting would be more discreet. He was worried about his script changes and the heavy bag of money was a further source of anxiety.

This inn by the river was patronised by the lesser intelligentsia: lawyers and wits, small business men and minor members of the court who enjoyed the eccentricities of the landlord. Bonus points – there were clean rushes on the floor, the tables and benches were a comfortable distance apart: one could have a quiet and private conversation if required. Usually Will enjoyed the atmosphere, but tonight he was uneasy, irritated by the attentions of Rupert the ape, which both drew the eye of the other customers and isolated him in his corner.

At last, he could stand it no longer. He fought Rupert for

possession of the inkhorn and got up. He threw some coins on the table, fastened the inkhorn to his belt, decided against wresting the quill from the ape's wrinkled black fingers and, heavy wallet clasped under his arm, made his way to the door, Rupert knuckling along behind him. He was stopped at several tables to acknowledge acquaintance, exchange gossip and jokes and endure heavy-handed raillery regarding his friend from Gibraltar. The clinking wallet was burning a hole in his side, sweat beaded the prematurely balding head under the feathered hat.

'Got your new play in there, Will?' called someone. He started, turned to answer and collided with a man striding through the door.

Nicholas Talbot had arrived.

He was more than usually splendid tonight, Shakespeare saw. He wore a velvet cap with an ostrich plume that brushed fetchingly against his cheek, threatening to entangle his baroque pearl earring, and a furred cloak thrown negligently back over a doublet of black Florentine double-velvet resplendent with embroidered carnations. Breeches and boots were soft fawn leather and his codpiece fashionably discreet.

In a gloved and tasselled hand he held a large red-and-green parrot in a cage.

Ducking under the lintel, Nick greeted Will with a smacking buss on each cheek, Italian style, and the parrot yelled, 'Give us a kiss! Give us a kiss!' Will recoiled and Nick grasped him by the elbow and drew him back into the room, calling for the landlord and holding up the parrot, to the delight of the clientele.

'A present for you, Barney,' he shouted. 'To keep my friend

298

Rupert amused.' He clattered the cage down on a table. 'Watch your fingers, the old devil's got a beak as sharp as his wits.'

The landlord and his wife and daughter, the potboys and most of the customers, crowded round the table, slapping Nick on the back and trying to get a view of the parrot.

'-----' yelled the bird. ' ------ your ----------' The landlady shrieked, clapping her hands over her daughter's ears and hustling her out of the room to a roar of laughter. Will backed out of the crowd and sought obscurity by the door.

'What light from yonder window breaks—' continued the parrot. 'Kiss my arse—'

'I have endeavoured to raise the level of his conversation,' said Nick. 'As you see, with only partial success. He is yours, my friend. Try him with French. Now, if you will excuse us, Master Shakespeare and I have an appointment with two charming ladies and a capon or two. They felt Lucifer here would be *de trop.*'

'*Merde!*' screamed Lucifer.

'Precisely. My apologies to your dame, Barney. A cloth over his cage will quiet him.' With which he fended off Rupert, who was taking an interest in the lining of his cloak, and made a graceful exit, drawing Master Shakespeare in his wake. He smelled expensive.

Once out in the street, Will rounded on him.

'What are you about! Are you mad? This was supposed to be a discreet meeting – now the world and his wife will know!'

'Of course. And they will talk about the parrot. What do you suppose was in the bottom of his cage? The inspectors at the dock were laughing so much they let us through in a blink. They are not letting even my couriers through without a signature these days. Unless you can get the Queen herself to sign for them, I must find a way. If you don't like it, fetch 'em yourself.'

Will subsided, muttering, 'I'm sorry. I hadn't realised.'

'You'll like these. Come on, I have a boat – and I really do have an appointment.'

'Who is it this time? A woman, or your friend at court? I happen to know your light of love is out of town.'

'Mind your own business. Stick to the playhouse, Will, and you'll come to no harm. Our author sends his regards, by the way. And if you make any more changes, I have his permission to chop off your inky index finger.'

Nick obeyed the curt summons to enter and pushed open the door.

There he was, the spider of Whitehall, little Robert Cecil, second Lord Burghley, feet dangling, floating his gossamer threads over half the world.

Cecil thoughtfully surveyed the tall, clear-eyed young man who stood before him, assessing the breadth of shoulder and the hand resting light and confident on his sword-hilt, the other tapping a feathered cap against his leg.

'Hm. I see what Ned Faulds meant. I doubted his judgment in recommending you for this task, but now—'

His melon-rind face was yellow in the candlelight and he was frowning.

'Let us hope all this growth has not stunted your intellect.' There was a little ship in a bottle on his desk and he stroked it with the end of his quill.

'Hm. Yes. Sit. You are recovered? Good. Now, there is much

you will not know. Let us take a little wine to help us through this dry stuff.' He gestured to Nick to pour for them both and settled back in his chair, legs dangling, one foot feeling for the footstool. Wary of all this familiarity, Nicholas placed the stool for him and poured the wine.

'The Queen is ailing, Master Talbot. She is thinking of the succession and will not discuss it. She may well fear her own death and feel that to speak of it will bring it closer. As we all do. Or it may be policy. As she says herself, people were ever prone to worship the rising rather than the setting sun. Now: at present we are at peace. It is for her advisers to look about them, to safeguard that peace and the present prosperity. The wrong choice may wreck our ship of state; sink it in the breakers of religious upheaval once again. Or bring war with our neighbours across the Narrow Sea.' He gazed into his goblet.

'There are a number of possibilities. As always, her Majesty prefers to juggle and keep her counsel. I think her wise – to announce a successor openly and too soon, well... As it is, the rival claimants must tread softly, and as long as I know where they are and what they are doing, I am content. One faction, however, is by nature rash and presumptuous. A pre-emptive strike would be their style. We must be ready.' He looked across.

'Are you following me?'

'Yes, my lord. In principle. But I don't know who you mean.'

'How could you? But any fool who studies history books or spends his time hanging around the Court listening to gossip could tell you. It is no secret who may consider they have a right to govern England. And Scotland. They each have their supporters. What we don't know is what they propose to do about it.' Cecil pushed a scroll of parchment towards him. 'Study that. You will see it is marked. Take your time.'

The diagram was very clear and quite alarming.

Cecil was watching him over the rim of his cup. 'Well, Master Talbot, what are your conclusions?'

Nicholas thought for a while, turning his goblet in his fingers. He did not find the question strange until afterwards.

'The French have ever been our natural enemy,' he said at last. 'The Narrow Sea divides us and we have lost our foothold in Calais. A Spanish monarch would plunge us back into religious chaos. So might—' He paused, wondering if he was digging a hole for himself. He was in deep water. 'I know little of the Scottish court, my stay was short, only that the King has kept his head and his throne for nearly thirty years. That must tell us something.' He added, musing, 'My mother was a Scot. A Melville.'

'Good thing she wasn't a Douglas,' muttered Cecil.

'My lord?'

'Never mind. Melville—' He made a note. 'A natural preference, then.'

'No, my lord. I know nothing of any kin north of the border. But we have been at peace with our nearest neighbours for a while now. The King seems to have struck a balance between his beliefs and the Catholics – could he make it work in England?'

'There are those, Master Talbot, who would prefer him not to try. As you saw.' He reached across, took the scroll, tore it in pieces and threw them into the fire. 'Remember those names and who is kin to whom – not easy, they all seem related to one another. Positively incestuous. On the face of it, your task is simple. You are to deliver a personal and private letter from the Queen to King James in person. To no one else, do you understand?'

'Why me, my lord?'

'You have caught the Queen's eye, and no doubt have caught his Scottish Majesty's as well if all I hear is true. You know how to conduct yourself and it is time to move you on. Keep your wits about you and your eyes and ears open. The Earl of Mar, who you have met, is a useful man – sensible. But trust no one, even if you find some kinfolk at court. An escort to wherever the King is – I understand he is on a Progress, his excuse for a hunting trip – as I say, an escort will be provided at Berwick and a pass over the border. Take men with you and leave discreetly, no need to kill your horses and draw attention. Any urgent message send to me post through Lord Hunsdon's son, John Carey, in the East March.' He handed over a packet and a heavy purse. 'Contacts and bribe money. The letter will be brought to you. You are on the Queen's business, Master Talbot. Fit yourself accordingly.' He nodded dismissal and Nick rose and bowed. 'Did they not teach you courtly manners in the playhouse? I shall send a dancing master. Practise!'

Nick returned thoughtfully to Shipwrights' Lane to find Toby returned, his booted feet stretched to the fire, his lanky length disposed at ease in the best armchair, a mug of ale in his fist. He raised it to Nick.

'This is the life, my friend. I confess I'm glad we met.' He rose, grinning, and came to meet him. 'Food on the way. You're looking very fine tonight, Nick. Been to see your dangerous dark lady?'

'I am the burnt child who fears the fire. I doubt we have seen
the last of each other – indeed I very much hope not – but I'm
not looking for that sort of trouble. I have enough. Any letters?'
Toby shook his head.

Alice brought in a tray loaded with food, and set the table
with platters and goblets, bobbing to Nick with a shy smile
of welcome, signing that his bed would be made ready. Nick
threw off his cloak and sat down to struggle with his boots.
They were new and an excellent fit and Toby took pity on him
before toeing off his own.

'You need a valet, Nick. And from the look of things you'll
soon have one. Tell me, how does a poor player pay for all this?
No, don't answer that. I said when I came, no questions asked,
and I meant it. But if you have troubles, share them. If you
like. Is it Mowbray again?'

'Let's eat.' He fetched a bottle of wine and the two young men
dispatched their meal in silence, elbows spread, only slowing
down when they got to the excellent blackberry pudding.
Tobias fetched his pipe from his pack and sat back, puffing
luxuriously. 'Well?'

'You first.'

'Very well. Lucius is most disappointed we had no trouble
on the way and business is booming. Your investment is safe.
What's next?' Nick got up, laughing, and fetched another bottle.
If he couldn't trust Toby the world was a sad place indeed.

'What's next is what looks like being a tricky enterprise.
I'd appreciate your help. Up to a point. Look, I'd better tell
you...'

He began at the beginning, how he had become embroiled

with Faulds, and through him Lord Burghley, and why he had made his choice. He told him about Rokesby and Kate. He left out any reference to Kit Marlowe, attributing Tom Walsingham's patronage to his political connections. 'It suits him. And we have mutual friends.' He explained the wretched business with Gerard and his own reservations about turning spy.

'I think Cecil knows about those. This business is different. It sounds – an interesting opportunity.'

There was a long silence, Toby apparently asleep. Nick selected an apple from the bowl and bit into it. Toby opened blue eyes, serious for once. His pipe had gone out and he refilled it thoughtfully.

'One thing seems to trouble you greatly, Nicholas. This business of Father Gerard. I did not understand that and you were in no case to speak of it. You say he feared he might recant. You saved him from that. It was a merciful end – you should not be uneasy. You took the devil of a risk for him as things are.'

'That's the devil of it, the way things are. I wish you could have heard the talk that night at Cobham. These are men who look ahead, Toby, thinkers. We are on the brink of something, my friend is right. The printing press has started an avalanche – when all men and women can read and reason and write down their reasonings and pass them on, surely then, surely, we shall see an end to this bigotry.'

'I can see a sticky end for you, friend, if you broadcast these ideas outside these four walls. What is your frequent saying? Establish your position. Why don't we get on and do just that. One step at a time, Nick. Oh, and by the way, show me a woman who can reason and I'll marry her.'

'I do know one,' thought Nick. 'I'm going to marry her myself.'

There was still no word from Kate. Nick had written again and was beginning to think of defying Cecil and going to Rokesby. It was a week before Cecil's letter arrived and if Nick thought he could relax a while and enjoy the peace of a household comprising the taciturn Toby, the ever-discreet Michael and his silent wife, he was mistaken. True to his word, Cecil sent a dancing master and for three hours a day he made Nick's life hell teaching him the manners expected at court and the intricate steps of the dance. Nick exorcised the man and his pomades with fencing practice and schooling the horses. Cecil's letter came when he was hanging over the stall in the yard with Michael, admiring Rowena's foal.

'I shall call you Hotspur,' he said, 'Little beauty. I think he'll be black, like his sire.'

'Aye, sir, his coat's coming already. She's done us proud.' A lathered horse drew up at the gate, blowing, and Michael tutted in disgust.

'No urgency to be apparent, I thought my lord said. Is that not right?' asked Nick. The panting messenger nodded, handed over a package impressively sealed and stitched and was off again, passing Toby as he went.

'Are we off?'

'Looks like it. Michael, take a message out to Sergeant Ponsonby will you? No hurry. We'll leave at first light.'

'Best get organised, then,' said Toby. Nick nodded and took the package inside to study. It contained two dossiers, one in code addressed to the King ending with the number 10, Cecil's codeword, and a letter with the Queen's seal. The dossier in clear was a list of contacts at the Scottish court, accreditation, a pass into Scotland and most surprising of all, a summary of Nick's Melville connections. It appeared he had a great-uncle who was Scottish ambassador to Elizabeth's court and two distant cousins, Colin and Charles, attending King James.

'Handy,' said Toby. 'Strange your father never mentioned it.' Nick shrugged. No doubt he had his reasons.

Chapter Twenty-Nine

Meeting with their escort at Shoreditch Nick and Tobias started north. The dawn broke misty and chill, the stubbled fields brown with a hint of pale green where vulnerable early shoots had been encouraged by the Indian summer, now long gone. Sheep in the new wool of winter coats scattered the slopes like grains of rice; naked trees stood with their feet in pools of red and gold. Apart from peacefully grazing cattle they had the world to themselves. This was the country Nick had sworn to protect and he fell in love with it all over again.

Only Nick had ever been further north than York, and Tobias had taken the precaution of including two Borderers in their company. 'It's as foreign as abroad up there,' he said. 'Even speak a different lingo. So I'm told.'

Fleeing south for some peace and quiet ('running away from

some piece of skulduggery, more like,' said Toby), Wee Ralphie Crawford did not exactly fit the elegant requirements of the Rokesby escort service, being short, square and bandy-legged with a fearsome scar. Nor did his low-browed compatriot, Jamie Turnbull. No one ever mentioned Jamie's nose. Both men were excellent scouts, however, and worth double their pay to O' Dowd. The rest of their small company was made up of pikemen and archers, hand-picked by Ponsonby. They were nine all told, a number sufficiently small to avoid attracting interest and a sufficient deterrent to opportunist attacks. According to Toby.

His theory appeared to be working and they made good progress. Each man had a remount carrying his gear, Nick not trusting to the availability of decent post-horses for so many. For the most part, the roads were appalling, rutted and broken, save for the occasional stretch of Roman paving. Fearghas ran free in the grass alongside, never far from Nick's boot. They maintained a steady cavalry pace, walk a mile, trot for two, canter for three, lead a while, sparing their horses, and once or twice a messenger flashed past them with a shout. They broke the journey at Stamford for a much-needed briefing, and again south of Nottingham. Once into the Dales, the landscape changed dramatically. Arable and pastureland gave way to crags and hillsides of grey stone, hedgerows replaced by miles of drystone walls badged with lichen and overhung with gorse. Leaning trees dotted the valleys and hillsides and the east wind blew.

Huddled in their cloaks they picked up speed. At the next inn, Tobias sloped off to speak to the innkeeper. He came back with two tankards of ale and dropped down on the bench where

Nick sat, with Fearghas slit-eyed between his knees, playing with the hound's ears.

'He doesn't reckon much to finding another decent inn. And the last messenger going south says the weather's closing in.' Nick shrugged.

'It was never going to be a good time of year. We've been lucky so far.'

'I'll see if I can find some rough weather gear and a couple more ponies. Make an early start, eh?'

The wind had a sharper bite when they set off again, blowing away the mists in the valleys. A weak sun made its appearance, and Jamie Turnbull lifted his nose and sniffed the air, shaking his head gloomily. Large birds planed overhead, choughs started up, chirring, flying low to the grass as the riders passed. Hares sat up and looked at them, deer showed a pale scut as they bounded away. Small game abounded and they fed well, sleeping at night rolled in blankets in a ring of horses. Nick had his pad out a great deal along the way, drawing, and had little of note to report in his journal. Their steady pace was eating up the miles and by the seventh day they were nearing Border country. The nature of the beasts they saw was changing, the cattle shorter-legged and shaggy, with wide horns, the sheep all colours from beige to parti-coloured, their fleeces long and draggled. Deer and goats roamed the hillsides, and later on Nick reined in to watch a pair of eagles circling a distant crag.

'It's all too quiet,' said Tobias and began to set a guard.

The country grew wilder and more inhospitable, flat viridian expanses of bog interspersed with outcrops of rock, clumps of brush and furze offering excellent cover. Nick called a halt and gave orders for the men to change horses and get on their fighting gear.

'Wondered when you'd wake up,' grumbled Toby. They certainly looked a troop not to be trifled with as they remounted and made sure of their weapons. Each man had a pair of wheel lock pistols, sword, dagger and pike and weighed another sixty pounds in the quilted jacks interleaved with plates of iron. Three of them were bowmen and slung their longbows across their backs, still faster in a fight than a crossbow.

They pressed on into border country, the low sun settling into the long northern twilight. The wind had dropped and fat flakes of snow began to drift down. It was ominously quiet as they passed a burnt-out farmhouse and a wrecked stone tower, and they forged on through what had been fertile cultivated land, now a wasteland of burned and trampled crops. Visibility deteriorated rapidly and Nick, consulting with Toby, sent the two scouts on ahead, waiting in what cover there was for the all-clear whistle, moving on from covert to covert, Fearghas leashed and quiet. It was wretchedly slow progress. The first snow had melted and now began to freeze, making the going treacherous. Nick had adjusted to the weight of his jack by now and was only miserably conscious of the snow creeping in down the back of his neck, chafing the skin.

They waited in the shelter of an overhanging rock for the next signal to proceed. It never came. Instead, Wee Ralphie appeared out of a flurry of snow, on foot and quietly leading his horse.

'Fair amount of movement up ahead, sounds like cattle, moving fast.'

'Make ready,' said Nick. 'Horses under the overhang and keep 'em quiet. Where's Jamie?'

'Taken cover, sir, like you said.'

Nick could hear them now, hooves drumming, beasts lowing and the occasional curse and whack of a stave. Nick dismounted and tied the hound to a sturdy branch. A smear of red grew and brightened on the underside of the low cloud.

'None of our business,' thought Nick, climbing back on to Nero. At that moment, one of their horses spooked and whinnied and two of the drovers wheeled their scrubby horses aside with a shout. In no time, their rock was surrounded with fierce hairy men, wielding swords and axes and yelling with throats of brass.

Like clockwork, the pikemen formed square, pistols ready, the archers behind. The shower of arrows and discharge of pistols stopped the charge for a moment and Nick and Toby drew swords and rode out with two of the others, two to each flank. Nick spared a thought for his friend, who always seemed to read his mind and then was in the thick of it, trying to drive their attackers towards the pikes. The move failed and Nick yelled to the pikemen to attack. They came on fiercely and fast, driving into the centre, laying about them, the bowmen picking their targets now. Nick dodged an axe and lifted Nero to strike with his hooves at a man behind Toby, slicing sideways as he did so. Their mounts were taller and heavier than their enemies' and in the barging and shoving it was beginning to tell. Even so they were outnumbered and the fighting was desperate. Nick took a jarring blow across the shoulder blades and another to the shoulder that knocked him forward onto Nero's neck as an axe whistled past his head. Nero plunged and kicked, Nick heard the crunch and a cut-off shriek.

The glow in the sky grew suddenly brighter and over the noise

311

of the fighting and the frightened bellowing of the milling cattle came the thunder of many hooves and furious yelling.

'So this is it,' thought Nick, parrying a blow and slashing the man's arm. 'Sorry, Kate...' He hacked and cut his way to where he could see Toby's fair head. Tobias had lost his horse and his helmet and Nick swung him up back to back on Nero.

'To me!' they yelled as one man and their men, blessedly disciplined, fought their way to reform as a ring of steel, breath blowing steam from man and horse. As they slowly gave way to get the rock at their back, a horde of screaming riders with torches swept past on both sides and fell on their attackers with a roar of fury. Nick did a quick headcount. Two down, one missing. He spotted Wee Ralphie on the ground in danger of being trampled and flung himself down. He ran through a forest of legs to drag his man inside the bristling circle of pikes. He couldn't see the other man and turned to fend off a marauder with hair bristling as red as his flaming torch, stopping just in time as the rider held up a hand.

The fight was over.

Some of the raiders were disappearing, hotly pursued into the dark, others lay in groaning heaps on the ground. The new arrivals turned their attention to rounding up the scattered cattle and horses, and the man facing Nick dismounted and approached. Tobias slid off Nero, staggered and came to stand at Nick's back. The man spoke at length. Nick, his ears ringing from a bang on the head, could not understand a word of what he was saying. He took off his helmet and as his head cleared he began to filter the dialect. Toby was quicker; he had fought alongside such men.

'He's thanking us for hindering the raid. These are his cattle and that is his home burning.' There was a gurgling scream as one of the newcomers struck down at a man on the ground.

'He's saying he hopes that's not one of ours. He says come back with him and he'll see us safe.'

'Safe! For the love of Christ, from what now!'

'He thinks there may be retaliation…what d'you reckon?'

'I reckon they're all mad.'

'We've nothing to lose if we go quietly. We can't take on this lot – they're in a blood-frenzy.' The chief had turned away and was calling his rampaging men to order. They came slowly back, putting away their bloodied swords, and gradually the beasts, sheep and goats among them, were gathered up and driven back with the prisoners the way they had come. A man with his cheek sliced open had found Oberon, Nick's remount, and seemed disposed to keep him until his chief caught him a buffet on the side of his head and extorted a garbled apology.

Of their own party, several were wounded, one seriously, one horse was dead and another had to be destroyed. Wee Ralphie had a broken leg. His fellow-countryman was still missing.

'Where is he?'

'He's a Turnbull, sir. Ye'll no' be expecting him to fight his kin.'

The smell of the burning homesteads stayed with Nick all the way to Wark. Tobias and he and the rest of their men had turned to and helped to build makeshift shelters for the wounded and dispossessed, in an atmosphere of silent anger. It was full dark again before the work was done. Red Robert Kerr and his men had given them food and shelter for the night and sent them on their way with an escort ('they murdering Elliots are about') as far as Kelso, where they followed the Tweed to Wark Castle. Sir John Carey, Warden of the East March, was meeting them there and had a party of the King's men to take Nick on to Smailholme where the King was staying for the hunt. Toby had no pass and would turn back at this point.

'A pity you missed my brother,' observed Sir John as they sat down to dinner. 'He's off on a hot trod – I doubt he'll be back before you leave. I'll pass on the news about the Turnbulls.'

'Hot…?'

'Raiding the raiders,' put in Toby helpfully. Nick snorted. The man always knew everything. He was going to miss him.

Chapter Thirty

In spite of an early start, the King had gone to bed when Nick clattered in with his escort. Glad of the respite, Nick unpacked the clothes suitable for an audience with the King, laid them out to give the creases a chance, saw Fearghas fed and watered, rolled into bed and slept soundly. Water and bread and ale were brought to him in the morning, and he presented himself brushed and washed and clean-shaven in the antechamber to the King's rooms. This was not the palace nor one of James' official residences, but the country home of Lord Abercrombie, councillor to the King. Nicholas looked about him, amused. Compared with what he had heard of the pomp and beggaring expense of a Progress made by Elizabeth, little appeared to have been done. The rooms here were plain and workmanlike, the chill of the stone walls mitigated with tapestries far from new. Solid furniture battered from years of use gleamed with recent polish, certainly, the air sweetened by fresh rushes on the floor, but no sign of ostentation. He was to find this typical of James' court; the only extravagance was indulged in by his wife.

A Gentleman of the Bedchamber approached and offered to relieve him of his letters. He refused politely.

'Your pardon, sir. I am to deliver this letter from my queen into the King's own hand.' Annoyed, the man stalked off and presently another came, and another. Nick stubbornly refused to part with the letter he had come so far to deliver. Did James mean to offer a snub? Some said he was harbouring resentment over his mother's execution.

This proved not to be the case. Admitted at last into the King's presence, he found an impatient James standing at the window with his back to him, tapping his fingers on the glass.

'My advisers are overprotective,' he said. 'A letter from my dear cousin is of the first importance.' He turned and his long sallow face brightened. Nick knelt. He had done his best with his appearance. The well-cut green doublet flattered him. His hair had grown and curled close to his skull like the poll of a bull, the tanned skin was reddened over his cheekbones by the recent cold winds and the cut over one eyebrow gave him a piratical slant. James came forward with his awkward gait, lifted and embraced him.

'I have not forgotten your last visit. You shall dine with us, Master Talbot. You have cousins at court – they have been summoned and will see you horsed. Yes, you see I am forewarned of your kinfolk. Our good friend Cecil has seen to that.' He left one arm round Nick's shoulder and drew him to a stool by his chair. It's true, then, what they say, thought Nick.

'The letter.' Nick drew it out and gave it to him. 'May I hope to take a reply, your Majesty?'

'We shall consider. We would keep you with us for a time. You shall have entertainment after your long journey.' He set aside his letter from Elizabeth and twisted to peer out of the window. 'The weather holds. We hunt the deer today, Master Talbot. You shall attend me later and tell me of our sister England. We must make ready now, the days are short. Go and find your cousins – we shall have sport!'

Nick bowed himself out, marvelling at the informality. It was lucky, he felt, to have caught the King away from court. James' love of the chase was well known, as was his liking for young men. 'Oh well,' thought Nick. 'I should be able to deal with that.'

He fetched Fearghas, and, directed to the stables, he found his cousins, Charles Melville and his nephew Young Colin, admiring his two horses. Both had the Melville features, Nick only the colouring and the eyes. Charles Melville was shorter than Nick, stern and unsmiling; Colin's face had not lost its childish roundness, snubnosed and freckled with an obstinate chin. Eager to find out more about his connections, Nick's questions were brushed aside.

'I see you don't need the nags we brought,' said Young Colin enviously. 'We heard about the boar-hunt. You've been lucky, cousin. Take care you don't get your comeuppance today.'

'Enough,' said his uncle. 'That is no way to speak. Welcome, cousin. Colin means only to remind you to watch your back. Others remember the boar-hunt – you were perhaps wise to leave when you did.'

'I had little choice in the matter, sir. It is a great pleasure to find kin of my mother, I thought I had none.'

'Your mother is not spoken of,' said the repressive Charles Melville. 'But blood-kin is blood-kin, and so you will find us. Stay back today.'

'I am not here to distinguish myself, cousin,' said Nick angrily. 'I shall do as I see fit.' Melville made a Scottish noise in his nose and turned away. Nick took the reins from a grinning groom and rode off, decidedly ruffled.

His plan to stay unnoticed was doomed to failure. The sight of Fearghas cantering on his leash beside Nero reminded a number of the court of the boar-hunt and several came to ride alongside and gossip. Lord Ruthven had left the court and they heard the old Queen was ailing. Francis Bothwell's wife was back. Was it true her husband had sought refuge in England? The troubles on the border were a little improved since the coming of the younger Carey. Had Nick met him? No? Pity Robert did not get on with his brother.

Fearghas was allowed to bring down a hare or two and towards the end of the day's sport, Mar dropped back.

'Welcome back, Master Talbot.'

'My lord.'

'You had a little trouble on the way.'

'A common enough trouble in these parts, I believe, my lord.' Mar smiled.

'Perhaps you are a tall tree to attract the lightning, Master Talbot. Why are you here?'

'To bring a letter from my queen, my lord, and bear back a reply.'

'Is that all?'

'My lord?'

'Very well, young man. The King favours you. Remember where your duty lies and you will come to no harm.' He cantered off with a wave and Nick made his way back with some food for thought.

The T-shaped board ran the length of the room, covered with tapestries, cushioned benches either side. Branched candles marched down the centre, flambeaux on the walls flared in the draught. Servants were laying silver platters heaped with meats of all kinds: venison, a great baron of beef, geese and capons swimming in their own fat, raised pies and pasties, custards and tarts and gilded marchpane, tall confections of spun sugar. Lord Abercrombie might stint on decoration, but he knew what was important. This was indeed a feast fit for a king. Toasts and more toasts were drunk as the meats cooled and when they set to at last, Nick had to endure a great deal of banter, good-natured and otherwise, when he produced his silver fork, brought from Venice.

'All the rage in Town,' he said airily, 'saves on the cleaning.' He got on with his food, keen to question Colin on this matter of kinship. The Melvilles seemed markedly reluctant to talk about it. By now, however, Young Colin was considerably the worse for drink and answered readily enough.

'It's quite simple, really. My distant uncle Andrew – sorry, Sir Andrew, was sent to the Tower – made himself unpopular with his preaching and evangelising – lives in Paris now. Well, *his* cousin Charles – same name as my father, rather confusing – had a sister Mary, the youngest. Now Charles and his brothers were killed in a raid and the place burned to the ground—'

'Who by?'

'Never mind. There was only Mary left. She was bound for the convent but Uncle Andrew intervened – against his beliefs, you see. So she went to France to marry this fellow my uncle had picked out. Thirsty work this.' He paused to fill both their goblets. Nick, a little lost among all these uncles and cousins, prompted him.

'Go on, you're getting to the interesting part. Mary was Sir Andrew's cousin—'

'Do you know, you keep a very cool head, cousin.' His speech was beginning to slur.

'My mother's name was Marie – it can't be the same person.'

'I suppose she Frenchified it when she ran off with Jack Talbot.'

'What!'

'I believe he was campaigning in Liège at the time. Suppose he was in Paris for some…er—' A servant offered a platter of meat and his other neighbour nudged him.

'The King raises his cup to you,' he hissed. Nicholas pulled himself together and bowed, accepting the wine but feeling it would choke him.

'You were a crazy bastard with the boar, Nicholas Talbot!' roared Colin, his cheeks flushed. He caught Nick's eye and sobered slightly. 'No, no, no, m'father says they were wed right and tight – Uncle Andrew saw to that, being a minister as he was. Married them himself, gather it was a fine scandal at the

319

time…she was practically at the altar with this count or some such.'

A skirl of pipes heralded the ceremonious entry of a broad platter of what looked like a bag-pudding in a steaming pool of gravy. The heat and noise and smell of humanity in the room were tremendous and Nick's stomach turned. He had had enough for one day.

'She must have been a fine, brave woman,' Colin went on, now arrived at the maudlin stage. 'Ask my uncle, he looked into it all when we heard you were coming – in case…you know—'

'I'm sure he did,' thought Nicholas.

A thin dark man at the King's side with hair down to his shoulders reached for a lute to begin a ballad of exquisite melancholy, and Nick was alone with his thoughts.

The song ended, the King rose to leave. Nick hauled up the indiscreet Colin and handed him over to his uncle, who was looking very grim.

'I'm pleased to see one sprig of the Melvilles can hold his drink. You're a young fool, nephew, be off with you and hold your tongue.'

'Who murdered my grandfather, sir?'

Charles Melville sighed. 'Colin and his loose mouth. That is not for you to concern yourself, Nicholas Talbot. It has been dealt with. Whatever lord Cecil sent you to do, get on and do it. And be careful.'

Fearghas pushed a wet nose into Nick's hand.

'That was a princely gift, my lad. Watch yourself.'

In the few days that followed, he roamed the castle and grounds with Fearghas, rode out hawking with Young Colin, gleaned gossip and wrote up his report. James summoned him from time to time for long sessions of question and answer about the state of things in 'our sister England', and talk of poetry and current ideas.

'This is a man of great intellect,' noted Nick in his journal, to write to Kate later. 'An unhappy man, albeit he seems to love his family. His queen spends money like water, money he does not appear to have. It is a poor country, but its people are great in spirit. I would rather be a friend of Scotland than her enemy.'

Chapter Thirty-One

The court moved on to Selkirk for more hunting and feasting. Robert Scott of Buccleugh was more open-handed than Abercrombie, and a ball was to be held on the last night before the hunt moved on to Liddlesdale. James had still not replied to the Queen's letter.

The dancing was a strange affair of twirling, leaping and kicking, hands on hips or overhead, mixed with the court dances he had learned. He was given a cup of wine and stood watching as the groaning and skirling gave way to a stately pavane. James had imported the volta from the English court and the tempo changed again. Nick had noticed a woman standing against the wall with a sullen expression. Among the heads all shades of red from sandy to deep auburn, her hair stood out black as a crow's feather. Her full red mouth was sulky and her foxy-brown eyes burned with impatience, her foot tapping the floor. His cousin followed his gaze.

'Marianne, Countess of Bothwell. French. Her husband is in France in disgrace. Come, I'll present you to her – she lacks a partner.'

Nick bowed over her hand and her expression lightened as he led her out to take their place behind a short stocky Scot manfully heaving up a woman twice his bulk. Nick smiled down at his countess. The volta was definitely a dance for a strong partner. He tried out his rusty French in a clumsy parody of courtly usage as instructed by the dancing master.

'I am persuaded you will fly like thistledown, milady.' To his surprise he was rewarded with a giggle and a flirtatious tap. They bounced down the set clapping and high-kicking and when it came to the volta he was ready. He grasped the bottom of her stays fore and aft as instructed, sorely tempted to put his hands elsewhere, whirled her high into the air and decorously set her down with no more than a stray finger out of place. He was about to apologise when her nail scratched his palm, her eyelids drooped and she smiled as she followed the pattern of the dance. Next time the steps brought them together he went a little further and as he brought her slowly down she leaned in to him, breasts squeezed together level with his mouth. He blew gently and she widened her eyes. He caught his cousin's eye over her shoulder. Colin winked and raised an eyebrow.

'Why not?' he thought. 'She knows what she's doing and I need a woman, by God.' The measure changed to a galliard and his lady leaned on his arm, leading him off the floor, fanning herself.

'Such an energetic partner,' she said. 'A breath of air, I think.'

She pinched the back of his hand and slipped away through a side door. After a moment, he followed. 'True to you in my fashion, Kate,' he thought. It was icy out on the terrace and he could not see the countess at first. He shrugged, about to go in. He was not going to hunt for her. Then he saw her footsteps plain in the snow and she was there, framed in the doorway of the tower, beckoning. He went to her.

'Will you dance again, my lady?'

'I know a better place for dancing, m'sieur.' He bent to kiss her and she broke away, laughing, and fled before him up a long winding stair. He caught her up in a small room with a curved outer side, hung with arras and with a fire burning merrily in the grate. A tray of food and wine stood ready. She had vanished into the bedchamber beyond where the only light was a banked-down fire. They made great play with laces and buttons and Nick would have prolonged the game, but the room was chill on their heated flesh and they burrowed hastily under the quilt to dance the oldest dance of all.

That first encounter was urgent and satisfying: they lay entwined in the half-dark recovering themselves and murmuring quietly. She ran her hand idly down his body and stopped as her fingers found the puckered groove along his ribs. She started up.

'I would see you—' Nick heard the rattle and scrape of the tinderbox, light bloomed as she lit candles. He pushed himself up on the bolster, enjoying the plump outline of her body curving to stir the fire. She came back to him shivering and lay beside him questioning and numbering his scars until he pushed away her exploring hands and resumed a more leisurely exploration of his own.

He woke later to find the candles guttered, the fire out and the room bitter cold. Marianne was in the doorway, wrapped in the quilt over her petticoats, his clothes in her arms, listening. He could hear the animals outside beginning to stir. Angry with himself for falling asleep, he got up and went out to her. She held out his shirt.

'Quickly, my maid will be coming. Here, dress by the fire—' A sword scraped on stone and she broke off, fear widening her eyes. The outer door closed softly and booted feet ascended the stair. Terrified, she thrust him naked behind the arras and fled into the other chamber to bundle his clothes under the bed. Cursing himself for a fool, Nick had no time to do anything other than stay where he was as the door opened and someone, a heavy man by the sound of him, entered the room.

'You are up betimes, my dear.'

Her husband? He was supposed to be in France.

'I heard the horses, Francis.'

I wish to God I had, thought Nick. This is a ridiculous situation to get myself into.

'Why are you here, my love – the risk—'

'No one knows. Nor must they. Don't stand there shivering – cover yourself. I want you out of here, I am expecting company.'

'But Francis—'

'Hurry. Never mind your maid; you'll have to dress yourself for once. Tell no one I am here. Do you understand?' Nick listened to him bundling her out of the room and throwing logs on the fire in growing dismay. He was freezing, all the hairs on his body erect, and he clenched his teeth to stop them chattering. Presently the door opened again and two pairs of boots crunched on the rushes. Stools scraped.

'We shall not be disturbed,' came the first voice. 'You were not seen?' Nick pricked up his ears.

'No, my lord.'

'Well?'

'Everything is in train, my lord. All that is needed is the time set. The route is unchanged?' Nick's treacherous nose began to tickle and he pinched the bridge fiercely, breathing shallow through his mouth.

'The King leaves in an hour. He stays at St Mary's for the hunt and should be at the Devil's Beef Tub at dusk. If all goes as planned, they will be awaiting him at the Hermitage for a long time.' An obsequious chuckle. 'How many men have you?'

'Enough, my lord. One good shot will do the trick. With the King down, surprise will do the rest.' Nick had forgotten he desperately wanted to sneeze and strained his ears for a name. He could see nothing through the web of the arras and dared not move to find a chink.

'You will only have one chance. You trust your marksman?'

'Longnose Wattie is the best. He takes the papingay every year.'

'Ruthven will be close to the King. He must not be harmed. That is understood?'

'Yes, my lord.'

'To it then.' Money clinked. 'The rest when it is done.' Boots tramped and the door closed. Naked as he was Nick had never felt more vulnerable. He could not feel his feet and he was sure something unpleasant was crawling up his leg. *The King was to be assassinated.* He was in possession of vital information and was completely helpless. Francis Stewart, Lord Bothwell was still in the room. If he didn't make a move soon Nick was going to have to, speed and surprise his only weapon – he had to stop the King leaving. Bothwell was moving about, he seemed to be locking something away. There was the slither and drag of a heavy cloak. Yes – the door opened and shut and Nick was out and into the other room dragging on his clothes.

He hopped across the floor struggling into his boots and pulled at the door.

It was locked. Unbelieving, he tugged with all his strength and could not budge it. He looked round for something to force it and could find nothing, not even a firedog. He ran to the embrasure in the outer wall and peered out. His head swam and his scalp prickled. It was fully fifty feet down to where fresh snow carpeted the terrace. Nick had a poor head for heights, even the top gallery in the theatre troubled him, and he drew back, the backs of his knees trembling. He raced into the bedchamber to find that no better, an embrasure and a sheer drop to the frozen moat. He sat on the bed for a moment to collect himself. Think. Surely Marianne would be coming back, or a servant.

'The King leaves in an hour.' That was what – twenty minutes, half an hour ago? He could not afford to wait. He went back to the door to examine the lock, perhaps lever it off or manipulate the key. The key was missing and the lock on the other side. Where in God's name was Marianne? Last night had been madness.

He made himself calm down. Taking a deep breath, he went back to the embrasure. It was narrow, made for an archer. He was too broad. No, just an excuse, he could go sideways. The

He risked a glance down. It was a very long way and he looked at the wall instead. There was what looked like a rainspout about ten feet down to his right and beyond, another embrasure. For the first time he examined the cracks between the massive stones. They were full of frozen snow. His biceps were cracking with the strain of supporting his weight, he must find a foothold – and soon. Winding the end of the sheet round one wrist, he let himself down to hang full stretch, brought up a trembling hand to take the knife from his mouth, and reached down as far as he could to drive it into a crack. He had to scrape away snow and ice before he could get a purchase and his shoulder was on fire by the time he had forced the blade in far enough. It bent, but took his weight and he gained momentary relief. The bitter cold was affecting his grip and his hands were beginning to slide. The thought of the next step appalled him. He pressed closer to the tower for friction and let go of the sheet. There was a moment of weightlessness and then he had grasped the knife and swung across to the waterspout. Spreadeagled, he sought with his foot for the top of the embrasure. It was free of frost and gave him a toehold. His calf began to cramp and not thinking what lay below he freed one hand, found his dagger and drove it in as far over as he could reach. He was directly above the embrasure now and he almost shouted aloud – this one was barred across. He got both feet on the bar and the relief was such that he could let go of the spout, find another handhold and pull out the dagger. The effort almost unbalanced him and he teetered dangerously before driving the point in further down. He stepped down the crossbars, cursing them now for preventing him climbing in. He stood on the sill, working out the next move. His hands were growing numb with cold, whatever he did it would have to be quick. He let himself down the bars and grasped the sill, sobbing with fear and effort, scrabbling for a foothold. He could find none, and fighting down panic he had no choice but to rely on his dagger again. Reaching down he drove it in and clung to it with both hands. This time he found a ledge for his foot and this small respite gave him a burst of reckless confidence. He remembered the clasp in his doublet and wrenched it off. Using it to scrape away a sizeable crack he was able to ram in his numbed hand and wheedle out the dagger. He did it again. And again. Next time he risked a look he was almost there. He pulled out the faithful blade and let himself go, sliding down the rough stone to land in a heap in the snow.

No time to nurse his bleeding fingers, he was up at a staggering run for the stables, planning as he went. Thankfully the man assigned to him was there, reverently brushing Nero and minding his gear. Nick shouted to him to saddle up, scrabbling in his pack for pencil and paper and yelling for a messenger. The Earl of Mar was with the King and the only person Nick thought he could trust was his own cousin. He gave the frantically scribbled note to the page who came running, fought his way into his jack, snatched up sword and helmet and leapt up on Oberon, calling to his own man to follow.

The fleeter Oberon soon outdistanced the groom and Nick dug his heels in unsparingly, thundering hooves pounding come on, come on, come on. He dared not fail.

Sitting with the King in court, sometimes beside him, sometimes with James' hand on his knee, he had absorbed some knowledge of the man: his reserve and dry humour, his scholarship and distaste for violence, his desire for peace among his nobles and his even-handed dealings with the warring religious factions. He seemed to Nick the ideal man to unify the two kingdoms, he must live to do it. He galloped on, his sweat-soaked doublet clammy and cold under the jack, eyes and nose streaming from the bitter wind.

He saw them at last, at the head of the green bowl of turf that must be the Devil's Beef Tub. He shouted and the words were torn from his lips and blew back on the cloud of his breath. He called on Oberon for one last effort and the great horse responded, gaining on the hunting party with every stride. No time to talk – they crashed through the rearguard and Nick launched himself at the King and bore him to the ground.

'Lord Almighty, I've laid hands on the sacred person of the King of Scotland,' he thought as they crashed into the snow. 'The man who thinks he's appointed by God – a hanging offence at least—' He looked up into a circle of pointy steel.

'Ambush—' he croaked, flinging up an arm. From both sides of the valley yelling men were pouring down the hillsides. The King beneath him had not moved. Was he dead? The Earl of Mar was roaring orders, hooves trampled perilously near Nick's head. Abercrombie and a man Nick did not know were bending and tenderly lifting James, who was stiff with shock. The arrow meant for him had gone through the plate of Nick's jack, the point nestling uncomfortably under his shoulder blade.

'Lucky it wasnae a crossbow, you'd be deid,' said the man who was hauling him up.

'Longnose Wattie wins the papingay every year,' said Nick, high on adrenaline, and stretched out a hand to the King. He was immediately felled by a crashing blow to the head.

He saw nothing of the onset of Charles Melville and his

men, or the roaring yelling Grahams and Elliots coming from the west. Carried in a jolting wagon with the other wounded, he was haunted by dreams of ravening red lips and Oberon faltering under him. He dreamed of Marlowe and the hot Italian sun, he was stuck to the icy stones of the Tower.

He came awake to find himself lying on a thin pallet of straw, his hurts roughly bandaged and a heavy chain round his ankles. Pale snowlight filtered through a slit in the wall. The cell stank. He stank. His head was splitting, he was cold and there was a tight feeling in his chest. He pulled himself up and tried to stand. The foul smell came from the drain in the corner and a wave of nausea brought him to his knees, vomiting. His stomach was empty and nothing came up but a thin stream of bile, burning his throat. He was thirsty. Time passed and the slit darkened. Someone nearby was groaning piteously. Extreme hunger and thirst were the only indication of how long he had been there. Memories of his sojourn in the Tower came to plague him and he could only put his trust in his kinfolk and his own innocence – not that innocence would count for anything. Long hours passed and by his reckoning it was past the King's bedtime and any chance of reprieve when the peephole squealed open, keys rattled and Charles Melville stood in the doorway. Involuntarily he crossed himself at sight of Nick.

'Mother of God, this should never have happened – strike off those chains! The King wishes to see you – but not in this state. Can you walk, cousin?' Nick tried one or two steps. 'Good. I will make your apology. Come—'

Attended by the King's physician and presented with an

exquisite suit of clothes, Nick was able to wait on the King at the banquet held to celebrate the monarch's safety. Young Colin came to help him dress, finding him coughing and his swollen fingers fumbling with the buttons, Fearghas anxious and whining at his hip. He told Nick how the countess had come to his uncle with the story of her husband's return. Letters had been found in the tower room.

'Bothwell's insurance policy. Lucky for you. If he went down he was not going to be alone. Names, meetings, everything.'

'Who struck me down?'

'Ruthven. He's in jail.'

'Bothwell?'

'Gone. His wife too, now, banished from court.'

'Oberon?'

'Lame but mending. Not gone in the wind. Not like you, you madman!'

He sat beside Mar at the King's right hand, the gold chain of the Order of Merit across his shoulders and a moiety of Bothwell's confiscated property in the north-west in his possession. Fearghas would not let him out of his sight again, and had not joined the sprawling heap by the fire, but lay with his head heavy on Nick's foot. He went with them when the King himself led Nick out to select a mount from his fine stables. Nicholas chose a solid, seventeen-hand gelding, light bay and well bred. He named him Caesar.

'Wait 'til Toby hears about this,' he said to himself.

The King kept within doors for the next week, nervous after this third attempt on his life, and Nick had a chance to recover. He had a troublesome rheum and a cough that would not leave him. Nevertheless, he was summoned often to the King's side, entertaining him with talk of plays and poetry, listening to James speak of his philosophy of nationhood, and shown the work in progress, James' *Basikon Doron*, in which he set out for his son his ideals of kingship. It was written in a beautiful hand, soon to be published. Nick was more than ever glad he had been in the right place at the right time. In a sense.

He asked at last if there was to be any reply to the Queen's letter.

'Of course, we had forgotten why you are here. We have it in mind. Once it is written we shall lose you, Master Talbot. We shall remove to Selkirk in a day or two. You shall have it then.'

Nick was impatient now to have done with this task and go home. Another birthday had come and gone and it would soon be Christmas again. He knew better now than to make promises, he planned to surprise Rokesby. He took leave of the King in Abercrombie's stronghold and made his way along the river valleys to Berwick, accompanied by his cousins and his faithful hound.

In a seaport almost hemmed in by the weather, he met again with the Lord Warden, who asked him to take letters and dispatches back to London. Reluctant to expose his horses to the rigours of the worst winter in living memory, he left them to Melville's guardianship, who swore to treat them as his own and send them south as soon as the weather allowed. Reassured and saddled with the very important person of the French ambassador, he took ship for Harwich.

Chapter Thirty-Two

It was a terrifying passage, the only dubious advantage the strong wind that blew steadily from the north. Rigging and decks were encased in ice, the sails heavy and unwieldy. Two crewmen were lost overboard in an attempt to free the tackle and the master gave up any idea of manoeuvre and sailed a dogged line south. In the cabin alongside Nick's the Frenchman lay moaning and praying: Nick could sleep only in snatches for the keening of the wind and the scream of the rigging. No hot food was to be had as the ship pitched and rolled and fought its way forward. He lent a hand where he could, mostly below decks trimming ballast, a fearsome back-breaking job that at least kept him out of the wind. The cold was such that when they were driven perilously close to shore, he could make out a frill of grey ice at the water's edge. The deerhound made himself comfortable on Nick's bunk and was a blessed source of warmth to curl up against.

They stood in at last to Harwich, the ship so disabled by now that boats had to come out to row them in. Nick had the ambassador carried to the nearest inn, where the warmth and hot food revived him a little. Nick turned in with Fearghas and slept for twelve hours. Waking in a room grown chill, he rolled out of bed to stir up the fire and stood over it, coughing and taking stock. Areas of his skin were raw with running sores from over a week in the same sodden salty clothes; most of his wardrobe was ruined, lice-ridden and stained with seawater and mildew. Thank God the horses were safe. Hot water was brought and he sent for dry clothes and asked for his leather gear to be cleaned. Presently he sat over the fire, clean and wrapped in the quilt with Fearghas' head on his knee and wrote up his journal. It would be some time before his companion could travel and he added this to his report. His face was too sore to shave so he did his best with scissors. Feeling better, he dressed and went to find breakfast.

''S been the coldest winter in living memory,' confided the landlord over the mulled ale. "Til the next one,' thought Nick. It was true, winters were getting colder. Roll on Verona.

Fearghas was bolting a huge bowl of gently steaming meat. The landlord was still prophesying doom. 'They say the Thames will freeze. No shipping. That's the last French brandy you'll see for a while, my lord, and they're slaughtering cattle for want of fodder. Grain'll be short next year—' Nick halted this jeremiad with a handful of coins and went to hire a horse to take him to London. He left money for the care of his companion and set off.

The ride was further purgatory and he stopped only to change horses, attend to Fearghas' pads and again to hand in his report and letters at Whitehall.

The docks were still for once, the incessant hammering silenced as he rode, weary and saddle-sore through Deptford to Crosstrees, Fearghas cantering at his side. The windows of the house were ablaze with light. He could hear O'Dowd from the gate, and he bent to open it. The hinges squealed, and the sound of the hooves on the cobbles brought Toby out at a run, calling for Michael. Speechless, Nick slid to the ground, his feet almost too numb to walk.

'Body of Christ, Nick! What happened? No, never mind, let's get you inside. Come on, hound.'

'What's all the shouting?'

'O'Dowd's come to report,' said Toby. 'I have explained to him twice that although Alice is dumb, she isn't deaf. Soup, Alice. Brandy. Warm the bed.'

Nick walked unsteadily into the parlour to find O'Dowd comfortably settled at the table with food and wine, surrounded by a mess of papers. He came to embrace Nick and thump him on the back. Fearghas growled at the back of his throat.

'Good dog, good dog. I hear you had good sport in the Borders,' he roared. 'Wait 'til you see what I've brought ye!' He threw open the lid of a small iron-bound chest to reveal a pirate's hoard of coin and plate. 'What d'yer think of that? Hey? Hey?' Nicholas was staggered. He fumbled for a chair and sat down. He had not dreamed their enterprise would burgeon like this.

'It's net, not gross,' shouted O'Dowd. 'Everyone's paid, Ponsonby's got a bonus, and we've three more trips in hand!'

'I can afford a new pair of boots,' said Toby. 'You look as if you need a drink, man. With your looks, my brains and O'Dowd's brawn, what did you expect?'

Nick shook his head and drank to the pair of them, feeling almost too ill to care.

The next day dawned far too bright, and Nick stumbled downstairs at noon squinting against the glare and nursing a thunderous headache. Shaking with an ague, he went outside and scooped up handfuls of snow, rubbing them on his face and letting it melt in his mouth. Fearghas was cantering around, hunting for new smells and rolling in the snow. Indoors a pile of letters was waiting for him on the table and he was trying to focus when Toby lounged downstairs, breezy and infuriating.

He clapped his hands for Alice and Nick tried not to flinch.

'What's next?'

Nick looked up, a letter with an imposing red seal dangling from his hand.

'I'm summoned to Court,' he said, and slid gracefully off the chair.

Chapter Thirty-Three

Toby and O'Dowd hid his boots and clothes and refused to let him travel anywhere until he was better. By the time they judged him fit, his horses had arrived safe in the care of Young Colin Melville, sent by his exasperated uncle to acquire some Court polish and if possible a rich wife. His arrival caused major disruption to the household and it was not until he had been packed off to find his mentor, Robert Carey, that Nick was able to read his other letters. There was a worrying note from Kate, long delayed.

Dearest Nicholas.

Daily we hope and pray for your safe return. You have been away so long we fear you have forgotten us. There is so much I long to share with you but I wonder if the boy I knew has vanished from me. Hugh tells me a young man such as you must have his freedom to make his way in the world, this I have always known, but I wonder if Rokesby will ever be world enough for you. Could our quiet woods and rich pastures, our small interests, ever hold you now? I fear not and I despair of seeing you again. There is something you should know that I cannot write.

Come home soon, Nicholas, your loving Kate.

The letter stayed fretting the back of his mind all the while he was making ready to obey the summons to Court. The tone of it was so different from the Kate blossoming under the teaching of their old owl. Was she sick? Hugh's letters said nothing of any trouble of that kind. There had been no choice but to obey Cecil. He could only hope to finish this next business quickly, whatever it was, and return to her. Nothing would stop him this time. He provided himself with a suitable wardrobe, wrote to Tom Walsingham with enclosures to Rokesby, and to Marlowe, promising a speedy return, and wondered what Cecil had in store for him this time.

Unwilling to arrive at court with his new clothes splattered with mud, Nick elected to take Nero. The four of them laboured over the stallion's appearance and turned him out in splendid style, mane and tail braided with yellow silk, his coat glossy and hindquarters patterned, tack polished and gleaming. Satisfied, Nick just had time to cram on his best suit of clothes, pull on his boots and go, riding proudly over the bridge.

No need for passwords and crested buttons this time, his name was on a list. For some reason this made him uneasy. Passed from lackey to page to steward, he threaded his way towards the heart of the Palace. The corridors were lined with groups of men, some idly talking, some with heads close together. You could cut yourself on the tension.

'Toby would be totting up the amount of bullion they're wearing,' thought Nick. No one appeared to pay him any attention, but he felt the questioning looks, the shrugs, the sly glances. The liveried man conducting him rapped on a pair of ornately-carved doors and bowed him in. The audience chamber was not as large as he had expected. The high ceiling was carved and coffered, the walls hung with fine tapestries lit by a row of plain glass windows down one side. It was crowded. The brown velvet throne was empty.

Nicholas looked around. The furs and jewels here were several degrees more costly than those he had passed, but worn with a casual flourish. There was not an ill-looking man in the room, all young gallants flirting idly with bored-looking women. Not unlike the Scottish court. The lady Rosalyne was not there. There was a subtle frisson as Nick entered; a sharpening of awareness, a straightening of already straight backs. He resisted the impulse to fiddle with his clothes. The black double-velvet from Marlowe had been tailored to an impeccable fit, his linen starched and immaculate. He could do no more, and stood still, left hand on his sword-hilt, the other relaxed at his side, waiting.

A good-looking man detached himself from a group paying court to a statuesque beauty and crossed the room towards him. He had a limber, swordsman's walk and a charming smile. He bowed with an admirable flourish.

'Robert Carey, at your service.'

'Nicholas Talbot, my lord.'

'I know. But I am no lord, Master Talbot. A mere penniless knight, hoping to catch my cousin in a sweet and giving vein.'

'You know me, sir?'

'I know of you from my brother. I'm sorry to have missed you, and all the excitement. I hope John entertained you well. I hear you distinguished yourself. Are you here for the tournament?' Nick bowed in return.

'I have no skill in jousting, sir.' This was not quite true. He had had much fun as a boy jousting piggyback with a wooden lance on Sergeant Ponsonby's brawny shoulders. How he would fare on horseback with a larger heavier weapon he was not sure. Sir Robert was still speaking.

'We must amend that, sir. You are adept with sword and rapier, I'm told. You must allow us to complete your knightly skills. Do me the honour of meeting in the tourney yard when this interminable audience is over. If our knees are still functioning, that is.'

'Our knees?'

'I have knelt two hours or more at her Majesty's pleasure and stood four more. School yourself, young sir, no fidgeting, yawning or farting, if you please.' This last was spoken with a smile as the elegant figure moved off. There was a stir near the doorway and a wave of kneeling crested with feathers as caps came off and headdresses curtseyed. Elizabeth, Queen of England had arrived.

She was followed by her councillors, sober men, clad for the most part in black, ravens against the bright plumage of the court. Cecil was of course among them and his watchful, tired eyes found Nick, narrowed and moved on. Nick watched as for the next three hours courtiers and petitioners came and went, bowing, kneeling, making courtly speeches of fulsome praise, more often than not sent empty away. No one spoke unless spoken to by Elizabeth herself or an usher, and Nick began to see what Carey meant.

Dinnertime came at last and the Queen retired to her Privy Chamber. When they had thankfully sat down, eased their backs and eaten, Carey hauled him off to the practice yards behind the palace.

The practice yard was fully equipped with a quintain and rings, archery butts and a sanded area for wrestling and swordplay. The warm friendly odour of stabling came from a row of low buildings to one side and Nick saw a magnificent gelding being led out towards a bulky man in half-armour. He turned, putting on his helm and Nick recognised lord Mowbray. Mowbray saw him and paused for a moment before turning aside to the mounting block.

'Come,' said Carey. 'A bout to warm us and then we'll see.' He was stripping off his beautifully tailored doublet as he spoke, and down to his shirt and hose, was beckoning Nick to where other sweating pairs trying for a fall were wrestling with grim determination.

The two were well matched. Nick's wrestling was the no-holds-barred, dirty tricks variety, which he hesitated to use in these surroundings but after Carey tried one or two himself, he left his manners and fought back. After a swearing sweaty half-hour, they stopped by mutual consent and Carey sent a page for ale.

'Swordplay later. Come, we'll break a lance or two. You have a horse?' Nick spread his hands.

'Here somewhere.' Carey summoned a page.

'Find Master Talbot's horse. Now, armour. You are broader in the shoulder than I but my breastplate should fit, try it.'

Nick found that by letting out the buckles he could move fairly comfortably, if that was the word, and he put on the proffered helmet, mounted Nero, took a lance in his hand and prepared to make a fool of himself. As the lesson progressed and he struggled to master the twelve-foot lance and put it through the ring, a grinning crowd gathered. When he managed to hit it he discovered that, if he was not fast enough, the leather sandbag balancing the target came round and caught him a buffet on the back of his head. After being knocked out of the saddle a couple of times, to mocking laughter, he began to get the hang of it, at which point Carey jumped off his horse and fetched their swords from the heap on the ground. Two lines formed up. A fencing-master came towards them with a pair of face-guards. Nick, sweating hard, made to shed his armour and was stopped.

'Queen's orders. She don't like her young men marked.'

'Bit late for that,' thought Nick.

If the smirking courtiers thought the armour would be a handicap, they were wrong. Nick was used to practising in a fighting jack, sixty pounds of plated iron leaved between quilted leather. The fencing-master placed him opposite a young man in helmet and breastplate of polished steel that hurt the eyes, engraved and embossed with silver. The master lifted his blade and the bouts began.

Old Jem in his heyday had been reckoned one of the finest swordsmen around and he had taught Nick well. Cavalli had added the necessary polish. Even in the playhouse or on his travels, Nick had rarely let a day go by without practice of some kind, and he loved the feel of the sword in his hand, the judging of a distance, the mental effort. It was good to be facing a trained opponent.

'Watch the eyes,' Jem had told him. It was difficult with the shadow of the helmet and the guard and he watched the body language as well. To his disappointment, his first bout was quickly over, his opponent disarmed. He worked his way up the line, and, more evenly matched at the end, the last bout was stopped by the fencing-master. His opponent, an older, more seasoned fighter than the others, came to where Nick was unbuckling himself and listening to the master telling him where to improve. He banged Nick on the back with a genial grin.

'You should be counselling me, Carlton,' he said. 'I was within an ace of defeat. My thanks for saving my face.'

Carlton turned away smiling.

'Thomas Grey of Wilton. I know who you are. Word goes round.' A page came round with ale and Grey took two tankards and gave one to Nick.

'Your health, sir. I look forward to taking my revenge tomorrow.' He downed his ale in one swallow, saluted with his blade and stumped off.

Nick flung his sword up into the air in sheer exuberant joy and it wheeled, winking, once, twice, thrice before fitting back snug into his hand as if time was reeling backwards.

'Hmm,' said Carey, who had been watching. 'Good trick. Can you juggle as well?'

Nick laughed. 'Have you seen this?' He sheathed his sword and pulled out Marlowe's gift to him.

The farmuk (or yo-yo, as the English would christen it) unfurled its string and fled up and down it, vertical, horizontal, round the world and back into its smug wooden shell, over and over.

The Queen had been watching him at play with her Robin from a window and presently a page came doubling across the yard as a captivated Carey stood untangling knots.

'Your presence, sir, the Queen requires it.'

Startled, Nick reviewed his sins, bowed to Carey and strode after the page back into the palace. Carey followed at a more leisurely pace, smiling to himself. He knew his Elizabeth.

She was sitting stiffly on her brown velvet throne, her face a white mask with blackcurrant eyes. The room was deathly quiet. On of the courtiers had a four-fingered red mark on his cheek.

'Show us your plaything.'

Nick stepped forward, knelt and offered up his sword.

'No, fool. Get up. The thing that flies.'

Sheepishly he fingered out the farmuk, thinking to have it confiscated as if he were a boy at school with a catapult.

'Make it fly.' Nick looked round at the staring court.

'*Show us!* Make it fly!'

Trembling, he made sure there were no knots left in the string, gave the old woman his best smile and unloosed the farmuk, praying to himself. In the silence, the farmuk obligingly hissed up and down, before, behind, round and round and smacked back into his palm. The hooded eyes followed its flight and the withered cheeks cracked into a smile. There were a few titters and she glared round.

Nick went on one knee and offered it on the flat of his hand as if it were an apple for Rowena.

'A scientific experiment, your Majesty.' She nodded and a page stepped forward and conveyed it to her. She examined it.

'What does it prove?'

'A mathematical force in nature, your Majesty. It is a toy also.' She looked around.

'We would be alone. Master Talbot, remain. And you, my lord Burghley.' The room cleared as if by magic, leaving only Cecil and a lady-in-waiting.

'Approach, Master Talbot. Teach us.'

Trying to control his trembling hands, Nick showed her how to hook the string over her finger and give the little jerk to start it. He knew it took patience that the Tudor temper did not have to master the trick of it. But her fancy was caught and she made him show her again and again until the little golden globe obeyed her.

She gave a sudden cackle.

'You have amused us, Master Talbot. And I was watching you at work with my cousin Robin. Yes.' A pause. 'My lord Cecil tells me you have done us much service in Scotland and, I understand, elsewhere. Give me your sword. Kneel.' She touched him lightly on the shoulder.

'There are many battlefields, Sir Nicholas. Are there not?'

'Do you speak of the heart, your Majesty? My queen is conqueror there.'

'You learn fast, young man. A pretty conceit. Pray do not turn yourself into a courtier too soon, Sir Nicholas. That would be a waste. You may rise. Have no fear, they shall not dub you knight of the – what is the pretty thing called?'

'A farmuk, your majesty.'

'A heathen name. We shall find another word for it. No sir, you are honoured like your father for your service to your country, and so it shall be known.' She turned to Cecil. 'See to it. Young man, your action over the border has set my mind at rest – for the moment.' The lady-in-waiting came forward with a scarf of silver tissue.

'Wear this at the tourney.' She sank back in her chair and the little golden globe dropped from her hand and rolled across the floor. 'You may retire, Sir Nicholas. Remain at court.' She waved a jewelled hand at Cecil. 'Deal with him.' She extended the hand to Nicholas and in a daze, he knelt and kissed it.

Outside, Cecil turned to him with a face of stone and handed him a large packet bound with pink ribbon.

'The paperwork. The glebe lands round the Rokesby estate are yours and your heirs. Look out for Mowbray, they were his. You have already thwarted him once. Possibly twice.'

'What does all this mean, my lord?'

'It means, *Sir Nicholas, lord Rokesby*, you will now always deal directly with me. In a different capacity. Your use to me is now circumscribed. You are conspicuous, sir, and have caught the Queen's eye. Unsought-for, I know, but – unfortunate. You will be the object of envy. You will be watched and should conduct yourself accordingly. Incidentally, everything will cost you twice as much.' He flicked the gauzy scarf. 'You had better win at the tourney. Go and practise or you'll get yourself killed. And no more play-acting – unless it's at court at her majesty's pleasure.' With which he limped off through the anteroom in his crab-like gait, leaving Nick to run the gauntlet of curious stares and smothered laughter as he made his way through the press.

A Gentleman of the Bedchamber came to meet him and conducted him with all ceremony to a tiny panelled room with a narrow truckle bed in one corner and another stretcher bed under it. These were his quarters, he was told, and his belongings had been sent for. Evidently 'remain at court' meant just that.

'Don't worry,' said Carey, leaning in the doorway. 'Come the tourney this place is so crowded even a broom cupboard is fought for. You will be able to slip off to live in your own home like a gentleman and not a court rat and no one will care a jot. I may come with you. Come to supper. Wine and a few cards.'

Kate's letter had been burning a hole in Nick's side. This latest twist in his fortune confirmed what had been in his mind since Italy. He had known then what he wanted and now had something worthy of her to lay at her feet. If she would have him. He looked over her letters to him, full of words of steadfast affection. Was that enough? He would know when he saw her. He wrote:

My own sweet Kate,

I can at last unpack my heart of the dreams I have long held for us. I am Knighted, Kate and you shall be my lady if it so pleases you. Your letter just come troubles me - if the Queen had not bidden me to stay at court I would be at your side tomorrow. She must be obeyed, sweetheart. Do not think me a feeble lover who swears and swears and is forsworn. If the fates permit I shall be with you straight after the tourney, where I am commanded, a little month but it will seem an age to one already so long away. Whatever ails you, my brave Kate, stand firm. Such safety as can be hoped for in these times is ours, the ills we can face together, if you are willing.

My thoughts have ever turned to you, my loved one, as the needle to the North Star. At times of the deepest despair you have come to me and given me aid. What I have been about, I cannot tell you, only that constraints have so hedged me about to keep me from you that I can only beg you of your wisdom to forgive me.

Faithless I may have been but not fickle. You are the still centre of this whirling world, Kate and so I would be fixed. I have been too far away from you for far too long. You often ask if I have found a bride. I think I have always found one and not known until now. Wear this ring as a sign of our betrothal if you can still love me and I will come as soon as I am able. You are my first and only true love, Kate. Write to me at Crosstrees to tell me my fate.

Your adoring, penitent Nicholas, faithful in his fashion.

I see in this poor letter I take no account of what may be in your heart. If I must come a-wooing, beloved, I will do so joyfully, and not look between the lines for your answer, but in your eyes, so you do not refuse me out of hand.

Yours ever, Nick.

He made a packet of the letter and his signet ring, wrapped it strongly and sealed it and then sat pondering on how to send it. There was no one here he would trust. He decided to wait until he could contact Tobias. The next escort was not due to leave just yet, there might be time. Chafing at the delay, he made it his business over the next few days to cultivate one of the older ladies-in-waiting. Flattered by the attention, and in touch with her Majesty's day by day activities, she agreed to let him know when there was opportunity to slide off on his own affairs. The first too-brief escape gave time only to take Nero up onto the heath and gallop. The atmosphere at court was stifling. The Queen's courtiers were not precisely her prisoners but certainly they danced to her capricious tune.

At last he was able to ride to Crosstrees and find Toby. He found his friend dressed in all his own new finery to visit Lady Caroline. That friendship had prospered, but Toby dolefully confessed he was only one of many suitors.

'M'way of life don't suit,' said Tobias. 'Like you and your Kate. They don't want a husband who's footloose and fancy-free while they sit at home rocking the cradle.'

'That is going to change,' said Nick. 'That's why I am here, to crave a favour. I am reluctant to break into your leisure, Toby, but I need something taken to Rokesby – I am asking Kate for a betrothal. I have position now, lands, money. I have plans.'

Laughing, Toby clapped him on the back. 'Excellent news! I take it you want me to play Mercury—'

'And to stand up with me if she is willing.'

'Give you joy, Nicholas, she will not refuse you. I'll go gladly.'

'When it chimes with your own affairs. I have been so long in the wooing…look, Toby, read this letter. This was the spur.' Toby's face grew grave as he read.

'Something was amiss,' he said. 'So long ago. You have heard nothing since?' Nick shook his head. 'Then all is probably well. Bad news always travels fastest, you must have noticed. I'll go first thing tomorrow.' The two friends rode together, full of eager talk, as far as Westminster, where Toby rode off, waving his hat, to meet his lady. Nick watched him go, smiling. He could not see Tobias as a married man.

That night, returning hospitality, Nick entertained some of the acquaintance he had made at court. Carey was there, and his protégé d'Arblay, Robert Southwell and some of the wilder young men, who were ardent gossips. Idly, Nick wondered how it came about that he should have fallen heir to some of Mowbray's lands, and set off an avalanche of speculation.

'Rumour has it he sired a bastard on the lady Rosalyne and the Queen wasn't pleased. Neither is he now – pleased as punch 'til he saw the babe, never managed it before y'see—' the voice tailed off. The light shone full on Nick's face, lighting the green eyes and chestnut hair.

'What of the lady?'

'Married my lord Sexton straight off, says the child is his. Got his colouring.' With a wicked grin, 'Similar to yours, Rokesby.'

'Perhaps he's half-Scots too. That reminds me, Robert, what have you done with my cousin?'

'Young Colin Melville? Sent him for schooling. He's a young barbarian – you can have him back, Nicholas, he'll make you a squire for the tourney. D'Arblay here will keep him in order. Have you done anything yet about armour?' The talk drifted into the usual channels and Nick relaxed. If he allowed barbs like that to stick, he would soon resemble a porcupine. Carey lingered after the rest had gone.

'Tell me, young Rokesby, did it never cross your mind to make use of your connections here at court?'

'My connections?'

'You are naïve, Nicholas. Gilbert Talbot, Earl of Shrewsbury – you are related. Did it never occur to you?'

'My father attached no importance to it—'

'Obviously not, he was going about things differently. But you – you might use it to your advantage. I notice my lord Cecil is none too pleased at your elevation. You are slipping out of his grasp, Nicholas. You have only to make an advantageous marriage and he must ask nicely for what he wants. I have my ear to the ground, you see, I make what headway I can before I'm packed off back to the Borders.'

'I am already promised.'

'Nonsense. You are in no position now to marry where you will. Is she suitable?' Nick hesitated. 'Ah. Think hard, youngster. It won't do to take your eye off the ball now.'

Tension was mounting in Nicholas. He could not take the tourney seriously, it was a game, an annual entertainment for a public holiday. It had been postponed once because of the weather, and now, as Carey predicted, the palaces were packed, every available space taken. Nick practised daily in the tiltyard and went home to Deptford at night, his thoughts with Toby and the success of his mission. He should be on his way back soon—

Chapter Thirty-Four

Blessed with a good eye, excellent co-ordination and willing to take risks, Nick learned fast. He had grown into his full strength now: he could draw an eighty-pound longbow and his old fighting jack was too small. O'Dowd found him some supple, workmanlike armour that fitted and cost a small fortune, and Nick had his father's sword reforged with a tang and blade of Toledo steel. Nero took to this strange new activity to the manner born and by the time the building of the lists was finished and the order of jousting posted, Nick was ready to try his luck.

He had no thought of winning this competition in this company: as long as he did not disgrace himself and his queen's favour, he would be content. Young Colin had shaped up passably well as a squire, restrained from the worst excesses of family partisanship by the cool charm of d'Arblay. Carey was hugging himself. His young friend had worked and trained like a demon, he was young and fit and hungry – a natural. The men of the court were wily and seasoned fighters, experienced in this kind of sport, but perhaps grown a little lazy for lack of real challenge. One or two young gallants fancied their chances, but had not been seen much in the practice yards.

Carey laid more than he could afford in bets at excellent odds.

The day of the tourney dawned grey and overcast, the grip of winter finally broken. It was ideal conditions for men sweating in a carapace of metal. Nick was wound up with excitement. His pavilion was pitched next to Carey's, his two squires were there, brave in their livery and bearing his father's blazon. 'The readiness is all.'

Young Colin had won a minor battle and the red and white of the Melvilles floated beneath the black and gold of Talbot with its crest of a hooded eagle. His horses were gleaming, still in their winter coats, splendid in their black and gold trappings. The great deerhound lay at their feet like a heraldic beast. All that could be done had been done, and Nick stood in the opening of the little tent watching the show as Elizabeth entered to a blaze of trumpets. Stiffly upright in cloth of silver she mounted the steps specially built for her and settled in her place. The silvery gauze of the scarf she had tossed so casually to Nick fluttered on the crest of the helm Young Colin was carrying, and Nick suddenly saw the enormity of what he was doing. He fell victim to the worst kind of stage fright and if he hadn't been in full armour would have rushed round to the latrines. He managed to control himself and grabbed a mug of ale from a passing potboy.

The procession began and gallant after gallant rode out to salute his queen. The first wore an overdress of feathers in the likeness of a swan, and declaimed a long poem in honour of Elizabeth. He was followed by others, bears, mountebanks, lions and one daring unicorn complete with virgin. This last was Carey, whose eulogy earned him a prize and a favour to wear. lord Mowbray arrived, perilously late, and did not take part.

The noise was indescribable and the sudden hush when the trumpets sounded for the first bout took Nick by surprise. After the long build-up, the action was fast and continuous. Heralds announced each contestant with full title, the rod went up, lances were couched and two half-tons of horse and armour hurtled together with an echoing crash. Losers out of three bouts cantered or were dragged off the field; the next pair taking their place.

A newcomer, Nick was early in the lists. White-faced, he stood still while Young Colin laced on his helm with trembling fingers, pulled on his gauntlets and climbed aboard Nero. D'Arblay handed him his first lance with its bold black and gold stripes, grinned up at him and slapped the horse's rump as it passed. 'This is the real thing,' thought Nick. He added the combined speeds of two galloping horses and calculated the impact when the lance, albeit blunted, hit him, and felt sick. Too late now. He squeezed into the trot.

His first opponent was Lord Seymour, a cocky young blood who had boasted that he would 'swat the upstart Rokesby like a fly'. Facing an approaching black and gold thunderbolt with an unwavering point, the boaster lost confidence and aim at the last moment and found himself flat on his back. The first black and gold flag was fixed on the tally.

Carey crossed Seymour and then the next two, off his list. 'Keep it up, Rokesby,' he breathed. The draw was such that he would not be likely to meet Nick himself until later, if at all, but in the event, both his borrowed horses went lame and he was forced to withdraw. Nick, visor up and scarlet with excitement, offered him Oberon, but Carey grinned and shook his head.

'I've no wish to meet you in the next, my friend. Watch out for Mowbray, he's got some dirty tricks. Go for his head if you can, it makes him nervous.'

The trumpets sounded and Nick snapped down his visor, wheeled and took the fresh lance from d'Arblay, who had completely lost his sangfroid.

Mowbray, formidable in orange and sky-blue, trotted into the lists. He wore the latest in French armour, inlaid with gold, and bore an unusual shield, heavily curved. Three scarlet plumes sprouted from his helm, the mark of a former champion, and he rode a heavy-set Cleveland with feathered hocks. Altogether a sight to strike terror into any novice. Nick settled into the saddle, checked his girth and gear and gave Nero the office to begin his trot. He'd back his horse against any other. Into the canter, he couched his lance, aimed at Mowbray's helmet and quickened into the gallop before Mowbray was out of trot. Mowbray's lance glanced off Nick's shield and he rounded the barrier to see his opponent lying back over the Cleveland's rump. The man raised himself slowly and his squires came running. There was an interval while an undented helm was fetched and Nick used the time to quench his thirst and check Nero's legs. The bouts were best of three, he would change mounts after the next one.

Mowbray, boiling with fury, his vision blurred and dizzy, vowed to serve his enemy the same physic. Nick watched him thundering towards him, dipped his shoulder, aimed for the bottom of the fancy breastplate and urged Nero into a sudden spurt. He took Mowbray's lance in the left shoulder, almost spinning him out of the saddle and Mowbray, unseated, was left sitting on the ground totally winded. He was not a popular man and the noise in the stands grew tumultuous. The Queen had her hand over her mouth. Carey crossed off Mowbray. One more to go: Leicester, last year's champion. He had even made a bet that black would be among the winner's colours. Bruised and breathless, Nick took off his helmet and slid awkwardly off Nero to make a fuss of him. A herald in Leicester's colours approached the Master of the Tourney. Leicester was injured and would withdraw. Nick had his back turned when two of the Queen's heralds approached, trying to wheedle out a splinter that had gone between the joints of the harness. A scroll rapped his shoulder.

'The Queen waits to greet her champion.'

'What!'

'You've won, man – Leicester's withdrawn—' His two squires-for-the-day were almost crying with excitement and the effort of maintaining suitable decorum. Dazed and in quite a lot of pain, Nicholas walked out to stand before his queen, clutching the silvery scarf in his fist, followed by his squires with the horses. She nodded and an equerry brought to him an embroidered glove on a cushion. A handsome trophy with the prize money followed and he struggled to hold them and lift them to the shouting crowd. The equerry seemed to be waiting for something and presently leaned forward to murmur, 'You ride round the field of honour, my lord.'

'Oh.' A block was brought, he clumsily handed the prizes to Young Colin, who looked fit to burst, and hauled himself aboard Nero again. He twisted the scarf round his arm and set off to a wild Caledonian yell from Young Colin, a huge grin lighting his face as he realised what he had done. Perhaps Kate would be proud: he imagined her gentle mockery and quiet pleasure. He would see her soon. Christ, he'd be glad to get this splinter out.

Carey was delighted. He'd won a hatful of money and his cousin Elizabeth looked kindly on his new protégé. He had been right, a young man to cultivate.

Nick had won two horses, one of them Mowbray's Cleveland. He would give them to Toby and O'Dowd, the Cleveland was the ideal sort for O'Dowd. 'Wait 'til Toby hears about this,' he thought. 'I'll never hear the last of it.' He made Carey a present of a bolt of plum-coloured Italian velvet and shared out the prize money among the team. He would have preferred Kate's womanly touch to deal with the splinter but it was out at last and he put on his best doublet and dragged himself off to the feast. Mowbray was apparently unhurt but not present. The feasting went on far into the night. Nick left d'Arblay in charge of Young Colin, who was already half-drunk and joined Carey to get a little drunk himself.

Chapter Thirty-Five

Late the next morning, he dressed to go and find Toby, surely back by now, and then ride for Rokesby. James' gift horse, Caesar, was fresh and he trotted eagerly into the stable yard at Crosstrees. There was no one about and Nick looped his reins over the fence and trod round to the front of the house. He pushed open the door and ducked under the lintel.

Tobias was there, talking to a slender, grave-faced woman with a child at her knee. She was beautiful, fine-skinned with tendrils of auburn hair escaping her cap. The child turned, tow-headed and green-eyed with the beginnings of the Talbot nose. He cried out and began to run towards Nick with a wide gappy grin and hesitated at sight of the huge hound. Nick stared for a moment, a line from Shakespeare or someone floating through his head. He flung out his arms and shouted, 'Why, there's a wench! Come on and kiss me, Kate!' The woman stood silent, her hand to her breast, unmoving. Tobias came forward and said helplessly, 'She's married, Nicholas. She married Hugh Shawcross last month—' Nick turned blindly and walked out of the house. He did not hear the little boy begin to cry. Tobias followed him.

'We thought it best she should see you, speak to you herself.'

'That is *my* son...'

'You have stamped him in your image. Come back, Nick, let her explain.'

'What's to explain. It is a good match.'

'In name only. Shawcross cannot – he told me – Nick, he is willing to have it set aside. He has written—'

'Is she willing?'

'Come and speak to her.'

Kate was still standing by the fire. Fearghas was stretched in front of it, suffering the child to stroke him. Tobias enticed the lad with promises of apples and horses and took him tactfully off to the stables. Very white and stiff in her brocade skirts and embroidered stomacher, dressed as became a lady in her position, her hair confined in a starched cap, Kate walked away from him and stood looking out of the window. He remembered the last time he had seen her, flushed and naked in his bed, her hair loose about her shoulders, watching him make ready to leave. 'I shall not watch you ride away this time, Nicholas,' she had said. He would not speak first, he stood trying to control his breathing, waiting.

'We did not hear for six months,' she said at last. 'Your letters came last week. The seals all broken. We thought you were dead. And then Tobias came.'

'Would you have waited? Worn my ring?'

'You know the answer.'

'How long did you mourn me?' he asked savagely, and could have bitten his tongue.

'What do you want of me, Nicholas – after all this time, what do you want?'

'You have read my letters. You know my innermost thoughts and hopes and desires. You know I love you, Kate, and you know what I want and now cannot have. I know you, Kate, you will not break a promise, nor can I ask it, but every bone, every beat of my heart wishes you were mine. And you have borne me a son. Why in God's name did you not tell me!' She was in his arms, weeping. A thread of her hair stung his cheek.

'You were such a boy, Nick, so eager to be off in the world and make your fortune.' She tried to laugh. 'Was I to chain you to a hearthstone, make you something you are not? You would have grown to hate me. And I was right, look at you. I thought we had time – and then we heard you were hanged or banished… Hugh could find out nothing. We waited and searched, there was no word from you. I knew you would have written if you could. And then Hugh was ill – he worried your child would have no name.'

'What is his name?' She looked up at him. 'Jack.'

A deep abiding anger was building in Nick. He sat her down on the window seat and moved away. He did not trust himself to speak. 'I see now,' she went on. 'There was no proof, only silence. Until last week.'

'Too late for us.' He crossed to the cupboard and poured wine. 'Am I right?' he said, giving it to her. 'You would not let Shawcross set aside this sham marriage? You could be free.'

'No, Nicholas. I will not leave Hugh. He needs me. He has treated me always with kindness and respect. I cannot repay him so cruelly. And you were not there.'

'As I thought. True and tender Kate. Well, I will see you safe home, but I would like the boy to know me a little. Will you rest here a while – I will send a message to Hugh.'

'He knows Hugh is not his father. I have spoken of you, often and often.'

'A few days, Kate. Time to think.'

Jack was a merry child, given to rainbow moods of chuckling and tears. Brought up on tales of the father who would come one day, he accepted this giant with green eyes and a high, bony nose who crouched down to play knucklebones and took him up to tell stories. He sat on Nick's knee and watched the farmuk do its magic tricks, listening to the rumble of his deep voice, leaning against the slow steady beat of his heart. He was not allowed to ride Fearghas. He learned tantrums did not work. He leaned from safe arms to feed carrots and apples to the horses and sat, a long way up, in front of his father to ride out. Careful of his position and his own son, Hugh Shawcross had done none of these things. At nearly four years old, there was a gap in Jack's life and this man filled it.

Nicholas thought. He came together with Kate at mealtimes, which was as much as he could manage. Tobias would be leaving soon to escort the next group and then Nicholas would ride to

Rokesby. He would set out his plan for Jack's future. He visited a notary and signed papers to make sure Jack would bear his name and title and inherit his lands and money. He would discuss with Shawcross ways of providing for Kate. Tobias offered to come with them to Rokesby; his friend at times was like someone cast adrift.

'Who would take the escort? Toby, let one thing at least be constant – apart from Kate's wedding vows that is. More than one of us three must give business some attention.' And there is Kit, he thought. I have Kit to think of. 'I will take the next one.'

Tobias was glad to leave. He could hardly bear to watch Nick with the little boy and the tension at mealtimes was like a drawn bowstring. He longed for something to snap. They were courteous to each other and to him, told amusing stories and made conversation until Toby wanted to scream. On his last night, they were drinking to the success of the journey, and Kate leaned across Nicholas, smiling, to clink glasses. Nick got up abruptly and left the room. Toby found him later in Rowena's stable, dry-eyed, his hair wet from the pump, his arms round her neck. Toby withdrew quietly and left him alone.

In the end, Nick took Michael along and they set off with Jack in the crook of Nick's arm, clutching his farmuk and warm in a fold of his father's cloak. He fell asleep and woke crying for his mother. Once there he wriggled to be back with his father on his big white horse. They humoured the child and after a while he settled for the solid safe comfort of his father's body, strong arms that would not let him fall. His parents did not speak much: they had told all there was to tell. Nick was struggling to lay a foundation for an existence without Kate, planning that as soon as he had settled things with Shawcross, he would take up the reins of his life and return to Italy and Marlowe. He wondered what Kit would make of it all. Weave it into a play no doubt. He could only admire his Kate for her steadfastness, hate her and love her the more. He strove to admire Shawcross for his generosity and subdue the worm of jealousy that gnawed at him. He felt like murder.

They rode on, resting for a night then on once more. Michael smoothed the way, made arrangements, paid bills, tipped ostlers and kept his counsel. He was never a chatterbox and Nick's frozen face did not encourage conversation. Nearing the outer reaches of Rokesby, they rode through the village of Lower Rookham, Nick noticing a number of new buildings. The church steeple had been repaired, barns had new roofs. Cottagers stopped what they were doing and came out with their children to see this exotic tawny-haired stranger in his fine velvet and furs, the great red hound loping beside, the beauty with her babe and trim manservant. Fat cattle and sheep peered from their neat shelters, or grazed the new grass: lines of ploughing striped the fields like red corduroy, hazed with lime green. In the distance he could see the pink and white froth of orchards and the waving tops of hop poles. Spring was come at last.

It was almost dark when they came to the outskirts of Rokesby itself. He handed Jack, fast asleep, to Michael, and trotted on. A false sunset glowed pink on the underbelly of cloud to the west, and he set spurs to Oberon, up the rise to where he might see. There was a tight, hard lump in Nick's chest.

Rokesby. The house that Jack built, thought Nick. For me and my sons and my sons' sons. And I shall not live in it.

The English Succession

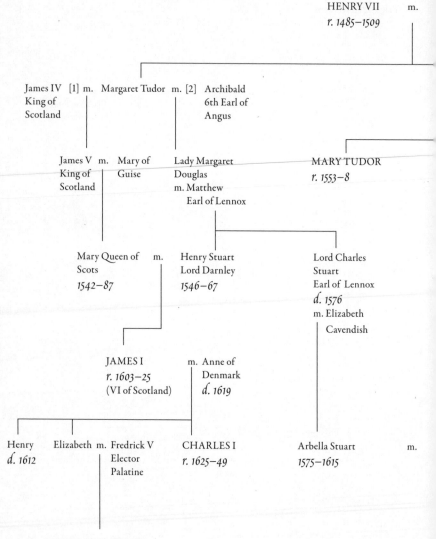

HENRY VII   m.
r. 1485–1509

James IV   [1] m.   Margaret Tudor   m. [2]   Archibald
King of   6th Earl of
Scotland   Angus

James V   m.   Mary of   Lady Margaret   MARY TUDOR
King of   Guise   Douglas   *r. 1553–8*
Scotland   m. Matthew
                                  Earl of Lennox

Mary Queen of   m.   Henry Stuart   Lord Charles
Scots   Lord Darnley   Stuart
1542–87   *1546–67*   Earl of Lennox
                                        d. 1576
                                        m. Elizabeth
                                           Cavendish

JAMES I   m. Anne of
r. 1603–25   Denmark
(VI of Scotland)   *d. 1619*

Henry   Elizabeth   m.   Fredrick V   CHARLES I   Arbella Stuart   m.
d. 1612   Elector   *r. 1625–49*   *1575–1615*
                          Palatine

HOUSE OF HANOVER

Elizabeth of York

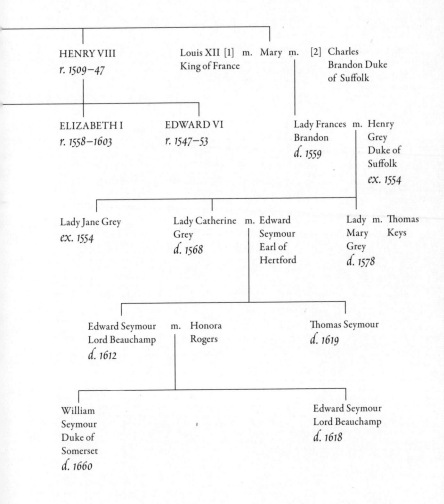

HENRY VIII
r. 1509–47

Louis XII [1] m. Mary m. [2] Charles
King of France   Brandon Duke
                                  of Suffolk

ELIZABETH I
r. 1558–1603

EDWARD VI
r. 1547–53

Lady Frances m. Henry
Brandon   Grey
d. 1559   Duke of
                 Suffolk
                 ex. 1554

Lady Jane Grey
ex. 1554

Lady Catherine m. Edward
Grey   Seymour
d. 1568   Earl of
                  Hertford

Lady m. Thomas
Mary   Keys
Grey
d. 1578

Edward Seymour m. Honora
Lord Beauchamp   Rogers
d. 1612

Thomas Seymour
d. 1619

William
Seymour
Duke of
Somerset
d. 1660

Edward Seymour
Lord Beauchamp
d. 1618

Bibliography

Cartographer's Map of Elizabethan London

The Life and Times of James VI of Scotland, I of England, Antonia Fraser, Weidenfeld & Nicolson, 1994

The Lodger: Shakespeare on Silver Street, Charles Nicholl, Penguin, 2008

The Steel Bonnets: The Story of the Anglo-Scottish Border Reivers, George MacDonald Fraser, Harper Collins Publishers Ltd, 1989

The Stirring World of Robert Carey: Robert Carey's memoirs 1577-1625, Rockbuy Ltd, 2005

And many more!

MORE FROM HONNO

Short stories, Classics, Autobiography, Fiction

Founded in 1986 to publish the best of women's writing, Honno publishes a wide range of titles from Welsh women.

Praise for Honno's books:

"a marvellous compilation of reminiscences"
Time Out

"A cracking good read"
dovegreyreader.co.uk

*"Illuminating, poignant, entertaining
and unputdownable"*
The Big Issue

All Honno titles can be ordered online at
www.honno.co.uk,
or by sending a cheque to Honno
with **free** p&p to all UK addresses.

ABOUT HONNO

Honno Welsh Women's Press was set up in 1986 by a group of women who felt strongly that women in Wales needed wider opportunities to see their writing in print and to become involved in the publishing process. Our aim is to develop the writing talents of women in Wales, give them new and exciting opportunities to see their work published and often to give them their first 'break' as a writer.

Honno is registered as a community co-operative. Any profit that Honno makes is invested in the publishing programme. Women from Wales and around the world have expressed their support for Honno by buying shares. Supporters liability is limited to the amount invested and each supporter has a vote at the Annual General Meeting.

To buy shares or to receive further information about forthcoming publications, please write to Honno at the address below, or visit our website: www.honno.co.uk.

Honno
Unit 14, Creative Units
Aberystwyth Arts Centre
Penglais Campus
Aberystwyth
Ceredigion
SY23 3GL

All Honno titles can be ordered online at
www.honno.co.uk
or by sending a cheque to Honno.
Free p&p to all UK addresses